Stephen Booth is the internationally bestselling, CWA Dagger-winning author of the acclaimed thrillers featuring Cooper and Fry. The series is in development as a TV programme. Booth lives in Nottingham.

STEPHEN BOOTH

DROWNED LIVES

sphere

SPHERE

First published in Great Britain in 2019 by Sphere

1 3 5 7 9 10 8 6 4 2

A CIP catalogue record for this book is available from the British Library.

Hardback ISBN 978-0-7515-7628-3
Trade Paperback ISBN 978-0-7515-7629-0

Typeset in Meridien by Palimpsest Book Production Ltd, Falkirk, Stirlingshire
Printed and bound in Great Britain by Clays Ltd, Elcograf S.p.A.

Papers used by Sphere are from well-managed forests
and other responsible sources.

Sphere
An imprint of
Little, Brown Book Group
Carmelite House
50 Victoria Embankment
London
EC4Y 0DZ

An Hachette UK Company

www.hachette.co.uk
www.littlebrown.co.uk

For Lesley, as always
And for everyone whose family history has
surprised them!

Prologue

First I see the animal. Its body is a hunched grey shape, outlined by the glow of a lantern and the shadows moving slowly on wet bricks. Billows of warm breath swirl in the fog as it trudges under a bridge to the clatter of its own hooves. Soon I hear the leather harness rustling on its flanks, the line of twisted hemp creaking and sighing as it tightens over the swingletree. I catch the scent of fresh manure, mingled with the tang of earth matted in the animal's hair and the aroma of oats in its nose tin, moistened by its breath.

Thirty feet behind, the stem of a boat drifts into sight. It moves in silence, but for a murmur of water caressing the keel. A coating of coal dust clings to the oak boards, and the lantern light catches the roof of a squat cabin, where the arc of a tiller rears over the stern.

And then I notice the man. He's a ghostly silhouette, staring ahead, his eyes fixed on the horse as he judges the curve of the bank and braces the tiller against the pressure of water. There's a stillness in his manner, an air of concentration as he reads the motion of the boat. When his face emerges from the mist, I recognise the pain that deadens his eyes. It's the look of a man who has faced betrayal, a man who knows all about fear.

My body aches with tension at the relentless tread of the horse and the slow drift of the boat towards the bridge. Through a gap in the fog, a wooden bollard appears on the wharf for the steerer to tie up his line. Stacks of unmarked boxes lie decaying on the cobbles, slippery with mould.

The second figure barely stirs. His face is invisible behind the collar of a worsted greatcoat as he stands in the shelter of the bridge, his sweat drying cold on his forehead and a faint wheeze in the back of his throat. A chill strikes into his bones from the freezing water and he moves his feet slowly, one after the other, flexing his toes to stop them from going numb. He turns his head to follow the boat and waits for the horse to pass, praying that the fog will muffle his breathing and the painful pounding of his heart.

And finally, I see one more thing. It's a six-foot boat shaft, tipped with an iron spike, gripped in a waiting hand.

My thoughts are tainted by these images. They've grown in my mind like ancient ghosts breathed into a raw, quivering life. They sound and smell too real to be illusions. They're trying to convince me they're actual memories.

Yet all this began in that brief instant when the old man's eyes first met mine. I realise now that he'd already been able to see these images himself, and perhaps he'd been seeing them for years. He was preparing to transfer them to me, like a dying ancestor handing down the secrets of the tribe. My reluctant hand was the next in line. Refusal had never been an option.

There was just one moment when I had the chance to walk away, a second of hesitation when I could have drawn back from the edge. I might have gone back to my Victorian semi, to the constant struggle to pay the bills, to the micro-waved meals for one in front of the TV, and the tedious tick of the carriage clock that reminded me constantly of my parents. It wasn't much, but it was my own life, and I was used to it. If I'd been asked, I would have chosen to keep it.

But I *had* hesitated, and it was too late. When a voice called my name across the Fosseway restoration site, my shabby, ordinary life sank into that evil-smelling mud where the dumper truck had reversed and churned the earth into a morass. During the weeks that followed, it seemed I would never stop floundering in my efforts to reach firm ground.

Andrew Hadfield was among the work party that day. He'd straightened up and spotted me before I could walk back to my car. He was pointing me out to a tall, elderly man in a dark overcoat who stood at his side. And then Andrew shouted the words I couldn't help but hear.

'Hey, Chris! Chris Buckley! There's someone here who's dying to meet you!'

I'd been turning over a paragraph in my mind, something about the first small step in a project to re-create a waterway that had lain buried beneath the Staffordshire countryside for forty years. I should have known that no matter how much you dig, or what ancient facts you unearth, you can never restore the past completely. There always have to be compromises, and a great many lies. But, like those muddy enthusiasts shovelling out the first lock of the canal, the knowledge wouldn't have stopped me digging.

'Come on, Chris,' called Andrew. 'Come over and say hello.'

A gust of chilly wind blew across the fields, and the afternoon sun had slipped behind a mass of grey clouds building up from the east. I was cold and tired, and I wanted to go home. But politeness made me move towards Andrew and the stranger, the sort of courtesy that becomes an obligation. That, and my other major fault – curiosity. An almost fatal combination, as it turned out.

It seemed only a short flicker in time from then to the moment I found the police standing at my door, two hard-faced detectives with nothing but questions in their eyes. That movement was all it took to precipitate my headlong plunge through two centuries of bitterness and hatred, decade upon decade of guilty secrets, and an endless thirst for vengeance.

That step taught me the meaning of betrayal. It took me right to the brink of despair.

And then it showed me death.

1

February 1998

Lichfield, Staffordshire

It was all about family in the end. That's how it began, and that was how it finished, too.

There are some families that seem to last forever, perpetuating themselves in infinite generations, son after son marching through the centuries, fecund and proud. They branch off and flourish in great clumps like wild flowers seeding themselves on the wind, until their teeming progeny populate vast swathes of the countryside. But other families are destined to die out, to fade and vanish into history. They wither on the branch like blighted fruit, until just one shrivelled apple is left. Such a family are the Buckleys.

The deaths of my mother and father, coming so close together, should have been a catharsis, a cleansing. When the stonemason added my father's name to the headstone in the graveyard at St Chad's, it was a symbolic act that swept the board clean, giving me a chance to start life afresh. Instead, it felt more as though an emptiness had fallen on me, a heavy blanket through which I could barely remember my former life.

It also left me with no family that carried the Buckley name. I had no brothers or sisters, no broods of nephews and nieces. There weren't any uncles or aunts on my father's side, and no cousins. And, of course, I had no wife or children of my own to inherit the house, or the carriage clock.

So there was just me. Christopher Buckley, thirty-two years old, single and always likely to be. A man who was about to be made redundant from his position as an Information Officer with Staffordshire County Council. I was the last shrivelled apple, waiting for the next stiff breeze to knock me off the branch. And trying my best to avoid the wasps.

True, there were many friends and acquaintances I'd made over the years in the newspaper, magazine and PR businesses – some former colleagues at the *Lichfield Echo*, fellow free-lancers, councillors, all the contacts I'd cultivated. And recently there were some members of the Waterway Recovery Group I'd come to know through visits to their sites, and asking a lot of questions about a subject that had sparked my interest.

But how many of these people would waste a day coming to my funeral, as my father's old work colleagues had? Precious few of them. There would always be something better to do. An urgent meeting, the kids to pick up from school, some unmissable daytime TV game show. But it wouldn't matter to me by then, would it? A dead man needs no friends.

There was one person who would certainly come to my funeral. She'd make a point of sobbing into a handkerchief during the service, nodding sorrowfully at the platitudes of a vicar who didn't even know me. And she'd be weeping buckets as they carried my coffin out to 'The Chorus of the Hebrew Slaves' from Verdi's *Nabucco* – a piece of music I've chosen specifically because I want to make them all cry. No laughing at my funeral, thanks very much.

My next-door neighbour, Rachel Morgan, was divorced and lived alone, like me, in a house much too big for her in a neighbourhood she knew little about and cared for less. Even I could work out from her frequent appearances on my doorstep, on one pretext or another, that she wanted friendship, maybe more. Yes, Rachel would come to my funeral. She would come out of the fellow feeling that one lonely person has for another, but she'd believe she was there as something more.

It was Rachel who happened to be raking dead leaves from her front lawn that cold February morning when I left the house to look for updates on my current stories. I write a few theatre and book reviews for the local papers, but they barely bring in a few pounds. Feature articles for some of the glossy magazines had become my current interest, mainly because they pay well. All I needed was an angle, and a few good photos. Now and then, it was possible to hit lucky.

'Good morning, number six.'

Rachel had tied her red hair back off her face in a yellow ribbon and was dressed in jeans and a baggy sweater.

'Morning, number four,' I responded automatically.

'Off taking more pictures then, Chris?'

'That's right,' I said, patting the camera bag stupidly, as if she hadn't already spotted it.

Our houses are a pair of Victorian brick-built semis, like many others in the Gaia Lane area of Lichfield. Some of the houses have little wooden balustrades on their upper storeys, as if they were trying to hint at the existence of proper balconies like those of their larger neighbours round the corner. Each pair has a plaque built into the brickwork between the bedroom windows, recording a date in the first decade of the twentieth century and a romantically rustic Victorian name – The Hawthorns, Oaklands, Rosemount. Our pair are Maybank, 1910. It must have been Rachel who started the ridiculous habit of addressing me by the number of my house, but it seemed churlish not to respond the same way.

'Where are you off to today then?' she said.

'Oh, the usual.'

'Hilton, is it? Cyril the Squirrel and his friends in their tree houses?'

There were only two on-going stories I could rely on, and they were loosely related. One was the efforts of the restoration group to re-create the abandoned Ogley and Huddlesford Canal that had once run through Lichfield – a huge task that seemed about to become impossible in the face of plans for the country's first toll-paying motorway. The South Staffordshire Link Road would cut right across the line of the canal.

The other story was a series of protest camps set up near Hilton by environmental campaigners determined to save countryside threatened by the road. Bit by bit, the Under Sheriff of Staffordshire was clearing them from their tunnels and tree houses with the help of armies of bailiffs and police. But every time they had to retreat from a site, the protestors set up camp somewhere else and defied the law to do its worst. The game had gone on throughout January and February.

Rachel was interested in the link road protest. In a way, she was typical of the readers I aimed my articles at.

'Trees and the environment versus the road builders,' she said. 'Whose side are you on, Chris?'

'I don't have to be on anybody's side. A journalist makes it his business to see both sides.'

'Oh, yes?'

She tossed a rakeful of dead leaves into a wheelbarrow with a dismissive gesture, condemning the limp and useless mass to the compost heap. I took this to mean she didn't think much of my trite remarks.

'Look, the protestors have a point, obviously,' I said. 'We've lost enough of our environment already, and somebody has to take a stand. And why on earth do we need yet more roads, when they'll only create more traffic?'

Rachel looked up at me then, her eyes expectant, using the prongs of her rake to turn over some decaying beech

8

foliage. The leaves were an attractive chestnut brown on top, but when she turned them over, their rotting black undersides were exposed and tiny slugs and insects fell away, wriggling to escape the light.

'But at the same time,' I said, 'if you've ever seen the cars and lorries crawling through places like Brownhills and Walsall, you'll see why a new motorway is needed. It's a nightmare for people living in those places. There are two opposite viewpoints, both with justification. So there's bound to be conflict. And that's what I'm reporting.'

She smiled at me, nodding encouragingly. I knew I'd done exactly what she wanted, and allowed her to provoke me into conversation, pushing me to express an opinion and show my feelings. I could never figure out how she did it, or why.

'You shouldn't take your job too seriously,' she said. 'People want some entertainment with their news.'

'Even in the *Lichfield Echo*?'

'We all need a bit of fun.'

'I'll look for a pile of leaves to kick,' I said.

Rachel frowned at me, concern forming little creases around her eyes. She'd been giving me that look a lot since my father's funeral.

'I know it's been hard,' she said. 'But it's been three months, Chris. You need something. Your friends—'

'I have to go now,' I said. 'Work to do.'

She sighed. 'All right, then. Have a good day.'

I walked towards the little car port at the side of my house. The Escort isn't fond of cold mornings, and it took three or four attempts to start. It was already ten years old and rarely serviced, and I hardly dared to look at how many miles were on the clock. But replacing it wasn't a possibility right now.

Rachel waved to me as I pulled onto the road, and I raised a hand in acknowledgement. I suppose I could have had worse neighbours than her. It might have been a house full of screaming children next door, or students smoking weed every night with the stereo turned up full blast. Or it might even have been a couple with a patio barbecue and an urge for midnight DIY, just like the neighbours I'd left behind in Stafford two years ago. But if there'd been anybody like that in the other semi at Stowe Pool Lane, I wouldn't have stayed in the house when my father died.

Rachel had been divorced for five years. She'd worked as a librarian until the cuts began, and now she was a part-time receptionist at a vet's surgery. I gathered she also put some hours in at a charity shop for cancer relief. At weekends, she went with a couple of girlfriends to folk concerts at the Guildhall to hear Bellowhead or The Albion Band. The previous November she'd roped me in to see *Pirates of Penzance* staged by Erdington Operatic Society at the Civic Hall. How she'd managed to persuade me, I couldn't remember. But somehow I ended up humming 'I am the Very Model of a Modern Major-General' for weeks afterwards. *I know the kings of England, and I quote the fights historical. From Marathon to Waterloo in order categorical* over and over again. Well, I say 'singing', but no one would want to hear me sing.

That fateful morning, I'd decided to make the canal restoration my first stop. The day was turning out clear, with a pale blue sky and a bright February sun. The weekends had been constantly wet for weeks, and I hadn't managed an opportunity to photograph the latest stage of the work. Reinstatement of a buried lock was now being extended to the site of the old Fosseway Wharf, where vast expanses of undergrowth had to be cleared.

There was a work party from the Waterway Recovery Group on site all week, and I knew a hired JCB had begun to haul the soil and assorted debris from the canal basin. Thousands of tons would have to be shifted before the structural condition of the abandoned wharf could be assessed.

10

It seemed a good chance to capture the first sections of brickwork being exposed.

The WRG were all volunteers. They were many things in their ordinary lives – teachers, solicitors, bus drivers or factory workers. All they had in common was a willingness to give up their spare time to labour in the mud for no reward other than knowing they'd made a small contribution towards a bigger scheme.

Canals seem to hold a fascination for many people. As more of the Ogley and Huddlesford Canal emerged from its premature grave, dozens of volunteers were coming forward to help, organisations were finding funds to support the project and businesses were showing an interest. Not long ago, the whole subject of inland waterways had been a mystery to me, but I was beginning to grasp the appeal.

I'd already recorded the progress on the restoration of the lock. The early stages had been the most fascinating, as digging parties moved onto a completely filled-in site. Trenches had been dug to locate the wing walls of the lock, and one trench had hit a soft spot which turned out to be the paddle frame and drop shaft a couple of feet below ground. A trial hole on the land boundary exposed the distinctive orange brickwork of the arch above the approach ramp to the old bridge.

Restoration had suffered a setback when plans in the British Waterways archives revealed a three-foot-wide land drain had been cut through the head walls and inverts of all three locks in the Fosseway flight. The drain had caused damage to the head walls, and the floors of the lock had been partially cut away. A survey showed that just over three feet of masonry had been taken off the walls of the lock, creating yet more work for the volunteers.

By now, things were different. The lock had been fully excavated and repaired, including the weir and by-wash. Thanks to the land drain, it even contained water. A stile and picnic table were being erected, and work was under way to re-establish the towpath.

If you're trying to be a freelance journalist, it helps if you can take your own pictures. Part of my inheritance had gone on a good Nikon 35-millimetre SLR camera. Since my photographic skills were self-taught, I'd adopted a technique explained to me once by an old newspaper staff photographer. If you shoot off enough exposures, one or two of them are bound to come out all right, he said. So I keep shooting whenever the conditions are right and the opportunity arises. And occasionally they do come out okay.

I set up my tripod and took pictures of the lock site for a few minutes without taking much notice of the activity. There were twenty or thirty people around, most of them anonymous in overalls or thick sweaters and jeans, and all wearing white hard hats. There were a few vehicles coming and going, and a dumper truck reversing on the lockside. It was only when I'd finished off a film and was packing my camera away that I became aware of Andrew Hadfield. He was a recent recruit to the restoration team. An architect by profession, he'd proved a valuable addition. Today, he was taking an interest in the visiting volunteer work party.

Andrew waved to me from the head of the lock, where he stood with an old man at his side. If only I'd taken that gesture as a warning instead of an invitation, things might have been different.

'This is Chris,' Andrew was telling the old man as we squelched towards each other. 'He's our resident reporter and chronicler. He gets us in the news now and then, when he can spare the time from his other work. Theatre and book reviews he does as well. He's a cultured chap, you see.'

There was something in the tone of Andrew's voice that told me I ought to have gone back to my book reviews right then and let my brain wallow in the familiar words and sentences. Books and plays are a series of worlds in which to escape, where reality is kept at bay, at least for a while.

The old man was stepping forward, his shoulders stiff inside his overcoat. He picked his way carefully over the mud, tapping his stick on the broken bricks. The sound was like the ticking of a watch, slow and relentless, like the old carriage clock back at Stowe Pool Lane.

'You don't know me – do you, Christopher?' he said.

'No, I'm sorry. I don't.'

I hadn't been called Christopher for a long time, not since my father had died three months before. It wasn't a name used by friends or workmates, and certainly not by strangers who'd just been introduced. It was a name used only by family, and a family was something I no longer had.

Andrew laughed in delight at my expression, and took my arm to pull me closer to the old man.

'I've got a surprise for you, Chris. This gentleman is Mr Longden. He's an old friend of the family.'

'Really? A friend of *my* family?'

I looked at the old man again. There wasn't anything out of the ordinary about him, nothing that should have given me that strange, uncomfortable feeling when I first saw him. Despite a slight stoop, he was as tall as Andrew, over six feet. He wore an old coat, buttoned up tight against the chill, and leaned on a strong stick with a well-worn ivory handle in the shape of a ram's head. His white hair was thinning on top but he'd allowed it to grow thick round his ears and on the back of his neck. A woollen scarf worn inside his overcoat didn't hide the fact that his shirt collar was too loose on the sagging skin.

'Yes, my name is Samuel Longden,' he said. 'Have you heard of me?'

The question seemed important to him. But it didn't take much thought before I answered.

'Not at all.'

A mixture of reactions passed across his face. Pain, disappointment, resignation – and some other powerful emotion I couldn't name, but which made him thrust his body forward, so that he could grasp my hand in his cold, dry fingers. I stared at him in amazement as the old man leaned in and spoke with a sudden intensity.

'Christopher,' he said. 'You don't know what it means to me to meet you at last. Because there's only you left now, you see. Only you.'

2

We sat in my Escort, parked in the lay-by on Fosseway Lane, close to the level crossing for the branch line to Brownhills. Andrew had been too pleased with himself, too intent on being part of our conversation, for me to want to linger at the lock site where he could listen to what Samuel Longden had to say. So I'd invited the old man into my car on the pretext of the cold, and he'd readily agreed.

The Escort had taken quite a hammering over the years. The inside trim was showing signs of wear, and the body-work was full of chips and scratches that were revealed whenever I took it through a car wash, which wasn't often. Most worrying at the moment was a strange rattle in the engine at low revs. I didn't dare take it to the garage, for fear of what they might find wrong, and how much it would cost.

The heater worked, though, and gradually we began to warm up. The old man sat hunched in his overcoat, staring out at traffic passing over the level crossing. Once we were in an enclosed space, I became aware of a smell about him – not the stale, unwashed odour I might associate with old people, but a sort of mustiness, a suggestion of mildew, like a stack of old books in the cellar of a second-hand bookshop.

'It's fascinating to see the old canal re-appearing after so many years,' he said. 'Wonderful. It's history coming full circle. This was Lock Eighteen, wasn't it? Fosseway Lock?'

'No, Fosseway is number seventeen. Eighteen is Claypit Lock. Across the road there, to the south.'

'Of course.'

'And just beyond that is the site of Fosseway Wharf. It's completely overgrown now.'

He looked at me with a smile. 'You've become quite an expert, haven't you, Christopher? Very admirable.'

The windows of the car were starting to steam up, so I wound the handle down on the driver's side to let in a bit of the cool February air.

'I'm not an expert on anything,' I said. 'Journalists rarely are. The restoration provides good copy for me, that's all. So I've made it my business to know a bit about the history of the Ogley and Huddlesford.'

He propped the handle of his stick against the scuffed dashboard. The grey hair on the back of his neck curled onto his coat collar, and his large nose had turned pink with the cold. His eyes were watering slightly, and he pulled a tissue from his pocket to wipe them. Though he was an old man, there was nothing feeble about his voice. It was steady and clear, with a local accent distinguishable under an educated veneer.

'Just one lock dug out so far, and a new bridge, isn't it? What do you think the chances are of restoring the entire seven miles of canal?'

'Very slim,' I said. 'Oh, they've got the enthusiasm, that lot down there. But just think of the cost. We're talking ten million pounds at least, and the estimate is rising by the year. Where's the money going to come from? Most of the line of the canal has been filled in, parts built over completely – factories, housing estates, garden centres, you name it. Locks have been broken up and bridges demolished. And that's not to mention the new link road. It will cross the track of the canal twice, and the restoration trust has to pay for bridges, if they want them. It seems obvious to me that it's more work than a handful of volunteers can possibly manage. We'll all be dead long before there are narrowboats passing through Lichfield again.'

'I see you know how to talk like a journalist. But I've been told your heart is in it, and I think they're right.'

'Who said that exactly?'

'Oh, people I've asked about you.'

I didn't like the sound of that. There were no dark secrets in my life, but the idea that anybody had been going round asking questions about me felt uncomfortable all the same.

The old man made no attempt to wind down his own window. He continued staring straight ahead while the glass misted up and blotted out his view of the road. His eyes had a faraway expression. I didn't know what he was looking at, but it wasn't anything in the real world.

'Are you really a friend of my family?' I said.

He turned towards me then, and fixed me with those pale eyes. He smiled, showing a set of teeth that must have been his own, judging by the unevenness and the staining of the enamel on his front incisors. For the first time, I noticed the short, white whiskers on his upper lip where he'd failed to shave properly.

'Yes, Christopher. I'm Samuel Longden.'

'The name still means nothing to me, I'm afraid. My parents never mentioned you.'

'And you never met your grandfather, of course.'

'He died long before I was born.'

'Yes, I know.' He turned away again and used the cuff of his overcoat to wipe a small, damp space in the condensation on his window. 'It's understandable, of course. But I thought I was just ignored, not forgotten entirely.'

His words sent a small, inexplicable shaft of guilt through my heart. But I couldn't see a justification for feeling guilty, and I shrugged it off immediately.

'You were a friend of my grandfather's then.' I realised

they must have been of the same generation, though my grandfather hadn't survived to anything like the age Samuel Longden had reached.

'I knew him very well indeed,' he said. 'Yes, your grandfather. George Buckley.'

'If you were a very close friend, I'm sorry that I haven't heard of you.'

'I shouldn't be too surprised. There were things that happened between us, between myself and your grandfather. They meant I was no longer welcome in the Buckley family. Now I can see I was never forgiven. "Unto the third generation" they say, don't they?'

He said this with such a note of despair that I felt sorry for him. I wanted to tell him something different, to assure him I'd heard of him after all, that my parents had talked about him often, and he'd been such a close friend of my family that I almost considered him an uncle. But I could assure him of none of these things. They wouldn't have been true.

'Perhaps you'd like to tell me about yourself,' I said, as kindly as I could.

He rallied then, shook his shoulders and gave a small smile. 'Of course. I must warn you, though – I'm happy to tell you a certain amount about myself. But there's something I want from you in return.'

And there it was. The trap. He thought he had a hold on me, and perhaps he was right. I was curious, and whatever it was he wanted, I was going to have to cope with it. I hoped he couldn't see the expression that passed across my face.

'That sounds like a deal.'

He was beginning to look better in the warmth of the car. A bit of colour returned to his face, and his shoulders relaxed. He caught me looking at him, and I got that frisson of shock again as our eyes met. It was as if I was looking at somebody I'd known all my life.

'You *have* seen me before,' he said, as if reading my mind.

18

'Though you might not have noticed me at the time. I've certainly seen you, Christopher.'

'I don't remember. I suppose it must have been a long time ago?'

'Not at all. It was three months ago. I was at your father's funeral.'

'What?'

'I didn't make myself known, of course. I wanted to come along because . . . well, because your father was George Buckley's son. I've always regretted that it wasn't possible for me to attend your grandfather's funeral. I knew I wouldn't have been welcome. But with your mother and father both gone, I hoped there'd be no one to object to my presence. I took a gamble with you, Christopher, as to whether you'd recognise me. But now I see that I worried unnecessarily.'

My father's funeral was still very clear in my mind. There had been few mourners at St Chad's. Even fewer had bothered to come the short distance from the church to the house at Stowe Pool Lane. Most of those who appeared were my mother's family, the Claytons and Bridgemans, the same tight-lipped middle-class couples from Birmingham who'd attended my mother's funeral a few months earlier. Their cloying sympathy had irked me, but the knowledge that it would almost certainly be the last time I saw any of them was a consolation.

There had also been some of my father's former colleagues – most of them rather depressed-looking men who'd been made redundant at the same time as him from the engineering factory on the Ringway industrial estate. None of those had come back to the house, so there had only been a small clutch of in-laws and one or two neighbours who were openly inquisitive about what I intended to do with the property.

As our silent group stood at the graveside, my mind had wandered over many subjects, none of them related to memories of my father. Like the neighbours, I was considering what

I'd do with the house. I could sell it, but what would I use the money for? The property was vastly more desirable than the grubby flat I'd shared in Stafford. The question was whether I could bear to live in a house full of reminders of my parents. It was this mental debate that might have made me seem reserved and withdrawn.

If I'd seen an old man among the gathering, white haired and leaning on a stick, I couldn't remember taking any notice of him. I did recall a flurry of excitement and alarm among some older in-laws as they queued to examine the wreaths. The occasion had been solemn and wordless until that moment, and the flutter of movement was like a raucous child bursting in and dancing round the hearse. I'd also been aware of the faces turned suddenly towards me, anxious or frankly prurient, waiting to see my reaction to something. The men had fingered their black ties nervously, the women clutched their handbags and tilted their hats into the wind as they studied me with avid eyes. But I hadn't known what it was they expected, and I didn't care. They'd wanted something I couldn't give them.

Then, looking at Samuel sitting next to me in the car, I had a sudden flash of insight, like that neurological flicker they call déjà vu. It was something I should have known at the time. Maybe, in a way, I had.

'You sent a wreath, didn't you?'

'Yes,' he said. 'There were some there who knew of my existence – your mother's mother and her brothers. They were aware of the split, though perhaps not the details. I suspect my name has become a sort of fable, mentioned only in whispers.'

'A split? That sounds intriguing. Something to do with my grandfather?'

'Your grandfather and me. That's the reason I was unwelcome.'

So there was a secret in the family. Was I the only one

who hadn't known about it? I felt a flush of anger at the thought of those chattering in-laws hugging a bit of knowledge to themselves. They'd known about it, and yet they'd eaten my sandwiches and sausage rolls and drunk my beer and said nothing. They'd muttered and winked to one another and uttered not a word. In the end, the only person who'd come forward to tell me the truth was the man himself.

I studied Samuel's distant blue eyes. I guessed it had taken some courage on his part, in the face of likely rejection.

'I suppose I was trying to draw attention to myself,' he said. 'I wanted you to be reminded of me. I wanted to see if you'd get in touch. I was foolishly hurt that I'd never been informed of your father's funeral. When you didn't make contact, I thought you still hated me.'

'But I knew nothing about you.'

'I see that now.' He sighed. 'It seems incredible.'

'I take it you don't live in Lichfield?' I said.

He frowned as his pale eyes focused on me, recalling my face. 'No. Well, I was born here in the town, in Tamworth Street, but my home is at Whittington.'

'Not far. What, five miles? Didn't you think of making yourself known before this?'

'Not while your parents were alive.'

'Was it such a terrible row that you had with my grandfather?'

'Oh, there was no row,' he said. 'Not really. We didn't need to argue. We both knew our relationship was over. There was no doubt that we would live separate lives from then on.'

'I don't understand. Are you going to tell me what it was all about?'

'Not now, Christopher. Soon. But let's take it slowly.'

A series of possibilities ran through my mind like a flickering slideshow. I recalled being told that my Granddad Buckley was an old soldier, and I imagined him being rigid and strict in his beliefs. What might have wrecked a friend-ship for a man like that? Some moral transgression, surely. I wondered if Samuel could be gay. It would have been enough, in those days. Perhaps that was why the old man was taking his time, waiting until we knew each other better before he told me the truth.

'Well, all right,' I said reluctantly. 'I don't want to tire you too much.'

He smiled weakly. 'You're right, I do get tired.'

The old man shifted uncomfortably, easing his bones, then reached for his stick. I could feel him withdrawing from me rapidly. He was sinking into the well of his own thoughts, where no one could reach him.

'I don't have the energy any more,' he said. 'There's a job to be done. And it needs somebody younger to finish it.'

I frowned, puzzled by the change of subject. 'What job?'

But he just smiled at me wearily. 'Would it be possible for us to meet again soon? Tuesday perhaps?'

I didn't have to consult my diary. A list of my appoint-ments for Tuesday would have read: 'Open post, feed cat, put out wheelie bin. Pay telephone bill (if possible).'

'That will be okay.'

'I'll tell you more on Tuesday then,' he said. 'I'm sorry to appear so mysterious. I wanted to make contact with you first, to see if we can work together.'

'Work together . . .?'

He held up a hand. 'I'd like to have the chance to explain it to you properly at another time. There are also some items I want to show you, which will help you to understand things better than anything I could say.'

I sighed. 'All right. Tuesday it is.'

So in the end, I had to curb my curiosity. Samuel asked me to take him to the bus station in Birmingham Road, where he could pick up a taxi to Whittington. When I started the car and switched on the wipers, the windscreen seemed to

22

have gathered a coating of grime as thick as if it had stood neglected for years.

We drove back towards Lichfield through the outskirts of Leomansley and onto the roundabout at the Western Bypass. An old clock tower stands in the Festival Gardens, where it was moved to make way for a new road, The Friary. I always think it looks a bit forlorn on its new site, a victim of progress, as if it had been banished to the bypass from the city centre for some unforgivable offence, perhaps for being too obvious a reminder of the passage of time.

I wasn't sorry to have the old boy off my hands by then. He looked ready to drop with exhaustion, and I was worried he might become ill if I kept him talking any longer. I didn't want to find myself looking after an invalid.

At the bus station, Samuel struggled out of the car and pulled himself upright on a steel barrier. He stared at me through the open door of the car, his eyes strangely out of focus. I don't know what he saw in my face, but suddenly a surge of anger went through him. He raised his stick above his head and brought it down with a clang on the barrier to get my attention. I was horrified to see heads turning our way from queues in the other bays.

'Stop it,' I said.

'It all depends on you now,' he barked. 'There's only you left.'

The old man lifted his stick again, and I thought he was going to set about battering the car. Unnerved, and frightened of an embarrassing scene, I slammed the door of the Escort and pulled sharply away from the kerb. In my rearview mirror, I saw the old man slump helplessly as two women came forward to guide him into a taxi.

3

Once Samuel Longden was out of my company, I began to wonder whether he'd just been spinning me a yarn. He was old, and perhaps not entirely in touch with reality any more. A little bit unstable. Besides, what did I really know about him, other than what he'd told me himself?

There was no evidence to back up his claim to be so closely involved with my family. On the contrary, my parents had conspicuously failed to mention him. I hadn't asked to see any proof, of course – it would have seemed incredibly rude. My emotions at being confronted by this man, a complete stranger who seemed so familiar, had completely swamped my journalistic instincts. I'd always been taught to check my sources, to get confirmation.

Back in 1987, I began my working life as a trainee reporter on one of the local papers. It was something I drifted into, just because an advert for the job appeared in the *Echo* in the same week that I returned home after graduating from the University of Birmingham. I'd studied Economics at Birmingham, but I never intended to be an economist. I wasn't alone in that. Most of the students I knew had no idea what they wanted to do when they went out into the real world – they were only concerned about whether their grants would last out and where the next party was happening.

It's different these days, I know. I think we were probably the last generation who saw no need to worry about the future. I'd certainly never concerned myself with the past. Part of my course was called Economic History, which dealt with the Industrial Revolution and all that stuff. Those were the lectures I skipped to spend lunchtimes in the pub.

I don't talk about my Economics degree now. It seems to tempt sarcastic comments about how bad I am at managing my own money. Now all that's left to me from those three years in Birmingham is some vague recollection in the back of my mind about the laws of supply and demand and the price mechanism, and a man called John Maynard Keynes.

But the world of newspapers couldn't keep me interested either. At least, not the *Lichfield Echo*, with its constant diet of council meetings and summer fairs. I felt cut out for better things than reviewing the amateur dramatic society's latest Alan Ayckbourn comedy or sitting in the magistrates' court in Wade Street all day long listening to the dreary details of shoplifting and speeding offences.

So after a few years I went into Public Relations, deciding there was no future in local newspapers. Who wanted to read the *Echo* when there was television and local radio and the internet? I took a job as a PR officer for the county council at their offices sixteen miles away in Stafford. The journey by car was a bit too much sometimes, and that was my justification to move away from home. It was ridiculous that I should feel I needed an excuse, but I did.

It was impossible simply to tell my parents that I wanted to leave home, even though I was nearly thirty by then. It took a calculated campaign, with numerous references to the appalling traffic on the A51, the notorious accident black spot near Rugeley, and the bad weather when the north wind blew across Cannock Chase and iced up the road. I told my mother how difficult it was for me after a hard day's work, and in the end she was almost relieved when I announced that I had the chance of sharing a first-floor flat in Stafford with a county council Information Technology Officer called Dan Hyde.

Dan was a real computer buff, and his enthusiasm was infectious. He'd persuaded me that the internet was the future, and there was a real killing to be made by the people who got in early. Six months ago, he'd told me he wanted to start a dot-com company aimed at businesses in the West Midlands. It couldn't fail, he said. And he wanted me to join him. All it needed was a bit of capital to get it started.

I knew very little about running a business on the internet, but Dan was persuasive. He showed me lots of articles about dot-com start-ups with mind-boggling figures for their estimated value within months of being launched.

I remember him smiling at me smugly as I boggled over another string of zeros behind a pound sign.

'See,' he said. 'We can make a killing. It's exactly the right time.'

'But this isn't real money, is it? It's only a notional value. No one makes any profit from a dot-com unless the company is sold.'

'That's why timing is so important. Right now, people are buying into the hype.'

'So we create hype? Is that what we're going to do?'

'Exactly. We build it up big, then after a few years we do an IPO, make our fortunes, and get out.' He rubbed his finger and thumb together. 'Easy money, Chris.'

'It sounds *too* easy.'

'Well, as I said, it needs a bit of investment to get it off the ground. We've got to rent some premises, hire a few programmers, invest in the right tech. After that, it's all about advertising and marketing. Creating that buzz. You'll be the perfect guy to write the website content.'

I looked again at the articles. Many of these dot-coms hardly seemed to be doing anything tangible.

'And you think an online auction site is the right choice?' I asked.

'Absolutely. Just like uBid or eBay in the USA. I showed you the figures—'

'Yes, I've seen them.'

'Fantastic, isn't it? uBid only launched a few months ago, and they'll be going public this year. We can do what they're doing, but here in the UK. There's a gap in the market.'

'They specialise in consumer electronics, don't they?'

'Yes, laptops, computer hardware, business equipment, cellphones. We can do all that too. At least at first, then we can see how it goes, decide whether we want to expand into other areas. It doesn't matter, because it's all third-party sellers. We don't hold any stock ourselves, everything is done online. A win-win situation, Chris.'

Then Dan had become exasperated with my hesitation.

'Come on, Chris, you know you'll love it,' he said. 'You were always the one who got excited about a new project. You can't—'

He stopped suddenly.

'What?' I said.

But he hesitated. 'Nothing.'

'What were you going to say, Dan?'

'Oh, just that you can't pass up this opportunity.' He shook his head as he sighed. 'The old Chris Buckley wouldn't have done.'

The old Chris Buckley? So who was I, this person standing here now? Apparently a different man from the one Dan Hyde had known, and perhaps everyone else I knew or worked with. In other people's eyes, I was no longer the same Chris Buckley I'd been a few months ago, the old Chris who got excited about a new project and wouldn't have passed up an opportunity. They didn't know what to do about that change. And neither did I.

I looked again at the dazzling figures.

'So what are we going to call it?' I said.

Dan smiled. 'I've already registered the domain. We're calling it *winningbid.uk.com*. It has absolutely the right ring to it. Makes people think about winning straightaway. And that's what we should do.'

His tactics had worked. Once I was on board, the project became the one thing that made my future seem brighter, a glowing vision of untold wealth in the not-too-distant future. It was like an oasis in the desert.

Gradually, I'd become convinced we were onto a real winner. Online retail was set to be a burgeoning market in the first years of the new millennium, and we were going to be right there at the cutting edge.

'We've got to do the job properly,' Dan had said. 'A professional marketing campaign, corporate design. Remember who our target audience are – we want high-grade businesses to come on board. Image is everything, Chris.'

So I'd gone along with the idea of employing a graphic design agency and a marketing consultancy in Birmingham, who charged the earth. My eyes had nearly fallen out of their sockets when I saw their quotes, which involved figures so large they made me dizzy with anxiety.

Dan had soon packed in his county council job to launch the website. He said *winningbid.uk.com* was going to make our fortunes – but only once we'd recouped the money we put into it and paid back the frighteningly large bank loan we'd just committed ourselves to, with both of our names on the agreement.

Offices had been leased on an enterprise park near Trent Valley Station. I'd visited the unit and gazed in awe at the empty space we intended to fill. Dan wanted to get the sign up on the building as soon as possible, and that was the first remit for our designers. Equipment had been ordered, and the next step would be to start hiring staff. The costs were mounting up, but we had a lot of interest in advertising on the website, and within a year we'd be well established and heading for profit. Or so Dan told me.

It hadn't been in the plan for me to part company with the county council quite so soon. Despite the bank loan and an investment from some anonymous backer Dan had found, there was no money in the kitty to pay me a salary – indeed, the flow of cash was entirely the other way for now.

Of course, there was no such thing as job security any more. I was on a fixed-term contract, and I'd known for some time that my term was coming to an end. The writing had been on the wall, and it didn't take a genius to read it. After all, I'd been one of those whose task had been to put the best possible gloss on cuts and redundancies in other areas. My contract ended in three weeks' time. And since I was owed fourteen days of my annual leave, I'd effectively already left the job. All that remained for me to do was turn up at the office for one last day, clear my desk and accept the ritual presentation from my colleagues.

So that was how I ended up back home in Lichfield. It was the last place on earth I wanted to be, but the flat in Stafford had become a luxury I could no longer pay for and would soon have no need for, once *winningbid.uk.com* went into profit.

There were no outright recriminations from my father that I'd failed to stick to a career, no 'we told you so', just a continuous cool, unspoken atmosphere of disapproval. My mother had died a few months before, the sudden onset of stomach cancer taking her away before my father even knew what was happening. I looked after him for a while, a duty I could never have imagined until it happened and there seemed to be no choice. But he faded rapidly. It was a heart attack that took him one night as he watched television in his armchair. I'd been at the pub with some friends, and I found him cold and stiff when I let myself back into the house at about half past eleven. 'The Big Match' was still blaring away on the TV screen.

At least, everyone said it was a heart attack. But they hadn't seen him droop and fade once my mother had gone. They didn't see the disappointment and resignation in his eyes when he looked at me every day. The fact is, my father hadn't thought it worthwhile to carry on living. Not for my sake, anyway.

His death had helped me financially, of course. With no prospect of another full-time job after my contract ended and *winningbid.uk.com* draining every spare penny, my dead parents were now subsidising the cost of my board and lodging, as if I was a teenager who'd just left school, rather than a man in his thirties. The small amount of money that came to me in my father's will would have to keep me going for the next twelve months.

Meanwhile, I was trying to cover my options by earning a bit of extra money as a freelance journalist, and that was hardly lucrative. Even my modest lifestyle was gradually eating into those few thousand pounds my father had left me. The car was getting old, the household bills were piling up, and I spent too much over the bar of my local, the Stowe Arms. By the time I said goodbye to my colleagues at Stafford, I would be practically penniless. Thank God there was no mortgage to pay on the house in Stowe Pool Lane.

But things would change. Life would get better soon. When our dot-com was the success that Dan and I planned, all of this would be forgotten.

4

When I got back home after leaving Samuel Longden at the bus station, I parked the Escort under the car port and went in through the back door – a habit I'd got into, because this route wasn't overlooked by the windows of the house next door. Rachel might sometimes be seen lurking in the back garden, but in winter she couldn't be out there all the time.

My parents' aged black cat, Boswell, hovered around me in the kitchen until I fed him his Whiskas, then I sprinkled some fish food into the heated tank in the sitting room. The fish had been my father's hobby. They're supposed to be relaxing, but I can't say I ever noticed any beneficial effect on his temper.

I went into the front room, which I've converted into a makeshift office, with a computer on the table and a few bookshelves. I pulled the South Staffordshire phone book out of the sideboard and ran my finger down the 'L's until I found 'Longden, Samuel' next to an address in Whittington, a village five miles east of Lichfield.

Then I went out again and drove up Beacon Street to Safeway, where I filled the car up with petrol, wincing as my credit card crept another £30 nearer to its limit. I wandered around the aisles of the supermarket with a wire basket for a while, forcing myself to stock up with the essentials – coffee, milk and toilet paper, and enough frozen meals to last me a week.

I didn't want to go back to the house after that. It was getting dark, and when I looked at my watch it occurred to me the work party from Fosseway Lock site would be in the pub by now after their day's work. I wanted to know how it was that Samuel had come to find me. The person to ask was Andrew Hadfield. It was probably time I bought him a drink anyway, to keep him sweet. Finances would just about stretch that far.

The canal work parties normally retired to the Pipe Hill Inn on Walsall Road. Not every pub appreciates a score of sweaty, muddy labourers trampling over their carpets, but the Pipe Hill was also used by walkers heading for the Heart of England Way. I found Andrew in the middle of a small group of WRG volunteers, many of them women. The people on these weekend parties tended to be teachers and office workers, whose idea of fun was getting up to their knees in mud on their days off. During the summer, there were two-week camps when dozens of volunteers came from Italy, Germany, the USA and Spain to spend their holidays labouring.

'Chris. Nice to see you again. Come and join the party.'

Andrew looked as though he'd already sunk a few pints of Marston's Bitter. The high colour in his narrow face from a day out in the open was heightened by the beer. He was in blue jeans and an open-necked red-check work shirt, showing off his lean hips and wiry arms. During the week he commuted on the train from City Station to his architecture practice in Birmingham. But at weekends he seemed to have made it part of his job with the restoration trust to help supervise these work parties. Looking at the flushed faces and bright eyes of some of the women around him now, I wondered if they were the reason for his dedication.

I bought a round of drinks, noting that the women seemed to be getting through a large quantity of Smirnoff Mules and Metz, judging by the empty bottles on the table. I slid

Andrew's pint across and managed to squeeze into a spot opposite him. The bodies close around me smelled of sweat and soil, overlaid with cigarette smoke and the mingled sweetness of alcohol and feminine scents.

'Had a good day, then?' I asked.

'Brilliant!' they all said, practically in unison. One or two of them looked meaningfully at Andrew and laughed. He grinned at me, and I half-expected a conspiratorial wink.

'We're getting on well. We really got down to business today, didn't we, girls?'

More laughter. I smiled tolerantly. They were a group who'd bonded by tackling a hard physical task, not to mention roughing it at night in a youth centre somewhere, and were now relaxing together. They deserved their fun. But in the process they'd become an intimate little unit of the kind that always makes someone outside the group feel uncomfortable, an unwelcome intruder who doesn't even understand their language.

'You know what you can do with your shovel,' said a female voice. General hysterics followed, and I tried to laugh along with the in-joke.

'I wanted to ask you about the old man, Andrew,' I said finally, when the crowd thinned out for a trip to the loo.

'Who? Oh, Mr Longden. Quite a touching reunion, Chris. I don't think I've ever seen you so gob-smacked. I take it the old chap came as a bit of a surprise?'

'Like a bolt out of the blue.'

'And other journalistic clichés, no doubt.'

'I wondered how you happened to meet him.'

'Actually, I'd seen him hanging around the lock site a few times. We get the occasional spectator, you know. Asking their damn fool questions usually. You know – "who let all the water out?", that sort of thing. It's no problem really – we like people to know what we're doing. But this old chap wasn't that sort. He was different.'

33

The loo party returned and fussed about taking orders for another round of drinks. I let one of them persuade me to have another half of Marston's. That would be my limit, at least while I was driving, and until I could get to my local back home.

'How do you mean, different?' I said.

'Well . . .' Andrew frowned as he thought about it. But his concentration slipped as he watched the women at the bar, and I had to drag him back to the conversation.

'The old man, Andrew.'

'Yeah. Well, he never said anything for a while. In fact, he didn't move around much, just stood there propped on his stick in that old overcoat. No matter how cold it was, he would stand there, staring. He didn't look well to me. Physically, I mean. A bit frail. Almost as if he wasn't all there, too. But he's an old friend of the family, isn't he, Chris? You must know him.'

He looked puzzled at my insistence, and I could see he was starting to get bored with the subject.

'But how did you get talking to him, Andrew? If he wasn't asking questions?'

'Oh.' He waved a hand vaguely at the rest of the group. 'One day a couple of the girls got in conversation with him. He was interested in the history of the canal. But way back, you know – right back to when it was built. They were out of their depth. And so was I, to be honest. Then somebody mentioned your name. "Chris Buckley might know stuff like that. You should talk to him," they said.'

I tried to picture the moment. Had the old man looked surprised to hear my name mentioned? Or had it been what he was expecting?

'I can tell you, he got so excited, I thought he was going to have a seizure on the spot,' said Andrew. 'And then today he came back again, and there you were. Cue the great reunion. Fate, eh, Chris?'

'Yes.'

But was it really fate? Or something more deliberate, with little left to chance? You might say I have a cynical and suspicious nature. But I had the feeling I was the object of some clever manoeuvring by a person who knew exactly what he was doing. And the manipulation had started even before we'd met.

I drained my beer and told Andrew I had to be going.

'Sure you won't have another? We'll be here for a while yet. The girls are just getting into the swing.'

'No, I'm driving.'

'Oh, so I see.' Andrew peered out of the window and sneered at my old Escort parked near his bright red Jaguar XJS. 'I suppose you have to save your energy for pedalling.'

I didn't humour him with an answer, but my ears grew warm at the giggles from around the table. They were all well on their way to getting drunk, and I was far from it. The world seems a harsh and lonely place when you're the only one sober.

'This old family friend of yours, Chris,' said Andrew as I stood up to leave. Suddenly he looked more clear-headed, and his eyes were assessing me. 'Do you think he might have a bit of money, then?'

I shrugged. I didn't know what to say. His question had struck straight to the heart of what I'd been thinking all afternoon, but hadn't yet admitted to myself. Suddenly I'd found an elderly friend of the family in a frail condition. A man who was almost like an uncle, and who was, by his own admission, not poor. *'There's only you left,'* he'd said. Only me left for what? That was the question. It's a sad fact that poverty can make you see the chance of money in everything.

'Well, like I say,' grinned Andrew, seeing my expression, 'it could be fate.'

5

I woke up on Monday with a thick head after staying until closing time at the Stowe Arms. I'd become involved in a game of darts with some of the regulars, and recalled having lost money on a bet when my darts had bounced all over a board I could barely see by that time. Sure enough, my wallet was empty, and my pockets were cleaned out of change. I knew my current account was already overdrawn, which meant I would very soon be raiding the dwindling savings account.

After a few cups of coffee, I set about putting together an article on the advancing restoration of the Ogley and Huddlesford Canal, which I intended to try on one of the waterways magazines – *Waterways World* perhaps, or *Canal and Riverboat*. With a picture or two, it might earn me a few quid. It was peanuts, but everything counted.

With that thought in mind, I unloaded the film from my camera and set off to clear my head with a walk into the city centre to drop the film off at Boots for twenty-four-hour processing. Rachel was cleaning her front windows, and she called a cheerful 'good morning'. I surprised her by not heading for my car, but walking away with a perfunctory wave. With the first blast of cold air, my thoughts were starting to stir again in a rational manner, and I couldn't do with being interrupted by one of Rachel's interrogations.

I was unsure exactly how to play the situation at the

moment, but I knew that I didn't want Samuel to come to the house in Stowe Pool Lane. Not just yet.

I suppose it was a defensive reaction – I was reluctant to let him penetrate any further into my solitary life and upset my routine. It was a means of keeping him at arm's length. Instead, I'd arranged to meet him on Tuesday outside the bookshop in the Cathedral Close. He'd expressed a wish to see the cathedral properly for the first time in many years. I had no objection. On a Tuesday, it should be quiet enough. But I'd have to be careful not to let him tire himself so much that he was driven to an embarrassing outburst of the kind that had ended our last meeting. That had almost made me decide not to see him again.

So when Tuesday morning came, I walked up Gaia Lane towards The Close. The day was bright and clear again, and birds were clustered on the water – ducks and geese, gulls and swans, and a handful of smaller birds. Coots or moorhens, I was never sure which.

A few people ambled around Minster Pool on the perimeter path, some walking their dogs, others in pairs, deep in conversation, all huddled up in their coats against the cold or the intrusion of the outside world. Work was still taking place high on the south side of the cathedral, where scaffolding seemed to have been in place for months.

The old man was waiting outside the bookshop, gazing up at the three great sandstone spires they call 'the Ladies of the Vale' and the vast Gothic facade of the west front, which never fails to awe me. The carvings that cover the stonework are rows and rows of kings and saints, sculpted by medieval craftsmen who laboured for years to create their masterpiece. A vast well of love and devotion had been poured into that structure of wood and stone.

Samuel was still in his black overcoat and carrying his ivory-handled stick. But there was fresh life in his face, as if

37

he'd spent the intervening hours sleeping and recharging his energy.

'How old is the cathedral?' he asked. 'I can never remember things like that.'

'There's been a cathedral here for thirteen centuries,' I said. 'This one was started about 1195.'

'More facts from your journalist's bag of tricks.'

'That's right.'

'Ah, but you're not a journalist any more, are you, Christopher? My information is a little vague.'

'In a way. I leave my job at the county council in three weeks' time. I'm trying to earn some money as a freelance while I get a new project off the ground.'

He nodded as he stared up at the soaring spires. 'It took them a long time to build, I suppose.'

'A hundred and fifty years, I think.'

'A very long time. Generations. It must have taken an awful lot of commitment and patience. But they built it to last, didn't they? Did you check up on me, Christopher?' he asked. 'I assumed you would. Are you satisfied now?'

I flushed instantly. 'I'm satisfied there is such a person as Samuel Longden.'

'I see.'

I knew I must have hurt him. I was throwing his approach back in his face. I had no idea how hard it might have been for him to make himself known after so many years of rejection and isolation. I couldn't meet his eye. It seemed such a cruel thing to do to an old man who'd only sought out his friend's grandchild in his last years.

'It's just a precaution,' I said. 'You know a lot about me, but I know nothing about you at all. I didn't even know you existed until two days ago.'

'I do understand. But I think I can put your mind at rest on all counts.'

'Do you want to go inside and have some tea?'

'Do you mind if we walk for a while?'

'Not at all, if you're sure you want to.'

'Perhaps a slow perambulation around The Close?'

I soon discovered what a perambulation was. Our progress was slow, and Samuel wanted to pause often, to admire the cathedral from a different angle, or to study the buildings around The Close – the Bishop's Palace, the Cathedral School, the Deanery. At other times, he seemed simply to want to rest, or gather his thoughts, as he began to tell his story.

He was eighty-three years old, born during the Great War, in which his father had fought and died, like so many others. When he left school, Samuel had gone to work for Seward's, a small independent brewery at Sandfields on the Birmingham Road, which has long since disappeared. The Lichfield area was known for its brewing industry in those days, as its water supply was ideal for ale making.

Samuel proved a bright and capable boy, and he'd caught the eye of old Benjamin Seward, the brewery owner, who'd encouraged him to learn every aspect of the business. The Second World War had intervened, but on his return Samuel had become a manager and gained influence in the company, which expanded its chain of pubs and became very successful. Seward made him a partner, and when the old man died, he left Samuel in sole charge.

Many independents had been bought out by the larger brewery chains by then, but Samuel had decided to hang on. The Sandfields brewery and its small string of traditional pubs became more and more valuable, until in the late 1960s he finally sold to a national company based in Burton on Trent. Now the Lichfield water was pumped to Burton for the breweries. But the sale had left Samuel extremely well-off.

'We used to move goods by canal at one time,' he said. 'Seward's was built backing onto the Ogley and Huddlesford. Barley and hops came in by boat, and barrels of beer went out the same way. We switched to road transport, of course, because it was more efficient. That was my decision, in the late 1940s. I suppose we helped to hasten the end of the canal trade.'

'What have you been doing since you sold out?' I asked. 'It's a long time to be retired.'

He smiled. 'I've never been a man to sit and stagnate. I've had several other projects. And I suppose I've been fortunate, in that I've been able to spend time with my family.'

'Ah, you're married?'

'I was.'

I could see the pound signs retreating from me rapidly at this news. Of course, there was no reason why I should have imagined Samuel to be as alone as I was. No reason, except the gut recognition of a man losing the ability to communicate with the outside world.

'And I suppose you have children,' I said. 'Grandchildren perhaps?'

He ignored me as if I hadn't spoken. It seemed his mind was running along a different track entirely, which allowed no room for irrelevant small talk.

'Christopher,' he said, 'there's something I find very difficult to talk about. I hope you'll understand and forgive this in an old man. It's something you need to know, but it's very hard for me to find the right way to tell you.'

'To do with your family?'

He was peering at a figure of King Charles II in a stone alcove. It was Charles who ordered the restoration of Lichfield Cathedral in the seventeenth century, but time had eroded his face into a grotesque mask, unrecognisable as human.

'To do with your grandfather,' said Samuel.

Now it was my turn to stop. 'George Buckley? Like I said, he died long before I was born.'

'George was a good man, a clever man. Much cleverer than I ever was. We attended the same school, but he was

40

older than me and a hero in my eyes. He went away to university while I was still at school. Then he married his wife, Mary, in 1938.'

'My grandmother? I never knew her either.'

Samuel nodded, as if absorbed by his own recollections. 'Yes, 1938,' he said. 'And your father was born just over a year later, at the start of the war. When George enlisted to fight the Nazis, he was a happily married man with a young son. When he returned, his life had been shattered.'

What did that mean? I had no idea what my grandfather had died of.

'Shattered?' I said. 'By a war injury?'

'No. His life was destroyed by what Mary did.'

I was so astonished I didn't know what to say. When Samuel set off again, walking slowly towards the western end of The Close and Bird Street, my feet seemed frozen to the ground for a few moments before I could catch up with him.

'I don't understand,' I said again, though I was starting to sound like an echo of myself. 'Mary? You mean my grandmother? What did she do? I know nothing about any of this.'

'I realise that. There are a great many other things you need to know too.' Samuel looked at me sadly. 'But you're right. To understand, you have to know the story from the beginning. There has to be a start somewhere. But not there – not with Mary. That wasn't the start of it at all.'

Some of the medieval buildings around The Close were distorted out of shape and bulging dangerously with age. They looked as warped and out of proportion as my life felt just then. Was it me, or had the world suddenly ceased to make any sense?

By the time we got to Bird Street, Samuel was starting to flag. I'd been watching him for signs of abnormal behaviour, but so far he'd seemed only harmlessly vague and rambling.

41

To keep him like that, I tried persuading the old man to stop for a coffee.

'Let me buy you lunch,' he said.

I looked at his old coat and his creased trousers. 'There's no need. I'll pay.'

'Believe me,' he said, 'I may be many things, but I am not a poor man. Choose a place somewhere and I'll treat you to lunch. I can afford it, I promise you.'

'Well, okay.'

Samuel looked at the pedestrianised street and waved his stick at the 'For Let' signs over some of the shops.

'I don't get into the city too often,' he said. 'But Bird Street used to be a busy shopping area. Now it's mainly pubs and restaurants.'

'Since the Three Spires precinct opened, it's on the wrong side of town.'

We settled on the White Hart, because Samuel thought the dishes chalked on the board outside looked plain and English, unlike some of the others. There was a dining area separate from the bar, but the place was busy and we had to wait a few minutes for a table. I bought a pint of Marston's bitter for myself and a bottle of Guinness for Samuel.

He wandered off to find the toilets while I was at the bar, and I was reminded that he was an old man in his eighties.

When he returned, he fumbled a pair of spectacles from a case deep in a pocket of his overcoat to read the menu. He waved away my tentative concern about prices with an impatient grunt and told me to have whatever I wanted. There seemed to be a constant gnawing in my stomach these days which was never satisfied. My body told me it was the pangs of hunger. So I chose a sirloin steak, hoping I wasn't taking advantage of the old man. For himself, he ordered salmon, which reassured me.

Over a few sips of Guinness, Samuel stared at a portrait of Lichfield's most famous son, Dr Samuel Johnson. Every corner of the city seemed to hold some personal meaning for the old man that I couldn't fathom. Johnson inspired him to one of those baffling non sequiturs I was already coming to expect.

'Did you know that, as a young man, Dr Johnson refused a request by his father to look after his book stall at Uttoxeter market?' he said. 'The guilt stayed with him for the rest of his life. The story is that Johnson stood bare-headed in the rain for several hours in the marketplace when he was quite an old man in his seventies. It was a penance, you see. It was the only way he could atone for his guilt. It's one of the scenes depicted on his plinth.'

'I've heard the story. You can't live in Lichfield without having Dr Johnson thrust at you from all directions.'

I wondered if I should mention my own favourite Johnson quote, which goes: 'I remember when all the decent people in Lichfield got drunk, and were not the worse thought of.' It's a slogan on the wall of the arts centre – except that whoever wrote it couldn't spell 'remember'.

'But what has that got to do with my grandparents?' I said.

He heaved a deep sigh with many years of practice in it. 'Mary left your grandfather a long time ago. They only had six years of marriage, and for much of that time your grand-father was away in the war. He hardly knew her as a wife at all. Not that Mary was a worthy wife to him.'

It made me uncomfortable to hear the way he talked about her. It didn't make any sense, since I'd never known her, whereas Samuel obviously had. Why should I feel defensive about her?

I'd met my grandparents on my mother's side, the Claytons, but never my paternal grandparents. I was racking my mind to try to remember whether I'd been told that Granddad and Grandma Buckley had both died, or whether Mary just hadn't been mentioned. As a child, I might have made the assumption that if one of them was dead, the other must be too. Why else would they have been so absent from my life?

'Why?' I said.

'Because,' said Samuel, 'no woman should have done what Mary did.'

6

This was all too much. People split up every day, didn't they? Even in my grandparents' time, it can't have been so unusual. But Samuel was making a big thing of it. I saw no reason why I should sit and listen to him condemn a grandmother I'd never known for something that must have happened decades ago.

His tendency to over-dramatise was starting to get on my nerves, as well as his cryptic evasiveness. He could have told me the facts straightaway, but he was trying to force me to ask questions, as if he thought he could capture my interest that way. I didn't want to play his games.

And underneath it all, I thought I detected the bitterness of a man who'd been deceived in love himself. Presumably even Samuel Longden had been young once.

'What about your own wife?' I asked.

'Oh, I married rather late in life. My wife, Alison, died ten years ago, in a car crash on the A38. She was travelling with my secretary, Karen Mills, when their vehicle hit an articulated lorry that had crossed the central reservation.'

Samuel smiled sadly at his tragic memory. I felt as though I ought to apologise for being so ignorant, for forcing him to explain it all and live through the pain again.

'My parents didn't tell me any of this,' I said.

'So I gather. I can't really say it surprises me. None of your

45

family came to Alison's funeral. No Buckley had spoken to me for over forty years by then.'

'You haven't told me what caused the rift between you and my grandfather. Was it something very petty?'

'Why do you say that?' he asked sharply.

'It often is, isn't it? You know, a row over some trivial issue that escalates and gets out of hand, until neither side can see reason. It often seems to happen between close friends and within families. It's almost as if people are just waiting to seize on something as an excuse for a row.'

'Christopher,' he said, with a shake of his head, 'you talk as though you have a vast experience of family life.'

'Ah, I see what you're saying. You think I know nothing about families, right? How could I? But it's my job to inquire into other people's lives. And what I see depresses me immensely. The family is a vastly over-rated institution, in my view. Some of the situations that people create for themselves are beyond belief – and all in the name of family. Well, I'm *glad* to say that I haven't experienced it personally.'

'Was your relationship with your own parents good?'

'Well . . . I think so.'

I looked away towards the city, where the cathedral spires towered over the medieval street pattern. They were inarguably solid and enduring, a symbol of the stability and permanence I'd once longed for.

'I'd like to think it was too,' said Samuel, though I could tell he didn't believe me.

I realised he wanted more than anything to talk about my family. He wanted to know about them, to hear my memories, to find out what they'd been doing all those years since he'd last seen them. I realised, with a sinking of the heart, that most of all he wanted to hear they'd spoken of him sometimes, that they hadn't just wiped him from their minds. And I knew I couldn't give him what he wanted.

46

What he told me next confirmed my worst fears. It carried the sound of an obsession.

'I suppose it might have been because I was cut off from them, but I developed an enthusiasm for researching your ancestors,' he said. 'There have been many Buckleys in the Lichfield area over the years. Most of them were tradesmen and business people in a small way. But they've suffered fluctuations in their fortunes. Rather erratic fluctuations.'

'Like all families, I suppose. There are bad times and good times.'

'Perhaps. But I don't think so, not in this case. I don't think the Buckleys were ever quite like other families.'

I looked at him, but his face was impassive. I realised there was no point in questioning him – it only seemed to send him off on a tangent. I would have to wait patiently for him to tell me more.

The food came, and we were silent while we ate. Samuel picked carefully at his salmon, slicing the pink flesh with slow, deliberate strokes of his knife. He had an air of single-minded absorption now that was slightly unnerving. For a while, I was the one who'd ceased to exist.

Then Samuel sat back and reached for his drink.

'You may be interested to hear that your great-great-grandfather was once what they called a "number one" in Victorian times,' he said.

The words meant nothing to me at first. Number one what? Did he mean that my ancestor was a leading figure in the area? A number one? The phrase had a familiar ring, though. I'd read it somewhere, and only recently. Samuel watched me while I put two and two together, and the phrase clicked into place.

'You mean on the inland waterways? He worked on the canals. Am I right? A number one was a man who owned his own boat rather than working for the big carrying companies like Fellows, or Morton and Clayton.'

47

'That's right. They were the true canal folk, the ones they called the "water gypsies". They resisted the spread of the large companies for a long time. As a young man, Josiah Buckley operated a pair of narrowboats, the motor *Willow* and its butty, *Hazel*. The Ogley and Huddlesford was his home "cut", but he worked all over the Birmingham Canal Navigations.'

'Coal carrying, I suppose?'

'Mostly. He and his wife Hannah raised five children on board those two boats.'

'Amazing.'

'Most children stayed to help their parents. But some were sent onto the bank to live with relatives, to get a proper education.'

'My great-grandfather?'

'Yes, your great-grandfather. His name was Alfred, and he was the youngest child. His father had expanded the business, until he owned a small fleet of boats serving the collieries in the Cannock area. But then Josiah died. The oldest son, Thomas, tried to keep the boats going for a while, but small carriers like the Buckleys were doomed. After they sold out to a bigger company, Thomas was out of a job by 1905. He would only have been thirty then. There was work, of course, but he had no skills other than as a boatman. He could never expect to be more than a labourer, and that was a humiliation for a former number one. But his brother Alfred became a respectable mercer, a trader in textiles, and Thomas went to live with him for a while.'

'How did Josiah Buckley die? Was he killed fighting in one of those endless Victorian conflicts? The Crimea, the Boer War?'

'It might have been better if he had,' said Samuel. 'But canal work was an important trade and he escaped being called up.'

'What, then? I suppose there must have been many illnesses the boat people were prone to.'

'And dangers, Christopher. Canals and boats were always hazardous. In fact, Josiah ended up drowned in the cut. No one knows how it happened. There was a suggestion at the inquest that he was drunk, which was nonsense. Josiah Buckley was an abstemious man, a teetotaller, and he must have known better than anyone that you had to be careful on the bankside as well as on deck. But, like many canal people, he was quite unable to swim.'

Samuel paused, but only to take a ragged breath. 'He went missing one night, you see. Hannah would have been sick with worry. She had the children to look after as well. But there was nothing they could do. Next morning, Josiah's body was pulled out of the water from behind a lock gate. They said his head had been battered against the wall by the pressure of water when the sluices were opened. His face was quite unrecognisable.'

Suddenly feeling a bit queasy, I reached out and finished my beer in one gulp.

'It was reported that shortly before his death Josiah had been involved in a fight with another boatman,' said Samuel. 'He'd made himself unpopular with rival carriers by winning a lucrative contract for transporting coal to the power stations. But it seems he was just more efficient and better organised than the others. Probably more honest, too. There were some who didn't like that.'

I wiped my hands on a napkin, trying to see what possible relevance all this could have to me nearly a hundred years later.

'How far back have you traced the Buckley family?' I asked.

'They tell me it's possible to trace some families back to the sixteenth century, with a bit of luck,' said Samuel. 'But I confess I've never tried. I got as far as the late eighteenth century. Then I stopped.'

There was something very final about the way he spoke the last phrase. I felt a growing certainty that at last he'd reached the crux of what he'd come to talk about, the thing all this had been leading up to, ever since we'd set eyes on each other across Fosseway Lock.

'Aren't you going to ask me why I stopped, Christopher?'

'Somehow, I feel sure you're going to tell me.'

'Indeed.'

He took a sip of his Guinness with a hand that trembled noticeably. I could see the brown liver spots covering his skin like a spattering of dried blood, and I had a sharp sense of his advanced age and frailty. His energy was draining from him, and he looked what he was – a tired old man. Part of me wanted to tell him that we should leave it for today, that we could meet again and continue our conversation, like two people who intended to carry on a close relationship indefinitely. But my mind shied away from the intimacy that suggested. Besides, my curiosity made me want to urge him on, to get to the end of the story. I couldn't be left hanging.

The same thought seemed to have occurred to Samuel. He took a great breath and clasped his fingers together, as if to draw the remnants of strength from his body.

'I stopped because I came across something that was far more interesting than unearthing some seventeenth-century peasants. More interesting even than discovering which side they were on when Cromwell brought the Civil War to Lichfield. I discovered a great injustice. And those who were responsible have escaped retribution. Until now.'

He paused, and looked at me with a triumphant gleam in his tired eyes.

Well, that pretty much settled it. The old man was plainly mad. Why else would anyone be obsessed with seeking retribution for some injury he imagined had been done centuries ago? What was the point?

'I need to explain to you how things must be put right,' he said. 'But first you have to learn what was done wrong. It's ironic, of course. But unavoidable.'

50

'Do you realise how infuriating it is when you talk in riddles?' I snapped, my patience at an end.

He looked contrite. 'I'm sorry. It will all become clear, I promise.'

He finished his drink in silence. I waited for things to become clear, but they remained as murky as the dregs in the bottom of my glass.

'My grandmother, Mary,' I said at last.

'Ah, Mary,' he said. 'She had the most striking eyes. The way she looked at you—'

'Yes, yes. But what did she do that was so wrong?'

'She betrayed your grandfather, Christopher. She betrayed him with another man, despite the fact that he was desperately in love with her. She left him in the cruellest way possible.'

The way he talked about her was surprising. The word 'grandmother' had created an automatic picture in my mind, and Samuel's version of her didn't fit with my image of an imposing old lady. I suppose things like this went on, though, even in the 1940s.

'But there was a worse betrayal than that,' said Samuel.

'Worse?'

'Oh yes. Much, much worse.'

I stared at him doubtfully, conflicting reactions stirring up turmoil in my mind. But I couldn't look at the old man for long. I had to turn away to avoid the sight of his tears.

'What do you mean?' I said.

He brushed at his eyes with a handkerchief. 'No, I'm sorry. I can't tell you now. I thought I had the strength, but it's too much.'

'All right.'

As we left the pub I glanced again at the triple spires of the cathedral. Yes, it had been built to last. But I'd neglected to tell him that the Parliamentarians had bombarded it during the Civil War, destroying the roof and the central spire. Cromwell's troops had smashed the stained glass windows, turned the lead into musket balls, and stabled their horses in the chapel before looting the place and leaving it a ruin. Sometimes, a grand appearance hid a much more sordid story.

Samuel took my arm as we walked towards the taxi rank in Bore Street. His hand felt thin and bony as it grasped my elbow. I was starting to feel sorry for him, and that wouldn't do. He'd demonstrated sufficiently that he was someone I didn't want involved in my life. I shied away instinctively from public displays of emotion and instability. My mind was busy working out ways of keeping him at a distance without offending him too much.

'I still don't understand what you want me to do,' I said. The old man turned those weak blue eyes on me, but I hurried on before he could speak. 'But, look – I have to tell you here and now that I don't have the time to get embroiled in complicated history projects. My time is fully committed.'

Samuel looked at me sadly as I explained about the dot-com start-up, and its financial implications.

'It's going to take all my time and effort to make it a success,' I said. 'And that means *all* my time.'

He nodded as if he understood. 'Of course you think that now, Christopher. But when you understand everything, you'll feel quite differently.'

'I don't think so,' I said firmly.

'I know you will.'

Samuel rapped his stick on the pavement for emphasis as he dropped my arm. But there was no power in the gesture, no real anger. As I watched him go, I felt confident I'd made my position clear. I had no intention of getting involved, and he knew it. I had my own concerns, and my own life to lead.

But fate was about to take hold of my boring life and give it a vigorous shake.

When Samuel Longden walked away towards the taxi

rank, he looked like an old man who'd exhausted himself, who'd walked too far and talked too much. And no more than that.

He certainly didn't look like a man who was about to die.

7

And now I see a seething of dark water as the sluice gates open at the tail of a lock. A woman stands on the counter of a narrowboat moored to the bank. Her arms rest on the hatch and her rough hands twist and clench as she stares into the gathering dawn.

A pair of Black Country joey boats are waiting to pass into the lock, and a ripe smell hangs on the morning air. The joeys are carrying night soil, smuggling the nauseous substance away from the towns under cover of darkness. Their planks are green with mould, clumps of moss grow on the black-tarred sides, and the gunwales are bent out of shape from repeated impacts on lock sides.

The woman's own boat is scrubbed and clean, with the name *Willow* and a registration number smartly painted on the cabin. Inside, the wood is smooth and varnished, carefully scumbled to give the impression of wood grain. An oil lamp hangs on a bracket, its light reflecting from the wood, while lace-edged plates gleam on the brass rails.

At the boatwoman's foot is a hot stove, its chimney leaking smoke as grey as the light now creeping over the roof of the warehouse beyond the lock. A coal box drawer is pulled open to form a step down into the tiny cabin. The box is almost empty of coal, but there are several tons of it beyond the back wall of the engine hole, where the hold is full of a cargo loaded at the Cannock pits.

A long skirt rustles against the cabin doors, and the woman's black boots move uneasily on the counter. Below, in the cabin, a small white face turns up towards her and begins to speak, a plaintive sound like the mewing of a cat. The woman shushes it abruptly, the anxiety clear in her voice and the rigidity of her movements.

When the joeys have passed, they leave a wash that sucks the keel of the narrowboat against the bank. The woman continues to stare straight ahead, past the exhaust funnel, along the top planks and the box mast, to the triangular cratch at the stem of the boat, nearly seventy feet away. Her eyes watch the towpath for movement, but there is none.

She turns and looks behind her, where the sky is still dark. The butty lies close to the stern of the motor, deep in the water with several more tons of coal for the power station near Coventry. She can see the water cans on the roof of the back cabin, where two more children are asleep in the claustrophobic warmth. The curved wooden tiller has been tilted upwards, shipped out of use.

As I watch, I know the woman should have been standing in the well of the butty, not on the counter of the motor, which is usually her husband's place.

Finally, the joeys are safe in the lock, and a boatman hauls on the balance beam to close the tail gate. The dark water heaves and churns again, releasing lumps of debris and blobs of foam that show white and ghostly in the grey light.

And something else is released too, as the massive gate moves slowly away from its recess in the wall of the lock. There's something darker than the water, and oilier – something that bursts in a small slick on the surface. A metallic smell mingles with the stench of human waste, and the woman's throat tightens as her hands grip the edge of her shawl.

Then a shape breaks the surface. It rolls and wallows, black and glistening, bobbing like a broken fender. It looks like a lump of rope, but it uncoils into the reality of human limbs and sodden clothes and floating hair.

The light of dawn is still too faint to make out the face that turns in the water, pale and gaping. But the woman knows the truth already. She's looking at the body of her husband.

8

'On the roads this morning, traffic is particularly heavy on the A38 and A5. Watch out for hold-ups at Muckley Corner and the Weeford Roundabout. And the weather for South Staffordshire today is: cold and wet.'

I turned off the radio and pulled on my old waxed jacket, ready to go out. The word was that the Under Sheriff and his bailiffs would begin clearing the tree houses at the third camp near Hilton this morning, no matter how wet the weather. In fact, the rain would be on their side – the protesters would be staying inside, and there would be fewer supporters on hand to hinder the operation.

I had to be there, on the off-chance of getting that crucial human interest story – a pregnant woman manhandled by the bailiffs perhaps, or the notorious Squirrel arrested again. There was also a chance of being on the spot for just the right photograph, one that the nationals would snap up. Some hopes. With my luck, there'd be so much else happening around the world that the protesters would be relegated to a paragraph on page 30. But still, I had to be there.

As I drove away towards Gaia Lane, a figure in a red waterproof and hood stopped on the pavement and waved to me. It was Rachel, out walking old Mrs Norton's cocker spaniel, Jed. Automatically, I acknowledged her greeting, though she probably wouldn't even see me through the streaming windows.

Most of the rest of the day I spent tramping about in the rain on the edge of a muddy field, watching very little happen. The bailiffs seemed reluctant to move in, and when they did eventually decide to get on with it, the tree people put up no resistance. The constant drizzle blurred the scene, creating a dismal atmosphere in which there were only shades of grey, no black and white confrontations to provide the striking image I wanted.

Later in the afternoon, a mist began to develop. By then I was chilled through and rain had trickled down the neck of my coat, soaking my collar. The wellingtons I'd brought with me in the boot of the car were caked with clay. I decided to go home and change.

There was a meeting I had to attend that night in the community hall at Boley Park. Although the tree houses and tunnels of the eco-warriors had attracted most publicity, the road scheme had also brought together a consortium of local councils and community groups calling itself the Alliance Against the South Staffordshire Link Road. The Alliance was pursuing a legal challenge against the road, which it hoped to take to the Court of Appeal.

The hall was already crowded by the time I arrived, and I spotted Andrew Hadfield across the room with other members of the trust. The WRG work party had gone home by now, and these were the real activists, dedicated to promoting their cause on every occasion, by whatever means they could.

Tonight was notable because one of the local MPs from an area crossed by the new road had turned out to support the campaign. His presence on the platform had attracted a good crowd, included a sprinkling of press.

There was nothing like a high-profile personality to attract publicity to a cause. And the MP, Lindley Simpson, was as high-profile as you could get in this part of Staffordshire. He was a rising star in the New Labour government, one of Tony Blair's generation, who'd already become a junior minister in the Department of Agriculture. How much he knew about road schemes and transport policy remained to be seen, but at least he was there. An MP for a constituency in the vast, sprawling West Midlands conurbation around Birmingham, he might have been expected to be in favour of the new road, so his support was regarded as a coup for the Alliance. But maybe it was just a public relations stunt.

The MP sat at a table on the platform, alongside councillors. He was in his early forties, well-groomed, with short fair hair, and he was wearing a smart dark suit and a bright red tie. His manner was a little too slick for me, his smile exaggeratedly sincere. He behaved as if he was entirely at home in the spotlight, undoubtedly a man who'd been trained how to behave in the public eye. Lindley Simpson wouldn't open his mouth and say the wrong thing, or be caught off-guard. He was a media-friendly politician. In a few years' time, if he managed to keep his nose clean, he'd be a man of power and influence.

I took a seat at the side of the hall and spent some time studying the audience. To me, they were more interesting than the platform party, because they were a whole mixture of types. You could see the journalists, keeping their distance from the crowd, and the council officers clustering together as if afraid that they might find themselves taking the blame for something if they ever became isolated.

At the end of the front row was a group I couldn't quite place. There were a couple of men and a woman with black hair. They were behaving in a quiet, self-effacing manner, speaking to no one around them. They certainly weren't drawing attention to themselves. Yet it was that air about the little group that made me notice them.

After a while, I realised that they were exchanging glances with Lindley Simpson. Whenever the discussion moved on to another topic, the MP would glance to this little corner, like an actor looking for his prompt. Maybe he was getting secret signals about what his views ought to be. Were these people what the tabloid newspapers referred to as 'spin doctors'? Special advisors, press officers and the like? It seemed that every government minister had them these days.

When the meeting was over, Andrew Hadfield wandered over towards me. He was with another Trust committee member, Phil Glover, one of the organisation's real experts, an experienced civil engineer who'd masterminded the plans for the restoration. He'd drawn up a new line for the canal in places where the original route had been built over. In one section, a bridge had been lost in the middle of a concrete works, and he'd proposed a replacement route thrust-bored under a railway embankment some way to the south. Like me, most of the Trust members would never even have heard of thrust-boring. So Phil was a man whose brain I picked shamelessly for his technical knowledge.

They both greeted me like an old friend. They were useful to me, and in my business, that constitutes a friendship.

'What do you think, Chris? Is the Right Honourable minister on our side, is it just a load of politician's bullshit?' Andrew jerked his thumb at the front of the hall, where the platform party were conferring together in a self-congratulatory way.

'Lindley Simpson? It's a bit difficult to say, isn't it?' I glanced at my notebook. 'I'd guess there was nothing he said that couldn't be interpreted to mean whatever you want it to mean.'

'That's about the size of it, isn't it? All words and no action. The action's left to people like us.'

Phil smiled sardonically. I wondered what was going through his mind when he looked at Andrew. But all he said was: 'I suppose we need every kind of support we can get.'

The councillors on the stage were splitting up now as the

hall emptied. Simpson trotted down the steps to join his support team. One of the men half-rose from his chair to shake hands with him. I could see that he was quite a small man, maybe five foot six, with heavy shoulders and a barrel chest like a wrestler's, straining the seams of his jacket.

'Which reminds me,' said Andrew, 'how did you get on with the old man?'

'Oh yes,' said Phil. 'Old Mr Longden.'

I frowned. Did everyone know my business?

'There's something he wants me to help him with,' I said. 'Some kind of research project.'

'And are you going to?'

'I don't think so, Andrew.'

'Why on earth not?'

'Oh, he's very vague and mysterious about it. I found him a bit irritating, to be honest. Slightly unstable. I still don't know what his project is exactly, but my gut feeling is that it'll be more trouble than it's worth. He's not somebody I want to get involved with.'

'Are you sure? Are you really going to turn down old Samuel?'

I shrugged, watching the politician's group walking down the hall. 'Yes, I think I am. I've got better things to do with my time. More interesting things to think about.'

Andrew followed my gaze. 'Such as our tame MP?'

I didn't answer. My eyes had been moving from the tall, elegant Simpson, to the short, dark, muscular man at his side, and then to the other two people with them. It was the woman who attracted my attention now. From behind, all I'd seen was a curtain of black hair. But now, as they walked towards me, I was struck by her looks. Her eyes were almost as dark as her hair and set in a pale face with high cheek bones. She was taller than the thickset man beside her, and she moved with the grace he lacked. She had an expression on her face like someone who'd accidentally walked into the wrong bar and found herself among a bunch of drunken labourers. Her eyes were fixed on the exit, and she completely failed to see me.

As the group passed, the thickset man was saying something to Simpson that I couldn't make out. But the MP was turned half towards me when he replied, and I heard his words clearly.

'Yes. But it cuts both ways, Leo,' he said.

Rachel was lurking in the window of her half of Maybank when I arrived home. It was hardly unusual. But I hadn't been inside my house more than a few minutes when she was knocking on the door. She appeared to be in a state of excitement.

'Somebody's been to see you, Chris.'

'Oh?'

'An old gentleman. He came in a taxi.'

Immediately, my heart sank. There was only one old gentleman it could be, and I'd already made my mind up that I didn't want him coming to Stowe Pool Lane.

Rachel saw the look on my face and hurried on. 'He said he knows you very well. He just wanted to drop off a few things you'd need.'

'What things?'

'I don't know what they are. He didn't say. Since you weren't here, he left them with me. I hope that's all right,' she added, watching me with a bright eye and a cautious smile.

'Did this old gentleman give his name?'

'Mr Longden. He was very nice, I thought. Very polite. He had old-fashioned manners that you don't see very often these days. He said he was a—'

'—a friend of the family?'

'That's right.'

'So where is it, then? All this stuff he left for me?'

'Oh, it's still in my hallway. I think you'll have to help me bring it all round. There's rather a lot of it to carry, you see. The taxi driver had to bring it in for him.'

I let my eyes close against a rush of anger. What on earth had Samuel Longden dumped on me? What gave him the right to impose on me like this? He'd even involved my next-door neighbour, encouraged her to poke her nose into business that I'd rather she didn't know about.

'There are some files,' said Rachel. 'And a box. Mr Longden said it was all to do with a project you were helping him with.'

I sighed. 'I'm sorry if you've been put to any trouble.'

'Oh, it's all right. I liked the old chap. Not that I had much chance to talk to him. The taxi was waiting, and he had to rush off.'

I put the front door on the catch and walked round to Rachel's house with her. I could simply have stepped over the low wooden fence that separated our front gardens, but it was too valuable as a symbolic barrier to be treated in such a dismissive way.

Sure enough, a black file and a bulging A4 folder sat on a long wooden box in her hallway. I felt her watching me carefully to see my reaction. I knew she'd want to know all about Samuel and the nature of the 'project'. So I kept my face straight, trying not to show my despair at the weighty evidence of Samuel Longden's invasion into my life.

I hefted the box file, which felt as though it was loaded with house bricks, and added the blue folder on top.

'I'll come back for the box,' I said.

'It's all right,' said Rachel. 'I think I can manage that.'

'No, no. Don't try if it's full like these.'

But she picked the box up anyway, without any apparent effort. 'It seems to be empty.'

We trailed back to my house and I couldn't stop Rachel following me into the front room, since I had no hands free

63

to shut the door. I dumped the files on the dining table and she slid the box next to them.

'It all looks very interesting,' she said. 'Is it a big story you're working on? An investigation?'

'To be honest, I've no idea what it is.'

'Oh, but surely . . . Mr Longden seemed to think you'd know all about it.'

'I wish I did. No – scrub that, I wish I didn't know anything about it at all.'

She was starting to fumble at the lid of the file. She pressed the button and it sprang open, revealing a thickly compressed mass of paper under the metal spring that was supposed to hold it down.

'I'll look at it later, I think,' I said firmly. 'It's probably confidential material.'

She withdrew her hand reluctantly, her curiosity simmering. 'I suppose I'd better leave you to it, then.'

When Rachel had left, I lifted the lid of the file again and flicked through a few pages without actually reading anything. The file was crammed with papers, scrawled notes, cuttings from local newspapers and photocopies of pages from old documents and books. I pulled the elastic band off the folder and saw a stack of typewritten A4 sheets. It was a manuscript. So that was what it was all about – he was writing a book.

But my attention was drawn from the files to the box alongside them. It was an old box, made of something like oak, and about eighteen inches long by a foot deep, with a close-fitting lid bound in tarnished brass. In fact, it was a *very* old box, with the patina of age on it, the grain smoothed by many hands.

But the most curious feature was the three brass-plated keyholes on the front, only one of which contained an ancient iron key with an ornate handle. Three keyholes, but only one key.

Intrigued now, I turned the key. It moved slowly, but

without sticking. I heard the lock click, but the lid wouldn't move. I removed the key and tried to insert it in the middle of the three holes, but it wouldn't fit. I tried the third, with the same result.

So it must need three keys to open the box. Why would anyone make an item like that? And what would they keep in it? I ran my hand over the surface. The whole object was solid and heavy, and the wood felt as though it was very thick. There were no screws at its corners, only perfectly fitting dovetail joints varnished and smoothed over. When I tapped the lid of the box, it gave a deep, hollow sound.

Was it really empty? Why would Samuel Longden have sent it to me if it was? Without the other two keys, there was no way I could find out without forcing the lid and destroying what might be a valuable antique. And did it matter anyway?

I put the box back down and I stared at the other items covering my table. I thought I could detect the same musty odour that had emanated from the old man himself when he sat in my car at Fosseway. Mouldy books in the cellar of a second-hand bookshop. It was the smell of age, of thousands of forgotten words buried in paper-bound graves, waiting for somebody to open their covers and reveal their secrets to the light.

I shook my head. Some people might be excited by that smell. I wasn't one of them.

9

On Thursday morning I had my report to write up on the road meeting. But somehow the pile of files on the corner of my desk kept getting in the way. If not physically, then at least psychologically. They sat there reproaching me for not looking at them, until finally they'd irritated me beyond endurance. I picked the whole lot up and shoved them into a cupboard. The wooden box I couldn't find room for, so I put it on the floor and pushed it under the sideboard with my foot. Out of sight, out of mind. A good philosophy, in my opinion.

When I left the house later on, Rachel was there as usual, timing her appearance to coincide with my departure.

'Morning, number six. Are you all right?'

'Yes, but I'm in a rush.'

'I was wondering how you had got on with the files that Mr Longden left for you.'

'Got on with them? I haven't looked at them.'

'You're joking. Why not?'

'I've got better things to do.'

'Chris, surely you must have some curiosity?'

'Of course I have. But all this stuff . . . it's not something I can afford to spend my time on. They're just the scribblings of some cranky old man.'

'How do you know if you haven't read them?' she demanded.

'Look, I've met an ancient eccentric who rambled on about a research project he wants me to help him with, and I've seen a great heap of files that he's dumped on me totally uninvited. Therefore, the contents of those files are the scribblings of a cranky old man. No argument.'

'They could be very interesting,' she said.

'*You* read them then.'

She dropped her rake. 'All right.'

'No, no,' I said hastily, not having expected her to take me at my word. 'You can't. I'm giving them back to him today.'

'What? But that's terrible. He'll be really upset.'

'I don't care.'

She looked prepared to continue the discussion right there and then on the pavement, but I didn't have time. As I drove off in the Escort, I reflected that I ought to be grateful for Rachel's interference. She'd pushed me into making a decision. I would take the files and the box back to Samuel Longden, and I'd do it tonight. I wouldn't even consider looking at them any further.

After all, Samuel meant nothing to me. Why should I concern myself with someone else's past? It was the future that was important.

Yet for the rest of that day, there was an impression I couldn't get out of my head. It was an indistinct image of my grandmother, Mary Buckley. Whenever I thought about her, her figure seemed to blur and change, and I was unable to bring her into proper focus. I couldn't decide whether it was an actual memory, or a false picture produced by my imagination after listening to Samuel Longden's ramblings about her. Whichever it was, her ghostly presence was unnerving.

And Mary Buckley wasn't someone else's past. She was mine.

I collected my photos from Boots and dropped my article off at the *Lichfield Echo*, then wondered what else to do. I tried ringing Dan Hyde from a callbox, but there was no answer. There hadn't been an update on *winningbid.uk.com* since we'd signed the lease on the office space, and I was starting to worry he might have found something else to spend money on without consulting me. Financial anxiety gnawed at me constantly now, and I needed some reassurance.

Instead, I found myself driving towards Stafford, where I walked into the county council offices to retrieve some notes and a contacts book from my desk, even though I was technically on leave. It had occurred to me they were items which might have disappeared if I waited until my last day.

I was met with desultory greetings and embarrassed silences. My departure was a fact known to everyone, though nobody had openly mentioned it to me yet. I'd ceased to mind all this. Once I got it into my head that I'd be going, it seemed completely inevitable. I was merely waiting out my time until the end. If I was very lucky, I might get a bottle of cheap wine and a pat on the back from the Information Manager, followed by a 'good luck' card covered in forged signatures for all the people who'd forgotten to sign it.

Some of these people I'd worked with for quite a while, and I knew them well. There were two guys from Planning I used to play squash with every week. I wasn't sure when that had come to an end. Did they stop asking me, or had I lost interest? When I looked in their faces, I caught momentary glimpses of the good times we'd had after work, playing hard and laughing together, the way friends do. But it seemed like one more memory of the past now. What had happened to me?

In one drawer of my desk I found the remains of my last assignment – the proofs of some new leaflets that had been distributed to households explaining the council's policy on recycling. They were filled with cartoons of compost makers and bottle banks with jolly, smiling faces, mouths gaping wide in their eagerness to dispose of your rubbish for you. Nowhere was there a mention of a facility for recycling human beings in an environmentally friendly way. Now, as ever, people were merely dumped on the scrapheap.

The first thing I did when I got back to Lichfield was collect all the files from the cupboard and the wooden box from under the sideboard and stack them on the table. Light from the window glinted on the brass and the single iron key. The two empty keyholes drew my eye as if tempting me to try them again. But I didn't have the other keys, and I had no idea where to start looking for them. No one would be able to open this box, except perhaps Samuel himself. So he should have it back.

Well, there was no time like the present if I was going to do it. I looked up Samuel Longden's phone number in the book, but there was no reply to my ring. No one wanted to speak to me today. I wasn't in a mood to be put off by that, so I consulted my Staffordshire street map to locate his address in Whittington.

For once, I'd taken Rachel by surprise. She was nowhere to be seen as I turned the car onto Gaia Lane.

Ash Lodge was a tall, square-gabled house from the middle of the nineteenth century, its doorway shrouded with trees and hedges, and the drive covered in dead leaves. It stood in a quiet, narrow road that backed onto the Coventry Canal on the eastern side of Whittington.

I parked near the bottom of the drive and walked up to the door, crunching through the leaves. A high hawthorn hedge separated the garden of Ash Lodge from the next property, but through the bottom of the hedge I could see a neat gravelled drive that looked a good deal better kept than Samuel's. Of course, Samuel didn't have a car, so had little use for a drive.

I rapped a few times with a brass knocker, but couldn't

get any reply. There was a little electric bell push, but it produced no sound that I could hear from outside. I peered through one of the bay windows, seeing a room full of heavy furniture and a display cabinet packed with china. Most of it was Royal Doulton and Coalport, at a guess. I hoped Samuel had some decent security, because otherwise he was a sitting duck in this secluded spot.

When I went round to the side of the house, I realised I wasn't entirely unobserved. Here the hedge gave way to a fence which provided a view of the house next door. I could see a woman watching me surreptitiously from a kitchen window. I decided I'd better call round and enquire about the whereabouts of Mr Longden to establish my bona fides, otherwise my car number would be reported to the police. This definitely looked like a Neighbourhood Watch area.

The woman answered her door promptly, wiping her hands on an apron. She was middle-aged, with a heavy-hipped figure, and the hair straggling over her forehead was starting to turn grey.

'Yes?' she said.

'I'm sorry to bother you. I'm looking for your neighbour, Samuel Longden. Do you happen to know when he's likely to be at home?'

'Well, he doesn't go out much,' she said cautiously.

'I'm a friend of his. I've got something to return to him.' I gave her my most reassuring smile, and she seemed to relax a bit.

'I'm not sure,' she said. 'But I suppose he might have gone out with his daughter. He sometimes does that. I don't know what time he might be back. In fact, I haven't seen him all day, so he might have gone to visit his friend in Cheshire. Did you want to leave anything here for him? I don't mind.'

'No, it's okay. I think I'll just pop a note through his door.'

'All right.'

She watched me go back to my car, where I scribbled on

70

a page from my notebook. On one side I wrote: 'I'm sorry, but I can't help you with your project. Please contact me to let me know when I can return your files'. I popped the note into an old envelope, folded it over and wrote 'Samuel Longden' on the outside. Then I went back to his front door and shoved it through the letter box. As I heard the envelope fall on the mat, I turned and caught a glimpse of the woman next door still watching me.

Turning back into the village, I passed the White Swan pub. This seems to be the name of half the canalside pubs in this part of the world. A little further to the north, the Coventry Canal had once formed a junction with the Ogley and Huddlesford. Working boats would have been constantly passing up and down this stretch of water.

Now, since it was winter, there weren't even any pleasure boats – just a few ducks nosing around in the overgrown margins or dipping their beaks into the murky water for insects.

That night, Dan Hyde phoned me at home. There was an unfamiliar note of uncertainty in his voice, which rang a warning bell straightaway.

'Chris. Bad news.'

'Oh God, what?'

'Some problems with the start-up. It's the marketing company. They're being a bit awkward.'

'Awkward how?'

'I had a phone call from their top guy. Basically, they won't release rights to our brand assets until we pay their invoice. That's our logos, website design, advertising layouts . . .'

'Well, pay the invoice then. What's the problem, Dan?'

'The thing is – there's not much left to pay their invoice with. There's no revenue yet.'

'I know that. But that's what the start-up loan is for – the twenty thousand from the bank. Pay them out of that.'

'Well . . .' Dan suddenly sounded more cheerful. 'Tell you what, Chris, leave it with me. I dare say we can sort it out. I just thought you ought to know, that's all. In case you were wondering what was happening.'

'Okay, mate, you've let me know. But it will all be different in a few months' time, won't it? We won't have to go through all this once we get into profit.'

'Sure,' said Dan. 'Sure, it'll all be different then.'

10

It was only two days later that the letters arrived. It was a Saturday, and I'd stumbled blearily down to a breakfast of cornflakes and coffee rather late, having spent Friday night at the Stowe Arms playing pool with a crowd of regulars. As usual after a night out, my pockets felt lighter and my head several times heavier.

It wasn't until I was halfway through my second mug of coffee that I started to take notice of the mail I'd picked up as I passed the front door. Mail usually meant bills and bank statements, *Reader's Digest* prize draws, and offers of credit cards I couldn't possibly afford. But this morning there were two items that stood out. They gave off a subtle aura that said 'read me' far more effectively than any claims of 'Important', 'Exclusive' and 'You may already be a winner'.

The first envelope was long and white, with the address neatly typed, and instead of a stamp it had been passed through a franking machine that left the name of Staffordshire County Council imprinted in the top right hand corner.

With a churning feeling in my stomach, I slit the envelope open using my marmalade knife. It was a terse instruction to attend an appointment with the Human Resources department on a date that was two weeks away, the very day that I was due to return from leave. It didn't say what the appointment was about. But it didn't need to.

My brain was reluctant to consider the implications of the

first letter just yet, so I turned to the second. The envelope was smaller, and though not exactly used before, it looked faded, as though it had been sitting around for a long time since it was originally bought. My name and address filled most of the front in an unsteady scrawl, and the stamp wasn't stuck on straight. It was from Samuel Longden, in response to the note I'd pushed through his door two days before.

Though couched in almost formal phrases, his words made his distress obvious. He pleaded with me to reconsider. He hinted at revelations he'd yet to make which would undoubtedly change my mind. He talked about a mysterious disappearance, he repeated his claim of a great injustice. He begged me to meet him one more time, that afternoon at six o'clock in the market square, by the statue of James Boswell.

And he mentioned my grandmother's name too. Three times, like an incantation. I felt an odd shiver of apprehension when I read it, as if I might turn round and see Mary Buckley herself sitting in the corner of the room, fixing me with that stare.

I looked at the two letters, one in each hand. My brain might not have been working properly, but my hands told me the only thing to do. I dropped the first letter and read Samuel Longden's again. The only way to avoid thinking about the meeting in two weeks' time was to concentrate on the meeting today. Six o'clock in the market square?

But no – of course, I couldn't actually go. The idea was ridiculous.

As it happened, I was a bit early. Dusk was falling, and it was still cold, and I didn't fancy standing around outside shivering in the wind that blew down Dam Street towards the market square. Nearby in Conduit Street the Earl of Lichfield was already open. I slipped inside and got myself a seat by the window, where I could watch the corner of the square with a pint of bitter in front of me.

Although it had hunting prints on the wall and was right next door to a McDonald's, the Earl of Lichfield was in the *Good Beer Guide*, which was enough for me. From the pub, I had a view of the former Corn Exchange. Tucked under its arcade were a series of small shops – Fonebase, Supasnaps, a dry-cleaners, a clock repairers.

The first few sips of the beer made me feel better. The lethargy and muddle-headedness began to pass off as the alcohol seeped through my veins. I started to wonder what on earth I was doing there. A little nagging voice at the back of my brain was telling me I'd already made my judgement on Samuel Longden's project. So why was I going back on my decision just because an old man was upset about it? Let him find somebody else to help him with his crackpot idea.

An even more insistent voice was starting to remind me that not only was my dubious career as a county council information officer rapidly drawing to a close, but my hopes were pinned entirely on the future success of *winningbid.uk.com*. Although advertising bookings had been made, all that we had to show for it so far was the sign that had gone up on that empty building on the enterprise park. The reality was that I should be concentrating all my efforts on earning a livelihood, not wasting them humouring an eccentric old man like Samuel when there wasn't any money in it for me.

The more I drank, the clearer the situation became, and the more obvious it was to me that, if I was ever going to be decisive in my life, the moment was now.

Then I saw the old man arrive. He was walking slowly across the square from the direction of Dr Johnson's house, moving stiffly with the aid of his stick. He looked older and more infirm than ever, his black overcoat hanging from his body like a loose cape.

He gazed around for a moment, and I could see his breath coming in short puffs in the cold air. For a while, Samuel stayed on his feet. He read the plaques on the buttresses of the old St Mary's Church. I knew they commemorated four men who'd been burned at the stake in the square, including the last burning in England, that of Edward Wightman in 1612.

Samuel watched a family pass in front of him – the parents laden with shopping bags, their children dragging reluctantly behind. Then he settled himself on a bench directly under the Boswell statue. I looked beyond him to the solid bulk of the cathedral, a monument to nearly thirteen hundred years of Christian belief. Over the centuries it had swollen into an unfathomable Gothic immensity that filled the sky above Lichfield.

Samuel's arrival had frozen me with indecision again. I'd been on the point of getting up and leaving the pub to meet him on the bench. But my hand had automatically groped for my glass again, and sense returned as the beer touched my lips. I drained the last of my pint and ordered another. Then I sat down to watch the old man, as the dusk gathered and thickened over the city.

He must have been cold sitting there. He tapped the ground with his stick, and looked from right to left, raising his head hopefully every time someone passed. Once or twice he turned and looked directly towards the pub, but I knew he couldn't see me through the pattern of the glass in the window.

Gradually, the old man stopped hoping. It took over half an hour, but eventually I saw his shoulders slump. He rubbed a hand over his face and sat very still, staring at two children who were playing with the pigeons, chasing them in small, clattering flocks towards Dam Street.

I remained in my seat, barely aware of the increasing activity of the pub around me. I couldn't walk out into the cold air and end the old man's misery, yet I was unable to tear myself away from the window and the sight of his distress. My glass stood empty before me on the table, attracting curious stares from the barman and other customers. The street lights had come on, and the market square began to empty.

Finally, Samuel stood up. He moved with difficulty, and the paleness of his face and hands was startling against his black coat in the gloom. He left the square and walked towards the Corn Exchange, pigeons bobbing their heads and weaving round his feet. He moved slowly under the arcade only a few yards from where I sat, past the lighted windows of the clock repairers and the dry-cleaners, past Supasnaps and Fonebase. Two office workers on their way home stepped aside as he approached, recognising his weariness and air of defeat.

I knew why I'd been unable to go outside to meet Samuel. It was because he'd chosen the wrong place for the meeting, a place flooded with history and demands for remembrance. It symbolised what he wanted of me. I'd seen it all too clearly as he had stood and read the inscriptions on the plaques recalling the death of Edward Wightman.

Some people desperately want to remember. It can become the most important thing in their lives, that search for the past. But I wasn't one of them. I didn't want memories. I didn't want to remember any of it. All I wanted was to get on with my life and think about the future. I reckoned that was pretty reasonable, a perfectly rational ambition.

So I stayed in my seat and I kept watching the old man until I lost sight of him in the darkness.

For a moment, the world around me seemed suddenly empty. The pub, the other customers, the glass in front of me – they'd ceased to mean anything. Even the street outside the window looked unnaturally dark and deserted. There were still a few people passing by, wandering in and out of the lights, but they were all strangers.

I jumped up from the table, scraping the legs of my chair on the floor, and ran out of the door into Conduit Street, irrationally afraid that I'd left it too late.

At the corner, I stopped. There was no sign of the bent and weary figure I expected to see. A pedestrianised stretch of Bore Street ran down towards The Friary, while ahead of me was the Baker's Lane entrance to the Three Spires shopping centre. I looked at the row of benches located for people to rest on. Instinct told me that Samuel would have chosen that route, then turned into the arcade halfway along Baker's Lane.

But when I emerged at the end of the arcade and found myself outside the shopping centre again, I realised he'd evaded me. I was too late after all.

I stood for a few moments by the ugly, flat-roofed Civic Hall, which lay in darkness that evening. A dense clump of trees separated Castle Dyke from the bus station, and the area was silent, but for the hum of traffic on Birmingham Road. The overwhelming feeling of isolation made me reluctant to go any further.

Then I was startled by a sudden noise. It was a loud, racking cough, brought up from deep within the lungs of someone standing out of sight. I knew I wasn't alone. Now I was scared.

Quickly, I turned away to go back to the lights of the shopping centre. Behind me, a car engine revved until it screamed, tyres squealed on tarmac, someone shouted indistinguishably. I caught a glimpse of tail lights vanishing up Frog Lane.

On the way back to the marketplace, I heard the wail of a siren passing through the city, somewhere beyond the Three Spires. The sound echoed across the medieval streets – a shaft of howling modernity striking through the stifling grey blanket of history.

And first thing next morning, the police arrived on my doorstep.

11

There were two of them, just the way you always expect. Detective Sergeant Graham was slim, with a narrow, worried face. He had greying hair and the beginnings of a five o'clock shadow, but a vigilant look in his eyes. He wore a leather jacket and fawn chinos with a black belt. The female officer at his side was Detective Constable Hanlon, looking broad-shouldered in a padded jacket and a pair of jeans, with her fair hair scraped back off her forehead and a direct gaze that was probably meant to be disconcerting.

They turned up on the doorstep at nine o'clock. I'd only been up a few minutes, and I was still feeling groggy from lack of coffee. After they'd shown me their warrant cards, I let them into the house. As people must often do, I was wondering what I'd done wrong. In my case, drinking and driving invariably flashed through my mind when I saw a policeman, even when I hadn't been drinking. What else could it be? Was my tax disc out of date? Quite possibly. I couldn't remember.

But no. I had enough sense to know that two detectives wouldn't visit me at home for something so trivial. I had a panicky moment when I tried to recall what might be lying around the house that I wouldn't want them to see. A few weeks before, I'd stupidly invited back some people I met in the Stowe Arms, and one of them had passed round a joint. Could traces of it linger so long? There might also be a pornographic magazine lurking somewhere. But it was too late to worry about it now.

As I took them into my sitting room, my last thought was that their visit might be related to the road protest at Hilton. Had I been reported for trespassing perhaps? Had I seen something I shouldn't?

But in the next second, all my speculations went out of the window.

'Mr Buckley, we understand that you're acquainted with a Mr Samuel Longden.'

'Good God.'

'Sorry?' DS Graham looked intrigued at the reaction.

'I mean – yes, I am. It was a bit of a surprise, you mentioning his name.'

'What else did you think we'd come about?' asked DC Hanlon smartly. She thrust her hands aggressively into her jacket pockets as if she had two hidden revolvers pointing directly at my groin.

'Hanlon thinks everyone has a guilty secret,' said Graham, with a smile.

'It's just such a short time since I first heard his name,' I said.

Graham cocked his head. 'Perhaps we'll come back to that in a moment, sir.'

He said it like a threat. And I wasn't fooled for a minute by that word 'sir'. There's nobody like a policeman for infusing the word with whatever meaning he chooses to give it. DC Hanlon pulled her hands out of her pockets. But there were no revolvers, only a notebook and a ballpoint pen. In a way, I would have preferred the guns.

'So what's this all about?' I asked, knowing they must be the same words thousands of people use to police officers every day.

'We're investigating an incident last night involving Mr Longden. We'd like to ask you a few questions, sir. So that we can eliminate you from our inquiries, you understand.'

'Right.'

They both smiled then, as if at some police officers' in-joke. At this point, many householders might have offered them a cup of tea, but I wasn't feeling that way inclined. Until they arrived at my door, I'd always thought I was a law-abiding citizen, but these two made me feel positively seditious.

'Could you explain to us how you come to know Samuel Longden, Mr Buckley?'

'It's a bit of an odd story,' I said.

'Don't worry about that. We hear plenty of those.'

So they sat down, and I told them about the old man appearing at the canal restoration site, how he'd wanted me to do something for him, and the mysterious hints he'd dropped. They listened carefully, and DC Hanlon made the occasional note. But their faces were impassive, and they gave nothing away. For some reason, I didn't tell them about the files and the wooden box that still sat on my table in the other room.

'How many times did you meet Mr Longden?' asked DS Graham.

'Just the twice. The first time, when he approached me at Fosseway. And again two days later, when we met in the Cathedral Close.'

'Just twice. Hmm.'

'Yes?'

DS Graham wasn't trying to conceal the fact that he didn't believe me. 'Just twice. And the first meeting was only a few days ago. Would you say that was enough of a relationship to make you a friend of Mr Longden's?'

'No, not really.'

He looked at Hanlon, and Hanlon looked at her notebook. 'Yet three days ago you told Mrs Sylvia Wentworth that you were a friend of his,' she said.

'Sorry? Who?'

'Mrs Sylvia Wentworth. Mr Longden's next-door neighbour in Whittington.'

'Ah.'

'It *was* you, Mr Buckley, who called at Mr Longden's home on Thursday evening looking for him?'

'Yes, it was.'

'And you spoke to Mrs Wentworth, asking after the whereabouts of her neighbour.'

'Yes, I did.'

'And you told her you were Mr Longden's friend.'

'I – might have done.'

'Might?'

'Yes, I suppose I did. But it's just an expression. It's shorter than saying "acquaintance", that's all. It means nothing.'

'Would "acquaintance" describe your relationship with Mr Longden more accurately then?'

'Yes, indeed. Certainly.'

'Thank you. An acquaintance. But an acquaintance who was anxious to see Mr Longden about something?'

'Not anxious exactly.'

'But you called at his house. Peered through his windows. Questioned his neighbour. Put a note through his letter box.'

'There was something I wanted to tell him, that's all.'

'We have the note in our possession, Mr Buckley. It said that you couldn't help him.'

'That's right. That's what I wanted to tell him.'

'So why, then, did you arrange to meet Mr Longden again yesterday?'

I didn't have time to wonder how they knew all this. The question of who had known about the meeting we arranged in the market square was much too difficult for me to contemplate anyway.

'It was Samuel who arranged the meeting,' I said. 'He wanted to persuade me to change my mind.'

'About this project of his?'

82

'That's right.'

'And did he manage to persuade you, Mr Buckley?'

Now I did hesitate. How was I to explain to them that I hadn't gone through with the meeting? Could I tell them that I'd sat in the pub and watched the old man growing cold and disappointed, that I'd been a coward and hidden from an awkward moment? I could already see their contemptuous, disbelieving stares.

'I didn't turn up for the meeting.'

'Any particular reason?'

I shrugged, trying to avoid their questioning eyes. 'I just didn't want to meet him. I'd given him my message. As far as I was concerned, that was the end of it.'

'But you hadn't told Mr Longden that, had you?'

'No.'

'You let him think you'd turn up.'

'Yes.' Then a little glimmer of hope began to form. 'His letter only arrived that morning. It was much too short notice for me. I couldn't get there.'

There was silence in the room for a few moments. I'd just lied to them, and I was afraid they knew it. It must have been scrawled all over my face. DC Hanlon would be jotting my name down on her guilty secrets list. I needed to do something to distract their attention. Then I realised I hadn't asked the question they must be expecting from me.

'Has something happened to Samuel? Has he had an accident?'

'You might say that,' said Graham grimly, with that uneasy shifting of the eyes that communicated bad news.

'Is he . . . is he dead?'

'Yes, Mr Buckley. But as for an accident . . . at the moment we can't actually say whether it was an accident or not.'

'That's why we need to trace his exact movements during his last few hours,' said Hanlon, trying to pierce me with her glare.

'It's a real pity you didn't turn up for that meeting,' said Graham. 'You might have saved him, Mr Buckley.'

'What on earth do you mean?'

'He died shortly before six-thirty. If you'd turned up to meet him, you might still have been with him then.'

'Six-thirty? But—'

'Yes?'

I hesitated, holding back what I had been going to say. 'He was still in the city centre then?'

'Yes, he died in Frog Lane.'

'In the street? What happened?'

'He was knocked down by a car. A hit and run.'

The news shocked me more than anything I'd been imagining. 'Have you caught the driver?'

'No. We haven't been able to interview anybody else in connection with the incident yet.'

I didn't miss the 'anybody else'. Did they really think it might have been me driving the car that had run Samuel over?

'You must have some description of the vehicle?'

'Yes, there was a witness,' said Graham, with a hint of satisfaction.

'But you can't say whether it was an accident. Why not?'

'An inquest might say it was misadventure. If Mr Longden had wandered out into the road, for example. He was an old man – and rather frail, we understand. If he'd been waiting outside in the cold for a long time, he might have been unsteady on his feet.'

'The verdict might even be suicide,' said Hanlon. 'If he was distressed about something. If he was upset enough by your failure to turn up, say.'

'And then again, we can't rule out the possibility of a murder charge,' said Graham, and watched for the effect on me, which must have been clearly visible. 'Now shall we just go back to the beginning, Mr Buckley?'

84

I went through the story again. Their tactic was obvious. If you make a story up, you're more likely to make a mistake, to let slip an inconsistency, when you're asked to repeat it. There's a natural tendency to start embroidering the details. So I decided to be sensible and come clean. I told them I'd been in the Earl of Lichfield while Samuel sat in the market square. The detectives looked suitably shocked, and Hanlon made another note – guilty secret confirmed.

'So the last time you saw Mr Longden, he was walking towards the Three Spires shopping centre. Did he look as though he was heading anywhere in particular?' asked Graham.

'I couldn't say.'

'Was he hurrying?'

'No. Walking rather slowly. He used a stick anyway.'

'Yes, he *was* a rather fragile old man.'

I began to get irritated. 'Look—'

'Do you think he might have been heading towards the bus station?'

'Quite possibly. He might have been planning to get a taxi from there to go back home. Did you say the accident happened in Frog Lane?'

'Yes, near the corner of Castle Dyke,' said Graham. 'By the exit from the multi-storey car park.'

'I see.'

I was starting to piece the scenario together bit by bit. I could see Samuel tottering off, a little unsteady on his feet, his legs perhaps numb with cold. Maybe he'd been deep in thought, his brain going off on one of those strange tangents I'd come to recognise. He must have walked a few yards down Bore Street and cut through Tudor Row to reach Castle Dyke. And just beyond there he'd stepped in front of a car. Perhaps it had been driving down the ramp too fast, and the accident was entirely the driver's fault.

Somehow, the thought didn't make me feel any better. I

remembered too clearly the sound of the revving engine, the squealing tyres. And that deep, racking cough. Was it significant? Why didn't I tell these police officers? Because I didn't want them to know I'd been so close to the scene where Samuel Longden had died. I'd been much too close. If I told them, it would only double their suspicions.

'But you haven't found the driver?' I said.

'Not yet. We're checking all the possibilities.'

I sensed that something else was coming. 'Yes?'

'So would you mind if we had a quick look at your car while we're here, Mr Buckley?'

'You don't think—' But obviously they did. That was their job, after all. I was the last person known to have seen the old man alive. Perhaps I was also the person who'd run him over. Why not? They were obliged to be suspicious.

'That is your Escort we saw in the car port?' asked Hanlon.

'It is. Do you want the keys?'

'That won't be necessary.'

We all trooped back outside. I trailed behind them, not knowing quite what to do as they examined the exterior of my car, particularly the bodywork and bumper at the front, the trim on the door and even the wing mirrors. They also looked at the tread of the tyres.

'Where did you park your vehicle last night, sir?' asked Hanlon.

'The Bird Street car park,' I said promptly. 'Behind Iceland.'

Unfortunately, the Escort was of an age when it was starting to show quite a number of scratches and small dents, most of them completely innocent – a stone thrown up from the road, someone opening their door too close in a car park. All these little incidents left their mark. I wondered how they could possibly mean anything to the two police officers. Did their inspection mean there were injuries to Samuel that could be matched to a part of the car that hit him? Did they think there might be a match to that dent in the wing of my Escort? The idea made me shudder as I watched DS Graham scrutinise my paintwork, tilting his head from side to side to get a better view.

Eventually, they stood up and dusted off their knees.

'Well, I think that will be all for now, Mr Buckley. But we'd like you to call in at the station during the next day or two to sign a formal statement.'

'No problem.'

'Oh, and we may need you at the inquest.'

'Really? But I can hardly tell you anything about Samuel's death.'

'His state of mind immediately prior to the incident might prove to be important.'

'And his physical condition,' said Hanlon, who clearly had me pegged as an OAP molester.

'But how could anyone get away with running an old man down in the middle of the street and not even stopping?'

'It happens,' said Hanlon. 'Usually it's some drunk who panics and drives off.'

'Yes, I see.'

There was a significant pause.

'Which pub did you say you were in that night, Mr Buckley?'

The gibe had come from DS Graham. I flushed angrily at the insinuation. 'I told you. The Earl of Lichfield. And I wasn't drunk.'

'Was the pub busy?'

'Very quiet, actually.'

'No doubt the staff will remember you, then.'

They left me in no doubt they would check.

'We'll be in touch, then.'

'Yes. All right.'

They drove off, leaving me standing on my driveway in my shirt sleeves and slippers. It was a moment or two before I suddenly realised how cold I was, and a shudder ran through me.

It was obvious that I wasn't going to be allowed to forget Samuel Longden. Because there is nothing rational about guilt. And it was certainly guilt that had etched last night's scene into my mind, leaving me with a permanent recollection of a defeated, dejected old man shuffling painfully into the darkness, surrounded by a miasma of misery caused by me.

He'd looked like a man walking to meet his fate, a condemned criminal going to the gallows, with no hope of reprieve. He had, of course, been walking to his death.

12

'I noticed your early morning visitors,' said Rachel. 'Were they interested in buying your car?'

She'd knocked on the door only a few minutes after the police had left, making me panic that they'd decided to come back and arrest me. I almost didn't open the door, and it actually crossed my mind to escape by the back way and leg it across the gardens into The Charters. But I'd overcome the guilty response, and sense had returned. When I saw my neighbour standing on the doorstep, my first reaction was relief, then a burst of irritation.

'I hadn't even realised you were selling it,' she said. 'Are you getting a new one?'

'Fat chance,' I said.

'Oh. Well, they gave it a good looking-over, didn't they? I was surprised you didn't take them for a drive round. I usually want to sit inside and try out the seats when I'm buying a car.'

'Really? How interesting.'

'I couldn't help but notice, of course. I was just coming back from Mrs Knowles' house.'

'They were the police,' I said. 'And they weren't thinking of buying my car. They were deciding whether or not to take me in for further questioning.'

Rachel laughed, thinking I was joking. Then she saw I wasn't, and her eyes widened. 'Seriously? But what do they think you've done?'

I leaned closer to her, with a conspiratorial whisper. 'It could be murder.' That should send her packing, I thought. And serve her right for being nosey.

She gasped. 'You poor thing. That's terrible.' I felt her hand on my arm, and the next thing I knew she was in the house, leading me into the sitting room like a child. 'You sit down while I make a cup of tea, and you can tell me all about. It must be an awful shock, being accused of something like that.'

She vanished into the kitchen, and I heard the sound of water running and a cupboard opening as she located my crockery with an unerring instinct. I wasn't quite sure how it came about, but within five minutes I was sitting on my own settee telling Rachel what had happened to Samuel Longden.

Needless to say, she was riveted. She sat and listened with the kind of concentrated attention no one else ever gave me. Apart from the occasional word of encouragement or a small, probing question, she let me do all the talking. It was only as I re-lived the moments when I sat in the pub and watched the old man waiting on his bench that her eyebrows rose and she looked at me doubtfully.

'I know, I know,' I said, waving my hands defensively.

'That sweet old man.'

'Don't you think I feel guilty enough?'

'And he walked away from there . . . and died.'

'So it seems. I suppose if I'd gone out and met him, if I'd spoken to him, instead of being such a coward . . . If I had the courage to explain to him how I felt . . .'

'No,' she said briskly. 'It's no use thinking like that. If these things are going to happen, they'll happen. Accidents can't be foreseen or avoided. It's just fate.'

I wasn't so sure about that. But I hadn't yet fully acknowledged to myself what I feared about Samuel Longden's death. I certainly wasn't ready to share the fear with Rachel.

90

'The police can't seriously think it was you who ran him over,' she said. 'Not now they've met you.'

I wasn't quite sure how to take that. 'Thanks very much.'

'You're not the hit and run type, Chris.'

'Hmm.' Was that really true? Wasn't it exactly what I had done to Samuel in a way? A hit and run? I'd been trying to run away from our sudden contact. But I hadn't been running fast enough.

'So what about all his stuff now? What happens to that?' she asked.

'Stuff?'

'The files, and the box. All the things he left. You said you were going to give them back to him. What are you going to do with them now?'

'I hadn't thought about it. I suppose I'll get rid of them some other way.'

'We can read them first, of course. That would be all right, wouldn't it? He did give them to you. You owe him that, at least. It must have been what he wanted.'

Thanks to the tea and the opportunity to tell the story, I was starting to feel better. There might have been something in what Rachel said about owing Samuel a bit of my time to read the files. But there was a telltale word she'd used, that 'we'. It sent a shiver of horror through me. There wasn't going to be any 'we', if I could help it. Quickly, I searched for a get-out.

'There's a daughter,' I said at last.

'What?'

'His neighbour told me Samuel had a daughter.'

'You never mentioned that.'

'I forgot. It didn't seem important until now. But obviously I'll have to give the files back to her, won't I? Next of kin and all that.'

She looked disappointed. 'Did she live with him?'

'I've no idea. I'll need to find out.'

91

'We could just have a look at some of it in the meantime,' she suggested.

I shook my head. 'They're not mine. They were Samuel's. And so they must be his daughter's now.'

Rachel pulled a face. 'It seems such a shame. How can you resist taking a peek?'

'I'll survive.'

She stroked the wooden box. 'Tell you what, let me take the box and clean it up. It needs a bit of beeswax and a good polish, and some metal cleaner on the brass. It'll look beautiful then. It would make a real feature.'

'Rachel, it doesn't matter.'

She sat back, disappointed. 'So when will you give them back?'

'As soon as I can find someone to give them to.'

She was right, of course. I had an irresistible urge to go through the papers Samuel had left. I had no idea what I'd be looking for, but instinct told me something was waiting to be found in there. It was a half-familiar tingle I felt – one I remembered from my early days as a reporter, when I'd still been young and keen, when the excitement of knowing I was onto a good story was like a sexual thrill.

But I had to ignore it. It was a weakness of mine that I had to fight, that tendency to be sidetracked into some easy option, anything that meant I wouldn't have to face up to the difficult situations in my life.

Then I remembered Mrs Wentworth. I couldn't imagine how she might have known about the meeting Samuel had arranged with me. But it was certainly Mrs Wentworth who'd informed the police of my visit to Ash Lodge. I stood up and looked down at Rachel as if I'd never seen her before.

'In fact, I'm going back to Whittington right now,' I said.

Of course, I was doing quite the opposite of what I thought. The secrets that lay in Samuel Longden's manuscript were far from being the easy option.

*   *   *

Mrs Wentworth was surprised to see me. She looked frightened at first, as if she genuinely believed I'd killed Samuel Longden. Then her expression changed to one of embarrassment when I explained why I'd come. She still kept me standing safely on the doorstep, shivering in the wind.

'The police asked me who'd been to see him recently,' she said. 'I had to tell them about you. He never got many visitors, not in the last few years. In fact, you were almost the only one for a while.'

'It's all right,' I said. 'But did you tell them why I came?'

'Oh yes, I told them what you said, and that you'd put a note through his door.' Her face slipped slightly as she recalled that she wouldn't have been able to see me do that unless she'd been watching me from her kitchen window. But I wasn't bothered about that.

'Did you tell them anything else?'

'No.' She frowned, puzzled now.

'I'm not sure how well you knew your neighbour. Did you talk to him much?'

'Hardly at all,' she said.

'Had you spoken to him since I came that day?'

'No.'

'I still want to return those items to somebody. Do you know where Mr Longden's daughter lives?'

'Caroline? Oh, I couldn't say. Sometimes she stayed at Ash Lodge with her father, but not for a while. There's certainly no one there now. I seem to recall she was going away somewhere.'

'Can you remember where?'

Her brow furrowed. 'I remember thinking it was an awful long way away. It could have been Australia. Brisbane.'

I didn't set much store by her memory. She said 'Brisbane' as if it were some mythical country way off the edge of the world. I supposed it could just as easily have been Belgium or Burundi. I wondered if Mrs Wentworth had ever been out of England. Being stuck on an island can colour your perception of the world. I speak, of course, as a global citizen who once spent a holiday in Majorca.

'Did Samuel never go away himself?'

'Hardly ever. He mentioned he was going to see a friend in Cheshire once or twice, but he was only away for a couple of days. Apart from that, he was always here. Mostly on his own, unless Caroline came.'

'I suppose he was quite a lonely old man.'

Mrs Wentworth studied me thoughtfully. 'Caroline will get the house, I imagine.'

'Yes, she will.'

'And the kestrel.'

'Sorry?' I thought I must have misheard. It was the first indication that Samuel Longden had shown an interest in falconry. I peered over the high privet hedge towards Ash Lodge, expecting to see an aviary that I hadn't noticed before. 'Who's looking after it?'

Mrs Wentworth laughed, a strangely girlish giggle. 'The *Kestrel*. Did you think I meant a bird? The *Kestrel* is a boat. A narrowboat – that's what they call them, isn't it? It's kept on the canal down there.' She waved vaguely towards the garden at the back of the house. 'Old Samuel hadn't been anywhere on it for years, of course. But he still spent a lot of time down there. Tinkering about, I suppose. As men do.'

'A boat. I didn't know that. But it makes sense, in a way.'

As soon as I could, I thanked Mrs Wentworth and went back to Ash Lodge. I hesitated for a moment, then determined to check whether she was right about the boat. I made my way through the gate at the bottom of the garden and emerged onto a little path that led to the Coventry Canal. I knew Mrs Wentworth would be watching me from the windows of The Chestnuts, but I didn't care by now.

The boat was just where she'd said, tied up to a couple of bollards set into the canal bank, almost within view of the

94

upper floor of Samuel's house. *Kestrel* was a full-length narrowboat, almost all of its seventy feet being occupied by cabin space where the hold would once have been. But this wasn't an old working boat which had been converted. It was a more recent job, specially built as a pleasure vessel.

Kestrel was painted green and red, with white rope fenders at its stem and stern, and its name in decorative lettering on the cabin side. Steel shutters covered all the windows, and there was a large padlock on the stern cabin door.

But it was obvious the woodwork hadn't been re-painted for a while. In places the paint was starting to wear thin and the wood showed through. Streaks of green mould were creeping up the sides of the hull, and a pool of rainwater lay on the deck boards of the counter, where the steerer would stand to control the Z-shaped tiller. It was only short-term neglect, though – the effects of exposure to the weather. Not long ago, this boat had been in first-class condition.

I looked northwards along the canal. The water and towpath looked peaceful after the roads around Lichfield. I began to walk along the gravel path, enjoying being able to step out in quiet surroundings, with no one around. I supposed it might help me to think.

Within a mile, I reached Huddlesford Junction, where the Ogley and Huddlesford Canal branched off from the Coventry. It was in water for only a few hundred yards, until it came to a stop at a bridge. Beyond that, the line of the canal had disappeared under ploughed fields. A few narrowboats were moored on the opposite bank, near to where a bridge crossed the water. A middle-aged couple were polishing brasswork on a boat called *Rose Marie*, registered in Nottingham.

This was where narrowboats had emerged into the Coventry Canal after descending thirty locks in the seven miles from Ogley. This little junction had been a crucial link in the waterways network, connecting the Birmingham canals to the Trent and Mersey at Fradley, and to the Oxford and Grand

Union canals via Coventry. The area must have been thronged with boats at one time. Now the scene was tranquil, most of the pleasure boats moored here still locked up and shrouded for the winter.

I turned my back on the water and saw the Plough Inn across the road in the village of Huddlesford. I decided there was time for a couple of drinks before I walked back to Whittington.

A few minutes later, as I sat in the Plough and watched the dark water of the canal being flicked into life by the wind, I found myself reminded too vividly of the three-quarters of an hour I'd spent sitting in the Earl of Lichfield, watching Samuel Longden waiting for me. The old man had walked away and died. But the memory of him wouldn't leave me. It had embedded itself in what I suppose must have been my conscience. I wondered if there was a way I could dislodge the memory. The beer in my hand might work in the short term, but it wasn't the permanent solution I needed.

I sat and stared at the canal for a long time. But my thoughts were blown along as helplessly as the small waves on its surface were being driven by the wind.

13

The next couple of days passed in a blur. I was busy working, of course. The launch of the website was due soon, and we needed some content. So I could hardly concentrate on anything but routine, while at the same time being aware that significant events were happening that might affect my life. And then it came to Thursday morning.

On Thursdays I'd started to have the *Lichfield Echo* delivered. Sometimes the local hacks don't realise they've got hold of something that will be of interest to the nationals. Or their editors frown on the idea of reporters flogging stories they've written for their own papers. It means more opportunities for people like me, and every unconsidered trifle is potential grist to the freelancer's mill.

This Thursday morning, there was little in the *Echo* to interest me. The front page was concerned with a nasty assault on an elderly couple during a robbery that had gone wrong, and a report from the planning committee about the siting of a new supermarket. It was purely local interest.

But when I got to page five, a small item caught my eye. 'Inquest adjourned', it said. It named Samuel Joseph Longden, aged 83, of Whittington, and said that he'd died in a road accident a few days earlier. Cause of death was given as multiple internal injuries. The entire item was only three paragraphs long, and it concluded by saying that the coroner had adjourned the hearing until some future date, so that police could continue their inquiries.

By one of those coincidences that could make anyone believe in the action of fate, there was another item in my morning post that was demanding my attention. Not a bill, but a letter from a firm of solicitors in Lichfield called Elsworth and Clarke. They invited me to make an early appointment regarding a will. The will of Mr Samuel Joseph Longden.

The solicitors' offices were in St John Street. The modern-looking facade of smoked glass and pink brick concealed a rabbit warren of corridors that seemed stuck in the 1950s. Maybe the decor was deliberate, to give clients an impression of age and solidity, a reminder that Elsworth and Clarke were an old-established firm on the inside, though they were aware on the outside of the imminent arrival of the next millennium.

Mr Elsworth himself gave much the same impression. His desk might have contained a computer loaded with the latest electronic database package, but his mind was still a dog-eared card index. He motioned me to an uncomfortable chair and took off his glasses, which hung from a cord round his neck. His suit was an aged grey pinstripe, but his tie seemed to be a cartoon strip, in which I vaguely recognised Wile E. Coyote.

'Could I just confirm that you are Mr Christopher John Buckley, of 6 Stowe Pool Lane, Lichfield, Staffordshire? And that your parents were Arthur and Sheila Buckley of the same address?'

'Would you like to see some identification?' I asked, surprised. I felt like a young-looking eighteen-year-old being challenged in a pub as an underage drinker.

'A driving licence perhaps?' he said. 'Ah yes, that's fine.' He replaced his glasses to study my licence, made a brief note on a pad with his pen and handed the licence back. 'Just a precaution, you know. There's no great formality about the reading of a will these days. Even when it happens to involve substantial assets.'

I wondered what Mr Elsworth was like on a formal occasion, if he thought he was being informal just now.

'So I'll press straight on to the business in hand, if you don't mind,' he said. 'There's a clause in Mr Longden's will which is of interest to you. Also, there are one or two other items.'

'Go ahead.'

'You'd like me to read the relevant clause?'

'Of course.'

'Well, it reads: "And to my great-nephew, Christopher John Buckley, I leave fifty thousand pounds, in addition to all my manuscripts, notes, letters, and any other items which may already be in his possession relating to my work on a publication called *The Three Keys*. The bequest of fifty thousand pounds is to be conditional on the said *The Three Keys* being completed and published before the end of the year 2000, that being the two hundredth anniversary of the death of my ancestor, William Buckley."'

'Sorry, how much?'

'Fifty thousand pounds. Quite a generous bequest. I dare say it will come in useful, Mr Buckley?'

'Useful?' I laughed. 'It'll only save my life, that's all.'

My brain must not have been working too quickly that day. My surprise was so great at hearing my name and the sum of fifty thousand pounds mentioned in the same breath that it took me a few moments to track back to the beginning of the sentence and work out what else was wrong with it.

'Hold on. Did you say "great-nephew"?'

'That's correct.'

The great surge of hope that had washed through my body a moment before was instantly smothered, leaving me flattened and more hopeless than ever. But there was no point in claiming to be somebody I wasn't.

'You've got the wrong person then, Mr Elsworth.'

The solicitor removed his glasses and looked offended. 'I don't believe so, Mr Buckley.'

'I met Samuel Longden only a few weeks ago. I'm certainly not his great-nephew.'

'But Mr Longden was very specific. He gives your full name and address and the names of your parents, which you agreed were correct.'

I sighed. It came painfully hard to give up the chance of so much money. God knows I needed it. But I couldn't take it under false pretences. I had the sort of luck that meant I'd be found out and have to pay the whole lot back some time in the future, probably with interest. Redundancy and debt were quite enough, without a charge of deception and fraud to add to my troubles.

'Samuel Longden did seem to take a liking to me for some reason,' I said. 'But he was a very old man. I suppose his mind must have been wandering towards the end, and that led him to imagine I was a long-lost relative.'

Mr Elsworth pursed his lips as if I'd accused him of some legal misdemeanour. He replaced his glasses to refer to the front page of the will. 'This document was signed and witnessed in these offices on the 15th of June last year.'

My mouth fell open in astonishment. 'You must have got it wrong.'

'I assure you, Mr Buckley, there's no mistake. You say you met Mr Longden a few weeks ago. But clearly he knew of your existence some time before that. And he believed you to be his great-nephew. Also, may I state that this firm does not allow clients to draw up a will if there's any doubt about their mental condition.'

'I wasn't suggesting that, I'm sorry. But this is very difficult for me to understand. You did say fifty thousand pounds?'

'I see it's come as something of a shock.' The solicitor withdrew a white padded envelope from the folder. 'Perhaps this will cast light on the situation, Mr Buckley. My instructions are to deliver this package into your hands once the provisions of the will have been communicated to you.'

I took the envelope cautiously. It bore my name on the front in unsteady handwriting, along with the words 'Private and Confidential'. I recognised the writing from Samuel Longden's letter and notes.

'There's also one other item which I'm instructed to give you,' said Mr Elsworth. 'This is a copy of a document that one of the former partners of this firm witnessed some years ago in his role as notary public. My own father, in fact. It dates from the 3rd of March, 1949.'

What surprise was there to come next? I looked at the photocopy blankly, unable to make any sense of the gothic script, the copperplate handwriting and archaic language. 'I'm sorry, I don't understand what this is.'

'It's a copy of a notarised deed by which our client, Mr Samuel Joseph Buckley, changed his name to Samuel Joseph Longden.'

'You mean a deed poll?'

'A deed poll isn't necessary to change one's name. This document is all that's required, and it's perfectly legal. In fact, even this isn't strictly necessary, though it constitutes a very sensible record of date and intention. It rather adds weight to the late Mr Longden's claim of a family relationship existing between you, does it not? It appears his name was formerly Buckley.'

'But why? Why would he change his name? And if he was my great-uncle, why didn't I know of his existence?'

Mr Elsworth leaned back in his chair, his job done. 'I'm afraid I have no more information I can give you. However, this publication my client refers to . . . a biography of some sort, I presume? Another family member? I take it you do have in your possession the items to which the late Mr Longden refers?'

'Yes, he gave me a whole heap of stuff.'

'There's a clear implication in Mr Longden's will that there may be other documents you require to help you complete the project. As executor, I'm able to permit you access to Mr Longden's property, so that you may locate and remove any relevant items. That would be in accordance with the provisions of the will.'

'Thank you.'

'If you do require access, give my secretary a call and we can arrange a convenient time, Mr Buckley.'

'And the money?'

'I'm afraid it will have to wait for probate. It's difficult to say how long that might be. It depends how complex Mr Longden's estate proves to be. There are tax considerations, and the sale of the property of course. If there are sufficient liquid assets, it could be a different matter. But I suspect all that is rather academic, in view of the conditions on this bequest. You'll first need to produce a copy of the book Mr Longden refers to.'

'I have to wait, then?'

'I'm afraid so. The condition is specific that the book must be published before the legacy can be released. But I can't foresee any problems in that respect. Unless you're aware of any complications?'

I saw plenty of complications, but none that Mr Elsworth would understand. I shook my head.

'I understand the funeral will take place next Thursday,' said the solicitor. 'Again, the provisions seem to be rather unusual.'

'In what way?'

'It seems our client was well known for his connections with the inland waterways system,' he said, with the air of a man who'd been told of a particularly repulsive sexual fetish. 'So his funeral will reflect that. It was Mr Longden's specific request, and there's money set aside for the necessities in his will. It will be a novel occasion, no doubt. I'm not conversant with the exact details, but I believe you'll receive a formal invitation within the next day or two, Mr Buckley. As a member of the family.'

One last thing occurred to me, which showed my mind was working after all.

'Who gets the property? The house and all that?'

'The principal beneficiary.'

'And that is?'

Mr Elsworth smiled condescendingly, as if he were performing a huge favour for an ignorant fool who'd just walked in off the street.

'The main beneficiary of the will is a Miss Caroline Longden. Yet another of your relatives, I believe.'

14

After leaving the solicitor's office, I sat in the Escort for a while and opened the package Mr Elsworth had given me. I drew out a letter from Samuel Longden.

Dear Christopher,

By the time you read this, my part will be done. It's up to you now. I hope you will understand what I've been trying to achieve. It all has to be brought to an end.

I thought I might find some justification for what has been done to us. But I found none, Christopher. Perhaps I wasn't objective enough. Perhaps you'll discover some cause where I could not. I only found, at times, the efforts that the Buckleys made to fight back, to restore the family's position in society, just as I've tried to do myself in my own way. These things become more important as we get older and we develop a greater sense of perspective. 'Today' means less and less to old people, but 'yesterday' means more and more.

And then, in the course of my research, I reached 1800. It was in that year your ancestor, William Buckley, vanished without trace. It was said that he'd embezzled money, and that he'd fled to escape disgrace. But was that really so?

You might think that two centuries are much too far back in time to have any relevance. Am I right? Yes, it all seems ancient history to you at the moment, doesn't it?

Dead and forgotten. But there are people with very long memories, Christopher. People for whom a wrong is never forgotten, whether real or imagined. People who will pursue a vendetta for ever, as if the sins of the distant past can in some way be avenged by this continuing feud, and two wrongs can make a right. They seek an eye for an eye, though the guilt has been buried with the dead. Betrayal plants the desire for revenge. Vengeance leads only to bitterness. Evil breeds evil.

And there's something more than that. I truly believe there's a sort of family 'genetic memory' that we all have, a memory which can be recalled to life once we start to look into our past, and peer into the lives of our ancestors. All we need are a few reminders, little nudges that will re-awaken the recollection and cause pictures to re-form in our heads, however dim and half-understood. It could be a smell perhaps, or a taste.

Have you ever read Proust? Do you remember his madeleine – the cake that created an involuntary memory, containing the essence of his past? Well, I've tasted my madeleine. I discovered my genetic memory, Christopher. I hope you will too.

Your great-uncle,
Samuel Longden

My great-uncle. It seemed so strange seeing it written down, and in Samuel's own scrawl too. But it was confirmation of something I hadn't really believed when the solicitor told me. The old man had been my grandfather's brother. How was that possible?

Then I remembered Samuel telling me at our second meeting that his father had died during the Great War. He'd never mentioned a name. Yet that must have been Alfred Buckley the mercer, the youngest child of Josiah and Hannah Buckley. Samuel Longden's father was my own great-grandfather. His choice of words had been deliberate all along, a slow drip-feeding of information to mislead me and keep me wondering.

The old man had been a lot smarter than he seemed. And much more devious.

After I'd read the letter, I realised the envelope wasn't empty. A heavy iron key lay in the bottom – a key of a kind that I recognised. Attached to it by a short length of string was a green luggage label. Scrawled on the label, in the same hand that had written the letter, were just eleven cryptic words:

'Here is the second key. The third is in the lock.'

15

The meaning behind Samuel's letter sent an extra stab of guilt through my heart. While I'd been feeling misguidedly complacent about being alone and without a family, there had been this relative, who'd felt equally alone and unwanted, but with the added burden of old age. He'd lived alone, visited only occasionally by a daughter who was now gone to some distant part of the world. And he'd become obsessed with the past.

It was clearly an unhealthy obsession, for it had surely turned his mind. This was obvious to me from the tone of his words. Genetic memory? Proust and his madeleine? This wasn't just going off at a tangent, or the vague wanderings that old people were prone to. Samuel Longden had definitely been a bit cracked. He'd needed help, but not the sort of help I could ever have given him.

But what of me now? I'd spent the last few months adjusting to the idea that I no longer had any family. Now here was this old man who'd walked into my life and turned it upside down, and it was difficult to know how to react. I felt astonished and angry at myself that I'd been so brainwashed by my parents and believed there were no other living Buckleys. In retrospect, their insistence sounded false, a case of protesting too much.

But I'd been perfectly happy to accept the situation. Even relieved, if I was honest. I'd never enjoyed the duty visits to my mother's side of the family, or the obligatory get-togethers at Christmas, and I'd been glad there were none to be suffered on the Buckley side. It had seemed like an escape.

If only, just once, I'd heard my Great-Uncle Samuel's name mentioned, I might have started asking the right questions a bit earlier, when my parents were still alive to answer for themselves.

That night, and during the next day, I searched my memory for references to the missing side of my family. But it seemed a complete blank. As a child, I certainly couldn't recall having questioned the lack of Buckleys – being surfeited, I suppose, with the Claytons and Bridgemans, and all those suburban houses in Perry Barr and Erdington. I recalled plump cousins and middle-aged aunts smelling of face powder, all of whom I was obliged to kiss on family occasions like weddings and funerals.

But there had never been a get-together of the Buckleys, no visits to unfamiliar houses in suburbs of Lichfield or villages like Whittington, no beery uncles to shake hands with in return for a fifty pence piece. There had been no names and addresses of Buckleys on our Christmas card list. Or Longdens for that matter.

And yet here was evidence that they'd existed. At least two of them, Samuel and his daughter Caroline. No, make that three – Samuel's wife, my Great-Aunt Alison, had been alive until ten years ago. Did my parents not go to Samuel's wedding? Had they ever spoken to Alison? No matter what disagreement had alienated the brothers, Alison could surely have done nothing wrong. And had they really not attended her funeral, after the articulated lorry had severed her relationship to the Buckley family? But I knew the answer, and the thought made me unreasonably angry.

I'd always thought of myself as a man who looked only to the future, and never really wondered about my past. There are more important things than family, more urgent issues than relatives with whom you have nothing in common.

Now, I had a lot to think about. When I'd left the house that morning, it had been as somebody with no ties, a solitary offshoot of the wilting Buckley family tree. But it seemed I had to come to terms with a creeping hedge of relatives that had been lurking around me unseen, who were now getting closer.

Most of all, it was incredible that my Great-Uncle Samuel had exploded into my life and left it again in the course of a single week, like a wayward comet streaking across my universe. What, really, had been his intentions?

Once back in the house, I made my way up to the landing and lowered the folding ladder that my father had installed to give access to the attic. There was a big space up there, which could have been converted into an extra bedroom easily if I'd ever had any brothers or sisters. But there'd never been any use for it, except as storage for all the useless lumber that accumulates in a house over the years.

Since the death of my parents, I'd made no attempt to clear out the rubbish. In fact, I hadn't even bothered removing their clothes from the wardrobe in their bedroom. Some items could have gone to the charity shops, I suppose, but it hardly seemed worth the effort. Who wanted a few old suits and cardigans, or dresses impregnated with the familiar, sweet odour of my mother's perfume?

When I'd last been in their room, my mother's make-up and perfume bottles had still been standing on the dressing table in front of the mirror. My father hadn't moved them, and neither had I. Now they stood next to his hairbrush and his favourite cufflinks.

In the attic, though, was an old suitcase, which I could recall being brought out occasionally when I was a child. It contained two bundles of photographs. Some were of myself as a boy in the late 1960s and early 70s, all scuffed jeans and sulky stares as the Flower Power era passed me by. Some showed my parents on their wedding day, and later on holiday in Scotland or Majorca.

But there were other photographs too, which had never meant much to me – black and white prints of unfamiliar faces, figures posing stiffly outside the church where my parents had married, or staring with frozen expressions at the camera with their baggy suits and Brylcreemed hair. Most of the people had been nameless, and an explanation for their presence had never been offered. But that suitcase seemed to be the only place I could start looking for answers.

As soon as I opened the lid, a strange essence was released into the air – not quite a smell or a taste, but almost a movement. I knew I was becoming too fanciful. It was Samuel's talk of madeleines that had done it. Of course, an old suitcase full of mementos was bound to contain its own smell of age and history. It was a cloud of almost imperceptible dust particles that had risen from the contents to float in the light creeping through the dormer window. But recognising the simple reality didn't stop me feeling as though I'd just opened Pandora's box to let out a swarm of tiny demons.

'Hello! Hello-o-o!'

I jerked at the sound, scattering a handful of photographs in the dust as I returned to an awareness of my surroundings. I became conscious of the pain in my calves where I was developing cramp from squatting in front of the suitcase. I must already have been crouching there for several minutes, lost in a world that had been dead for many years.

'Hello!'

I knew straightaway that it was Rachel. No one else had quite that quality of instinctive heartiness to their voice. And who else would have the cheek to walk into my house uninvited, as if we were intimate friends?

I edged towards the trap door, wincing at the discomfort

in my legs, and looked down onto the landing. Rachel's face was turned up towards me, round and white, an expression of concern and puzzlement in her eyes. She had a furry black bundle clutched in her arms.

'Chris? Are you all right? What are you doing up there?'

'Just looking for something.'

'I couldn't get an answer at the back door, so I came in to see if everything was okay. Boswell was crying at the door.'

'Yes, he does that. He just wants a bit of attention, that's all.'

Before I could think of anything else to say, another twinge of pain went through my leg as the circulation began to return. Rachel noticed my expression immediately.

'Are you sure you're all right?'

'Yes, I'm fine.'

But the damn woman was already putting the cat down and starting to climb the ladder towards the attic.

'Gosh, what a lot of stuff,' she said, as her head appeared above the dusty boards. I tried to edge casually round so that the suitcase was hidden behind me, but it didn't work. Her antennae were working overtime.

'What's in there? Oh, old photos. I love old photos.'

And then it was too late. She would accept nothing less than that we should drag the suitcase down the ladder and set it out on the dining room table while we went through every one. I even left her to it for a while so I could feed Boswell and put the kettle on for a cup of tea.

While I was in the kitchen, I cursed myself for not locking the back door. Rachel had been a regular visitor to the house while my mother was alive, and later on had called on my father occasionally. Since I'd been on my own, she'd used every pretext to get back into the house. She knew every detail of my life.

'Doesn't your mother look lovely in her wedding dress,' she said.

'Does she?'

She was gazing with a fond wistfulness at my parents' wedding photos. I thought my father looked ridiculous in his tight trousers, narrow tie and pointy-toed shoes, with his quiff sticking up from his forehead like an early Cliff Richard. It was 1963, there was still a Conservative government and the Beatles hadn't yet had time to make an impact on fashions. If it had been a few years later, my father would have been sporting wide lapels, a fringe and a droopy moustache. I came along in 1965, when Harold Wilson was prime minister, American planes were starting to bomb Vietnam, and Rhodesia was declaring UDI.

In the photograph of the group outside St Chad's church, my mother had a long, straight bob – but, apart from that, she could have been a bride from any era in that traditional white lace gown. As to whether she looked lovely, I was the wrong person to judge. She was just my mother.

'There's snow on the ground,' said Rachel. 'They must have got married in winter.'

'February.'

'Was that a bad winter?'

'I wasn't actually there, you know. I wasn't even born. That was the way things were done in those days. Wedding first, babies later.'

She looked at me sideways. 'Yes, but it's the sort of detail you get to know, isn't it?'

'Not me.'

Yes, it had been a bad winter in 1962–63. The Minster Pool had frozen over and snow had turned Beacon Park into a vast Arctic waste, stranding the statue of Captain Smith of the *Titanic* in a snowfield that was normally the Museum Gardens. Birds had frozen to death in the trees, and villages had been cut off for days. My father once said it had reminded everyone of the winter of 1947, when Lichfield had relied on two horse-drawn snow ploughs to clear the streets.

But these weren't only things I knew. They were family memories. They came with the remembered sound of my father's voice. They were brought back by the sight and feel of the photographs, by the evocative but unidentifiable smell released from the musty depths of the suitcase.

'And this must be you as a little boy.'

Rachel was thumbing through the photographs again, turning over pictures of me standing in the back garden at Stowe Pool Lane, wearing knee-length shorts and a short back and sides. Then there was me on a bike in my school uniform, with a satchel on my back. And there was another me, the older teenager in jeans and a Wolverhampton Wanderers shirt, growing sideboards and trying to look like my Wolves hero, Derek Dougan.

The photos were starting to make me feel uncomfortable. To me, the past was an unpleasant necessity, not something to rake over and dissect with that awful mixture of mockery and fascination. It was if I'd spread my dirty underwear on the table for her to paw through.

Now she was laughing. 'I bet you were a real pain in the neck when you were that age.'

I said nothing while I drank my tea. She looked up at me, and mimed an exaggeratedly apologetic expression. 'I'm sorry, Chris – you were looking for something, weren't you? And I'm interfering as usual. Just tell me if *I'm* being a pain in the neck, and I'll go.'

'It doesn't matter.'

'No, no. Come on, what was it you were looking for? A nice picture of your mum and dad, perhaps. Was that what you wanted? Something to frame on the sideboard?'

What I really wanted was to grab the big wedding day groups and scan the massed ranks of relatives for a face that resembled the old man I'd met one morning at Fosseway. And I wanted to pull open the folded, yellowing envelope that Rachel hadn't noticed yet. I knew it contained a few older photographs, the tiny, square sepia-coloured ones that were the only surviving images of my grandparents on my father's side.

My Grandfather Buckley had died when my father was a boy – that much I knew. I couldn't even picture his face, and I desperately needed to search it for resemblances to the man who claimed to have been his brother, my Great-Uncle Samuel. There might even be evidence of the existence of Samuel himself. Could there possibly be a snap of George and Samuel together? There were photos in that envelope of people who'd never been identified to me, grim-faced men and women in old-fashioned, ill-fitting clothes who stared at the camera as if the lens might steal their souls.

Rachel must have been psychic, or perhaps she'd seen my eyes stray automatically towards the envelope.

'Ah, what's this?'

The next second, there they were, spilled in a casual muddle on the table. Faded images of unfamiliar faces. A spasm of pain took me unawares and made me catch my breath as I looked down at a picture of my father, aged about seven, uncomfortably turned out in his Sunday best for a parade of some kind. His hair was cropped at the sides, with a longer lock flopping onto his forehead. He looked scrubbed and starched and vaguely resentful in his baggy shorts, and his bare legs were scrawny and pitiful. One of his socks had started to slip and crumple on his shin. Trembling with an inexplicable emotion, I picked up the photograph and turned it over. On the back, in washed-out black ink, it said: 'Arthur. Visit by Queen Elizabeth, 1946'.

The next snap showed my father again a few years later, a gawky boy in a white open-necked shirt, sitting with a group of adults. All the men were in ties and braces, the women in flowered dresses, enjoying the sunshine on an outing somewhere. 'Whitsun 1949' said the scrawl. There was a solitary portrait of my grandfather, George Buckley, from about the same period. He was standing proudly outside his back door in polished boots and a dark suit, solemn and upright, a pipe clenched in his teeth and not a hint of a smile. There was undoubtedly a look about his eyes and nose that reminded me of the old man who'd claimed to be his brother.

But I knew how easy it was to convince yourself of these resemblances. How often had I heard people cooing over a month-old baby, finding its father's eyes, its mother's hair. Once, I'd been horribly embarrassed after remarking to a couple I was interviewing that their son looked just like his father – only to be told that the child was adopted.

'This George,' said Rachel, reading the back of the photo. 'He was a fine-looking man.'

'My grandfather.'

'Mmm.'

I knew she could sense my tension. She was far too sharp to miss the change in my mood.

'Did you ever know him?'

'No, he died a long time ago.'

'And why is he on his own?' she said. 'Where's your grandmother, I wonder?'

'I don't know.'

She was right. It did look a bit odd. It was the kind of photograph you'd expect to include a couple, a posed portrait of Grandma and Granddad for the family album. But there was no sign of Grandma. No portrait of Mary Buckley. I looked at the group photo, but there was no way to identify her among the other women.

'Have you any other living relatives on that side of the family?' asked Rachel.

I was waiting anxiously for her to turn up the next photo-graph. But when I didn't answer her question, she looked at me keenly, as if she could see right through me.

'Well, have you?' she said.

And then it all came out. Rachel was fascinated, and grew

excited as she listened. Her response made me feel better. Being able to tell somebody about it, talking it through out loud, made the situation clearer in my mind. And once I'd told Rachel, there no longer seemed to be any doubt in my heart that the old man I'd met really was my Great-Uncle Samuel. It seemed right for the first time.

'But that's wonderful,' she said. 'A long-lost relative. It's like a fairy story. But how sad that he died.'

'Sad, yes.'

'I'd have loved to have met him. Properly, I mean. I didn't know who he was when he came that day.'

She put the photograph of my Grandfather Buckley aside, and I could see the next picture in the pile. It was almost the last one, and it showed two boys with similar serious expressions. One of them looked about twelve or thirteen, the other a few years younger. They were leaning against a heavy wooden beam, like the balance beam of a canal lock gate. They both wore stout boots and flannel trousers, their hands thrust deep into their pockets, and the older one had a flat cap at a jaunty angle. The caption read: *George and Samuel, June 1925.*

'I researched my family tree a few years ago,' said Rachel. 'It was fascinating. There's an amazing amount of information you can find, but you need to know where to look, or it can take forever. I joined the local family history society for a while. If you're thinking of researching your tree, Chris, I wouldn't mind helping – if you want.'

I remembered that Rachel had been a librarian. She'd gone back to her career after the divorce, but her part-time job at a branch library had disappeared in the cutbacks. At one time, as an Information Officer, I'd been responsible for justifying those cuts to the public. Now we were in the same boat. The knife that had made those cuts had turned on me.

But there was no way I could agree to what she was

suggesting. The thought of my next-door neighbour burrowing through my family's past repulsed me. I started to regret having told her anything. I wished I'd found the strength of will to keep my mouth shut and ask her to leave before it went so far. Suddenly, the whole exercise seemed pointless and self-obsessed, and it was Rachel's fault for dragging me into it.

'No, I won't be doing anything like that, thanks,' I said. 'Look, the reason I'm going through this material – it's not because of an interest in my family history, or out of loyalty to Samuel Longden. It's not even because I feel guilty.'

'I never said it was.'

'The only reason I'm going to do anything at all is because I'm being paid for it. You see? I have to earn a living, and if that means raking through the lives of the long dead, then so be it.'

I began to gather the photographs together and stuff them back into their envelopes. I plucked the picture of George and Samuel from her fingers and tossed it in with the rest as if it was of no importance. Rachel looked a bit hurt.

'Now,' I said, 'I've got other things to do. If you don't mind . . .'

She got up, flushing slightly. 'That's okay. I've got to go out myself. I'll be calling at Tesco's, if you want anything fetching.'

'No thanks. I'm doing my own shopping later. I usually go to Safeway.'

'Fine. Fine.'

I got her as far as the front door before she tried again. There was a hint of desperation in her voice, a pleading note that made me grit my teeth. 'You won't be wanting me to help, then?'

'I don't think so.' Then I cursed myself for not being definite. 'No, I'm sure I won't. Thanks all the same.'

Her shoulders sagged. 'Well, you know where to find me,

if you change your mind. I'm not exactly a million miles away.'

Finally, I got her out of the door and down the path with a few perfunctory words of farewell. I bundled the packets of photos together and shoved them into a drawer of the mahogany sideboard, stuffed well in among the place mats and spare fuses and God knows what else my parents had collected. One day I would really have to clear it all out. Perhaps I should look at the small ads in the *Echo* to find somebody who did house clearances. Let strangers shift the lot and do whatever they wanted with it. I could make a fresh start, clear the house of memories.

Boswell wandered into the room, right on cue. I thought of him as my parents' cat, but in reality my father had never been able to stand him. Boswell had been restricted to the back garden and the kitchen, except when my mother let him sneak onto her chair while Dad was out. Now, the cat had full run of the house.

For the past three months, I'd known there was something deep and painful that my father had left in me, a splinter of memory festering under the skin, lodged in a place I couldn't easily reach. It was the cause of the constant dull ache in my heart that sometimes flared into those jagged twinges of agony that hit me when I saw the photographs of him as a boy. It was a pain that I couldn't cure until I'd erased him completely from my life.

16

It wasn't unusual for me to take a walk on Sunday morning. Normally I took a route down Gaia Lane towards Beacon Street. There were lots of new houses here, discreetly set behind walls and hedges, some built of red brick that blended with the older properties. Speed humps controlled the traffic, and the pavements were narrow. Trees overhung the road, and grey squirrels scattered dead leaves on the sheltered drives. Sometimes I turned northwards to the corner of Curborough Road, which led out to the estates of Chadsmead and Nether Stowe, built to accommodate the population explosion that Lichfield had undergone in the 1960s and '70s.

But in the middle section of Gaia Lane there were enclosed walks through to Cathedral Close and the playing fields. I had to pass some of the other Victorian semis. Their frontages were similar to Maybank, but none of them had a Russian vine like the one my mother had planted in the front garden, which now climbed over the roof and halfway up the chimney, clutching the fabric of the house ever more tightly in its spreading tendrils.

At Stowe Pool, sloping concrete sides ran down to the water, where the bank was occupied by a solitary angler. The sun was still low and glaring on the surface, and a stiff wind blew, swirling leaves around my feet.

The walk round the water prepared me for a visit to the graveyard. As the cold wind numbed my face and limbs, it also seemed to deaden my feelings, ready for the task of confronting my memories. The most recent section of the graveyard lay behind St Chad's Church. There were rows of marble gravestones, black and grey, most of them with fresh flowers where the occupants were still remembered, but some with nothing but wilted stalks after only two or three years in the ground.

The sandstone facing of St Chad's tower glowed almost pink this morning. As I passed the porch, a waft of polish reached me from the open door. I orientated myself towards a bright yellow skip that stood in a graveyard extension. The grass was neatly mown right up to the headstones, and I heard the sound of a strimmer from the opposite side of the graveyard. Some of the headstones were grouped together, with no visible graves. Space is at a premium in many grave-yards these days. There isn't room for too many dead people cluttering up our lives.

Although I hadn't been to the graveyard for several months, I had no trouble finding the stone I wanted. It said: 'In loving memory of' on the top half, and the section below it was divided into two. My mother's inscription was on one side – 'a devoted wife and mother, Sheila Buckley, died August 1997 aged 60'. The other side had been left blank when she was buried. The design had been my father's idea. But it hadn't stayed blank for long, before his own name had filled it.

'Well, Dad, you taught me about secrets. You said secrets were never to be told. I didn't realise you were keeping other secrets too. Did they eat away at you like they did at me?'

Oh yes, there had been so many secrets. Not only the existence of my grandfather's brother, which had been kept from me, but why Great-Uncle Samuel had changed his name. And since I'd read Samuel's letter, I had an uneasy impression of a great, yawning hole in my family's history where other mysteries lurked. *I thought I might find some justi-fication for what has been done to us. But I found none,* he'd written. But what had been done? And who did he mean by *us*? The Buckleys? Yet Samuel had tried to distance himself from the Buckleys, to the extent of taking another name. *Vengeance leads only to bitterness. Evil breeds evil.*

I shook my head in bafflement. I knew all about betrayal and bitterness. But surely Samuel couldn't mean me. He was talking about something that had happened much longer ago. He'd mentioned the year 1800. Two hundred years of bitterness and vengeance? It hardly seemed possible.

I'd been determined to look ahead to the future, but somehow the past kept intruding. Now I had to acknowledge that I'd been fighting a losing battle. The only way I was likely to have a future was by exploring the past, thanks to a ridiculous bequest from a long-lost relative. Despite my best efforts to avoid it, I'd have to confront the history of my own family. I'd have to open my eyes to what had formed me, the factors making me what I am.

I looked again at my father's grave. Yes, bitterness and resentment could last for two hundred years, if you lived that long. But it couldn't survive your death, could it? The stuff that Samuel had written about genetic memory was nonsense. I hadn't inherited any memory from my father of a great wrong done to our family. Quite the opposite. If such wrongs had existed, he'd deliberately kept them from me.

Another picture of my father rose in my mind, unbidden. It was the image of him that I least wanted to see, the one I'd never been able to remove from my thoughts since those days as a child, when the meaning of evil had been imprinted on my memory. It might not be quite what Samuel had meant, but my father had passed on the meaning of betrayal, the taste of bitterness, the desire for vengeance. He'd done it in his own peculiar way. But he'd certainly done it effectively. Standing there by his grave, I knew that the feelings he'd planted in me had merely lain dormant, almost unacknowledged, for most of my adult years.

Perhaps Samuel was right, then. I couldn't take revenge on my father. But if the evil could be explained, its power might be destroyed. If evil had bred evil, who had planted the seed?

I decided to assess the facts logically. Being realistic, what evidence did I have that the old man I'd met at Fosseway really was my Great-Uncle Samuel? True, I had the document Mr Elsworth had given me, testifying to Samuel's name change. That seemed to give him some form of official status as a Buckley, even if he'd turned his back on the name. And why should he lie? I couldn't see what he might gain from pretending to be my relative.

And, of course, there was that photograph. I'd dug it out again, to reassure myself that it existed. *George and Samuel, June 1925*. If I'd ever seen it before, I couldn't remember it. But then, I'd never taken much interest, and my father hadn't been one to reminisce about his family.

It was only my mother who ever brought out the old photos, on the occasions when in-laws were gathered and small huddles of grey heads had formed round the table to smile at the boyish faces of the Buckley men. I could have had no reason for assuming that the Samuel pictured with my grandfather was anything other than a childhood friend. How could I have guessed it was his brother?

I pictured Samuel Longden as I'd last seen him, walking painfully into the dusk on the corner of Conduit Street, pausing perhaps to lean on his stick. In my mind, his face was etched with pain and betrayal. In Castle Dyke, he didn't hear the car that descended so fast from the ramp of the car park. Perhaps it didn't have its lights on as it entered the street, and the driver failed to see Samuel in the dark, until it was far too late. I could see the impact of metal on a fragile body, the jerking of limbs, like a dummy tossed into the air. And then followed the sounds, the sickening thump of impacted flesh, the breaking of bones.

By the time Samuel hit the ground he would already be dying or dead, no more than a sack of clothing dropped on the pavement. I thought I heard a tinkle of glass from a shattered headlamp and the revving of an engine that covered a final cry from a dying man's throat. I smelled the blood from his cracked skull. I could almost feel the agony of his pulverised body. 'Multiple internal injuries'. An easy phrase to say. Not so easy to understand what it meant.

And then there were the actual memories. That deep, racking cough from someone nearby, the car I'd glimpsed accelerating away, and the street falling quiet. Only Samuel would have remained, still and lifeless, his body broken, his stick smashed in the gutter.

But the picture in my mind wasn't complete. There were crucial details missing, specific features I couldn't fill in. Who else had been in that street? What colour was the car, and what make? And whose face had been behind the windscreen?

I called again at the Fosseway restoration site. There was no Waterway Recovery Group work party this weekend, just the usual collection of volunteers, the dedicated few who came out month after month to wield their shovels and trowels.

In the last two weeks a new culvert had been installed to take a brook under the canal below Fosseway Lock. Sections of the old cast iron culvert, full of silt, had been removed, and most of the spoil had been taken to backfill behind the abutment. Several of the massive coping stones from the lock walls had been recovered too. They weighed up to four tonnes each, and it took a crane and a lorry to put them back into position. But there was much more brickwork to be restored.

Today, I could see that a JCB had exposed the footings of the bridge and the water channel. But disaster had struck when lumps of masonry got stuck in one side of the trailer, causing a wheel to sink into the soft ground and the trailer to keel over. A cluster of restoration workers were gathered round trying to free it from the quagmire.

One of the ways the Trust had been raising money was through a scheme for supporters to sponsor the steel pilings that strengthened the bank. The piles were stamped with the names of sponsors. I ran my eye over a few while I waited. They said 'Emma and Sam', 'Panzer Cat', 'Tony's Pile' and 'The Woollibotts'. A working party had been using a borrowed piling hammer, and claimed to have driven seventy-five piles in a single weekend.

Andrew Hadfield was among the workers, with a hard hat pushed high on his head. I finally managed to attract his attention from behind the safety fence and beckoned him over.

'Andrew, I've got something I'd like you to have a look at.'
'Oh?'
'It's in my car. Can you spare a minute?'
'This sounds interesting.'

We sat in the Escort, and I took the box off the back seat and placed it in his lap. Since my visit to the solicitor's office on Friday, I'd spent what seemed like hours staring at that box and wondering whether I should smash it open. I'd even brought a hammer and chisel from the garage with the intention of starting the job. But I'd laid the tools down again. I couldn't bring myself to damage the perfect grain in the wood, or to destroy something that had lasted intact for so long. It would have felt like sacrilege.

'Mmm.' Andrew lifted the box, turned it over, stroked his hand against the grain of the wood and stared at the three keyholes. 'I suppose if you just turn the one key . . . no, I didn't think it would.'

'We tried that,' I said.

'We?' he asked, cocking an eyebrow.

'A . . . friend of mine has looked at it too.'

'No, you'd need all three keys,' said Andrew. 'That's the whole point. That's why it was made like this.'

'What do you mean? What is it?'

'A canal proprietors' box. It's the sort of thing they used for keeping valuable items in, like deeds or share certificates, or the company seal.'

'Would that be valuable?'

'Of course. The wax seal was what made a document legally binding. Possession of the seal meant financial power. So the seal and its stamp were kept in a box like this, with three locks, which meant three proprietors had to be present to open it. They would each have their own individual key, you see.'

'It sounds as though they didn't trust each other very much.'

'Trust each other? The canal companies were rife with jealousy and rivalry, not to mention the opportunity for dishonesty and misappropriation of funds. You must know the history of some of these companies. The Ogley and Huddlesford had its fair share of disputes and scandals, but it was no worse than many others.'

Andrew hefted the box and shook it gently. 'No impressor in there, though. In fact, it seems to be empty.'

'That's what I thought, too.'

'An interesting curio,' said Andrew, handing the box back. 'If it still had its contents, it would be a real treasure.'

'And the keys, I suppose.'

'Well, to have all three keys with it would be a real achievement. Bearing in mind they'd be in the possession of three separate people. This box was deliberately made difficult to open.'

He looked at me as I returned the box carefully to the back seat. 'Are you going to try to find the other keys, Chris?'

'How would I do that?'

He laughed. 'I have no idea.'

I didn't tell Andrew there was another key in my pocket, and I'd already checked that it fitted the box. I'd decided there were some things I should keep to myself. I could harbour a

125

secret too. I had a good teacher in that art. But, as for a third key, I couldn't begin to imagine where I would look. I could sense that it might become an obsession, if I let it.

'I wonder where he got the box?' I said thoughtfully.

'Who?'

'Samuel Longden.'

'Is that where it came from? Well, well. He was a curious old man in lots of ways.'

'What do you know about him?'

'No more than anyone else. But there's been a lot of talk about him since he died. It seems everyone knew his name on the Birmingham Navigations and the Trent and Mersey, not to mention further afield. Boaters like to gossip when they're tied up together. You should see them rattling away to each other at a rally. Did you know the boaters called Samuel "The Captain"?'

'No.'

'Well, the old Captain was a bit of a character apparently. Eccentric, even. That sort of person always attracts a bit of talk.'

'Had you met him before?'

'Not until he started turning up to watch the work parties. They say he'd been off the water for a few years. Couldn't cope with a boat on his own any more, I suppose, at his age. They call it "having moss on the fender".'

'Did you ever come across his daughter?'

'No. Never met her.'

'Not many people seem to have.'

Andrew regarded me quizzically. 'Did Samuel Longden take his project seriously, then? The book business?'

'It looks as though he did,' I said.

'And you? Are you taking it seriously, Chris?'

But I didn't know the answer to that one.

17

Back at the house, I placed the box file and the blue folder on the table to look at them properly. It seemed I was going to have to read Samuel's manuscript for clues about what he wanted me to do.

But this was also the point of no return. Once I opened the folder, I knew I'd be committed. If I wanted to forget all about it, I could still put my coat on, walk out of the door and go down to the pub instead.

Then the phone rang. Saved by the bell, I thought stupidly. But it was Dan Hyde. After the ritual enquiries after my health, he came to the reason he'd phoned.

He rattled on about cash-flow and budget forecasts and credit control, another hold-up that would delay the launch of *winningbid.uk.com*. It was all stuff I didn't understand, and I'm sure he knew it. My name was on the loan agreement, though – and on the lease for the offices.

'So is it something I should be worried about right now?' I said.

There was a moment's silence, then Dan said, 'You'll need to start worrying about it very soon.'

I put the phone down and took a deep breath. Then I turned back to the bundle of manuscript pages. They lay on the table taunting me, hinting at mysteries and murmuring of a hidden past, just as Samuel Longden himself had done.

A curious old man, Andrew Hadfield had called him. That seemed to sum up Samuel pretty well.

But had Samuel's mind been up to the task of compiling a rational history on any subject, let alone his own ancestors? There was only one way to find out.

The pages of the manuscript were stapled together in chapters. I separated the first chapter of *The Three Keys* from the rest and carried it through to the sitting room. I settled down in an armchair with Boswell on my lap, and I began to read.

Samuel Longden began his account in the closing years of the eighteenth century, the height of 'canal mania'. It was a time of speculation, with a surge of wealthy individuals investing in businesses for the potential profit, and inland waterways were a boom industry.

In South Staffordshire, the Ogley and Huddlesford Canal was built principally for the transport of coal, linking local mines to the Coventry Canal at Huddlesford and to the Wyrley and Essington at Ogley Junction. The first proprietors were notable men from the Lichfield area, corporation members or county officials, often connected by mutual business interests, or by marriages between their children.

There were several pages in the manuscript about the leading proprietors, who seemed to me to have been a set of dubious and idiosyncratic characters. Anthony Nall, the first chairman of the canal company, owned a substantial amount of property in Lichfield as well as several coal mines, but his term as chairman was marked by acrimonious disputes with other proprietors and employees. His main ally was his brother Joshua, a merchant who became Deputy Lord Lieutenant of the county and later Chief Magistrate. He had a farm at Leomansley, where he was said to have lived for many years practising his flamboyant signature.

There was James Allwood, a doctor; Edward Wilkinson, an apothecary; Robert Sykes, landlord of the Angel Inn, the venue for corporation banquets and canal company meetings; and Adam Henshall, who despite serving as a magistrate himself was continually being told to remove the detritus of his grocery business – hogsheads and cakes from outside his warehouse in St John Street, and dung and stone from Market Street.

According to Samuel, an important figure was John Frith, a solicitor who'd been steward to successive dukes and was Clerk of the Peace. He had a flourishing law practice in offices near the Market Square. But Frith was elderly and not physically active, so his junior partner Daniel Metcalf took on the role of chief administrator and legal advisor for the canal company. Metcalf was only twenty-six, but was said to be very ambitious.

Other influential proprietors were the Parker family, merchants and exporters. When financial services became more organised, two Parker brothers, Isaac and Seth, developed into Lichfield's earliest bankers, and Seth was appointed company treasurer.

But it was the Reverend Thomas Ella who became the central character in the story. He was a prominent Lichfield personality, headmaster of a local school, considered 'a real gentleman and scholar', well known for his generosity and public spiritedness. He took snuff, gambled at cards and enjoyed brandy and wine. He dressed well, wearing black stockings of superfine cotton, silver buckles on his shoes, and silk handkerchiefs.

Ella was a Cambridge graduate and had wide interests. He was secretary of a circulating library and distributed periodicals like *The Universal Magazine* to gentlemen of the neighbourhood. In his later years he founded several charitable institutions. He was happily married, but there had been a tragedy in his family with the death of his newborn son, who lived only three weeks. Ella baptised him at a private service, but the child died ten days later.

Much of the early work in getting the canal scheme under way was done by Ella, described by Samuel as a 'visionary' whose efforts were tireless in persuading friends and acquaintances to put up the money. Out of their own pockets these men paid for 'Land for Wharfs and the making the same and also all Collateral Cuts, Basons, Reservoirs, Engines and all other Works and Conveniences.'

The proposed Ogley and Huddlesford Canal was to be seven miles long, with thirty locks. A 1794 Act of Parliament empowered the company to raise £25,000 from the sale of two hundred shares, and a further £20,000 if necessary – money that would be paid back out of charges for tonnage rates.

Then began the actual work. The design of the project fell to the famous engineer William Jessop, who accepted the role of Chief Engineer, though working simultaneously on several other canals. The survey of the route was carried out by one of Jessop's assistants, who must have impressed the proprietors with his skill, because he was subsequently appointed Resident Engineer.

Samuel quoted a recorded reference for a resident engineer as 'A person capable of conducting the business of a Canal through, viz, that he is a good Engineer, can carry an Accurate Level, and has a perfect knowledge of Cutting, Banking, etc, and also that he is a compleat Mason.' But he added that it failed to mention three important qualifications for the job – diplomacy, for dealing with irate or greedy landowners, the authority to handle uncooperative contractors, and an indefatigable taste for travelling.

Once the chief engineer had drawn up his specifications, he left for the next project, and the job of supervising the actual building of the waterway fell to the resident engineer. He worked on one job at a time, which usually lasted many years. By the time most of them finished their first major job, canal mania would be over.

As a result, the resident engineer became neither rich nor famous. He expected to get the blame if things went wrong, but very little credit when the canal was complete.

Samuel described the resident engineer chosen by the Lichfield proprietors as a young man, only thirty-two years old. Like Samuel, he lived in Whittington, where he'd seen the Coventry Canal being constructed as a child. This may have been his very first experience of the problems of theft and dishonesty, which bedevilled some canal projects.

The new resident engineer was a single man when he was appointed, but shortly afterwards he met his future wife, Sarah, a local woman, and they married in 1796. He was able to settle down near Lichfield and start a family.

Four years later, the proprietors of the Ogley and Huddlesford Canal were shocked to receive serious allegations of fraud against their resident engineer. Before they could act, he'd vanished under suspicion of corruption and embezzlement, leaving behind his wife and a young son.

And Samuel's chapter ended with the most vital information of all. That resident engineer's name was William Buckley.

18

Late on Monday morning I headed towards Frog Lane to make my statement at the police station. I had to wait for a while in the reception area, kicking my heels until they found someone with time to see me. There were a few other people sitting around on plastic chairs, but they looked more like long-suffering relatives than hardened criminals.

Eventually, I was taken into a tiny room with a view down a corridor along which the occasional police officer walked. A uniformed constable came through clutching a file. His face was pink, and he looked about sixteen. By the time I'd gone through my story again and he'd written it down word for word, the whole tale sounded pathetic, and I was sweating with embarrassment. I desperately wanted to make something up that sounded more convincing and wouldn't portray me as a cowardly fool. But there was nothing I could do that would make this youth regard me with approval, no words I could say that would restore my self-respect.

By the time I emerged from the police station, I felt as though I'd been subjected to the third degree with bright lights and hosepipes. But there had been nobody torturing me except myself. I'd seen my humiliation written out in black and white, and I'd signed my name to it for posterity.

It was the first time I'd been in the Frog Lane area since Samuel Longden's death. Part of me wanted to turn away from the scene as a place it was best not to see. But instead

I made my way to the corner of Castle Dyke, intent on punishing myself further, seeking the traces of blood stains or fragments of broken glass in the gutter. There were none, of course – the evidence had been cleaned up and tidied away. If only the city council employed someone who could wipe away the shame that was staining my mind and running in the gutters of my thoughts.

Just inside the entrance of the multi-storey car park was a small cabin, and I could see someone moving around inside. The car park was the type where you 'paid and displayed' by putting your money into one of the automatic ticket machines on the parking levels. There was no barrier to pass through at the exit, and no need to have any contact with the attendant. He was there merely for security, and to check on vehicles that had overstayed the time on their tickets.

When I knocked on the door of the cabin, a thin, middle-aged man in a uniform appeared, clutching a mug of tea. At first, he didn't seem to understand what I wanted. I got the impression that people usually came to the cabin because they couldn't find their car. But at last I got through to him that I wanted to know about the accident in which the old man had been killed the week before. His suspicions cleared when I mentioned I was a relative.

'Oh yes, terrible,' he said. 'Course, I didn't see it, you know. I told the police that. I was up on the top level at the time. I'm supposed to watch the cars that are in, not the ones that are going out. But I'll say this – some of them go at a hell of a speed down the exit ramps. It's like a Grand Prix circuit some nights. There's one bloke burns so much rubber off his tyres in here, you'd think he was trying to keep the Goodyear factory in work single-handed. And as for the noise—'

'You must be good at taking notice of people. Do you remember anybody in particular being around that night?'

'Not really. It wasn't very busy by that time. The shop and

office folk had mostly gone home, and the evening crowd hadn't arrived yet. The only thing I can remember . . . well, it doesn't mean anything.'

'What?'

'Well, when I was up on level two, I could tell there was a bloke fetching his car from just below, even before I heard his engine start up. That must have been right before the old chap was killed. Sound carries something terrible inside here, so I could hear it clearly. It made me think of my old dad, who smoked himself to death before anybody even thought to tell him it might be dangerous.'

'The man you heard . . .?'

'Yes, terrible cough he had. Terrible. I heard him quite clearly, right the way up to the top level.'

'The police said there was a witness.'

'Not me, anyway. Not really. There were a few people who appeared after the accident – not that they could do much to help the old chap. Though, now you mention it, there was a woman standing over on the corner there at the time. Maybe she saw what happened. I don't know if the police ever spoke to her.'

My next stop was the County Record Office, located on the upper floor of a library building in The Friary, which had once been the Friary School.

I climbed the stairs and pushed through double doors into a large room lined with shelves. Microfiche machines stood at one end, and an assistant was dealing with an enquiry at a desk near the door. There were one or two people sitting at tables or using the machines, but the room was almost empty. Walking past the enquiry desk, I found a series of shelves down one wall marked 'Local Studies', and located a section devoted to waterways history.

Since I was taking a logical approach to the problem, the first thing to do was check Great-Uncle Samuel's facts. If I did this at every step of the way, I'd feel much more confident that I was on the right track, that Samuel wasn't just sending me down a blind alley.

The formal notification of Samuel's funeral had arrived that morning. It gave no hint of the novel occasion that Mr Elsworth had forecast, except that on Wednesday the funeral procession would leave from the Red Lion Inn at Hopwas, instead of from Samuel's home at Whittington, as would have been normal. Somehow, the black-edged card made my errand seem more urgent. I felt as though I ought to begin my project before Samuel had completely departed. I had to grab the baton he'd offered me before it vanished from sight into the great black hole that was the past.

The Local Studies Library and County Records Office seemed like a good place to make sure the background of William Buckley was accurate. Presumably William was some sort of very distant relative, six generations away at least. Samuel had considered him important, though. He'd thought William Buckley and the year 1800 were where it all started, or where it all finished – his thinking seemed confused on the point. Samuel had at least given me the opportunity to start at the beginning, and move forward in time. I could establish that I was building on firm ground before I began to construct the House of Buckley.

My knowledge of the Ogley and Huddlesford Canal was confined to the present and the recent past – it had never occurred to me to research beyond its closure in the 1950s. But according to Samuel's manuscript, William had been the resident engineer on the canal scheme. At some stage, he'd vanished under suspicion of corruption and embezzle-ment, leaving behind his wife and young son. My ancestor had evidently been a notorious crook. So what was the mystery?

As I scanned the shelves, I quickly identified a couple of books that had chapters on the history of local canals, and I took them with me to one of the tables in the middle of the room. I pulled out my notebook and pen and began to take notes as I turned over the pages.

But I'd hardly begun to write when a presence loomed over my shoulder. It was the librarian from the desk, a tall woman with an overly large nose and her hair permed into short, tight curls.

'Excuse me, are you looking for something?'

'Yes,' I said. 'Something on local canal history.' I indicated the two books, to show her that I'd found something and therefore didn't need any help at the moment.

'These tables are reserved for people who book them for researching the archives,' she said. 'If you'd like to move over here.'

She ushered me towards a smaller table at the side, where some of the space was taken up by microfilm machines. Behind me, she straightened up the chair I'd vacated, pushing it exactly into line with the others at the row of empty tables. I almost expected her to disinfect it.

'I'm afraid you're not allowed to use a pen in here,' she said, as I settled down again. 'Only pencils.'

She offered me half a pencil, about three or four inches long, and I obediently put my pen in my pocket. Presumably I had the look of a book vandal who'd scrawl obscene messages in the pages. Maybe I would too, once her back was turned.

'And could you sign your name in the book at the desk, please.'

'I take it I'm breaking all the rules,' I sighed, as I began to get up.

'As long as you do it before you leave,' she said. And the look in her eye suggested it wouldn't be any too soon as far as she was concerned.

Finally, I was able to continue my notes, switching from blue ballpoint in mid-sentence to grey lead pencil. I'd have

136

to be sure to transcribe my notes onto the computer before they faded out of existence. And I'd have to be careful not to press too hard. I couldn't afford to break the point, as I certainly wouldn't dare go to the counter to ask for another pencil. There was bound to be a rule against it.

I found references to the origins of the Ogley and Huddlesford, and to some of the people who'd been behind the scheme – the Reverend Thomas Ella, Daniel Metcalf, and the Nalls. There were also those whose conduct was said to have brought the canal company into disrepute. Two men had been transported to Australia for theft when money was found to be missing from the company's accounts. But the resident engineer, William Buckley, had evaded justice for his suspected crimes.

The information tallied with what Great-Uncle Samuel had written. One of the books quoted several times from the Assembly Minutes of the Ogley and Huddlesford Canal Company. I took these assemblies to be a sort of Annual General Meeting. A footnote told me that the minutes were kept in the County Record Office, having been transferred there from the British Transport Historical Records. Unlike some of the other canal companies in the West Midlands, the more detailed minutes of the monthly committee meetings were missing.

I eyed the dragon behind the desk speculatively, then looked at my watch. It would have to wait for another day anyway. I handed in my pencil and signed my name in the book, so that I could be identified if any obscene graffiti came to light. The air on the outside of the double doors felt much fresher.

Back home in Stowe Pool Lane, I pulled out Great-Uncle Samuel's files and stacked them on my desk. The pile looked daunting, like a notorious Himalayan peak not to be tackled without a base camp and a team of Sherpas.

Nervously, I put aside the blue folder, which contained the unfinished manuscript. What was in the box file? Letters, among other things. Two of them, bound in string and written on thick, yellowing paper. The writing was difficult to read, and was beyond my patience to decipher. They really needed transcribing. In fact, there was a whole load of stuff here that ought to be put into proper order before I could begin to make sense of it. I needed some help.

There was only one place I could go. I tucked the file under my arm. Then I looked at the long wooden box and remembered Rachel's offer to clean it up. I picked that up as well, went out of the front door and walked round to number four.

Rachel looked a little less pleased to see me than usual. She was wearing a huge, baggy sweater and black leggings, with her hair scraped back off her face, as if I'd caught her doing a spring clean or a bit of DIY.

'Hello, number four,' I said.

'Oh, Chris.'

'Not interrupting anything, am I?'

'Well, actually—'

'If it's not convenient, I'll come back later.'

'What is it you want?'

It wasn't the sort of open-handed welcome I'd been anticipating. At first I didn't think she was even going to invite me in. But when I embarked on what was obviously going to be a lengthy explanation while standing on her doorstep, she sighed and took me into a sitting room rich in chintz and furnished in shades of green and gold.

'I don't see how I can help,' she said.

'You already know a bit about what's involved. You're the only person who's already halfway towards understanding the thing.'

'I'm not sure.'

'What it really needs is a professional touch. I don't know

where to start with this sort of thing. I want a family tree doing, I suppose, and a bit of proper genealogical research. I'm completely out of my depth. Won't you help me, Rachel? Think about it, please.'

'You know I'm going away to visit my sister on Friday, don't you?'

'Oh yes, of course,' I said, though I'd forgotten. 'But you've got time to make a start before then, haven't you? Maybe you could just have a look at the letters.'

She still hesitated. I knew an extra nudge was needed. I could sense she really wanted to help with the project, that she was genuinely interested in *The Three Keys*. But there was something stopping her from agreeing. I looked at the set of her jaw and the coolness in her eye and realised suddenly that it was stubborn pride. I recalled the hurt look in her eyes a night or two before, when I'd rebuffed her offer of help. Had she been sulking since then? Was that the reason I'd seen nothing of her for a day or two? I'd offended her, and she was feeling upset. She wanted one more thing from me, and I'd have to do it if I was going to get her assistance.

'Rachel – about the other night, I'm sorry if I was a bit abrupt with you. I've been under a lot of stress. I'm really sorry.'

She sighed, weakening. 'I suppose you'd like some coffee.'

19

In the centre of Hopwas were two pubs, situated on either side of the canal close to the Lichfield Road bridge. On one side stood the black and white Tame Otter, and on the other the Red Lion, both with tables set out in beer gardens on the canalside. There was a small wharf at the bottom of the Red Lion's garden, where a smart red and green narrowboat waited, its brasswork gleaming. I realised then what was going to be unusual about Great-Uncle Samuel's funeral.

A small crowd of people in dark clothes were milling around the beer garden, moving in slow, automatic patterns like feeding crows, silent and uneasy. Some of them turned to stare at me as I walked down the steps to join them. They noted my black suit and tie, saw that I was one of their group, and promptly ignored me.

According to a sign on the cabin, the boat had been hired from Streethay Wharf. Samuel Longden's coffin had already been carried from the hearse that stood above us on the road, and now it rested on the flat roof of the boat, secured with white cotton lines to rails that ran the full length on either side. The funeral director's men were gathered round the coffin, checking it was secure. Then they began placing flowers around it in great heaps of colour, piling them up until the boat was like a floating garden.

'He'd really like to have gone on *Kestrel*,' said someone

nearby, 'but nobody is sure whether it's in good enough condition.'

There was no one there that I knew, except for Samuel's neighbour, Mrs Wentworth. She was dressed in a black coat and a strange little hat, and she was accompanied by a fat, bald man who might have been Mr Wentworth. She caught my eye, but looked away without acknowledging me. Everywhere there seemed to be dark backs and unfamiliar faces turned away from me, and the atmosphere was thoroughly depressing. I glanced longingly at the back door of the pub, but it was only ten o'clock and the bar wasn't open yet.

I began a slow prowl towards the bank of the canal, searching for someone who might be a relative. Samuel's daughter Caroline must be here, surely. She would have flown back from Australia as soon as she heard of her father's death. But I had no idea what she looked like, or even how old she might be.

And what other relatives might be gathered that I didn't know about? Maybe I was getting paranoid, but everyone I looked at bore an imagined resemblance to a Buckley. And every one of them turned away from me or stared right through me, dismissing me as an intrusive stranger.

The funeral director was taking charge now, calling people together in a courteous but insistent tone, with the manner of a man used to being in control at such occasions. He was ushering mourners onto the boat via a short wooden gangplank leading into the saloon, where tables and bench seats were installed as if in a railway carriage or a motorway restaurant.

And now it was a simple matter of observation to see that the man was paying particular attention to a black-clad woman and her companion, urging them to take their places at the front of the saloon. As far as I could tell, the woman was about thirty years old, tall and dark-haired. She wore a suit with a knee-length skirt that was a little too tight to allow her to descend the steps into the boat gracefully. Holding her arm was a tall man with a heavy jaw and deep-set eyes, who looked at everyone with the same expression of contempt. At least it wasn't just me, then. But the one glimpse I caught of his dark eyes made me recoil instinctively, as if I'd turned over a damp stone and found something awful squirming underneath it.

I joined the throng of people and ducked as I stepped down into the boat. The saloon was lined with small windows for sight-seeing trips. Behind me was another door, which led into the rear cabin and out onto the stern counter, where a steerer stood with his hand on the tiller. He was dressed in mourning clothes like everyone else, though whether he was a genuine mourner or an employee of the funeral director, I couldn't tell.

The woman I took to be Caroline Longden was at the front, with a small group gathered protectively round her. From her age, I reckoned old Samuel must have been well into his fifties when she was born. But wasn't that what he'd said? That he'd married late in life? It occurred to me that, as a relative of the deceased, I should perhaps be at the front too, near the chief mourners. But I knew none of these people. They could all be relatives, for all I knew. This wasn't the time to push myself forward where I might be unwelcome.

I settled instead for a place near the stern, where two middle-aged couples joined me. They obviously knew each other, and I sensed they were people for whom Samuel Longden's death was not a great personal loss. Friends, then. Neighbours or acquaintances, perhaps, or even former employees. The man nearest me was wearing one of those peaked caps, like a weekend yachtsman. Although it was black, it looked strangely jocular and out of place, even on a boat.

Soon the diesel engine burst into life and churned the water under the stern, and we were under way. Across the canal, at the Tame Otter, and along the bridge above us, people had gathered to watch the boat move off. Some had cameras to capture the moment. As Mr Elsworth had predicted, it was a novel occasion.

From the bridge, we emerged into bright winter sunshine. There were private gardens on either side of the canal until we passed a small landing stage and moved underneath a line of silver birch trees stretching towards Hopwas School Bridge. The smell of garlic wafted from a moored narrowboat, and two children stopped their bikes on the towpath to stare and point at us.

Within a few more yards we'd passed out of Hopwas altogether into a rural stretch of canal, where the silence around us was palpable. The River Tame ran close to the canal, and woods rose to the west. According to a sign, this was the furthest reach of the firing range at Whittington Barracks. Another danger area.

Two swans with tags on their legs followed the boat under the next bridge. They eyed us malevolently and hissed at us quietly through orange beaks. The arch of the bridge was low, and sunlight reflected off the water onto its lichen-covered bricks. Past the bridge, the trees were different. They had rough bark, and their branches divided low on their trunks to reach out across the water. The passage of the boat set up slow ripples that spread out behind us and nudged the banks, stirring the weeds and disturbing a moorhen. A cool breeze sprang up on the open section of canal. Petals slipped from the wreaths and drifted onto the water like confetti.

The journey to Whittington took about forty-five minutes. As soon as the novelty of the boat had begun to wear off, I was able to study the other mourners closely. No doubt they studied me too. From a galley near the stem of the boat, a woman in an apron served us with cups of tea and biscuits, and the atmosphere became more relaxed, as it does on these occasions when refreshments arrive. The people sitting near me began to eye me curiously.

'So how did you know the Captain?' said the man with the cap, after the tea had done its job.

'I'm a relative.'

'Oh?'

They looked at each other, but carefully avoided looking at Caroline's party.

'His great-nephew.'

'I see. Were you close?'

'No, we hadn't seen each other until recently.'

'He was a grand chap,' said one of the women, her hat swaying as she nodded.

'The best,' said the other. 'No edge to him at all. He always had a friendly word for everyone he met. And he must have met plenty of people in his time.'

'Everyone knew the Captain.'

Now I had them placed. They were boaters, Samuel's fellow waterways enthusiasts, turning out to pay their respects. They introduced themselves as Eric and Barbara, Malcolm and Margaret.

'A few years ago the Captain was up and down this bit of canal all the time,' said Eric. 'He went everywhere. Braunston, onto the Oxford, down to the Trent and Mersey and the Grand Union.'

'There were still working boats on those canals until the late 1960s, maybe a bit later,' I said.

'He liked that.' Eric smiled at me. 'The Captain was a pleasure boater himself, of course. But he was disappointed when the working boats stopped. Of course, trade just died out. They couldn't compete any more.'

'Sometimes he had the girl with him too,' said Barbara.

We all looked towards Caroline. She wasn't a girl any more.

She looked mature and calm, and very much in control. The black suited her – it gave her an air of elegance and sophistication that made her stand out from those around her.

'Ah, but he hadn't been boating for a while.'

'A few years, certainly.'

'What made him stop?' I asked.

'Don't know.'

'Old age probably.'

'But he kept up his interest in the waterways.'

'Oh, he put a lot of money into them.'

'Yes, you could always count on him when it was needed.'

Their eyes turned on me again, openly speculative now. 'He had plenty of money, didn't he? The Captain?' one said.

I managed a non-committal shrug.

'I suppose it goes to the girl,' said Eric, studying the back of Caroline's head as she delicately chewed on a biscuit.

'I believe so,' I said. 'Most of it, anyway.'

They watched me, waiting for me to continue. A residue of funeral decorum held them back from interrogating me about my relationship to the rest of the family and exactly how much I was going to gain from Samuel Longden's will.

'Do you recognise any of the other people here?' I asked. 'Apart from Caroline.'

Eric indicated discreetly with the peak of his cap. 'Those two in the corner. Their name's Chaplin.'

'Frank and Sally,' said Barbara. 'I was speaking to them earlier on.'

'Some sort of relatives, aren't they?'

'He's Caroline's half-brother.'

'Ah, he'd be the son of Samuel's wife from her first marriage,' said Eric.

'She died, you know. In a car crash,' Margaret told me in a hushed voice.

'What about Caroline's companion?'

'I think he's her boyfriend,' said Eric doubtfully.

145

'It's Simon something,' said Malcolm. 'I heard her call him Simon.'

'Do you know his last name?'

Margaret moved across the aisle and held a whispered conversation with another couple. 'His name's Simon Monks,' she said when she came back. 'And he's not her boyfriend, he's her fiancé. They're getting married.'

We passed a farm and a scatter of buildings. A pair of carriages rattled by on the railway line from Lichfield to Tamworth as we approached the level crossing at Hademore. The canal took a swing to the west, following the contours of the land towards the rifle ranges on the heath, and running alongside the road as far as Whittington Bridge.

From here, although there was no obvious change in the waterway, I knew it reverted to the Coventry Canal from the stretch of Birmingham and Fazeley we'd been on. This was the detached portion of the Coventry, an anomaly left by a dispute between rival companies that had rumbled on for years.

'Not far now,' said one of the canal people.

Cups and plates were being cleared away. Visits were made to the toilets somewhere ahead of the galley. Gradually, the party remembered what it was assembled for. Some of us had forgotten what was carried on the roof, until we passed the sewage works and chugged along close to the houses in Whittington. People came out of their back doors to watch us, and an old man walking his dog on the towpath shouted to the steerer to ask whose funeral it was.

Word seemed to spread through the village. By the time we tied up at the moorings near Burton Road, there was a crowd on the roadside, almost blocking the traffic. They stood in the garden of a pub, right among the play equipment and a grotesque plastic tree with a twisted human face like something out of Tolkien's *Lord of the Rings*. Next to the pub was a pair of old lock gates set into the ground and a

146

sign that said 'Whittington Lock'. But there had never been any locks on the Coventry Canal, so these gates had come from somewhere else.

Whittington Wharf was just below the bridge. It was only a private house really, with a shed in the garden labelled 'site office'. But there was a landing place where space had been left for the funeral boat to tie up.

We waited while the men carefully lifted the coffin from the roof. The boat rocked in the water when it was relieved of the weight. They carried the coffin up the path to the road, where the hearse waited, then came back for the flowers as we all disembarked via the gangplank, smoothing our clothes self-consciously and casting our eyes down under the barrage of curious stares from the bridge. A policeman was on duty to halt the traffic and allow the hearse and funeral cars to move off. I found myself crammed into the second black limousine with the Chaplins and an unidentified old lady who'd spoken to no one.

Frank Chaplin was a narrow-shouldered man in his forties with curly ginger hair starting to recede from his forehead. He had a wispy moustache and a tendency to smile without showing his teeth, which made him look as though he was smirking. Every few minutes he shot back the over-long cuff of his black suit to look at his wristwatch. His wife Sally was dark-haired, with a generously built body restrained in a tight grey skirt and jacket.

'It's going to take all day,' said Sally, leaning across the seats to me as if she suddenly felt she'd known me all her life. 'Did you realise that? I've never heard of a funeral taking so long. Frank has had to take an entire day off work.'

'I suppose we could sneak off after the service.'

'No, we can't,' said Frank mournfully. 'We've left our car at Hopwas, haven't we?'

'That's a point. So have I. Perhaps we could ask the funeral director to phone for a taxi, and we could share it.'

147

Frank and Sally looked askance at the old lady, who seemed to be falling asleep. 'We can't do that. Obviously, it wouldn't be respectful.'

'To whom?'

'Caroline would be offended.'

'Ah yes. We don't want to upset Caroline, do we?'

Sally looked nervous. 'She seems a bit cool at times, but she's quite nice when you get to know her.'

I wondered who the old lady was. It would be just my luck if she was Caroline Longden's aunt, who said nothing but heard everything and had a perfect memory. The Chaplins seemed nervous of her – but perhaps they had no idea who she was either.

'Do you know Caroline well?' I asked.

'She's Frank's half-sister,' said Sally, as if it answered my question.

Frank looked a bit rebellious as we turned the corner at the crossroads in Whittington. 'She's a class above us,' he said. 'She moves in different circles, if you know what I mean.'

Sally hushed him. 'She's away a lot,' she said. 'She never wanted to stay in this area. But Samuel was different. He was a lovely old man.'

'No edge to him at all. So they say.'

'That's right.'

The hearse was slowing as it approached the parish church of St Giles. I saw a square tower with a small spire and a building in a hotchpotch of styles.

'Did you know about Samuel's project?' I asked. 'The book he wanted to publish?'

It was a stab in the dark. But I'd rarely seen anyone's face change as quickly as Frank Chaplin's did. He went very white, the blood draining out of his cheeks in a dramatic contrast to his black suit. He stared me at, horrified. Sally noticed his reaction, but was more composed. She reached out to grasp his hand on the seat.

148

'A book?' Frank said. 'What was it about?'

'Oh, the history of the Buckley family,' I said casually, trying to hide my curiosity. 'I'm carrying on the project for him, actually. Perhaps I could come and see you some time? There might be a few things you could help me with.'

The cars had stopped, and the doors were opened before Frank or Sally could reply. The old lady was helped out first, then the Chaplins. I saw Frank jump as the folding seat I'd been sitting on banged back into place. No doubt about it – he was definitely nervous all of a sudden. Very interesting.

We arranged ourselves into a ragged file and trooped through the churchyard to the porch. Sally passed me, offering her hand to the old lady to help her up the step. I felt a tap on my shoulder, and Frank's voice close to my ear.

'Come and see us at the weekend,' he said. 'Saturday would be a good day. Thirty-four Cop Nook Lane, Chasetown. We're in the phone book.'

I nodded, and the next moment we were in the dimness of the church, with a tune playing on the organ. We shuffled into the pews, and I saw that many of the seats were already full for the service.

The funeral held still more surprises for me. For a start, the vicar actually seemed to know the man he was eulogising. This was unlike the service for my father, when the clergyman had asked me for a list of facts to refer to, and had read them out like a bad actor stumbling over his lines.

The man at Whittington wasn't the incumbent of St Giles, I was told. Yet he spoke of Great-Uncle Samuel as if he'd been an old friend, talking of his successful brewery business, his love of the waterways, his boat *Kestrel* and the tragedy in his life when his wife Alison was killed. He offered sympathy to Caroline, and gave us the usual line about not being there to mourn a man's death, but to celebrate his life.

Later, an elderly man with a red face and a large moustache got up and talked about Samuel Longden's exploits on the waterways. He treated us to anecdotes about the days when Samuel was a novice boater and had wedged his boat firmly sideways across the canal and later grounded it on a weir for three days. He also told a complicated story in which the Captain left his windlass slotted onto the paddle spindle, then nearly sank his boat through a badly fitted weed hatch, whatever that was. He struck just the right note for the members of the congregation behind me, who seemed to be boaters to a man and woman.

The speaker went on to list examples of Samuel's generosity, both to individuals and to causes he thought were worth supporting, including the restoration of the Ogley and Huddlesford Canal, to which he'd quietly contributed large sums of money for a number of years. He ended with a reference to the South Staffordshire Link Road and how Samuel Longden would feel if it was allowed to go ahead and sever the line of the canal. This brought murmurs of approval from around the church, and roused the congregation to a fine pitch by the time the coffin was carried out.

The time we spent at the actual graveside was mercifully short. Samuel went from dust to dust, ashes to ashes, in the way of all burials. Nobody commented on how ironic it was that a man who had been so concerned with water should be committed to the earth.

But there was one thing that struck home to me, as it did for no one else there. It was something that left me confused about my feelings. For here I was at the funeral of my great-uncle, and I was supposed to be mourning the passing of a relative. Yet the name on the headstone was Longden. At no time during the service did anyone mention this fact – that the man known as Samuel Longden was actually a Buckley.

20

'It might be what Samuel wanted, but really . . .' said Sally Chaplin as we were ferried back to Whittington Wharf.

The boaters were enjoying themselves now, chatting more loudly as they got back on the boat for the rest of the journey. They knew they were headed for the funeral lunch.

Soon we'd passed through Streethay and under the A38 and were approaching Fradley Junction. For want of anything else to do, I looked for the names of some of the boats moored on the final stretch of the Coventry. There was *Lily*, *Excalibur* – and, for some reason, *Billabong*. One of the men jumped off our boat to operate a little black and white swing bridge that gave pedestrian access to the opposite side of the canal.

Then we'd emerged into the junction and the canal widened out into a rectangular basin, with an enclosed dry dock on one side. Ahead of us was the Swan Inn, a white-walled pub overlooking the junction with the Trent and Mersey. It had china swans in the windows and an Ansells brewery sign over the door, with wooden rails lining a concrete landing area. Benches were set up outside under the arches of a former warehouse where Swan Line Cruisers had its offices. Several more boats were moored in front of the warehouse, painted with green roofs, white cabin sides and red gunwales. They were the Swan Line's own boats, built for holiday hire.

The scene was peaceful, with no more than the soft lapping

of the water as the wind blew it towards the gates of Junction Lock. Some of the people who'd been at the church in Whittington were waiting for us on the mooring. They'd come by car, driving up the towpath side from Alrewas or Fradley.

Inside the pub, a buffet had been laid out in a side room and a crowd of people swarmed around the tables. I held back for a while to allow others from the boat to get in before me. I was still feeling like an unwanted stranger, a sort of Banquo's ghost at the feast. I had the ridiculous feeling that if I pushed myself forward a bit too hard, if I presumed too much or spoke to the wrong person, then the whole mass of them would turn round and hound me out of the place. They say there's nowhere more lonely than the middle of a crowd.

So I kept to myself, circulating round the room discreetly, clutching a plate of food and keeping my distance from Caroline Longden and her companions. The boaters I'd spoken to smiled as I passed, but they were mostly concerned with catching up on gossip with acquaintances. The Chaplins saw me, but lowered their heads self-consciously to their plates of sandwiches and sausage rolls. As bottles of wine were opened, the room gradually filled with animation and noise, leaving me isolated on a tiny island wherever I happened to be standing. Some sort of impenetrable bubble surrounded me, separating me from everyone else. I longed for the end of the whole charade. Although I was a Buckley, I didn't belong here.

Inevitably, I soon found that I was drinking too much wine. Who could resist it when it was free – paid for, presumably, from Great-Uncle Samuel's will? Each glass I picked up seemed to empty itself in minutes as my hand moved regularly to my mouth to give the appearance I was fully occupied. I've never been accustomed to drinking wine in any quantity. It was that, I think, which made me talk too much.

152

I'd attached myself to the periphery of a group of boaters. They were talking about flights and staircases, lift bridges and stop gates, and something called the West Midlands Ring. I stood and listened, and nodded wisely at everything they said. They didn't exactly welcome me into their circle, but the way they ignored me was less threatening than the deliberate shunning of Caroline's group. Conversation turned to the restoration of the Ogley and Huddlesford and the evils of the South Staffordshire Link Road. A woman near me expressed the opinion that the MP, Lindley Simpson, would make a big difference to the campaign. 'He'll stir them up in Westminster,' she said.

'You've fallen for the famous Simpson charm,' said a man opposite her. 'He's not married, of course, which makes him highly eligible. They say the constituency party membership has doubled in the last few years, with all the Simpson groupies joining up.'

'He backs the project all the way,' protested the woman.

'Oh come on – he's just another clever politician. He'll ride the bandwagon for a while if he thinks it'll help his popularity with the voters. He'll work hard for the canal project for as long as he can get something out of it. But as soon as it looks like getting into trouble, he'll abandon it and we won't see him for dust.'

'A bit like William Buckley,' I blurted.

There was an immediate silence as members of the group turned to stare at me as if I'd just broken wind.

'He was the resident engineer on the Ogley and Huddlesford Canal,' I said. 'When the canal company ran into financial problems, he took the opportunity of embezzling money and disappeared completely. He even abandoned his family.'

In my half-oiled state, I imagined myself to be a unique authority on the fascinating subject of William Buckley, even though I'd never heard of the man until a few days before. So I was annoyed when members of the group turned aside and began to drift away, the way they might from some drunken bore. In a moment, I would have lost my listeners.

I leaned towards the woman who'd praised Lindley Simpson and spoke to her in what I thought was a confidential tone.

'Actually, I'm writing a book about William Buckley, you know.'

She took a step back from me, wrinkling her nose at the gust of pickled onions and wine-laden breath that reached her. Obviously I hadn't spoken as quietly as I thought, because faces turned towards me, and I suddenly had an audience again.

'William Buckley was my great, great, great, great, great grandfather,' I said.

I had no idea whether I'd used the correct number of 'greats'. Once I'd started, they just seemed to keep coming. In any case, I'd never bothered to work it out. I only knew he was a long way back. But these people seemed impressed by the information, and their attention made me feel wanted.

'That's fascinating,' someone said. 'When is it coming out?'

'Didn't you say you were Samuel Longden's great-nephew?'

The last question had come from my friend Eric, who was looking at me suspiciously, as if I'd been telling him tall stories.

'That's right. Didn't you know Samuel was actually a Buckley?'

'No, I can't say I did, old chap. It sounds a bit unlikely, to be honest.'

'It's true. It's his book. Well, he started it. He changed his name, you see.'

'Why would he do that?'

'Well . . .' I floundered for an answer, and saw them turn and smile knowingly at each other.

Then I noticed Andrew Hadfield standing behind Eric. He

hadn't been on the boat, so he must have come directly to the service, or to the pub.

'Andrew! Andrew knows about it, don't you?' I said.

But Andrew grinned and shrugged apologetically at the remaining boaters. 'A good spread they've put on, isn't it, Chris? But I think it's probably time for you to go home.'

Then I was standing alone again. Caroline's fiancé, Monks, gave me a long stare across the room. I flushed, knowing that I must look a complete fool.

I wandered around for a while longer until I noticed that the room was beginning to empty as the mourners dispersed. I clutched my glass of wine tighter, aware that I was more than slightly drunk. I wondered how I was supposed to get back to my car at Hopwas, and guessed that it probably wasn't a good idea to try. A taxi home would be the right thing. Or maybe I could cadge a lift from one of the waterways crowd who'd skipped the boat trip.

Then I heard voices nearby and turned to see if it was someone I could ask. I found I was looking at Caroline Longden and Simon Monks.

Since my mouth was already open, I was unable to close it again without uttering some inanity.

'Oh, hello. I'm sorry.'

They looked at me as if I was some vagrant off the street who'd gatecrashed the wake. Monks gave me a menacing snarl that sent genuine tremors of fear through my befuddled brain. Caroline, though, had a nice line in supercilious eyebrow lifting.

I addressed her directly. 'I'm Chris Buckley.'

'Yes, I know who you are.'

'We're related,' I said, knowing I sounded completely pathetic, but unable to stop myself. 'Long-lost relations.'

'I hope, after today, that you might stay lost,' said Caroline.

I thought this was rather unkind, and told her so.

'Unkind? Do I need to remind you that we're at my father's

155

funeral? Do you think you were kind to my father? Don't you think that your unkindness contributed to his death?'

'Well, I—'

'No, don't answer. I don't want to hear what you have to say. I know about the meeting he'd arranged with you on the day he died. He told me about it on the phone. He kept me up to date with what he was trying to do. I thought he was making a mistake from the start by approaching you, but I was unable to persuade him against it. He had such faith in you. And purely because you were a Buckley.'

'It was you who told the police then,' I said, a light dawning at last.

'Yes, of course it was.'

'I'm sorry about the meeting. I mean about not going through with it. I know it must seem awful to you.'

She waved aside my excuses. 'When you failed to turn up, he must have thought you were refusing him the right to continue with his family history.'

'The right? No, I don't see it that way. He'd asked for my help, that's all.'

'He needed your help, yes. But he also desperately needed your approval. Don't you see that? Perhaps my father was naive in some ways. He expected the same effort and consideration in return that he always gave to others. He would certainly have thought you'd take the trouble to read the manuscript, at least. He couldn't have conceived that it would be so unimportant to you that you wouldn't even have looked at it.'

She was growing more angry as she spoke, and I could only lower my eyes and fidget nervously. 'So naturally, he would have taken your failure to show up as your considered answer to his plea. He thought you'd snubbed him, that you'd rejected his appeal outright. Perhaps he was convinced in the end that you knew who he really was and you were turning your back on him, that he was still unwelcome in the Buckley

156

family after all those years. That you, too, saw him as a traitor. It must have been a very bitter blow.'

Monks took her arm, and urged her away towards the door. But Caroline couldn't resist one final, wounding shot. 'My father had pinned his hopes on you, Christopher,' she said. 'And you let him down. It must have been his dying thought.'

21

The cold air outside the pub did little to clear my head or stop my hands from trembling. The encounter with Caroline Longden had left me shaken. The depths of her animosity had been undisguised, and her words had bitten deep. On such an occasion, there was no way to answer back, no words I could use to justify myself. I could only bite my lip and hang my head, and get away from the confrontation as quickly as possible.

Now I stood on the edge of the canal basin, staring blankly at the Swan Line boats, letting the wind numb my face and dash the occasional burst of spray on my feet. The bright colours of the boats seemed to blur in front of my eyes, green merging into white, and red into green, like a nauseous kaleidoscope.

I realised it had been a bad mistake to come to the funeral. I'd felt alone and shunned from the moment I arrived on the landing stage at Hopwas. Apart from the boaters who'd spoken to me, the reaction had been an attempt to freeze me out. The Chaplins had seemed afraid of me somehow. And Caroline openly despised me. I knew myself well enough to recognise the beginnings of the maudlin phase that followed too much alcohol. I was starting to feel very sorry for myself.

'Excuse me.'

I turned at the sound of a voice and saw a woman. Now,

she certainly wasn't on the boat. I would have noticed her. She was small and dark, with glossy hair and a way of moving in her short black skirt that was very distracting. She was staring at me curiously.

'You're Chris Buckley, aren't you?'

'That's right,' I said, feeling the grin slip onto my face a bit too readily. The wine had numbed my lips, and I was afraid that I might be leering. 'The very same.'

'I was hoping to get a chance to talk to you.'

'Here I am. Talk away.'

She looked around at the mourners still leaving the pub. 'Could we walk on a little way?'

There were people further down the towpath, so we walked to the footbridge at the head of Junction Lock to cross to the Coventry side. The bridge moved slightly as we stepped onto it, and our footsteps reverberated on the iron plates.

'I understand you're a bit of an expert on the waterways,' she said, pausing in the middle of the bridge to gaze out over the water. Her words were almost an echo of something Great-Uncle Samuel had said to me the first time we met.

'Not at all. In fact, today was the first time I'd been on a narrowboat.'

She frowned, slightly puzzled. 'But surely . . .' she said. 'It is true, isn't it? I mean, you *are* finishing the book for Samuel Longden?'

Beneath us was a narrow drop between sheer brick walls covered in blackened moss and dripping with water. The wine had made me a little unsteady on my feet, and I was glad of the rail in front of me. As I looked down into the chasm, I instinctively reached out to clutch it for safety, afraid I might tumble into the murky water. I was unfamiliar with the height of the rise in locks on the Trent and Mersey, but this one looked particularly deep from where I stood. The space between the walls seemed barely wide enough for a narrowboat to pass through. Anyone who fell from here would brain themselves on the unyielding brick before they ever hit the water.

'Yes,' I said. 'The famous book.'

I forced my feet to move, and within a few paces I'd crossed the bridge and was back on solid land. A path rounded the corner of the house and followed the line of the Coventry. *Lily*, *Excalibur* and *Billabong* were ahead of us. *Billabong* had a thin trail of smoke rising from its funnel, indicating that someone was on board. I imagined it must be pretty cold living on a narrowboat during the winter. Cold, and inescapably damp.

'I don't know about famous,' said my companion. 'Not yet anyway.'

'Do you have a particular interest?'

She smiled apologetically. Her smile was everything I'd hoped it would be, full of life and subtle promise. 'Perhaps I should introduce myself,' she said. 'My name is Laura Jenner. I know Andrew Hadfield.'

'Ah. So I suppose you already knew about the book before I mentioned it in there.'

'Andrew told me, yes. It's an interesting story. About you and Samuel Longden, I mean. Meeting up after all these years. But Andrew wasn't certain whether you were going to go through with the project.'

'I wasn't sure myself when I spoke to him.'

'But you're sure now, are you?' she asked seriously, as if the answer was important to her.

I thought of Caroline and her contempt for me, her refusal to discuss the book. There was no reason why I should worry about her feelings on the subject. Whatever I did would make no difference. Then I remembered the Chaplins, and their reaction to the mention of the book. I already had a chance to visit them on Saturday to talk about it. Not only was I committed to the book by the promise of Great-Uncle Samuel's money, I'd already started my research.

160

'Yes, I'm sure.'

'That's good.'

But just when I expected her to explain why, she went quiet and said no more. She stopped at the swing bridge, and put her hands on it to try to move it, but didn't have the strength. Her hair swung across her cheek and emphasised the impression I'd got when I first set eyes on her face outside the Swan.

'I've seen you somewhere before, haven't I?' I said.

'God, that's an old one.'

'No, really. Was it at one of the restoration sites?'

She looked at me strangely, pushing the hair away from her face. I noticed a faint scar that ran from her forehead into her scalp. 'It might have been, I suppose.'

'It's funny, though. I think I would have remembered the occasion. Your face is one I wouldn't forget.'

She smiled sceptically. No doubt she was used to getting compliments from men all the time, but I couldn't help it. Laura was dazzling me.

We'd reached a section of towpath opposite Fradley Wood. By unspoken agreement, we turned and began to walk back again towards the junction.

'Or have I come across you somewhere else? Where do you work?'

'I've been working as a researcher for a television company in London, but I'm in between jobs at the moment.'

'I know how it feels.'

'You too? The worst thing is there isn't even anything useful I can do to keep my hand in, rather than sitting around idle while I'm looking for work.'

'I see.'

She looked at me, concerned at my pained expression. 'Are you all right?'

The truth was that the pressure of the alcohol was straining my bladder. Though I was reluctant to part from Laura, I

161

was going to have to slip away before there was an embarrassing accident.

'I'll have to pop back inside. Will you wait a minute?'

'Sure.'

I tried to sneak unobtrusively through the pub, hoping not to be noticed by the last few mourners lurking near the bar. But I failed badly. I was in the gents, feeling the flood of relief against the porcelain, when I heard the door open and sensed a threatening presence just inches from my back. There are few places you feel so vulnerable as standing at a urinal, and the intimidating growl in my ear made me almost splash my shoes.

'Driving home, friend? No? Pity. You might have ended up in a ditch. You'd be no loss to anybody, from what I've heard.'

I rolled my eyes nervously over my shoulder, but didn't really need to see him to know it was Simon Monks.

'What do you want?' I said.

'Only one thing. You've caused enough grief in Caroline's life already. Stay out of it from now on, okay? I don't want to hear that you've been doing anything to upset her. Anything.'

He remained standing close behind me, making no pretence of being there for a genuine purpose. My flow of urine was reduced to a trickle as my bladder contracted with apprehension.

'Are you threatening me?' I asked feebly.

Monks laughed as if I were the star act in the cabaret. Then he leaned closer to speak into my ear, a repulsively intimate gesture that brought his hot breath onto the back of my neck. 'Just remember, if Caroline doesn't want you to publish this book – it means *no book*. Nothing.'

I closed my eyes, waiting for something to happen. But after a shaky moment, I heard the door close and realised he was gone.

I waited a few minutes after Monks had left, trying to control my breathing and splashing cold water on my face. To regain a bit of self-respect, I had to walk back out of the pub without my legs giving way. But amazingly, by the time I got outside a smile was creeping back onto my face. While I'd been thinking about how I could safely show Monks that I wasn't so easily intimidated, a very tempting prospect had suddenly opened up in my mind, involving Laura Jenner.

To my surprise and delight, she was still waiting for me, leaning on a rail to watch the water.

'Laura,' I said. 'I wonder if you'd be willing to help me?'

'What with?' she said, turning to stare at me.

'The book, of course. Samuel Longden's book.'

'Why do you want help?'

'I need some family research doing. And since you're in London anyway and at a loose end – I mean, between jobs – you could do a bit of research for me at Somerset House, or wherever.'

'Registers of births, marriages and deaths haven't been kept at Somerset House for a long time,' she said. 'They're at the Family Records Centre now.'

'There you are, you see,' I said triumphantly, as if her knowledge had clinched the argument.

She didn't answer directly. 'So you're definitely taking the project on?'

'Yes, I am. It's what Samuel wanted. He said so in his will.'

'I suppose there's a lot to do.'

'Absolutely. And I can't do it all on my own. I need some-body to follow up leads, do the research, talk to people. You'd be good at that, I'm sure. I wouldn't be able to pay you until the book was published, though.'

'I don't want money,' she said.

'Are you willing, then?'

'I don't know. It's not the sort of thing I had in mind. It's a bit parochial.'

I was hurt at that. 'It could be really interesting. Following the development of a family through two centuries, charting the rise and fall of six generations. It's like a snapshot of social history over the last two hundred years, with a human perspective.'

She laughed. 'It's nice to hear somebody being so enthusiastic about a project. But then you're personally involved, aren't you?'

'Did you come in your own car, Laura?' I asked.

'Yes.'

'Will you do one thing for me?'

'What is it?'

'I came here on the boat, and I left my car at Hopwas. Will you drive me back there and let me talk to you about it a bit more?'

'All right.'

The sight of Laura's car surprised me. I'd never imagined that television researchers had well-paid jobs, but her lime-green Mercedes made my Escort look sick.

The combination of the cold, the brief exercise and the encounter with Simon Monks had sobered me up, but when we got into Laura's Merc I felt a bit dizzy again. Cars come to smell of their owners after a while, and I became very aware of her heady scent in the enclosed space, as well as the proximity of her hand as she operated the gear lever. By the time we were headed away from Fradley towards Lichfield, I was amenable to anything. But Laura began to give me a thoroughly professional grilling.

'So how far have you got, Chris? With the book, I mean.'

'Not far. I haven't had the chance, to be honest. What with the will and the funeral, not to mention the police, it's all been a bit of a whirl this past week.'

'The police? How do they come into it?'

'Well, don't you know how Samuel Longden died?'

'A car accident, wasn't it? It was in the paper.'

164

'Yes, but not an ordinary accident. A hit and run. They've never traced the driver, as far as I know. The police interviewed me because I was one of the last people to see him alive. In fact, it was the police who broke the news to me that Samuel was dead, when they came to see me next morning. It was quite a shock.'

'But they haven't bothered you since?'

'N-no. I had to go to the police station to make a statement. But I only saw some PC, not the detectives who came to my house.'

I was hesitant because of the tone of my meeting with DS Graham, which gave me the impression they hadn't eliminated me entirely. I'd been expecting a second visit. I'd even begun to imagine that people passing in the street or sitting in cars in Stowe Pool Lane were watching me. Under surveillance, wasn't that the expression?

Probably someone taking an objective view would say my reaction was the result of a guilty conscience. I desperately wanted to ask the police about the witness who'd seen the accident, but I had enough sense to realise that such an enquiry from me would immediately raise their suspicions several notches. And no police officer in his right mind would give the identity of a witness to a suspect. It was a frustrating fact, because the woman the car park attendant had seen standing on the corner might be the key to the whole thing.

'But you've read Samuel's manuscript, haven't you?' asked Laura. 'You must have had time for that.'

'Only the early stuff about the canal company proprietors and the appointment of William Buckley as resident engineer.'

'William Buckley, yes. The manuscript is a long way off being finished, though, isn't it?'

'Is it? I don't know. What makes you say that?'

'Well, it must be. Otherwise why would Samuel want you to continue it?'

'Hmm, true.'

'And there are other documents?'

'Yes, lots.'

'Letters?'

'Some.'

She nodded. 'Good.'

'Why?'

'Letters are true contemporary documents. A direct record from the time, unlike anything that might have been written since. They're original source material. Very valuable.'

'They're rather difficult to read,' I said. 'I've asked Rachel to transcribe them for me.'

She braked suddenly, as if a cat had run out into the road. I didn't see any cat, but I'd been admiring Laura's profile all the time she'd been speaking, and wondering how she'd got the scar. I hadn't even realised that we were already approaching Whittington.

'Who's Rachel?' she said.

'My next door neighbour. She can type, you see. She was interested in the project, and I thought she could be helpful transcribing the letters. That's all. It's not a problem.'

I wasn't sure why I was sounding defensive about Rachel. Could I really be imagining that Laura was jealous? Were two helpers one too many?

'Is that all she's doing, Chris?'

'Well . . . she did say she'd do some family history research for me. The Buckley family, I mean. Rachel is a trained librarian.'

'I can do all that.'

'But I've told Rachel—'

Laura cut across me. 'It would be better if we just kept this between the two of us. The fewer people involved the better.'

I was ready to go along with anything, yet I was wondering why this was so important to her.

'Don't you agree?' she said.

166

'All right.'

We drove on a bit further, and soon we were in Hopwas.

'Was there anything else that Samuel left?' she asked.

'Oh yes, there's a box. Did Andrew tell you about that?'

'Yes, he did. Very interesting.'

'I'll let you see it some time. But there doesn't seem to be anything in it.'

Laura drove into the car park of the Red Lion, where I'd left the Escort. She declined the invitation to go in for a drink, which was probably for the best, since I'd sunk too many already.

'I'll be in touch,' she said. 'I'm sure we're going to enjoy working together.'

I was sure too. I thought I was going to enjoy it very much.

'By the way,' she said, 'you realise what it means if the inquest comes in with an unlawful killing verdict?'

'No, what?'

'You're unlikely to get probate through until the killer has been identified.'

'Why, for God's sake?'

'A murderer isn't allowed to profit from his crime, such as by inheriting the estate of his victim. So probate is likely to be delayed until they're sure none of the beneficiaries are going be charged. Think about it.'

I thought about it. 'Oh, right. Well it's not asking much, is it? To earn my fifty grand, all I have to do is finish the book, publish it – *and* prove who killed Samuel Longden. It should be a doddle.'

When I got home, Rachel had returned the first letter to me. She'd pushed it through the door while I was at the funeral. I slid the letter from its protective plastic envelope. It was written on thick paper that felt warm and alive in my hands, and the handwriting was in faded black ink, scrawled in busy, slanting lines across the pages. The writing was difficult to read, and the flourishes blurred in front of my eyes. I turned instead to the neatly typewritten sheet attached by Rachel. For the first time I read the actual words of my distant ancestor, William Buckley.

22

Pipehill, Lichfield, Staffordshire. Thursday 2nd Jan. 1800.

To Reuben Wheeldon Esq., Warner Street, Ellesmere, Cheshire.

My dear friend,

I have to report that there seems no end to the troublesome dispute in which the Company finds itself. The Colliery Arm constructed at the behest of Mr N. has been the source of considerable disagreement. For myself, my Estimate shewed that the expence of completing the Navigation might bear little Proportion to the Benefits which would result from it. The failure of the Works has resulted from the want of that vigilant attention which has latterly been bestowed on the construction of the new Reservoir at Cannock Heath.

I am most inclined to impute the Failure to the actions of Mr N. himself. But to attempt to state precisely the cause or the continued causes of this failure would be in vain. If we could compel confession from the Many who were employed in the execution, much light might be thrown on the Subject, but their secrets are buried in the ruins. My Assistant Engineer complains of unreasonable interference on the part of Mr N. and his agents. I know I can maintain my ground on every Position, and have little Doubt that the evidence will enable me to convince the Committee of the rights of this matter. I pray that we might avoid an action in Chancery Court, of which there is much talk at present.

The latest news is that Mr N. has obtained a new Ally in his Cause. Though I entertain as high an opinion of his Judgement as any Man can, both of his knowledge and good sense, yet I am convinced that he has been misled in his association with such a man as M. presents himself to be.

But who is M., you ask? M. is a Gentleman but lately come to the City seeking employment. His Appearance I cannot adequately describe to you. His Manner of Dress puts me in mind of our own Doctor Johnson, as depicted in Mr Boswell's *Life*. He commonly wears a full Suit of plain brown Clothes with breeches fastened at the knee with a silver buckle and black worsted stockings. He wears a very wide brown cloth Greatcoat with vast Pockets, a Beaver Hat and Hessian Boots.

He differs from Johnson, however, in that his figure rather more resembles that of Gentleman John Jackson or some other of those Fighters whose names and likenesses are recorded in our Popular Journals. The gossips report that he was obliged to retire from the Ring on account of a weakness of the lungs, and they say the Ladies are wont to faint away at the sight of him, for fear of his savage visage. Would that M. were of as civilised and sociable a Nature as the good Doctor.

Of my family, of whom you so kindly enquire, I am able to send you good tidings, which I hope will give you satisfaction. Sarah is well and contented with her lot. Her Happiness was evident on the occasion of our Son's first birthday some weeks since. You will easily comprehend that Edward is a great source of pride to us both. I pray that you may set eyes on him for yourself soon.

Your friend,
Wm Buckley

170

23

Chasetown seemed to consist of one main road with a few shops and pubs. Streets of housing backed on to a trading estate with a Goodyear tyre factory and a new Safeway supermarket. Beyond them lay an expanse of heathland on the edge of Chasewater itself.

I turned past Chasetown Football Club's ground into a neighbourhood of small bungalows, with bare trellises on their front walls and dark conifers in their back gardens. A man was walking a dog, and children were playing in the yard of a school.

Number thirty-four was a brick bungalow exactly like all the others. It had an open garage to one side, with a brightly polished blue Vauxhall Cavalier parked inside. There was a neat lawn, lined by flowerbeds planted with severely pruned rose bushes. In February, it looked damp and dead and devoid of colour. The bungalow itself was built in the 1970s or 80s, with white woodwork and an imitation cartwheel propped outside the bay window.

Sally Chaplin answered the bell. She had her shoes and coat on, ready to go out, and she didn't look pleased to see me.

'I don't know why you want to talk to Frank,' she said. 'I really don't.'

'It was Frank who wanted to talk to me,' I pointed out.

'Well, as far as I can see, he's just using it as an excuse to stay at home and get out of helping me with the shopping.'

'I'm sorry, I didn't mean to disrupt your arrangements.'

'We always go shopping on Saturday morning,' she said.

'Perhaps I should come back another time.'

'Oh, it doesn't matter. You'd better come in.'

I stepped onto a hallway carpet that smelled of Shake 'n' Vac, and stood near an imitation mahogany hall table while Sally shouted into a back room.

'Frank! He's here. And I'm off now.'

'Will you manage all right, love?' Frank's voice drifted towards us from a distance.

'I'll have to, won't I?'

'Sorry.'

'You might as well go on through,' she said to me. 'You'll find him in the conservatory, of course.'

Frank was watering a row of geraniums that were thriving in an atmosphere that verged on the tropical. The bungalow itself had been warm, but in the conservatory the heat and humidity made my skin prickle. There were cacti on shelves along one side, and trays full of seedlings under plastic sheets dripping with moisture. The air smelled of water and damp soil, and that pungent, fruity scent peculiar to geranium leaves. Many of the plants were in abundant flower, despite the season, and their sprawling colours were in startling contrast to the regimented aridity of the front garden.

'This is my territory,' said Frank. 'Sally says the plants attract flies. Not to mention spiders. But it's all part of nature, isn't it?'

'I gather I'm keeping you from the shopping.'

He laughed. 'Don't worry about that. She'd much rather do it without me. She just likes to make a point.'

'Well, thanks for giving me your time.'

'Well, we're almost relatives, aren't we? In a way.'

'I suppose so.'

He smiled at my hesitation. 'But who'd want any more of those?'

'You're Alison Longden's son from a previous marriage. Am I right?'

'That's it. I was ten when Mum and Dad got divorced. I didn't much like the thought that mum had another baby and it wasn't my real sister. I felt jealous, I suppose. You know what teenagers are like.'

He stroked the leaves of a big pelargonium with pink flowers that he'd just finished watering. He was looking at it as he might have done at a favourite pet. I didn't suppose there was a cat or a dog in the house. Too much mess.

'After a while, we lost touch,' he said. 'I decided I was going to live my own life, as you do at that age. Then there was the accident.'

'The car crash.'

'It was a tragedy. She was a good woman. Everyone liked her. Old Samuel was devastated.'

Frank replaced his watering can under a tap and dusted his hands.

'It was Samuel I wanted to talk to you about really, Frank,' I said.

'Yes. You must have a lot of questions.'

'Could we go into the house? It's a bit too warm in here for me.'

'Sally says so too. Actually, I thought we might go for a walk. Down by the reservoir. We can get a breath of fresh air.'

'Whatever you like.'

We turned the corner from Cop Nook Lane into a road that came down past the football ground. From here, the heath stretched to the reservoir, with narrow footpaths skirting the edge of the water and winding up and down sandy slopes that were thick with clumps of gorse.

'This is a peaceful sort of place,' I said.

'At times,' said Frank. 'But you wouldn't want to come here at weekends in the summer. It's full of kids taking drugs and having sex, and God knows what. You can't move without tripping over them in every hollow.'

The wind stirred the empty husks of seed pods on the branches of the gorse, causing a dry rattling sound all around us. The noise made me feel uneasy. It was like the rustle of surreptitious movements in the undergrowth, or a hundred snakes slithering over pebbles.

'No one here now, though,' said Frank. 'They don't bother coming when it's cold.'

Across an inlet I could see small yachts pulled up onto the shore, their masts folded down onto their decks. In the summer the water would be thick with boats, and the light railway would be running on the opposite bank, while crowds flocked to the amusement park at the southern end of the reservoir. The Anglesey branch of the Wyrley and Essington Canal still linked Chasewater to Ogley Junction. That short branch had once been the feeder to provide water from the reservoir to the Ogley and Huddlesford. Unlike the Ogley, the feeder was still there, and it was in water too.

'But you don't mind the weather, Frank?' I said.

'I think it's bracing. It clears your mind. That helps you think.'

'Helps you remember too, perhaps?'

'Oh, I don't need any help doing that.'

There was a great scar in the earth between the reservoir and the town, and to the north I could see the remains of a vast tip from an abandoned quarry. The line of an old mineral railway could still be followed, where its embankment had once taken it right across the reservoir. The walls and chimneys of the trading estate rose behind us, and the constant buzz of distant traffic reminded me of the proximity of the main Cannock Road. Despite the expanse of heath, nature was a relative stranger here. We were surrounded by the ineradicable signs of industry. The rattling of the gorse was no more than a pitiful gesture of defiance.

'Shall I start with my first questions?' I asked, when Frank had been silent for a while.

He seemed to wake from his thoughts and plucked a twig full of seed pods from a branch. Still he didn't meet my eye.

'I said I knew there must be a lot of questions you wanted to ask. But I must warn you, I might not have the answers to give you.'

'At least let's try, now we're here.'

'If there's anything I can tell you that will help.'

'You know about the rift in my family, don't you?'

'Yes, I picked up on it in my early teens. I suppose I must have heard people talking about it. I can't remember now if it was my mum or my dad. It certainly wasn't Samuel. He never spoke about his family at all. There were none of them at the wedding, though of course it was only a register office affair. That alone was enough to cause people to talk.'

'He was calling himself Longden already by then.'

'Oh yes. I never knew him as a Buckley at all. In fact, it was Caroline who told me, when we went to see her after Samuel died. It was a bit of a surprise. But then Samuel had always been a surprising man.'

'You must have learned something about his past?'

'There were some things he talked about. What particularly did you want to know?'

'Anything, Frank, anything. Remember I didn't even know of his existence until a couple of weeks ago.'

He pursed his lips and rested his back against a tree. 'Strange that. A bit hard to believe.'

'I find it difficult to believe myself. But it's true. His history is almost a complete blank to me. I know he made a lot of money in the brewery business.'

'That's right. He inherited a brewery in Lichfield from some old chap he worked for. Business picked up again after the war. Then he sold out to one of the big Burton breweries in

175

the late 1960s, when things were really booming. He made a packet, by all accounts.'

'He would still only have been in his fifties then,' I said.

'I reckon he kept himself busy using his money to make more. Some people have that knack, don't they? Not me, though.'

'What do you mean? Investments?'

'He certainly talked about the stock market as if he knew what he was doing. But he had other interests as well.'

'The inland waterways, for example.'

Frank sniffed. 'I never understood what he saw in that myself. But yes, he bought himself a boat, didn't he? A narrowboat.'

'Yes, *Kestrel*.'

'I know those things don't come cheap.'

'Yes, I've seen it. I'd guess maybe seventy or eighty thousand quid's worth.'

His eyebrows shot up in amazement. 'Really? That much? It's almost what my bungalow is worth.'

'He must have been serious about it.'

Frank nodded sourly. 'Somebody as wealthy as that – well, money doesn't mean to them what it does to us. They spend those sort of amounts on a whim.'

'But this wasn't a whim of Samuel's. Not from what the vicar said at his funeral service. And all those boaters who went . . .'

'No, you're right. He was keen. I think he spent less time with the boat after he married my mother. She took his attention for a while, and then Caroline came along.'

'Alison meant a lot to him, Frank.'

He pulled himself away from the tree and began to walk again, following the curving path. 'I know she did. It destroyed him when Mum was killed in the crash. But at least he had Caroline. She was seventeen when Mum died.'

'A difficult age. Especially for an old man to deal with.'

'He was seventy-three when it happened. You'd have

thought it might have finished him off. But Caroline became the centre of his life. Her and *Kestrel* anyway. He took her on the boat with him all over the place.'

'I remember the boaters saying that. They knew him as the Captain. I suppose it was a mark of respect.'

Frank hesitated. 'Maybe,' he said. 'But I always thought it came from his wartime service.'

I frowned. The Second World War was a very long time ago, and it hardly seemed relevant. There were more immediate things that I needed to know about.

'When did he develop this idea about the book?'

'That I don't know.'

'But you knew he was working on it.'

'I knew he was working on something. But you could never tell with Samuel what it might be next. He was a bit unpredictable, especially after Mum died. He was never quite the same.'

'Old people do get more eccentric. But I know what you mean – he tended to go off at a tangent at a moment's notice.'

'Like I say, he was a surprising man. You, too, Chris. Perhaps you take after him.'

'Me? How am I surprising?'

'Well, for a start, you turned up at Samuel's funeral, large as life. We never expected you to, not after what Caroline said about you. We felt sure you'd stay away. But no, you faced it out. I'm not sure I'd have been brave enough to do that, knowing that people were talking about me behind my back.' He shrugged apologetically. 'Well, you know the way they do.'

'Yes, I know.'

'And you didn't stay in the background either. We seemed to see you everywhere, mingling with the other mourners. And then, in the end, you even talked to Caroline.'

'She had nothing good to say to me.'

'Still. That was what made me think you might be determined enough to see this thing through. A lot of people wouldn't. Me, for one. But you, Chris . . . I have a feeling you won't be stopped from going on with Samuel's book.'

'Would *you* want to stop me?'

'If I thought I could, yes. I'd try to persuade you, but I don't think you'd take much notice of me.'

'It would depend on what your reasons were.'

'There you are, you see. If I told you that, there'd be no point in trying to stop you.'

I frowned again, more puzzled by the minute at his attitude.

'In any case,' he said, 'there are others who'll try harder to stop the book. Much harder.'

I turned at a sudden rattling of the gorse bushes that was so loud I thought a crowd of football supporters were rushing down the slope. But it was only the east wind getting up, chilly gusts that stirred the water on the shoreline. We reached a small, sheltered pool and crossed a causeway of stone slabs set into the water. Something splashed into a dark corner of the pool. A moorhen maybe, or a water rat.

'Frank, there's nothing in Samuel's book that anybody could possibly worry about being published,' I said.

He stopped abruptly in front of me, making me lose my balance slightly on the causeway and dip my foot in the shallow water. It was very cold.

'Isn't there?' he demanded, and watched my face intently.

'No.'

He relaxed and turned away. He mumbled something to himself. It sounded like, 'He might have changed his mind then.'

'It's a history,' I insisted. 'A hundred or two hundred years old. Ancient stuff. It just happens to be about Samuel's ancestors. And mine.'

'All right, all right.'

'But I didn't come to talk about the book. I want to ask

you about Samuel. What caused the rift between him and my grandfather? Why did he change his name? Why didn't I know he existed until it was too late?'

He carried on walking, loping easily up the embankment with his back to me.

'Frank!' I shouted. 'Why?'

He turned then at the top of the slope, his thin figure outlined against the grey sky, with his sparse hair lifting untidily as the wind plucked at him.

'I can't help you, Chris. I know nothing about that.'

His attitude really made me angry. It had been his idea for me to come to Chasetown. He'd led me on, and he couldn't let me down now.

'Can't or won't?' I said. But he didn't answer. His gaze drifted away from me, out towards Chasewater again. But there was nothing out there for him to see. 'What are you frightened of, Frank?'

He shook his head and turned to descend the far side of the banking. I scrambled after him and ran a few yards until I caught him up and laid my hand on his shoulder. We were looking down on the streets of Chasetown, spread out before us.

'Tell me. I need to know.'

'There's nothing for me to worry about, if all you're writing is history. But if you're digging up secrets that ought to stay buried, then we've both got plenty to be frightened of. If that's the case, then don't try to involve me and Sally. We don't want to know. I'm only telling you what I told Samuel.'

Frank seemed calmer now as we walked along the embankment, back towards the football ground and the car park.

'What did Samuel tell you about the book?'

'Not much.'

'He must have told you something to make you so worried. But there's nothing in the manuscript to concern yourself about. There's nothing about anybody living, even.'

As we approached the road, we saw Sally pass in the Cavalier on her way back to Cop Nook Lane. The back seat of the car was stacked with Safeway carrier bags.

'Fine. Let it stay that way then. Let the dead stay dead. Don't try to dig them up.' Frank's eyes followed the Cavalier as it disappeared. 'I think it would be better if I didn't invite you back inside. Sally, you know . . .'

'No problem, Frank. Thanks for talking to me anyway.'

He caught the sarcastic tone. 'I know I haven't been much help. You'll have to find someone else to answer your questions.'

'But there isn't anybody else left.'

'Except Caroline.'

'Yes,' I said. 'There's Caroline.'

He hesitated for a moment before we parted. Then he surprised me by sticking out his hand to shake mine, as if we were two businessmen sealing a successful deal. It was a firm, warm grip, and in a strange way it reassured me. It made me feel I was in real communication with another human being who understood me. It made me believe, for once, that I wasn't completely alone.

24

I'd arranged to meet Laura at lunchtime in the Jarvis George Hotel, where she was staying until she went back to London. This was one of the most expensive hotels in Lichfield, and I wondered again where her financial resources came from. Hadn't she said she was unemployed? Clearly unemployment didn't mean quite the same thing to her as it did to me.

She was waiting for me in the bar with a bright red drink on the table in front of her. She offered to buy me a beer, and I didn't object.

'Not drinking wine today, Chris?' she said.

'I don't make the same mistake twice.'

'What have you been doing today, then?'

'I went to see the Chaplins. Or at least Frank Chaplin.'

'Was he helpful?'

'Not in the least.'

'That's a shame. There aren't many other relatives to talk to, are there? Apart from Caroline, of course.'

'Yes, Frank pointed that out as well. But there must be other avenues.'

'Relatives should always be the first line of approach. They can give you information which will save an awful lot of time and point you in the right direction for your research.'

'Caroline wouldn't want to talk to me.'

'Do you think she might speak to me instead?'

She said it casually, and it didn't quite register at first. Then I put down my beer and grinned at her.

'Does that mean you're going to help?'

'I thought about it last night. It does sound quite interesting. But I'd only be able to give a certain amount of time to it. If a job comes up, I'll have to drop everything, you understand.'

'Of course, of course. Anything you can offer will be gratefully received.'

'So what about Caroline? I could present myself as an independent researcher.'

'Mmm. I don't know. She might resent a stranger interfering just as much as she resents me.'

'Let's leave that for now, then. It might be worth considering later.'

She pulled out her notebook, in which a page was covered in jotted notes like subject headings, complete with under-linings and asterisks and question marks. I was impressed by her organisation. She'd certainly given the project some thought. In fact, I was so irrationally pleased that I almost forgot my beer in the simple enjoyment of sitting and listening to her speak.

'The way I see it, there are basically two ways we can approach your family history,' she said.

'Right.'

'Obviously, we have to start from a known point. But we're lucky in this case, in that we have a certain amount of information about both ends of the line.'

'I'm sorry—?'

'What I mean is, the usual way to trace a family tree would be to start with yourself as the known point. You then work backwards from your parents' wedding certificate to their birth certificates to get information about *their* parents, and so on as far as you can go, picking up as much detail as you can about each individual. Then you can

182

gradually fill in the tree. That way, you're going backwards through history. Right?'

'That makes sense.'

'The other way is to move forward. Since we know something about William Buckley and his immediate family, we could start in 1800, and come forward. It means you're less likely to miss collateral relatives such as brothers and sisters, who could be important in this case.'

I nodded admiringly. 'You sound as though you really know what you're doing. Which approach do you recommend?'

'It depends.'

'On what?'

'On how much you know about your parents and grandparents. Can you provide full details of their marriages and births? Have you got certificates or documents? If so, how far back?'

'Ah. There may be a problem there.'

'You'd better tell me.'

I explained to her about the mysterious rift in my family, and the secrecy that still surrounded it. I told her I'd never been one to wonder much about my ancestors until now. She looked more shocked at that than anything.

'You don't sound very inquisitive,' she said. 'Most people like to know as much as they can about their ancestors.'

'I don't understand why.'

'It gives them a sense of identity. Don't you feel a need for that, Chris?'

'My identity is what exists now. It doesn't owe anything to ancient history.'

'I take it you've heard of genes and chromosomes?' she said drily.

I held out my hands. Why was this so difficult to explain? 'Look. I may be made up of genes and chromosomes. But once I was formed, that was it. It doesn't matter where those genes came from. They might as well have fallen together

183

by accident, as far as I'm concerned. What's the difference between that and a series of couplings between people I never knew over periods of history that mean nothing to me? It doesn't affect my identity to know whether a distant ancestor was a beggar or a prince. My genes are my genes, and I'm the product of *now*, not then.'

Laura simply shrugged at my little speech. 'Fine. It's a very blinkered outlook, but a point of view all the same. At least you've thought about it. But if you're not interested in your ancestry, why are you doing this?'

'Fifty thousand pounds, that's why. I'm not researching my family history because I want to know about my ancestors, but because I'm getting paid. I need the money, I don't mind admitting.'

She made a note in her book. Another subject heading? 'Mercenary tendencies as a Buckley family trait'?

'We'll start at the beginning then, shall we? With William Buckley, the engineer.'

'Okay.'

'If I'm going to do some research, I need to get up to date with all the information you already have. So I need to read Samuel's manuscript.'

'Oh.'

'Anything wrong with that?'

Nothing, except that I'd loaned it to Rachel. Now I'd have to get it back from her.

'No. No problem.'

'And William Buckley's letters?'

'I think I told you, they're being transcribed by my neighbour.'

'You said it was a friend.'

'Well, yes.'

'How long does it take to transcribe a few letters?'

'I'll ask her how she's getting on.'

'The originals would be preferable. And we'll see how we go from there, shall we?'

She closed her notebook and finished her drink.

'Another?' I said. 'Whatever it is?'

'Thanks, but no. I've got a lunch engagement.'

'Oh, right.'

'Are you okay, Chris? Disappointed with a lack of progress so far? We'll soon change that.'

'No, it isn't that. Well, I suppose it might be. Frank Chaplin was a bit of a letdown.'

'You won't find me a letdown.'

'I'm sure.'

She gave me her smile as she rose from the table. I gazed up at her, wondering who her lunch engagement was with, and whether she'd have dinner with me one night, if I had the courage to ask her.

'We'll talk again soon,' she said.

'I'll look forward to it.'

When I got home, there was a message on the answerphone from Dan Hyde. Far from seeming worried, his voice sounded positively gloating as it echoed tinnily from the machine.

'Er, Chris. We've got a crisis. The thing is, I had a phone call from Poole House Design again. They won't release the designs for the website until we pay their last invoice. Now some of our advertisers have cottoned on to the fact that *winningbid.uk.com* won't be launching any time soon. Word gets round, you know. The phone here has been red hot. They want their money back, mate.' He paused. I could have sworn that he was breaking off to take a drink. I could almost taste the alcohol myself. 'If we don't cough up pretty quick, we'll be taken to the cleaners. What we need to do is hold Poole House off for a while. We have to promise them something, give them a prospect of being paid back. Call me with your ideas, mate.'

I abandoned plans for defrosting a chicken tikka and walked

up to the Stowe Arms for a pie and chips in the sort of surroundings that could take my mind off things for a while. The effort to distract my mind took all afternoon – and it wasn't entirely successful.

25

I noticed the BMW parked outside Maybank as soon as I turned the corner from Gaia Lane. It's the sort of street where you notice these things, even when there isn't a thickset man sitting at the wheel watching you with a covert intensity.

He was out of the BMW quickly enough to waylay me between the gate and my back door. I don't know why I felt threatened. He could have been another policeman, or he could just as easily have been a Jehovah's Witness or an insurance salesman. But my instinctive reaction was to seek an escape route as he approached. My key was in my hand, and I was looking round for Rachel, as if she might be a guardian angel watching over me. But for once, she was missing.

'Mr Buckley?'

'Yes?'

'Christopher Buckley?'

'That's me all right.'

'My name's Leo Parker.'

'Oh?'

Then I stopped looking past him at the road and focused on his face. I recognised him then. He was the man who'd been with the MP, Lindley Simpson, at the meeting in Boley Park Community Centre. The squat shape and heavy shoulders under the dark coat were unmistakeable.

'I wonder if you could spare me a few minutes.'

'Well . . . I'm not sure.'

'Don't worry,' he said. 'I'm not selling anything.' He held his hands out to show they were empty and gave me a sincere smile that was meant to be disarming. But all it did was make me look uneasily behind me at the door of Maybank, finger my key, and wonder whether I could still make my escape. At the sight of that politician's smile, I became convinced that he was on a lobbying exercise to persuade me write something favourable about Lindley Simpson, or some other cause that would benefit Leo Parker. I was about to come under a bit of gentle pressure, and I could do without it right now.

'I want to talk to you about Samuel Longden,' he said.

I stared at him in amazement. I heard the door of number four open and close, and the familiar footsteps began to descend the path. They slowed, and stopped somewhere near the gate. I could imagine Rachel's antennae springing to life and tuning in to our conversation as she became aware that I had company. I saw Parker's eyes flicker past me, and the polite smile became fixed on his face, though his eyes didn't change.

'You'd better come in for a minute,' I said.

'Thank you.'

I took him into the sitting room. It's a room I don't use very much, not since I've been on my own – my computer and books and the TV are in what used to be the dining room, which is at the front of the house with a view of the road. The sitting room is a part of the house which most captures the memory of my parents, with its three-piece suite in a dull yellow fabric, a glass-topped coffee table, and even the old tiled fireplace from the 1950s. I had a vague memory from my childhood of the traditional three porcelain ducks winging their way across the back wall, but maybe I was just imagining them. The room always smelt musty, as a result of a damp patch of carpet under the bay window where rain got in through a crack in the glass.

188

It was also a cold room, but I didn't want my visitor to be too comfortable. The only operative heating was in the fish tank set into an alcove next to the fireplace. My father's neon tetras and black mollies still swam in there. The only time I came into this room normally was to feed the fish or clean their tank. Occasionally I'd sit for a while and watch them as they twisted and turned aimlessly, gaping through the glass in their helpless captivity, preserved in an unchanging environment for the rest of their lives. Lately, I'd been looking at them with envy.

'Ah, fish,' said Parker. 'I'm told they're very restful.' He spoke like a visiting minor royal, automatically seeking something of interest to make conversation about. He was thinking 'This man has a tankful of tropical fish in his house, therefore he'll be won over and trust me more if I show an interest in fish.' It's an old trick. It's one that insurance salesmen learn – which was exactly what Parker claimed not to be.

'So. Samuel Longden,' I said. 'You have some sort of connection with him?'

'Yes, of a kind.'

'Are you a relative?'

'No, no. Simply a friend,' he said.

'I see.'

'A close friend.'

I hoped that he couldn't see the disbelief on my face. From what I knew of Great-Uncle Samuel, this man was not the sort of person to be his friend, close or otherwise. But then, what did I know of the long spell between the death of my grandfather and the day Samuel had approached me by the side of the lock at Fosseway Lane? Perhaps he had, indeed, become the sort of man to associate with the likes of Leo Parker. This Parker definitely looked like a politician to me. And I had no idea about my great-uncle's politics.

'Did you have some interest in common?' I asked. I cursed the conventions that prevented me from asking outright the

189

questions I wanted to put, for fear of appearing rude. Parker smiled again, as if acknowledging the same convention.

'Certainly. A shared interest in history.'

Though the smile stayed on his face, his words laid an even deeper chill on the air of the room. That one phrase left me in little doubt what he'd come about. Samuel Longden's obsession with the past was attracting a lot of unwelcome things into my life, and I was counting Leo Parker as one of them.

'And what can I do for you exactly?'

'Let me explain. I've been helping Samuel with a certain project. History, as I say.'

'Your shared interest.'

'Exactly. It has involved quite a lot of research, a great deal of hard work collecting documents and information. All this work was intended to lead to a book eventually.'

'I see.'

'Well, the long and short of it is that, now Samuel is dead, it obviously falls upon me to complete the project. But it seems that a large part of the material we worked on together may have fallen into other hands in the meantime. It would be a great shame, of course, if all Samuel's work were to be wasted. And mine, of course.'

'And your point is?'

'Well, Mr Buckley, I'm anxious to track down the material. Files, papers, parts of the manuscript. Quite a large amount of material. I really need it back.'

He looked very relaxed, with his feet spread out on my parents' mock goatskin rug. But I sensed that I somehow had the advantage of him, that he wasn't quite sure of his ground. Did he even know that Samuel claimed to be my great-uncle? Maybe Parker had only guessed that I might possess what he wanted and was trying his luck. If so, a straight bat should see him off.

'I don't think I quite understand why you're talking to me about this.'

'I thought . . . well, I know that you had made Samuel's acquaintance recently.'

'And how do you know that?'

'Oh, he mentioned it,' said Parker airily.

'When?'

'I can't remember exactly. Recently. Your name came up, and I gathered he was considering asking your opinion on the prospective book. He chose you because you're a journalist, an independent and impartial observer, so to speak. Not to mention your interest in the waterways. Probably he was hoping you'd cast an eye over the manuscript before you returned it.'

I stared at him as steadily as I could, waiting for him to continue.

'Perhaps,' he said, 'Samuel might even have been considering the possibility of a small payment as a consultant. An editor's fee, even. I think that might have been in the old chap's mind, don't you? But he got confused sometimes. He might not have made it absolutely clear what he intended. And, of course, I'm sure he never really meant to let the whole file of material out of his possession.'

He was beginning to sound more and more desperate. The hints about money proved that he was on shaky ground and appealing to my baser instincts. At any other time, the suggestion might have been tempting. It's money for old rope, editing. But I already had my meal ticket lined up in the form of Samuel Longden's fifty thousand pounds.

Boswell strolled into the room, rubbing his black fur against my legs to remind me he hadn't been fed. He took one long, disdainful look at my visitor, flicked his tail, and walked out again.

'Mr Parker,' I said, 'I really don't think I can help you. You may or may not be aware that Samuel Longden left me certain items in his will, which I was not expecting. You might think these relate to the same project you're talking about. I wouldn't know. But obviously my first concern is to follow Samuel's wishes as expressed in his will. And his intentions are quite clear – he wanted me to complete the project for him. If you're in any doubt about that, I suggest you contact his solicitors, Elsworth and Clarke, for clarification.'

The smile had been slipping from Parker's face for the last few seconds, and by the time I'd finished speaking, it was gone completely. Instead, his jaw had tensed into a hard line, abandoning any pretence of civility. The expression in his eyes hadn't changed, because the smile had never spread beyond his teeth.

'You may find the items were not Samuel Longden's sole property in the first place for him to bequeath to you,' he said.

'I suppose you could challenge the will, if you think you could prove that.'

'Perhaps I should.'

We stared at each other for a moment. I was trying hard to look much braver than I felt. Then Parker turned aside, ostensibly to admire the tetras and mollies in the tank against the wall. His heavy shoulders relaxed again gradually, and the smile began to twitch the corners of his mouth. He looked at me sideways, almost shyly.

'Look, Christopher, we've got off on the wrong foot, and it's entirely my fault. I suppose I ought to come clean.'

I noted the sudden switch to my first name, but I didn't like the presumed intimacy any better than the oily courtesy.

'That sounds like a good idea to me.'

'What I've just told you isn't entirely true.'

'Go on,' I said, far from surprised.

'When I first introduced myself, you asked me if I was a relative of Samuel Longden's, and I told you I wasn't. That's true, strictly speaking. But it's a little more complicated than that.'

'Perhaps you'd better explain.'

He sighed. 'There's something I should tell you. But this is very difficult for me. The subject is rather sensitive, both for myself and my family, just as it was for Samuel. I suggest it could be something you yourself are quite unaware of. Even though Samuel Longden was your great-uncle.'

I knew his ploy had been a calculated change of tactics. But I had to admit that he'd caught my interest now. I needed to hear what he had to say.

'Will this take long?' I asked.

'A little while,' he smiled.

'You'd better sit down then. I'll make us some coffee.'

'That would be very civilised.'

Leo Parker settled himself on one of the yellow armchairs, close to the fish tank, where his eyes could follow the flickering movements. During the next few minutes, I began to wonder if his eyes moved away to watch the fish at moments when he was lying, but I possessed no facts to check his statements against. I had to accept what he told me at face value, for now.

'Did Samuel ever mention my stepmother to you?' he asked as I returned with a tray.

'Why would he?'

'Her name was Mary,' he said. 'Mary Parker.'

I stopped in mid-stride, almost pole-axed.

'Mary—?'

Parker smiled as he casually let slip his bombshell.

'She was also your grandmother.'

I felt him watching me like a hawk, and I couldn't stop myself flushing with irritation and embarrassment as I clattered the tray down and slopped some coffee into a saucer.

'I'm talking about your grandmother, Christopher,' he repeated, as if I was deaf or stupid.

But I wasn't either of those things. I was just thunderstruck, the way he'd no doubt intended me to be.

193

'Of course,' I said finally. 'But did you say . . . your stepmother?'

He inclined his head. 'Your grandparents separated and divorced. Mary went on to marry my father, Matthew Parker.'

'So our families are related.'

'I'd describe them as inextricably entangled.'

'I had no idea,' I admitted. 'I knew that Mary left my grandfather when they'd only been married for a few years and already had a son, my father. But what happened to her afterwards—'

I must have looked sceptical, because Parker felt the need to convince me.

'I can assure you it's true. She married again.'

'To *your* father.'

'Yes.' He hesitated. 'Suffice to say that your grandfather's marriage to my stepmother had its problems. Their separation was very sad. There were things that caused a lot of distress within the family, aspects I don't really want to go into. You see, I'm hoping to avoid any more distress.'

As I recovered from the shock, I found the only emotion left in me was that profound sense of irritation.

'Surely that must all have been many years ago,' I said.

'Oh, the late 1940s.'

'It's all been over and done with a very long time ago. It can't mean anything to us now.'

'That's where you're wrong, I'm afraid. I do wish it were true, but I fear that Samuel may have been planning to re-open old wounds.'

'I can't imagine that was his intention.'

'But, as you said yourself, you knew very little about him.'

I had to acknowledge this was true.

'What I'd like to assure myself of,' he said, seeing me weakening, 'is the fate of any documents or papers relating to my stepmother, or to my father. Any letters, perhaps?'

'I've seen nothing of that kind,' I said. 'Nothing at all.'

This was quite true, as I'd yet to examine the files, apart from the first few pages of Samuel's manuscript. It was rapidly becoming apparent, though, that I'd have to face the task soon, to find out what everyone found so interesting.

'Are you quite sure?'

'Mr Parker, until a few minutes ago I hadn't even heard of your family.'

'Yes, you said so.' He waited, his lips pressed together in frustration, but his courteous exterior holding. 'I know it's an imposition, but might it be possible for me to have a look for myself?'

I bridled possessively. Much as I wanted to pump Parker for anything he knew, the attempt to poke his nose into what I was doing was outrageous.

'I don't think so.'

'But—'

'I think you're going to have to trust me. Allow me to use my own judgement on any documents I come across, whoever they might mention.'

'Oh, I'm sure I can trust you, but—'

'You see, my great-uncle has given me a very specific task to carry out, to complete a book. This is a historical work, about one of my own ancestors, as I understand it – not a biography of Samuel Longden, and certainly not an account of his private life or his marriages. Anything relating to your family is hardly likely to be relevant, is it?'

'I hope not.'

'So I'm afraid we'll have to leave it there.'

'Very well.' He stood over me, his shoulders hunched unhappily. I got to my feet, to feel at less of a disadvantage.

'I can see you're not entirely reassured,' I said.

'I'm sorry. If you understood the circumstances . . . But I can't really explain it to you. At least take my card in case you change your mind.'

As soon as I'd got him out of the house, I went into the

front room and looked at the files that had been delivered by Great-Uncle Samuel. What was in that musty heap of paper that was of such interest? Did something in there really hold dark, intimate secrets about Leo Parker's family? Something that involved my grandmother Mary in particular? It seemed unlikely. There might be a clue about the split in my own family, though. That would be interesting, given the lengths that everyone involved had gone to in order to hush it up, to erase it from history altogether.

But Parker knew something about it, or wanted me to think he did. And if he knew, then other people must do, too. Perhaps there was something here, in these files, that would help me to ask the right questions. At last there was a little chink of hope that might cast light on my family. And I had Leo Parker to thank for it.

I looked at the window as I caught a movement. I was just in time to see the driver's door of the BMW close and the car begin to drive away.

I was thinking about my grandmother Mary, trying to sort out my impressions of her, which had become much more fluid and confusing after talking to the two people who'd actually met her – Samuel Longden, and now Leo Parker.

I remembered that suddenly wistful remark of Samuel's when he'd mentioned her. *'She had the most striking eyes. The way she looked at you—'*

And then I remembered her. It was like suddenly recapturing a detail of a dream long after I'd woken up. I couldn't recall what the occasion was, but a distinct presence had just slipped into one of my childhood memories – an image of a quiet woman who nevertheless seemed to dominate our sitting room at Stowe Pool Lane, regardless of who else had been there.

I saw a forbidding figure sitting upright in an armchair, her hair tightly permed, her clothes redolent of some old-fashioned scent that I'd never smelled since and would always

196

associate with a sense of trepidation, a feeling that something awful could happen at any moment. It seemed to me that the adults had all been uneasy in her presence. As a result, I'd been a little frightened of her, and tried to avoid attracting her attention.

But she'd noticed me all right. She'd possessed such a piercing gaze that I felt she could see straight through me, knew every secret in my heart, disapproved of every boyish misdemeanour. How old had I been then? Very young, I thought. Four or five perhaps. Small enough to be propped on a kitchen chair in the corner of the room and told to keep quiet. It must have been some family gathering, but there was no wedding or funeral that fit the bill from that time. Had she visited us one Christmas in a last, futile attempt at reconciliation with the Buckleys?

If so, no one had ever told me she was my grandmother. And she'd never come back again.

26

'I only want the manuscript, Rachel,' I said. 'You can hang on to the letters for now.'

Rachel had barely managed to get her coat off after arriving home from the vet's surgery when I called round at number four. She looked surprised, but rather pleased. It was quite a reversal, finding me watching out for her arrival.

'You've decided to read it properly at last, have you?' she said.

'I've read some of it,' I said defensively.

'All right, where did you get up to then?'

'I've covered William Buckley.'

'Up to the point he disappeared?'

'Well, yes.'

'And what did you think?'

I shrugged. 'What is there to think? He vanished. There had been suspicions that he was fiddling the books, and defrauding the canal company. The committee were told he'd run off with some of the money.'

Rachel glared at me and put her hands on her hips like an irate schoolteacher. She had a high colour in her face from the cold outside, and her hair had fallen loose. She always seemed to be dressed more smartly these days than I was used to.

'Do you want me to do all the work for you?' she said.

'No. But William seems to have been dishonest, a criminal. It's not much of a thing to find in your family history.'

'Perhaps.'

'Did *you* read the second part of the manuscript?'

'Yes, but the main part of the story has nothing to do with William Buckley. It's about a different period altogether. Victorian.'

'Is it?' I said.

'Yes, it's about Josiah Buckley. He was William's grandson. Josiah was found dead in the canal, but there's a mystery about how he died.'

'I know. Another mystery. That's typical of the old man – going off at another tangent. But what happened to William? Does he just leave us hanging?'

'It seems so.'

'What can we do with incomplete information?'

'I've been through everything,' she said. 'I've been through all the notes and all the papers. Then I went to look up the canal company minutes.'

'In the County Record Office?'

'Yes, of course.'

'I hope you had better luck there than I did. They made me feel like an Egyptian tomb robber.'

She frowned at me impatiently. 'It's quite simple, as long as you follow the rules.'

'Right.'

'Anyway, the interesting thing is that only the assembly minutes are archived. The committee minutes are missing.'

'I saw that. So what's the difference?'

'The assembly only happened once a year, and all the shareholders could attend. The committee ran the company's affairs on a day to day basis, and they met at least once a month, sometimes twice. There must have been committee minutes, but they don't seem to have survived when the Ogley and Huddlesford was taken over by the Birmingham Navigations in the 1840s.'

'That must have been a blow to Great-Uncle Samuel. They would be full of information.'

'Absolutely. But I've copied the assembly minutes from the relevant period, until after William Buckley disappeared. I think if we sit down together with the minutes, William's letters, and Samuel's notes, we might be able to piece something together.'

'Come on, then.'

'What, now?'

'Unless you've got something else to do?'

'No, I'm just surprised at this sudden burst of enthusiasm.'

'I need to get on with it. I'll explain why later.'

'I suppose it's best now anyway, since I'm going to be away for a few days.'

Rachel made some coffee, and we spread the contents of the files out on her sitting room carpet. We put Samuel's incomplete manuscript to one side, stacked up the letters from William Buckley in the middle and the photocopies of the assembly minutes on the other side. We ended up with an untidy pile left over – notebooks, photocopied documents, clippings from old newspapers.

'Rachel – have you come across any mention at all of my grandmother, Mary?'

She shook her head firmly. 'None at all. There's nothing about Samuel's own life or his immediate family. Why? Did you hope there would be?'

'No, quite the opposite.'

'Why?'

'It doesn't matter.'

'All right. What we should try to do is get everything into chronological order and see how they relate to each other.'

'That sounds very organised.'

But it didn't work out like that. Within minutes, we'd both been distracted by individual items as the fascination of the voices speaking from the past took hold of us. We lost track of time as we sat on the floor exclaiming at intriguing items that we passed back and forth to one another, or laughing at the archaic language. It was as if we'd been transported two hundred years into the past by a pile of mouldy paper. I began to get an inkling of Great-Uncle Samuel's obsession.

Gradually, a picture of William Buckley emerged. Rachel made notes as we went along, calling out snippets of information or interesting details.

As Samuel had written, William's father had obtained him an apprenticeship with a contractor in Tamworth, who already had a business working on canal projects. Within a few years he was sent to be trained by the great engineer William Jessop. He learned surveying and map drawing skills, and in time he became assistant engineer on a big tunnelling project on the Leeds and Liverpool. Jessop was evidently pleased with him, and when the great man agreed to take on the role of chief engineer for the Ogley and Huddlesford Canal, he recommended William as resident engineer.

I was immediately struck by the fact that William was only thirty-two when he was appointed – the same age as me. My ancestor seemed to have achieved so much in a short life, whereas I . . .

'Are you still with us, Chris?' said Rachel.

'Yes, of course. Carry on.'

When William Buckley married Sarah, the daughter of a local businessman, the canal company provided him with a house at Pipehill, and he was able to settle down within a few miles of his birthplace at Whittington. The couple's only child, Edward, was born in 1798.

But, like so many other early canal companies, the proprietors of the Ogley and Huddlesford began to run into financial difficulties. Some of these were caused by inflation, some by shareholders defaulting on payments, or absconding without paying their debts, or going bankrupt. Other problems involved devious or dishonest contractors.

But the documents revealed that there was also a long-standing dispute with one of the company's own major proprietors, Anthony Nall, who owned several coal mines with wharves served by arms of the canal. Nall had been elected chairman of the canal company, though some must have regretted it in the light of subsequent events. It seemed remarkable, from a viewpoint two centuries later, that the chairman should have been involved in such a bitter dispute with his own company without being replaced or thinking of resigning. Nall had an influential brother, too – Joshua, who'd been made Deputy Lord Lieutenant of the county.

The dispute seemed to have begun over the water supply, a common problem on early canals, which had come to a head with the building of a wharf at Fosseway. The Nalls were suffering from severe water shortages at their coal mines, for in 1799 the most that could be promised on the summit pound where the mines were situated was enough water for fifteen-tonne boats. Eighteen months later Anthony Nall petitioned Parliament for a Bill to permit him to bypass the canal by building a railway.

But the Ogley and Huddlesford scheme relied on carrying his goods. Fosseway Wharf had been built largely to serve Nall's limeworks, and the company claimed that he was bound by agreement to transport his lime by the canal, as well as coal from his mines and corn to his brother's mill. For some reason Anthony Nall had abandoned use of the wharf after a couple of years. Perhaps his lime quarry had closed. In any case, the company found it was no longer benefiting from the tolls and tonnage rates. The committee ordered the company secretary, Daniel Metcalf, to begin proceedings against Nall.

It was clear that the dispute had concerned William Buckley greatly. There seemed to have been some suggestion that his estimates for the building of the Fosseway wharf were wildly inaccurate, and this was the reason the company was losing money. William defended himself strongly. And he redeemed himself by uncovering a fraud that was being perpetrated by

202

two of the proprietors themselves, which had drained the company of much of its resources.

It was Rachel who came across a reference in the assembly minutes.

'This is interesting,' she said.

'What's that?'

She was reading about a disaster that had hit the canal company in 1799, when the embankment of the reservoir at Cannock Heath had burst. According to the newspaper report: 'the water swept everything before it in the line it took through Shenstone, Hopwas, Drayton &c till it fell into and overflooded the Tame at Tamworth. At Blackbrook, seven miles from the reservoir, the new stone bridge was blown up; numbers of sheep and some cattle were drowned. The damage sustained is calculated at many thousand pounds. At Hammerswich, near Lichfield, the meadows are twelve inches deep with the gravel the water brought down'. The report was dated 10th June 1799.

'Is that Chasewater Reservoir?' she said.

'Yes, they reinforced it when they rebuilt it after the flood, and it's lasted perfectly well ever since.'

'That's lucky for the people living near it.'

'Hundreds would be killed if it happened now,' I said, thinking of Frank and Sally Chaplin in their house at Chasetown. 'The population of Burntwood has multiplied vastly since then.'

At some stage, Rachel had produced a plate of cheese and tomato sandwiches, a chocolate cake and a bottle of Buxton Spring Water. I wondered briefly whether I was keeping her from something else she ought to be doing. But she made no complaint, so I said nothing.

Then I noticed there was an oddity in the sequence of minutes. The records showed that a meeting had taken place in January 1800, four months before the normal time of the annual assembly.

'What's going on here?' I said, frowning at the handwriting that followed. 'It says it's a special meeting.' I turned back a page to the previous assembly. 'There's no mention of it earlier on. It must have been called some time during the summer.'

'Well, generally a certain number of members can get together and call for a special meeting, or the chairman can do it himself. Yes, it's here, I think. On the request of five proprietors under standing orders. Then the proprietors are named – there's Geo Wilkinson, Wm White, Adam Henshall. And there are our old friends, Anthony and Joshua Nall. There was a proposal that "the Conduct of certain members of the Committee has been such as to merit the Approbation of the Company present".'

'Hello? What were they getting steamed up about this time?'

'Oh, blah, blah . . . blah, blah. Mmm. It seems they'd discovered the company was owed more than four thousand pounds by defaulting proprietors. It says here they thought there was "great Neglect somewhere to have allowed so large a Balance to become due".'

'Four thousand quid or so?' I said. 'What's that in modern terms?'

'Multiply by fifty, that's the usual reckoning.'

'Two hundred grand? Not to be sneezed at.'

'I'll say. Remember the original amount raised to start the canal was only £25,000. And the shares were worth £125 each,' said Rachel.

'Right. So that's a pretty big chunk of shares not paid for, isn't it?'

'Or a big chunk of money gone missing somehow.'

'And does it say who's taking the blame for all this?'

'Not clear. Not from these minutes anyway.'

'Was William Buckley there?' I asked.

'Yes, his name's on the attendance list.'

'I wonder which side he was on. His letters don't give any clue, do they?'

'January 1800?' She opened the box file and turned over the letters. 'This second one's from 14th January that year. But if he had any idea about it, he doesn't mention it to Reuben Wheeldon.'

I leaned over her shoulder to read the second letter. 'Oh yes, he does. Look at this: "God give me patience, but I have been in so uneasy a state of Mind as not to be fit to write. Things have happened lately of great Perplexity." Later on he says: "I am extremely sorry to have given you any uneasiness, but I will call on you tomorrow week. I hope also to bring you the documents of which I spoke."'

'So he was going to visit Wheeldon. I wonder how long he stayed away.'

'Why?'

Rachel had turned past the special meeting to the next page of minutes. 'It's just that William Buckley's name isn't on the attendance list at the next assembly meeting. And it was the first assembly he'd missed in four years.'

27

Pipehill, Lichfield, Staffordshire. Tuesday 14th Jan. 1800.

To Reuben Wheeldon Esq., Warner Street, Ellesmere, Cheshire.

My dear friend,

God give me patience, but I have been in so uneasy a state of Mind as not to be fit to write. Things have happened lately of great Perplexity, and I walk about the room by the hour in great emotion. Would to Heaven that I had not taken up the cause of righteousness, but I do not count upon any Happiness in the present hour. Why am I to be thus insolently called to account? Am I not at liberty to please myself?

Though I entertain as high an opinion as any man can, both of N.'s knowledge and good sense, yet I am convinced that he is entirely wrong on this occasion, and I am persuaded that if he had seen the state of the Works he would not have decided as he has. He deservedly stands too high in the Public Esteem to be afraid to confess an error when he is advised of it. I sincerely hope I have converted at least some among the Proprietors – the very existence of the Canal now depends on their determination.

As for the Chief Engineer, the Committee wrote to him to insist that he allow nothing but the most pressing circumstances to call him away, which he promised he would do, but he has neglected his promise. I am most inclined to impute the failure generally to the want of the necessary diligence, though Danger and Difficulties are constant attendants on the Works, and credit and satisfaction are always Strangers. But I believe the Company behaved harshly in refusing arbitration over and over again and sticking to the letter of the contract in spite of inflation.

I am extremely sorry to have given you any uneasiness, but I will call on you tomorrow week. I hope also to bring you the documents of which I spoke.

Your friend,
Wm Buckley

28

On Sunday morning I went looking for Andrew Hadfield at Fosseway. I wanted to ask him about Leo Parker, and what his connection was with Lindley Simpson. I'd found Andrew a valuable source of information, and I knew he'd seen Parker at the Boley Park meeting.

But for once, Andrew was missing from the work party. Phil Glover shrugged when I asked where he was. He was too busy examining a large brick chamber constructed inside the head of the lock to allow the drain water to cascade seven feet to the lower level. It was the last obstacle before the completion of the lock.

I realised I'd have to catch Andrew on the phone, and Phil reluctantly broke off to find his number for me.

While I was at the site, I took a closer look at the lock. Another row of sponsored pilings had been hammered into the bank just beyond the wing walls. There, among the inscriptions on the pilings, I saw a familiar name. 'Samuel Longden 1916–1998'. It was brand new, put in during the last few days, presumably paid for by Caroline, since her father's death. But it made me look closer at the other inscriptions, remembering that Samuel had been known for his generosity to the restoration scheme. Had he sponsored pilings during his lifetime too?

A few yards further along I found them, close to the bottom entrance to the lock. There were two, and they were poignant. 'Samuel Buckley' said the first. It was almost the only written record of Samuel's previous name, apart from the document which Mr Elsworth had given me. The piling next to it recalled Samuel's other fascination. It was inscribed simply '*Kestrel*'.

I remembered Mrs Wentworth, Samuel's neighbour, who'd told me about *Kestrel*. There was something else she'd said, which was nagging at me. It had been the first time I called at Whittington, and it was only a very brief conversation. 'He might have gone to see his friend in Cheshire,' she'd said. What friend? If Samuel had been visiting an old friend recently, I needed to know who it was. He could be the ideal person to talk to – someone outside the family, without the prejudices that went with it.

I drove to Pipehill before I found a phone box, cursing the fact that I couldn't afford a mobile phone. I had to get Mrs Wentworth's number from directory enquiries, and when I dialled I was connected to a British Telecom Call Minder service suggesting I might want to leave a message. I left my name and home phone number, reminding her who I was, and asked her to give me a ring.

But I couldn't wait in the house and hope she rang me back. The need to be doing something was itching in me, and there was one person who hadn't been telling me what he knew. It was time to exert some pressure on the family.

There was no reply at the bungalow in Cop Nook Lane, but the blue Cavalier was standing in the drive. I walked down the side of the building and peered through the glass of the conservatory, but there was no sign of Frank among the dripping foliage. I figured that if Sally was out somewhere, there was only one place Frank was likely to be.

I drove into the car park near the football pitches and walked up the slope towards the old railway embankment to look across the heath. At first the whole area seemed deserted. But when I got to the top of the embankment, the panorama of gorse bushes, sandy hollows and water spread out before me, and I saw Frank almost immediately. I recognised him only by his ginger hair, a small strand of it moving in the breeze. He was lying on the ground, close to the crest of a rise, sheltered by some clumps of whinberry, and only his head broke the skyline.

I couldn't figure out what he was doing at first. But something stopped me from calling out to him. Instead, I set off down the embankment and made my way across to the spot where he was lying. He didn't hear me coming, and he seemed totally absorbed in something beyond the rise. Was that a pair of binoculars he had in front of his face, or a camera? Quite likely he was a keen birdwatcher, to go with the fondness for plants. What birds would be out here, in this dry heath, among the empty, rattling seed cases of the gorse?

The impression was so odd that I walked right up to Frank without saying a word. It was only then that I saw beyond the slope, and into the hollow beneath the whinberry. A movement in the coarse grass resolved itself into a tangle of pale limbs and a pair of naked, thrusting buttocks. At the same time, I saw Frank was pointing a camera with a long lens propped against the ground.

'Jesus Christ!'

Frank rolled over suddenly, his eyes wide and frightened, as he pulled the camera to his chest. His reaction made me duck in guilty unison, pulling my head below the whinberry in case the couple below should look up at the noise. Frank was white with shock, his eyes bulging with fear.

'Chris! What the hell do you think you're doing?'

'I was going to ask you the same thing, Frank.'

He looked angry at first. Then he grinned weakly, looking for a bit of boys-together complicity. 'I'm not doing any harm.'

But I had no sympathy. 'Does Sally know about this?'

'Of course not.' Immediately, he looked frightened again. 'For God's sake, you won't tell her, will you?'

'What would be the point of that?'

'You swear?'

'Yes, whatever.'

'Thanks, Chris. You're a mate.'

I shook my head, baffled by the pathetic sordidness I'd stumbled into. 'I just don't want to know about it.'

'What was it you wanted anyway?' said Frank. 'Did you come to ask me something? About Samuel Longden? I wasn't very helpful yesterday, I suppose.'

He was suddenly all too eager to please. And I found that I really didn't want to ask him questions about Samuel any more, in case he gave me answers for the wrong reasons. Then we both might regret it later. But I still had to find the friend in Cheshire.

'Oh yeah,' said Frank. 'I remember something about him.' He scratched his head, miming his effort to come up with an answer for me. 'Samuel used to write to him, mostly. But he did go and see him too. Cheshire? That sounds right.'

'Can you remember his name?'

He looked crestfallen. 'I don't think I ever knew it. Sorry. Is it important?'

'It might be.'

Frank's confidence seemed to be coming back, now that I'd promised to keep his secret.

'Well, I'll let you know if I remember.'

'Of course you will.'

He looked at me slyly, trying to push his hair back into position against the wind. This was the man who, only the previous day, had made me feel I wasn't alone. How quickly new-found allies can turn out to have feet of clay. And how quickly you can find you feel more alone than ever.

'But you know how it is, Chris. There are some things you forget.'

'Yes, all right, Frank. I know how it is.'

* * *

When I got home, the phone was ringing. It was Mrs Wentworth, sounding nervous at the aggressive note in my voice. Despite my message, she seemed unclear who I actually was.

'It's Christopher Buckley, Mrs Wentworth. Samuel Longden's great-nephew. I called round to the house, you remember?'

'Oh yes. How are you? I do hope the police—'

'Yes, that's all right, Mrs Wentworth. They're not bothering me now. I think I must have been given a clean bill of health, though they don't take the trouble to tell you that.'

'I'm sorry.'

'It's not your fault. You were just being a good neighbour. But there was something I wanted to ask you.'

'Yes?'

'When I spoke to you the first time I came, when Samuel was out, you said he might have gone to see his friend in Cheshire. I think those were your words.'

'Yes, that's right. But I don't think he can have gone to see him that time. Samuel usually told me when he was going to be away, so I could keep an eye on the house.'

'Did he leave you a name and address, or a telephone number for this friend, in case you needed to contact him in an emergency?'

'Well, it wasn't as if he was away for long periods, you know. Only a day out.'

'So you don't know who this friend was?'

'Well . . .'

'It's quite important that I trace him.'

'Well, he did mention the name, actually.' Her voice grew fainter, as if she'd turned away from the phone. 'And it's funny, but . . . well, I think his name and address is on the back of it.'

'Mrs Wentworth? Are you still there? On the back of what?'

There was a thump as the phone went down, then echoing

212

footsteps as she walked across the hallway of her house. The footsteps came back again, there was a rustling sound, and the phone was retrieved.

'Yes, I was right. It is.'

'What is? I'm sorry, you've lost me.'

'The postman left it,' she said. 'The normal mail is still being delivered to Ash Lodge, but this came by parcel van and the man couldn't get it through the letter box, so he left it with me.'

'Left what with you?'

'The parcel, of course. And it has the name and address of the sender on the back. Such a good idea, I always think. If it goes astray and has to be returned, the post office don't need to open it to find out who it came from, do they?'

'And are you saying this parcel is from Samuel's friend in Cheshire?'

'I'm almost certain this is the name. It sounds familiar. And it *is* in Cheshire.'

I was groping for a pen and a piece of paper in my pocket. 'Could you read it to me?'

'Oh yes. It's from a Mr Godfrey Wheeldon.'

'Wheeldon, did you say?'

'Yes, does it mean something to you?'

'Well, it might be a coincidence.'

'The address is The Old Vicarage Nursing Home, Bennington Road, Ellesmere, Cheshire. Do you want the post code?'

'No, that's all right, Mrs Wentworth. Thank you.'

'Are you going to speak to Mr Wheeldon, dear?'

'I hope so.'

'Well, I wonder if you'd ask him what I should do with the parcel? I was going to pass it on to Caroline next time I see her. But I don't know when that will be, and Mr Wheeldon might want it returned to him, now that Samuel is no longer here, mightn't he? I don't know if it's anything important, but it's one of those padded bags.'

29

Finally, as the last job of the day, I had to ring Dan Hyde back. We exchanged guarded greetings. Our friendship didn't look likely to survive a crisis facing our business venture, like a marriage falling apart on the death of a child. It was almost too easy to blame each other.

Dan sighed. 'The thing is – there's not much left to pay Poole House's invoice with. The ad revenue won't cover it.'

'I know that. But that's what the start-up loan is for – the twenty thousand from the bank. Pay them out of that.'

'Well . . .'

'We have enough left in the account, surely?'

'Well . . . no, actually.'

I shivered, appalled at the significance of this latest blow. 'There must be.'

'There have been a lot of expenses, Chris. We had the lease to pay, and equipment to buy, not to mention the marketing consultants and the employment agency. There were legal fees. And the phone bills have been astronomical.'

'Are you telling me there's nothing left?'

'A few hundred, that's all.'

'But, hang on, what about the investment from our anonymous backer?'

He mumbled something I couldn't make out, as if he'd moved his mouth away from the phone.

'I can't hear what you're saying, Dan. What about our backer?'

'He pulled out.'

'What?'

'Our backer has pulled out, Chris.'

'How can he do that, for God's sake? Surely you had him tied down to some agreement? Didn't you have it in writing?'

'Not exactly.'

'You mean someone can just pull the plug on us at the drop of a hat?'

'I suppose he must have seen the way things were going.'

'More than you did, then,' I said angrily.

'Come on, Chris. I know it's a mess—'

'A mess? If only we could have kept going a few more months. You always said that, didn't you? Six months, and we'd be in the black. Didn't you mention that?'

'Of course I did. But once they think you're a bad investment, these guys drop you as quick as hot coals. You know what it's like, Chris.'

'No. It's perfectly obvious to me now that I've never known what it's like. And I don't think you ever did either, Dan.'

'Chris, I've done my best. I'm sorry it hasn't been a success. I was trying to help, you know?'

'Help?'

'I was worried about you, mate. You needed something to bring you out of your slump – everyone could see that. I thought this would be a great project to look forward to, something we could both get excited about. I'm really sorry. I was sure we had things worked out.'

'*You* may have had things worked out.'

I could hear him breathing slowly down the line while he thought about that. 'What exactly do you mean?'

'How do I know you haven't been lying to me all along?

I reckon you could have been having me for a complete fool. Well, you can sort the mess out yourself, mate.'

His voice no longer sounded apologetic when he said: 'Hold on, we're partners in this. Fifty-fifty all the way. And that *is* in writing.'

'Bastard.'

'There's no point in being like that. We're in it together, and that's a fact. So you'd better start counting your pennies, Chris. This is going to cost us a fortune before we get ourselves out of the shit.'

I closed my eyes and clenched my fist. If he'd been there in front of me, I might have punched him in the face by now. But I had to know the extent of the disaster.

'How much do we owe?'

'Well, there's the bank loan, of course. Twenty grand, plus interest.'

'Right. But we can pay that back in instalments, at least.'

'Yeah, but . . .'

'What? Spill it, Dan. Tell me the rest.'

'There's still Poole House. If we don't pay their invoice, they won't release the designs in time for the launch. And if we don't launch, our advertisers are going to want their money back.'

'So we'll have no ad revenue to rely on either.'

'Not a penny.'

'How much are we talking about?'

'We owe them six thousand pounds.'

'I haven't got half of that.'

'Well, I haven't got any of it. I've been putting my own money in, and it's all gone. I'm totally broke. It's up to you now, mate.'

'There's no way I can find six thousand pounds. No way.'

'If you can't, it's court for both of us, and bankruptcy. They'll make you sell the house, I expect. I only rent a flat, remember. I've got no assets to dispose of.'

'This is a disaster. How the hell did it ever get to this?'

'It was always a gamble. It didn't come off, that's all. It was the wrong time. In another couple of years, we could try again.'

'You must be joking. I wouldn't touch anything ever again that you were involved in.'

'Hey, it's not my fault, mate.'

'Isn't it? You kept telling me we were on to a good thing. You kept saying you'd done the market research and we'd make a killing. Those were your exact words.'

'So I was wrong. It's just one of those things.'

'Crap. You've been a totally devious bastard over this, Dan.'

'Calling me names isn't going to help. We have to find a way out of the situation we're in.'

'A loan from the bank—'

'We've already got one, remember? And that's the next thing. Once the bank gets wind of the fact we're in trouble, they'll be calling in the loan. That's another twenty grand.'

'Oh great.'

'If I were you, Chris, I'd start thinking about putting that house of yours on the market. Unless you can find somewhere else to lay your hands on a few thousand quid in the next few months. Otherwise, I suppose I'll be seeing you in court.'

First thing on Monday morning, I went to Mr Elsworth's office. I needed to ask him some questions. Rather to my surprise, I was shown in to see the solicitor almost straightaway.

'Mr Buckley, how nice to see you again. I do have a few minutes, if there's something I can help you with.'

'It's about the conditions in Samuel Longden's will.'

'Ah yes, that rather unusual bequest.'

'I'm wondering how rigid the conditions are.'

'In what way?'

'Well, the deadline. The book has to be published within

217

the next two years, and a copy delivered to you so the money can be released from the estate.'

'Yes, I'm afraid the book must be published by the year 2000, that being the two hundredth anniversary of William Buckley's death, I gather.' He gave a dry, humourless laugh. 'I say "must", but only if you intend to claim the bequest of fifty thousand pounds, of course.'

'And if I don't?'

'Well, if you decide you don't wish to make a claim, or you're unable to satisfy the executors that you've fulfilled the conditions, the relevant amount will be reabsorbed into the estate and added to the residue inherited by Mr Longden's principal beneficiary.'

'It will go to his daughter, Caroline.'

'Quite so.'

'Mr Elsworth, this is proving to be a major task. You realise it takes time to approach publishers, and even more to convince them you have a book worth publishing? Getting to the production stage can easily take another eighteen months. And I haven't even started writing the book yet.'

'Yes, so I believe. It's true you don't have much time, Mr Buckley. But then, there's nothing like an approaching deadline for focusing the mind, I find.'

That sounded a bit rich coming from somebody in the legal profession, whose sole aim, in my experience, was to delay things as long as possible to maximise their fees. But I decided to let it pass. I couldn't risk antagonising Mr Elsworth, because I needed his help. Besides, I had enough enemies already.

'Also, you realise that if nobody is interested in publishing the thing as a commercial proposition, I'd have to spend money myself on having it produced?' I said.

'I dare say.'

'Well, I can't afford to do that. My financial circumstances are rather difficult at the moment. Not to put too fine a point on it, I may be facing bankruptcy.'

'I'm very sorry to hear that, Mr Buckley. Very sorry indeed. How did this come about?'

'A business enterprise has run into problems. There are debts to meet. I don't see any way of being able to pay for the publication of the book myself. Unless some of Great-Uncle Samuel's bequest could be released in advance.'

'Ah.' He looked genuinely sorry. 'I really don't think I can help you. There's no provision in the will for releasing all, or even part, of this bequest in advance of the conditions being met.' He stared thoughtfully at the ceiling for a moment. 'Mmm. I suppose it might be argued that the executors have the power to make that concession on their own judgement.'

'But you're the executor, aren't you, Mr Elsworth?'

'I'm one of two,' he said. 'The other executor would have to be in full agreement before such a thing could even be considered.'

'And the other executor?' I asked. But I knew before he told me, and my hopes had already faded.

'Miss Caroline Longden.'

Caroline thought her father had made a serious error in asking me to help him, maybe even a fatal error. She was suspicious of me, and perhaps a bit jealous. No doubt she would like to ask for the papers back, but once she'd seen the will, it wasn't possible for her to do that. Yet as an executor of the will, she could make it impossible for me to get my hands on the money.

It had been only a faint hope to help me out of what seemed a deeper and deeper hole I was sinking into. But my meeting with Mr Elsworth had done one thing – it had finally convinced me that I'd have to concentrate my energies on the book. Circumstances had conspired to paint me into a corner, with no other options.

I'd rung Laura and arranged to take Rachel's notes to her at the George on Wednesday night. I presented them to her proudly, as if I was offering a bouquet of flowers. She looked through them quizzically.

'Who wrote this, Chris?'

'Rachel. That's my neighbour. It's her theory, not mine.'

'But who were these enemies? Why should William Buckley have had enemies? He was only the resident engineer. It couldn't even have been a business rivalry. Why should anyone have bothered with him, unless he really was a thief or embezzler? Even then, the law would have dealt with him. Penalties were pretty severe in those days, you know.'

'Hanging for stealing a sheep and all that. Yes, I know.'

'Hanging or transportation, in the case of theft.'

She threw Rachel's notes down on the table scornfully and picked up Samuel's manuscript. 'I'll read this during the next day or two, then I might be able to do something for you. Quite honestly, if that's the best you and your friend can do, it looks as though you need me. Otherwise, you're never going to have anything worth publishing. Next year or at any other time.'

'That's great.'

'Shall we meet up next weekend? How about Sunday?'

'Well, actually, I've got to go and see somebody next Sunday.'

'Oh?' She looked at me sharply. 'Somebody to do with the book?'

'Yes, a friend of Samuel's.'

'Who is this? You haven't mentioned him before.'

I told her about Godfrey Wheeldon, pleased at the concentrated attention she gave to what I was saying. Though I hadn't spoken to the man himself, someone at the nursing home had assured me that Mr Wheeldon would be delighted to have visitors.

'And you think you'll be able to get anything out of this old man, do you?'

220

'Well—'

'I wish you luck. But you're not the most comfortable of people at meeting strangers, are you, Chris? Still, we'll have to arrange some other time to meet. Give me a ring if you like, but I might be away next week.'

I had a brainwave then, and couldn't wait to share it with her. 'Why don't you come with me?'

'I'm sorry?'

'Come with me to see Wheeldon. You can make up for my social deficiencies. You might be able to ask him questions I wouldn't think of. Don't you think you'd find it interesting, Laura?'

'Well, you could be right. And he lives where?'

'A nursing home a few miles the other side of Chester. We can get there in an hour or two.'

'All right then. Since I've nothing else to do.'

'Excellent. And when we get back, I'll take you to dinner as a reward.'

She smiled, and my heart gave a little lurch. 'We'll see about that,' she said.

30

Sunday couldn't come round fast enough as far as I was concerned. By Friday I was already eaten away with impatience, and I couldn't seem to concentrate on anything. And, unaccountably, I began to feel uncomfortable being alone for the first time I could remember.

I went into the office that morning, my last day as a council employee, and attended my meeting with HR. The news was exactly what I'd expected. Without too much sympathy, I was told that the days when the department could afford to employ three information officers were over. The time had come to bite the bullet and accept cutbacks.

The tone of the delivery was such that I was made to feel I ought to have known all these things already, which indeed I did. I had to admire the system that had left me in no doubt of my fate long before it came to the point of someone telling me. It saved embarrassing scenes.

Since I'd worked for the council for less than two years, the pay-off I'd get was negligible – certainly not enough to keep me alive for more than a few months. Unemployment was staring me in the face, and destitution was lurking at its shoulder.

The HR manager even had the nerve to ask if I needed any help to cope with my redundancy. Did she mean counselling? The word seemed to be on the tip of her tongue.

'Your colleagues say you haven't been yourself for some time,' she said. 'I believe there was a family bereavement?'

'Both my mother and father died within three months of each other.'

'Awful. That sort of trauma can have a lasting impact. Emotionally and—'

'Psychologically?'

She winced at the word. 'I wish we'd known sooner that you were struggling.'

'I haven't been struggling,' I said quickly, trying to sound confident, though my voice let me down with that sudden crack on the last word.

'But it's not too late,' she said, as if I hadn't spoken. 'We can still offer you help.'

I'd stood up then. I recognised when it was time to go.

My colleagues in the office practically ignored me, leaving me plenty of time to clear out the rest of the accumulated rubbish in my desk. At lunchtime, one of the IT team wandered in and tentatively invited me out for a drink at the local pub. But I declined politely. It wasn't his fault. It was just that I associated him with Dan Hyde, who'd worked closely with him until he had left the council. And Dan wasn't my favourite person at the moment.

At some point, we had to arrange a visit to see the bank manager about our loan and negotiate easier repayments over a longer period. The aim, as far as I was concerned, would be to try to delay things long enough for me to claim Samuel Longden's bequest. The other creditors would have to be stalled for a while.

Rachel had already been away for two days by then. She was staying with her family in Hendon, and looking forward to some visits to London theatres and musicals. *Miss Saigon* had been mentioned, and the highlight would be a matinee of *Cats*. Rachel had been excited about the prospect for weeks.

Without her, it was too quiet at Maybank. It was strange having no one watching me drive off in the mornings, and no *Riverdance* numbers thumping through the walls. There was nobody walking in through my back door at the most inconvenient moments, or keeping a check on my visitors while pretending to sweep the leaves from the path. No one to be concerned about my welfare.

I knew Rachel had a small group of girlfriends she went out with. It would be ridiculous to feel jealous, and wonder how much she was enjoying herself. I was perfectly fine here on my own, with the cat.

So I turned to my pile of CDs. I had Suede and Pulp on top of the stack, but I felt the need to go back a few years before Britpop. Ah yes, there were Bowie and U2, redolent of a different period in my life. *Achtung Baby* had the right tone to it. I turned up the volume to listen to The Edge's guitar and Bono singing about the end of world until he got to 'Love is Blindness', when it no longer felt so satisfying.

In Lichfield, a thin sprinkling of snow overnight had made everything look clean and new. But underneath was the same old winter mud, the same dirt-stained pavements. A town crier walked round the market square wearing a three-cornered hat and ringing his handbell, advertising an indoor market. *Big Issue* sellers stood on the corner of Baker's Lane complimenting passing businessmen on their suits to charm them into buying a copy of their paper.

I was already committed to completing the project bequeathed to me by my Great-Uncle Samuel. To contemplate anything else would have been too painful, even without Caroline Longden's efforts to twist the knife and Simon Monks's attempts at intimidation. But since the funeral, there was one part of the picture I hadn't quite got clear in my mind. Before I could come to terms with Samuel's death, I had to be sure how and why he'd died.

Finally, Sunday arrived and I set off early to collect Laura from the George. She looked a bit askance at the Escort, and I was uncomfortably aware of the contrast with her Mercedes.

But I could hardly have asked her to drive me to Cheshire. She was already doing me a big favour, and I was treading on eggshells trying to keep her interested.

The drive was nearly eighty miles, up the M6 and round the bypass at Nantwich to get onto the A51. As we crossed the Cheshire Plain, I found I was telling Laura all about myself. She had an undoubted skill at subtle questioning, winkling out everything she wanted to know without seeming intrusive, then listening with a flattering absorption, as if what I had to say was the most interesting thing she'd ever heard. Even as I talked, I congratulated myself on my coup in getting her on my side. She would be a great asset.

'So the business venture has gone down with a heap of debts, and now I'm on the dole,' I said. 'That's my story. I'm a bit of a disaster all round, really.'

It didn't sound very impressive, but Laura wasn't daunted.

'And your parents have died?' she said.

'Yes, in the last year. My father just three months ago.'

'I'm sorry.'

'No need to be.'

'Did you get on with them?'

'Does anybody get on with their parents?'

'Only if they don't have to live with them.'

'That's true. I found them almost tolerable while I was living in Stafford.'

'Was it your father or your mother you didn't get on with?'

'I don't know really.'

'It's usually one or the other.'

I watched the Cheshire villages spinning by. They had curious English names in this part of the world, and I saw signs for Tilstone Fearnall, Bunbury, and Aston juxta Mondrum. Laura looked at me thoughtfully, but didn't press me. I didn't mind talking to her about myself. I'd do it as much as she liked. But my parents weren't a subject I was comfortable with.

'What about you, then?' I said as we skirted the Delamere Forest. 'What's Laura Jenner's story?'

'I'm out of a job too.'

'Oh yes – the researcher's job. What happened?'

'It was just one of those things. A few projects were cancelled, and they didn't need me any more. It happens like that in television. In a few months' time, they'll probably be begging me to come back.'

'Are you local?'

'My family is from Cannock originally. I can remember walking the dogs on the Chase when I was little. But we moved away to a place outside Stourbridge. Dad runs a financial services business in Birmingham. He's done pretty well for himself, I suppose.'

She said it in the casual way that people do when they've come to take money for granted. I remembered the green Mercedes, and wondered whether she'd actually managed to buy that out of her researcher's salary, or if it was a present from Daddy.

'But for a few years I've been living in London, of course.'

'What made you come back to Staffordshire? Nostalgia?'

She laughed. 'Partly. But I'm not looking for my roots like you are, Chris.'

'I'm not looking for my roots either,' I said, offended at the very idea. It made me sound like some American tourist bolstering his uncertain identity by trying to prove he was related to Mary, Queen of Scots.

'Aren't you?'

'Not really. Well, not like you mean anyway.'

I noticed Laura had deflected my enquiry.

'But you didn't answer my question.' I said.

For the first time since I'd met her, she looked uneasy. A lot of people don't like talking about themselves, particularly if they've had problems in their lives or they don't have any

226

pride in what they've achieved. There were very few people I would have opened up to myself, for the same reasons.

'What do you want to know?' she said, passing the ball back into my court.

'What brought you back to Staffordshire?' I searched for the right words to use. 'A relationship?'

She tilted her head to look at me, as if she didn't recognise the word. 'Do you mean a man?'

'I suppose so.'

'No, there's no one here.'

'But someone in London maybe?'

'Of course, I've had my . . . relationships.'

'Children?'

Silence. I glanced at her, taking my eyes off the road for a second. Her expression had changed, a dark cloud passing across her face. I wondered if I'd touched a nerve. She wasn't quite so cool and composed as she tried to appear. Was this why she didn't like talking about herself?

'I'm sorry,' I said, concentrating on the road again.

'It's all right,' she said. 'No children. No husband, either. Plenty of relationships, good and bad. That's life, isn't it?'

'So they tell me.'

She paused. 'To be honest, Chris, I've never really known what I've wanted to do with my life. No job I've ever done has felt satisfying. Do you ever get the feeling that you're just drifting through life, bumping against one thing or another by pure chance, then spinning away downstream again? It's hard to know where I'll end up.'

'That's not necessarily a bad thing,' I said. I was thinking of my father, who'd worked for the same company all his life. A bit of spinning downstream might have made him a better person.

'Oh, but it could be,' said Laura.

When we got near Ellesmere, we passed under the M53 and over the Grand Union Canal into a residential area near

Wolverham. The Old Vicarage nursing home was what it said, a converted vicarage set in a street of Victorian detached houses. A new two-storey extension had been added some time in the last ten years or so.

A care assistant called Chloe showed us into a clean, neat room with white furniture and a large window that let plenty of light in. The room looked so bright and fresh that the appearance of Godfrey Wheeldon himself came as a shock. He'd wasted away until there was almost nothing solid underneath his layers of clothing. The skin had sagged on his cheekbones, and his eyes were sunken, though they glistened with life and curiosity. His hands and wrists were skeletally thin, and they moved constantly with a restless, nervous energy. Perhaps his body had concentrated all its energy in his face and hands – for his lower half was quite useless, and he was confined to an electric wheelchair that he spun across the room with twitchy jabs of his fingers on the controls.

'Samuel Longden, Samuel Longden,' he said after we'd introduced ourselves. 'Wonderful. I'm very glad you came.'

'You know he died, don't you?' I said, anxious to make sure of our footing from the start.

'Oh yes. His daughter phoned and told the people who run this place. They decided to break it to me gently. Silly beggars. Do they think death comes as a shock to somebody my age? I would have liked to have gone to Samuel's funeral, but it wasn't possible. I'm a bit trapped, as you can see, and it's a long way to Lichfield. Still . . . I'm sure it was a good send-off.'

'Samuel would have been pleased. They took him by boat on the canal.'

'Ah. Wonderful, wonderful.'

'How well did you know Samuel?' asked Laura.

'Oh, that's the funny thing. I suppose you'd say I hardly knew him at all. But Samuel was the only new friend I'd made for many, many years. Certainly since I've been in here. You'd be surprised how important that made him to my life. In fact, I don't expect you to understand it at all.'

'So it meant a lot to you that he visited. Did he come often?'

'Just three times, dear. Sad, isn't it? But the fact is that those three visits were the highlights of the past ten years for me. He was the last visitor I had, until you.'

'We'd like to ask what Samuel told you,' I said. 'I can explain why it's important, if you like.'

'I don't mind talking to you,' said Godfrey. 'I'll tell you anything. But only if you take me somewhere out of this place.'

'But is that all right?' I eyed his skeletal frame and the useless legs. 'I mean—'

'Don't worry, I won't die on you or anything like that. I'm allowed out, on account of my good behaviour. It's just that I don't have anywhere to go, or anyone to go with, which is not the same thing at all. Worse, of course. That's really being trapped. Is it a deal?'

'Okay.' I envisaged a quiet stroll somewhere nearby, and remembered the towpath we'd crossed a few yards from the nursing home. 'Do you want to go along the canal?'

'The canal? Are you joking?' snapped Godfrey irritably, spinning his chair. 'What would I want to do that for? I want to go to the zoo.'

'Where?'

'Chester. I want to go to Chester. They've got a good zoo there.'

'Yes, I've heard of it.'

'I'd like to see the animals.'

'Fine.'

With a flick of his finger he accelerated towards the door of his room, and we stepped back hastily out of his way. Godfrey swung the door back and shouted along the landing.

'Chloe! Chloe! I need a folding wheelchair. I'm going out.'

31

We manoeuvred Godfrey into the front seat of the Escort, and I managed to figure out how to fold the wheelchair so that it could fit into the boot, with the old man giving instructions over his shoulder.

'The handles fold back if you pull those little rods – that's right. Now lift the foot rests back and fold the seat up. Wonderful.'

The drive took us away from the Mersey estuary, with a short run down the M53 until we came off near Chester. The hills of North Wales were visible in the distance, with an unidentifiable peak still capped in snow glinting in a trickle of sunlight.

Laura and I shared the cost of Godfrey's admission to the zoo, and we wheeled him past enclosures of South American monkeys, orangutans and gorillas, and an area full of tunnels in the ground occupied by little prairie dogs. The air was sour with the scent of animal dung, and loud with the excited screams of children.

'I brought my grandsons here once,' said Godfrey, 'before I went into the Old Vicarage. The boys would have been about eight and ten at the time.'

'How old are they now?' asked Laura. But he didn't answer. 'What are their names?' It was probably the way she'd heard people talk to the elderly about their grandchildren, but with Godfrey it didn't seem to work. 'They'll be grown up by now, I suppose.'

'I suppose so,' he said, but there was something in his tone that suggested he'd withdrawn from the conversation.

'Don't they come and see you?' asked Laura.

Godfrey pointed. 'I want to see the big cats. I think they're over that side.'

Since it was the weekend, the zoo was full of visitors. Most of them were families – young couples with two or three children running around them, or older people struggling to keep up with their charges. Sometimes it was difficult to tell who was the most excited at the sight of a grinning chimp – the child or the grandparent. They were united in an ability to give themselves up to wonderment in a way the parents seemed to have lost.

'Yes, Samuel came to see me three times,' said Godfrey.

'Had you known him for a long time?'

'About a year.'

'That's not very long. I imagined you must have known him from years back. Weren't you connected with his business?'

'Me? Not likely. I worked as a tanker driver at the oil refinery up the road.'

'Runcorn? So how did you meet Great-Uncle Samuel?'

'He wrote to me, out of the blue. He said he was working on a family history project, and he'd traced my name.'

'But surely you aren't related to him?'

Godfrey started laughing and wheezing. 'Look at your face! Did you think you'd found another long-lost relative? Sorry to disappoint. Or perhaps it isn't a disappointment. Who'd want an old wreck like me in the family?'

I looked at Laura in perplexity as we passed the giraffe house with its towering doors like space shuttle hangars.

'You must have some link to one of the ancestors he was writing about,' she said, touching Godfrey gently on his emaciated arm.

'Almost right, dear. Well done,' he said, patting her hand.

231

'Only it was more that he thought one of my ancestors was linked to one of his.'

With his hand still on Laura's, he turned his face up to look at me. There was a twinkle in his eyes, as if he hadn't enjoyed himself so much in a long time.

'Would you like me to explain?'

'That's what we've come for,' I said impatiently.

'Now, now – allow me to have my fun. I'll tell you all about it. Look, there are the big cats, over there. Tigers. I like tigers.'

We pushed him towards the big cat enclosures and got as close as we could to the bars. We watched for a while as a male Bengal tiger paced up and down, his muscles rolling smoothly in his shoulders under his golden skin.

We parked Godfrey's wheelchair opposite the cage, where there was a bench for Laura and me to sit on. The old man seemed to slip into a reverie for a few moments as he watched the tiger. He was oblivious to the families passing in front of him, and had forgotten the two of us at his side.

'Samuel Longden,' he said eventually. He looked around vaguely, as if unsure where he was. 'Was it Samuel?'

I wondered if we'd made a mistake. Perhaps Godfrey Wheeldon's mind was too far gone for him to be any use. Though he had seemed lucid at the Old Vicarage, he was growing more vague by the minute. I had little experience with very old people, but I knew their rationality could fluctuate dramatically.

'Do you remember why Samuel first came to see you, Godfrey?'

His eyes focused on me again. 'Of course I remember. Do you think I'm ga-ga?'

'Certainly not.'

'Some of the old biddies back at that place are completely senile, you know. Totally over the bridge. But I'm not like them.'

'You had a link to one of his ancestors,' said Laura quietly.

'No, one of my ancestors was linked to one of his. You're not listening properly. It all started with some letters.'

'Samuel wrote to you?'

'No, no. These were old letters. From some ancestor of Samuel's to my great-great-great grandfather or something.'

'Reuben Wheeldon,' I said.

Godfrey clapped his hands in delight. 'You know!'

'Reuben Wheeldon was a friend of William Buckley, the resident engineer on the Ogley and Huddlesford Canal at the end of the 18th century.'

'That's right. William was an ancestor of Samuel's, as I said.'

'And of mine.'

'Well, I managed to figure that out,' said Godfrey scornfully. 'Being as how your name's Buckley too. I did tell you—'

'You're not ga-ga. Sorry, Godfrey.'

'Samuel had tracked down this Reuben's family, and eventually he came up with my name. He traced me here. I don't know how he did it, but there are ways, aren't there?' He looked to us for confirmation, and I nodded. 'He wanted to show me the letters.'

Godfrey began to cough. I was reminded of the car park attendant's account of a man with a hacking cough he'd heard on the parking levels just before Samuel was killed, the same cough I'd heard myself that night in Castle Dyke. It was an appallingly small thing to go on. It might have been a heavy smoker like the attendant's father, or a sufferer from a chronic condition like bronchitis or asthma. But it might just as easily have been a person with a bad cold, which had now passed off. The one bit of evidence I had could have been wiped out by a good night's sleep and a Lemsip.

The tiger had continued to pace throughout our

233

conversation. Where at first glance he'd seemed a powerful, noble animal, the more I looked at him, the more he diminished into a tired creature whose eyes contained a kind of hopeless longing.

'He doesn't like being caged either, does he?' said Godfrey.

The old man became tired of talking and made no objection when we suggested taking him back to the Old Vicarage. But before we left the zoo, I got Laura and Godfrey together in front of the chimpanzee enclosure and took their photograph, promising to send Godfrey a copy when I'd had it printed. But it was Laura I really wanted a token of.

We went up to Godfrey's room with him when we returned. I was about to write the visit off as a waste of time, but Godfrey had a couple of surprises for me. First, he pointed upwards with a bony finger.

'Lift down that old suitcase from the top of the wardrobe,' he said. 'They keep on at me to throw it out, but it has all my little mementos in it. You have to keep something to remind you, or your brain goes completely. Some of the folks here have forgotten everything they ever knew. They sit propped in front of the telly all day. In their minds, they live in *Coronation Street* or in the audience of *Blind Date*. Pitiful.'

The suitcase was brown and battered, and when we sprang the catches, the lid flipped open in a twisted shape, as if it had been heavily trodden on.

'There's all sorts of stuff in there,' said Godfrey eagerly. 'I've got a whole collection of cigarette cards. One set was famous cricketers from the 1920s. Samuel was very interested in those.'

'We haven't got a lot of time,' said Laura kindly.

He sighed. 'Yes, I know. We old folk can be a bore. You're interested in the letters, aren't you?'

Laura and I looked at each other. 'Letters from Samuel?' I said.

'No, no, from his ancestor.'

'William Buckley.'

'That's him.'

Godfrey passed me a brown A4 envelope. There were three letters inside – letters from William Buckley to Reuben Wheeldon. I glanced at the dates, and saw they followed closely the two I already had.

'I'd never heard of Reuben Wheeldon until Samuel mentioned him,' said Godfrey. 'He must be related to me, but it's too late for me to care now.'

'But the letters—'

'Samuel gave them to me to look after. I suppose he must have had his reasons.'

I remembered how I'd got Godfrey's address from Mrs Wentworth, and the package she wanted me to ask him about.

'You sent something to Samuel recently,' I said. 'It arrived after his death and was delivered to his neighbour. A parcel of some kind?'

'Oh, that.' He smiled. 'It doesn't matter now. It was nothing.'

'Are you sure?'

'Completely.'

Then there came a moment when Godfrey seemed to make a decision. It was as if we'd passed a test.

He said: 'Did Samuel mention a box?' He grinned when he saw me hesitate. 'The canal owners' box.'

'Yes,' I said, not sure whether I should tell him that I actually had it in my possession.

The old man nodded, tilting his head sideways as he looked at me. 'Samuel was funny about that box. He told me it was important, but he wouldn't say why. He could be very mysterious when he wanted to. Also, he made me keep these. But they'll only get thrown away when I kick the bucket. Take them, will you?'

He pulled something from a pocket stitched into the lid

of the suitcase. It was wrapped in a bit of newspaper, folded and sealed with tape.

'You're his family, aren't you?' he said. 'Family meant a lot to Samuel. With some people, friendship is more important. But with Samuel, it was the Buckleys above anything else. It was his family he always talked about, all the time. So I reckon you're the one he wanted me to give these to. He must have trusted you.'

I took the object from him. Even through the paper, I could tell straightaway what it was. Godfrey had given me a set of keys.

Laura and I ate a late lunch at a pub near Chester. While we waited to be served, I pulled the tape of the little package Godfrey had given me and unfolded the newspaper. There were two keys on a ring. Much to my disappointment, they looked nothing like the two big iron keys that fitted the canal owners' box. These were smaller and more modern, gold coloured keys like something made for a Yale door lock.

Laura watched me as I folded them back up and put them away.

'Not what you expected?' she said.

'It's hard to know what to expect any more.'

'I know what you mean.'

I looked up at her in surprise. Her tone of voice was different, a suggestion of some underlying sadness that I hadn't noticed before. I wondered what her story really was. All that stuff about walking the dog on Cannock Chase, her father's successful business – it was all too superficial. I realised I didn't know anything much about her at all. What reason did she give for being back in Staffordshire from her home in London? She didn't, did she? She'd evaded the question.

The trouble was, it only made her more intriguing. I needed to find out more.

We were back in Lichfield before the end of the afternoon.

I was wondering how to broach the subject of dinner and what we might do together in the evening, but Laura asked if we could call at Fosseway, and I postponed the subject.

At Fosseway, work on the lock was almost complete, and they were about to start clearing the earth and debris that filled the canal basin. Between the lock and the wharf had once stood a bridge, but it had been demolished many years before, leaving only the stumps of its buttresses, which now stood out from the undergrowth like broken teeth. Brickies were busy laying coping bricks on the wing walls of the bridge, while a new butyl membrane had been laid in the channel of the canal itself, and the towpath had been surfaced with crushed stone. The lock area was looking in good shape.

To one side, a tracked excavator and two massive six-tonne dumpers had arrived on the site, ready for the major job of tackling the basin and the wharf. The dumpers completely dwarfed the vehicle normally used by the restoration trust, and the excavator was even bigger. Equipment like this was expensive, but necessary. When the abandoned wharf began to re-emerge, it would all be worthwhile. Every bit of old brickwork was an encouragement, physical evidence of the past reappearing from its premature grave.

'We've had a chap down here today claiming to be your cousin or something,' said Andrew. 'He was asking a lot of questions. Seemed a bit jumpy, though. Odd sort.'

'Was he thin, with ginger hair, thinning on top?'

'That's him. A strange family you've got all of a sudden, Chris. Where are they all coming from?'

Laura looked at me quizzically.

'Frank Chaplin,' I said. 'Not really my cousin. He's Alison Chaplin's son.'

'What would he be doing down here?' she asked.

'I don't know.'

'Maybe he was looking for you, Chris. Perhaps he wants you to take him in for a while.'

'He'll be lucky.'

'You don't like him, then? What's he done to you?'

I bit my lip, annoyed at her inquisitiveness. I didn't mind when it concerned dead ancestors, but with living relatives it was a different matter. Even a step-cousin. There was no way I was going to drag out Frank Chaplin's sordid story for Laura or anybody else.

She shrugged and turned to go back to the car. I was about to follow her when Andrew took my arm to hold me back.

'Chris, have you heard about our big event tomorrow?' he said.

'What's that?'

'We've got our celebrity coming down for a visit. That's why we're working flat out today to make sure there's something to show him.'

'I didn't know you had a celebrity.'

'Yes, you did. You've seen him. You thought he was impressive. Our junior minister.'

'What, Lindley Simpson?'

'The man himself. He's asked for a guided tour, so some of us will be down here tomorrow to meet him. It'll be a bit of a photo opportunity, and the local press will be here. Why don't you come along?'

'I might do that.'

Andrew leaned closer. 'Nice,' he said, nodding his head towards Laura. 'Are you taking her out somewhere?'

'We're just coming back from a day out in Cheshire actually,' I said, pleased to have impressed him. 'A place you might know – Ellesmere.'

'I do know it – there's a big waterways museum there.'

'We didn't go to the museum. We were visiting a friend of Samuel Longden's.'

He raised his eyebrows. 'Somebody as exciting as the Captain, was it?'

I laughed. 'Interesting maybe. But I'd hardly call Godfrey

238

Wheeldon exciting. He's rather a lonely old man in a nursing home.'

'Well, that might be the fate for all of us one day, Chris. Don't keep her waiting, will you?'

I caught up with Laura and we walked back to the Escort, stepping to the side of the mud as far as possible.

'Where to next, madam?'

'Back to the George, I think. I could do with a shower and a change of clothes after all that mud and all those animals.'

'Yes, of course.'

'But then, later on – I think there was some talk of dinner? Does the offer still stand?'

'You bet it does.'

32

I didn't get back to Maybank until nearly one o'clock in the morning. I was feeling exhausted, but pretty pleased with myself. Having dinner with Laura had succeeded in pushing Samuel Longden and all those Buckleys completely from my mind for a while. I was tired, but bursting with self-satisfaction.

It was a feeling that wasn't to last long, though. The good things never do.

I saw the lights of the police car from Gaia Lane before I even turned the corner. It was parked in my driveway, and there were lights blazing, not only at number four but at my house as well, though I'd left it locked when I set off that morning.

A policeman intercepted me as soon as I pulled the Escort in behind his car.

'Would it be Mr Buckley, sir?'

'What the hell's going on?'

'Nothing to worry about, sir. You've had a bit of a break-in.'

'You're joking. What have they taken?'

'Not very much, it seems. Your next-door neighbour disturbed them.'

'Rachel? Where is she?'

'Having a cup of tea. She's a bit shaken up,' he said complacently.

'Was she attacked?'

'Nothing serious.'

'It may not be serious to you, mate.'

'I quite understand, sir,' said the policeman, unruffled.

He watched me as I walked through the garden and stepped over the fence to number four. 'CID will be here shortly, sir,' he called. 'They'll want you to go through your house with them to see if anything's missing.'

'Sure.'

Rachel was sitting at her kitchen table clutching a mug of tea, with a female police officer sitting across from her. The first thing that struck me was that the policewoman had taken her hat off, and it lay on the table between them like a chequered tea cosy. The second thing I noticed was that Rachel had been crying, and she had a bruise developing on the side of her face.

'Rachel – are you all right?'

'Chris, I'm sorry,' she blurted.

'What are you sorry for? They tell me you chased off some burglars.'

'Hardly. If I'd thought a bit quicker, I could have phoned the police straightaway, and they might have caught them.'

'It would be better to do that next time,' said the police-woman. 'We don't usually encourage people to have a go.'

Rachel touched the red patch on her cheekbone and smiled nervously. 'I suppose I was a bit silly.'

'Tell me what happened.'

'I'll make another pot of tea, shall I?' asked the police-woman cheerfully, edging aside to let me sit down. She wore a thick, ribbed sweater and her waist was hung with an awkward assortment of equipment that clattered as she moved.

'Well, it was a few minutes after twelve,' said Rachel. 'I was looking out of the front window, watching . . . well, I was just looking out of the window, when I thought I saw

241

something moving near your car port. I couldn't make out what it was, because the street lights don't reach that far. You really ought to get an outside light, you know.'

I noticed the hesitation when she'd almost admitted why she was at the window at midnight. It didn't take much imagination to guess that she'd been watching for me to come home, wondering why I was so late and trying to guess what I'd been doing.

'Perhaps you're right,' I said.

'Anyway, I went to the back window, in the kitchen here. I thought perhaps you'd come back without your car, that you'd broken down somewhere and had to walk. I waited a few minutes, but I didn't hear your door, and no lights came on. I started to think I was imagining things, or that it was only a cat I'd seen. But then I heard a noise.'

She took a swallow of her tea, and her eyes grew worried as she remembered the next few minutes.

'What sort of noise was this?'

'A sort of cracking noise. Not metal or wood. I couldn't place it at all, but I knew it just didn't sound right.'

'It turned out to be your kitchen window,' put in the policewoman, pouring me a mug of tea. 'Neat, professional job it was.'

She sounded almost admiring of the burglars. But I suppose the police see all sorts of break-ins that aren't neat and professional. You hear horrendous stories about the kind of gratuitous damage that hooligans and drug addicts do when they get into a house looking for money or small items to sell.

'But surely you didn't go out to see what was happening?'

'Well, yes, that's exactly what I did,' said Rachel. 'Stupid, wasn't it?'

'You could have got badly hurt.'

She touched the bruise again. 'I realised that too late, of course.'

242

'It's a pity you didn't get a good look at him,' said the policewoman.

'He was halfway through the window,' Rachel told me. 'Just his legs and his back half showing. I shouted out when I saw him, I think. He panicked a bit and started kicking out.'

'You surely didn't grab hold of him?' I said, looking at her bruise.

'No, he lashed out with his feet and caught me in the face. Then he kicked me again and I fell down. The next thing I knew, he was out of the window and running off. He was much too fast for me, and he'd vanished before I even knew what was happening. I suppose I was a bit dazed.'

'You ought to get medical attention,' I said. 'She ought to get medical attention,' I repeated to the policewoman.

'We did want to call a doctor,' she said.

'I refused,' said Rachel. 'It's only a little bruise.'

The policeman from outside stuck his head through the door. 'Mr Buckley? CID would like a word, if you don't mind.'

I went out and walked round to my side of Maybank. A woman was standing looking at the broken window. She turned to look at me as I arrived, and I recognised her.

'It's DC Hanlon, isn't it? I didn't expect to see you again.'

She gave me a curt nod. 'I had the bad luck to be the duty CID officer tonight, that's all.'

'And what have you detected so far?'

She carefully ignored the sarcasm. 'It sounds from what PC Fenwick tells me that the burglar didn't have long in your house. He was already coming out when your neighbour saw him. But he might have had an accomplice inside. You never know.'

'I, er . . .'

'Don't worry,' she said. 'PC Fenwick and his colleague have made sure there's no one still in there. They've even put the lights on for us. In any case, you've got me here to protect you.'

243

It didn't take long to see that the contents of the house were undisturbed. At least, the TV, stereo and computer were still there, which were the only things I had worth stealing, and there were no drawers pulled out or cupboards emptied. The only damage was the hole in the window.

'We'll get someone along later this morning to see if they can get any prints off the window frame,' said Hanlon. 'But frankly, it's unlikely.'

'I'm glad you're taking it seriously, anyway. I've always thought there were so many burglaries these days that the police hardly bothered with them.'

She gave me a thin smile. 'To be honest, it's the assault on Mrs Morgan we're concerned about. We always take violent crime seriously. A broken window is trivial in itself, but any evidence we could find to help us identify the perpetrator would be useful.'

'I see. So what do you do now?'

'I'm going to take a statement from Mrs Morgan.'

I waited in the front room, nursing a bottle of whisky, until I saw the police car leave, shortly followed by Hanlon's Renault. Then I nipped back round to number four and knocked on the back door.

'Are you all right, Rachel?'

She looked a lot better. Her eyes were brighter, with no sign of tears now and a bit of colour back in her face so the red mark didn't stand out as much. I sniffed the air, suspecting that she might have been at the whisky bottle herself.

'Come in a minute,' she said conspiratorially. 'They've all gone.'

'I know. I wanted to thank you properly.'

'What for?'

'Well, you were defending my property, weren't you? That was real good neighbourliness.'

She smiled. It was very quiet in the kitchen, almost cosy, now that the police had left and there were just the two of us. There's something about the early hours of the morning that makes you feel the rest of the world has disappeared.

'Did the burglar take anything then?' asked Rachel.

'We checked the usual stuff. All present and correct. I was rather hoping he'd have taken the old carriage clock, but he even left that. You obviously copped him before he got started.'

She looked steadily at me, and I felt she could see straight though me, that she knew exactly where I'd been that night and what I'd been doing.

'Never mind all that,' she said.

I gave in. 'Yes, you're right. The blue folder has gone. Great-Uncle Samuel's manuscript is missing.'

'Oh, no.'

I started trying to persuade Rachel to go to bed. She didn't argue too much, as she was clearly suffering from the same overwhelming tiredness that I felt, though from a different cause.

But first she started rambling about how lucky it was that Samuel's notes and the canal owners' box had been in her house, not mine. She seemed particularly concerned about the safety of the box. But that was ridiculous. I began to wonder whether she'd got a crack on the head after all. Concussion can do strange things to the brain, and the worst effects can sometimes be delayed. Who would even know about the box, and why should they go to the trouble of breaking into my house to get it?

'I suppose I'll have to re-create the entire manuscript from scratch,' I said.

'Not quite,' said Rachel. 'I still have the first chapter.'

'William Buckley and the canal proprietors? Well, it's a start anyway.'

'Did you tell the police the folder had gone?' she asked, reading my face again.

'No, I didn't.'

'Why not?'

'I don't really know,' I said.

I thought about it for a while, but my weary brain couldn't even analyse my own motives. 'Like DC Hanlon said herself, the attack on you is more serious.'

Rachel accepted this with a curiously pleased smile. She disappeared from the kitchen for a moment, then came back with the file and the box. The wooden surfaces had been painstakingly polished, so that it gleamed like bronze.

'They'll be safe in your house now,' she said.

At last I managed to escape without too many more questions and went back to number six to fix an old piece of board over the broken window, until I could get a glazier in. I was sure Rachel was right – I was safe from another break-in now, since whoever had searched my house had already got what they wanted.

Rachel's concern over the box made me wonder about the keys, though. I had two of them now, thanks to Samuel. Did someone out there have the vital third key, the one that would enable the opening of the box? I resolved to keep the keys separate from the box, just in case. I knew it didn't make sense. The thing was plainly empty in any case.

Seeing the box had reminded me of the keys that Godfrey Wheeldon had given me. There were two of them on the ring, but it had been obvious when I pulled them out that neither of them was anything like the two already in the locks. I tried them anyway. They didn't go anywhere near fitting. It had been far too much to expect.

I picked up the box and shook it. It was still empty, and no amount of imagination could convince me it wasn't. I shrugged my shoulders with weariness, pushed the box back into its place under the sideboard, put the keys away in a drawer, and went to bed.

* * *

I hardly seemed to have fallen asleep when I woke with a start. It was already half past eight, and I was going to be late for work. But then I remembered that I didn't have to go to work any more. It occurred to me that I knew this perfectly well and hadn't set the alarm. And finally, it dawned on me that it was the phone making all the noise.

'Chris? It's Sally Chaplin. I'm sorry to ring you so early.'

'That's all right.' Even in my groggy condition, I could tell from her voice that she was upset about something. 'What's wrong, Sally?'

'It's Frank,' she said, as if the two words explained everything. In a way, I thought, they did. But how much did Sally know?

'He's gone missing,' she added.

'How do you mean, missing?'

'I don't know where he is.'

'It's only half past eight in the morning. When did you last see him?'

'Last night. He stayed up watching TV after I'd gone to bed. He said he wanted to see the late film. It wasn't unusual for him to do that. I'm often asleep by the time he comes to bed. I think that might be the aim, really. Only this time, he wasn't there when I woke up this morning. He's gone, Chris.'

'Have you looked everywhere?' It sounded stupid, but it was the sort of thing people say, and my mind wasn't at its most original.

'I've looked all over the house twice. I thought he must have had a heart attack or something, but I couldn't find him. Then I drove out to the reservoir. That's where he goes, you know.'

'Yes, I know.'

'But he wasn't there either. I walked around for over an hour. Then I came back to ring you.'

'Why me, Sally? I don't know where he is.'

'You came to see him again, didn't you?'

I sighed. No point in lying. 'Yes, there was something I wanted to ask him.'

'I don't know what it was, but he was upset after your visit. I could tell. Did something happen between you?'

'Not exactly. I arrived at the wrong moment, that's all.'

She was quiet for a while. 'I see,' she said miserably. 'You know, then. You know what he does at the reservoir.'

'He didn't think you knew.'

'Oh, I've never seen him in action, but I don't need to.'

'I can't help you. I can't imagine where he's gone.'

'You didn't threaten to . . . expose him, did you?'

'Of course not.'

'I'm worried what he'll do. Something frightened him. He'd been reading in the paper about the canal restoration, some event at Fosseway. Did you talk to him about it?'

'No, nothing like that. In fact, I didn't really get to talk to him about anything.'

'Well, there's something that frightened him.'

By the time Sally hung up, I was completely awake and already sweating as if I had had a hard day. Frank wasn't the only one who was frightened. My imagination was filling me with an irrational fear, a grey, amorphous terror that had no source and no meaning, and certainly no escape. Somewhere out there, it seemed, danger was lurking.

There were several cars pulled onto the grass verge at the Fosseway Wharf site. Normally there would have been no one working there today. But it was a special day when Lindley Simpson MP was visiting to see the site for himself. The restoration group wasn't likely to let an opportunity pass to get publicity from a visit by a government minister.

Simpson hadn't arrived yet, and six or eight restoration group members were standing around with that anxious air of people expecting things to go wrong. I waved to Andrew Hadfield and one or two of the others I knew, and had a quick word with the chairman. He assured me the MP was on his way, though he was running a bit behind schedule. They'd had a call from his mobile, and they expected him in five minutes. The chairman seemed most concerned about the two photographers from the local papers, who were standing by their cars with their camera bags, looking impatient. They were on tight schedules, and needed persuading about the importance of the occasion to make them wait.

I took my own camera with me and went to have a look at how the restoration was progressing. The lock was complete, with its new walls and brick arches, and there were a few inches of water in the bottom.

Passing the bottom gates of the lock, I walked along a short stretch of cleared towpath to where they'd started work on Fosseway Wharf. The trees on either side were thick, and the wharf was out of sight of the road. A 'scrub bashing' party had been clearing undergrowth from the central area, where the basin itself had been filled in with hardcore and a layer of top soil over the years. On the eastern side, the remains of some brick buildings could be made out, and the sides of the wharf were emerging under the assault of shovels.

The big excavator stood nearby. It had already made headway on the mammoth task of digging into the countless tons of earth and rubble that filled the basin, exposing a muddy bottom churned into deep, oozing ruts. For today the excavator had been lined up ready to dig into the debris on the wharf side. A corner had been chosen close to the remains of the bridge, where there was less solid rubble to shift. In fact, with the weeds and undergrowth removed, the earth looked strangely white, as if it contained more lime than soil.

Andrew had been nominated to drive the excavator and was executing a few practice scoops with the shovel. For a while, I admired his skill in manoeuvring the huge machine, backing and spinning it round, steering it to within inches of the bridge abutments, even when it was loaded with a mountain of dirt and debris.

'He's here!' called somebody from the roadside.

There was a flurry of movement, and everyone gathered to greet the party that got out of the big black car. There were four of them altogether. A driver in a dark suit and white shirt got out and stood by the car. A tall man with watchful eyes cast a sharp look over the waiting crowd. Everyone seemed to get a once-over, including me, but especially the press photographers. He watched vigilantly as the other two men walked towards us. Lindley Simpson strode out confidently, clad in a stylish grey overcoat that toned with his hair, with a red and yellow tie the only splash of colour about him. Staying close at his side, heavy-shouldered and unsmiling, was Leo Parker.

For several minutes, Simpson listened carefully while the chairman pointed out the features of the restored lock to him. The little group posed self-consciously in suitable spots, moved on and re-formed into another pose, allowing me and the other photographers to get our pictures. The artificiality of it depressed me, and I soon decided I'd got enough.

As I was putting the camera away in the car, I heard a sound that sent a tingle of excitement up the back of my neck. It was a sudden, racking cough, deep from the lungs, and it carried clearly across the site. I turned quickly and ran my eye over the figures scattered around the wharf and lock. But the spasm had passed, and I couldn't identify the cougher.

Lindley Simpson was gesturing with one hand as he stood talking with the chairman of the restoration group. Leo Parker seemed to be questioning Andrew about a detail of the construction. They stood with their heads down, nodding in unison. There were other restoration group members standing in twos and threes, and nearest to me was Simpson's driver, who was leaning against his car, his gloved hand covering his mouth as if stifling a yawn. I looked around for the tall, watchful man. He was lurking to one side, standing on a mound of soil where he could keep the whole area in view. For a moment, his eyes met mine and something passed between us, cold and suspicious.

And then, in the background, there was another figure I hadn't noticed before. He stood on the far side of the wharf, just beyond the area where the undergrowth had been cleared. His hair stirred in the breeze, and his pale face was caught by the sun. I waved urgently.

'Frank!'

The tall man on the mound stared at me, then followed my gaze and saw the new arrival. He took a couple of determined steps towards him, but that was enough to make Frank look terrified and vanish into the trees.

I ran down the towpath and scrambled up on the stones of the bridge pier. But I knew it was useless – Frank was long gone.

'Who was he?'

I turned to find the tall man had followed me. He was right at my elbow, peering into the trees. 'Somebody I know. A sort of relative.'

'What was he doing?'

'That I don't know. He seemed to be watching something.' I looked around the restoration site, where people were throwing us curious glances. 'Or watching somebody.'

A few minutes later, everyone gathered back into a small crowd to see the excavator start up. Andrew climbed into the cab, while another of the group took charge of the dumper truck and a few others donned hard hats and stood around to direct operations. The aim was to unearth a token section of wharf to symbolise the next phase of the restoration.

It was another staged scene for photographs. One of the pressmen had already left, and I decided that it was time for me to call it a day as well. The trust had their own pocket cameras to record the event for their society newsletter.

As I climbed into the car, I was aware of some excitement among the party on the wharf, but I assumed it was just a minor earth collapse, or the dumper stuck in the mud again. I didn't wait to see what the latest mishap was, because I wanted to get back to Stowe Pool Lane and phone Sally.

So it wasn't until I read the front page of the *Lichfield Echo* on Thursday that I heard about the human remains they'd unearthed at Fosseway Wharf.

33

Pipehill, Lichfield, Staffordshire. Thursday 23rd Jan. 1800.

To Reuben Wheeldon Esq., Warner Street, Ellesmere, Cheshire.

My dear friend,

You earnestly inquire about the failure of the Works. This failure has happened for want of diligence, and I blame no one but myself for the consequence of having often seen much profusion of expence by an unnecessary consumption of Materials. I beg leave to observe that the longer I live, I every year see more into the reasons why estimates are generally exceeded in the Execution and how impossible it is without repeated proofs from experience to conceive how this can happen in so great a degree.

I think it common Justice that no one ought to suffer for the faults of another. I shall use every means that I can to have the Works efficiently re-established, and no expence attending it shall be charged to the Company. Painful as it is to me to lose the good opinion of my Friends, I would rather receive their Censure for the faults of my head than of my heart.

For my own part, I am harassed beyond endurance and hate the sight of the Post that brings me Letters. I am persuaded that the fault in the distressing affair lies partly at my own door. In my Pride and Zealousness I found it necessary to condemn what they have done as deficient both in honesty and good business. By so doing I have raised a Nest of Hornets about me, and I shall have much difficulty in combating the Prejudices of those who pay heed to their spite.

Now I find myself at odds not only with Mr N., but with Mr P. himself, whose regard it distresses me to lose, but whose bitterness is now turned against me. Outwardly he is all politeness, yet at every turn he seeks to thwart me.

With others of their mind they have set themselves against me. Hate is like a poisonous mineral, which eats into the heart, and I fear where their spite may lead them. Yet I am determined to persevere in my chosen course. Events leave me in no doubt where the true interests of Honesty and Justice lie, though this business may be the ruin of me.

You will easily comprehend, from these particulars, that the circumstances are more desperate than they are generally believed to be. The World has been deceived in that respect; and I scruple not to lay all the ill consequences on my own folly alone.

If you should have no objection to receive me into your house, I propose myself the satisfaction of waiting on you and your family and shall probably trespass on your hospitality for two or three days.

Your friend,
Wm Buckley

34

Gruesome find halts restoration scheme

Work on a major waterways restoration scheme was halted yesterday by the discovery of human remains.

Ogley and Huddlesford Canal Restoration Trust members made the gruesome find while clearing earth and debris from the site of the former Fosseway Wharf, near Pipehill. A Trust spokesman said the remains had been concealed in a heap of lime and were uncovered by an excavator driver. 'We were all very shocked,' he said. 'And work stopped immediately.'

Police say the body has not been identified and may have lain undiscovered for some time. They are appealing for anyone with information to come forward.

The incident happened during a visit to the site by Junior Agriculture Minister and local MP Lindley Simpson, who was on a fact-finding mission after recent protests by waterways groups against the proposed South Staffordshire Link Road.

Mr Simpson was unavailable for comment this week.

When I read the article, my first thought was of Frank. Had he committed suicide? But then I read it again, and I noticed the line 'may have lain undiscovered for some time'. That sounded like a police euphemism for a rotting corpse. Frank had been very much alive when the excavator had begun to dig into the lime.

That night Rachel came around again, clutching more notes and looking pleased with herself. These sessions were becoming a regular thing now as we set about re-creating Samuel's stolen manuscript.

Rachel had spent her time fruitfully in the County Record Office at The Friary. She'd scoured the parish register indexes for Buckleys and identified several members of the family in the records for St Chad's. Obtaining an address, she'd gone on to locate them at their Lichfield home in the historical 'snapshots' that were nineteenth-century censuses. For the first time, I saw the names of my great-grandparents, Alfred and Eliza Buckley, of Tamworth Street, Lichfield. Alfred was described as a mercer.

'Alfred's ancestors were a bit more difficult to establish,' said Rachel. 'His parents were boat people, remember.'

'Josiah and Hannah.'

'That's right. So he was probably born in the cabin of a narrowboat, like his brothers and sisters. But I did find a young Alfred Buckley in the 1891 census. He was six years old and described as the nephew of the people he was living with, the Bensons. I'd guess that Mrs Benson must have been the sister of his mother, Hannah.'

'So they sent him to live with his aunt and uncle.'

'Yes. I wonder why?'

'Probably Josiah and Hannah had too many children to cope with on the boats,' I said. 'It was called "putting a child on the bank". It probably meant that he got an education, at least.'

'Lucky for him.'

'But Alfred was left without a father,' I said. 'Josiah was killed.'

'Was he? How?'

I was remembering what Samuel had told me. Josiah Buckley had operated a pair of narrowboats on the Ogley and Huddlesford, but had ended up drowned in the cut. *There was a suggestion at the inquest that he was drunk, which was nonsense. Josiah Buckley was an abstemious man, a teetotaller . . . But, like many canal people, he was quite unable to swim.*

Samuel had described in detail Josiah's body being pulled out of the water from behind a lock gate. His head had been battered against the wall by the pressure of water when the sluices were opened, and his face had been unrecognisable. *It was reported that shortly before his death Josiah had been involved in a fight with another boatman. He'd made himself unpopular with rival carriers by winning a lucrative contract for transporting coal to the power stations. But it seems he was just more efficient and better organised than the others. Probably more honest, too. There were some who didn't like that.*

I repeated to Rachel what Samuel had told me, and she grimaced at the gory details.

'Well, Alfred did all right after that anyway,' she said. 'He was already a mercer by the time he married Eliza Shaw in 1911, and his address was the one in Tamworth Street. I also found an older brother, Thomas.'

'Yes, Thomas was the one who tried to keep the boats operating after his father died, but the business failed.'

'As a child, he seems to have lived on the boats with his parents. But he appears several times in the court records too. He must have been a bit of a bruiser – he was charged several times with affray, often fighting over women it seems. I also came across a paternity order against him. I only found him because Buckley is an unusual name. By the way, he was described as Thomas Buckley aka Thomas Pounder.'

'A pseudonym. I think it was quite common among the boatmen in those days.'

'Really? It sounds a bit suspicious to me.'

'Who are we to judge? I suppose they had their reasons.'

'Well, every family has its black sheep,' said Rachel.

'So both my grandfather and Great-Uncle Samuel would have been born at the house in Tamworth Street, I suppose.'

Rachel hesitated, seemed to consult her notes. 'That's the address your great-grandparents gave when George was baptised at St Chad's. It would help if we could get the later censuses, of course, like 1911 and 1921.'

'Why can't we?'

'The details are subject to the one hundred year rule.'

'Sorry?'

'They're confidential. They're not released until a hundred years have passed. So you won't see the details of the 1901 census until 1st January 2002.'

'We can't wait that long. Go on.'

'Okay. There was another child, a daughter, who died very young. That was very common too, of course.'

'And Great-Grandfather Alfred himself died, when?'

'Oh, not until 1947. But his brother Thomas died much earlier, in 1918. He was in France, serving with the Army Ordnance Corps. He was reported missing in action, presumed dead.'

'One of millions,' I said glumly.

'Army records show him lost in action near Bethune at the start of the Lys offensive in April 1918. The Germans used gas in those attacks, didn't they?'

'He would have been over 40 years old by then, Rachel.'

'Yes, and they didn't extend conscription to men over 41 until almost at the end of the war. The Military Service Act Number Two, April 1918. But records weren't terribly accurate then. He could have lied about his age to join up.'

'That would be a pretty stupid thing to do.'

'Men can be stupid at that age as well as at any other.'

'A mid-life crisis?'

'If that's what you want to call it. And we know this one was stupid on two counts – fighting and women. Whatever it was, he never came back.'

'It sounds as though Great-Grandma Buckley wouldn't have been too keen to have him back anyway.'

'It's a pity we can't ask her.'

I was impressed by the work that Rachel had put in. It was plain that she'd not only searched the parish registers and censuses, but had also hunted the Buckleys relentlessly through the court records and even the army lists. I could only guess at the amount of time and effort it had taken.

'Parish registers are okay, but they're incomplete,' she said. 'We really need to research the official registers of births, marriages and deaths. But they're in London, at the Family Records Centre.'

I considered the situation I'd got into. Rachel and Laura were both helping me. Laura knew about Rachel, but Rachel knew nothing of Laura. It was a position fraught with potential conflict and embarrassment. But I'd reached a stage where I didn't care about such consequences. The book was everything. It had become part of the fabric of my life now. I would have sacrificed all my relationships to it – even the house in Stowe Pool Lane, if it came to that. Which it might.

'I've got somebody handling that end of things,' I said.

'Oh?' Rachel looked surprised. 'Anyone I know?'

'No. A television researcher I met at Samuel's funeral. She lives in London, you see.'

'She?' said Rachel sharply.

'Her name's Laura Jenner. I persuaded her to help. The thing is, Rachel, this is all very well – but I need to find out more about Samuel.'

'Why?' she said, reluctantly accepting the change of subject.

'I feel I owe it to him. To record his life for posterity, along with William and Josiah.'

'And what's making you feel like that? You know practically nothing about him, even now.'

'That's exactly it, don't you see? I still know nothing about his life, even though I was responsible for his death, in a way.'

'But it wasn't you who ran him over, Chris.'

'The police suspect it might have been.'

Rachel snorted. 'That's the police for you. It's their job. They don't really think it was you, otherwise they'd have arrested you by now, wouldn't they?'

'Even so, it doesn't take away the guilt. I sat and watched Samuel walk to his death. I let him down. No, that sounds too easy. It was more than letting him down. I betrayed him.'

She lowered her notebook and gazed at me with a concerned expression.

'So that's why it means so much to you. It isn't just an intellectual exercise.'

I shook myself to try to pull my thoughts back together. I felt as though I'd been about to spill all my feelings out. It was a horribly tempting prospect, but dangerous.

'Well, I haven't researched Samuel,' said Rachel. 'But I've done some more work on William Buckley.'

'Yes?'

'And I've got a theory about his disappearance,' she said proudly.

'I thought you were leading up to something.'

A photocopied sheet fell from between the pages Rachel held. I picked it up and scanned it idly. It was just one of the many miscellaneous bits and pieces that were in Samuel's files. Some day soon, somebody was going to have to sort them into order and decide what was important and what was irrelevant. This sheet had a curious dark blob at the bottom which must have been a wax seal on the original. It was a certificate, and it said:

Share certificate: Number 120. Ogley and Huddlesford Canal Company

We, the Company of Proprietors of the Ogley and Huddlesford Navigation, do hereby certify that Wm Buckley of Lichfield, Staffordshire, is a Subscriber for and entitled to One Share in the said Undertaking, Number 120.

Given under our Common Seal at a General Meeting of Proprietors this 23rd Day of November 1798.

'I didn't know William Buckley was a shareholder as well,' I said.

'One share. I suppose it was a gesture of faith in the project. He was only an employee really. He was the resident engineer.'

'Still, William was in a position to be dealing with contractors, wasn't he? There must have been a lot of money within his power one way or another. So the temptation proved too much. He was only human, after all. He was in trouble, and saw a chance of making a run for it with a pile of money. I might have done the same in his shoes.'

'But let's examine the story. It's reported in an allegation to the committee that William Buckley arrived at the company stables in the early hours of the morning and made the stableman provide him with a horse. He harnessed the horse up and took a boat from the boatyard. The next day the boat was found abandoned at Fosseway Wharf, three miles away, with the horse tethered on the bank.'

'Fosseway Wharf wasn't in use, even then. It had been built in the wrong place, thanks to the dispute with Anthony Nall.'

'So why did he go there?' she asked.

'Well, for that very reason – because it was deserted and he wouldn't be seen. He was within walking distance of both Watling Street and the Walsall Road, where he could pick up a coach and be out of the area later that morning.'

'Taking the missing money with him?' said Rachel.

'Exactly.'

'Leaving his wife and an eighteen-month-old child?'

'Maybe. It could be in the Buckley blood. Look at Thomas.'

Rachel shook her head impatiently. 'Mmm. Try this one, then. In one of his letters, he tells Reuben Wheeldon he'd arranged to meet someone, but he doesn't say where.'

'The mysterious Mr P.'

'That's him. "At every turn he seeks to thwart me."

261

He was building up to a showdown with the person he thought was responsible for his trouble. I say he'd slipped out to meet Mr P. that morning, and Fosseway Wharf was the place chosen for the meeting, because it was isolated and quiet. William Buckley decided to go by boat, what else?'

I pictured the scene. A cold February morning, still dark, with perhaps a mist hanging over the water of the canal. William would have had a lamp lit on the fore end of the boat. He'd have chosen a good horse that would go on its own, if he was without a crew. What had been his intention? To return to the city with Mr P., having persuaded him to do the honourable thing? Or had he intended, all along, not to return to his home? Could he have planned some deal with Mr P.? Had they disappeared together?

But I knew that none of these could have been the case. It was clear from the letters that William Buckley knew he was in danger. With Rachel's eyes on me, I saw a dim picture forming as I imagined William Buckley docking his boat against the empty wharf. I saw another figure in the shadows, waiting for him to step off the boat perhaps, but with a different intention. Mr P.? Or someone else? Had William been courageous, but foolish? Had he gone willingly to his death? He'd told Reuben Wheeldon, *At every turn he seeks to thwart me.*

So what happened to William Buckley? Was he a thief, a fraudster? Did he defraud the canal proprietors of their money, abandon his wife and child, then vanish to avoid ending up in prison? A cowardly thief and deceiver, or a reckless, honest fool? Which was in the Buckley character?

'You think he might have been murdered?' I said.

Rachel nodded. 'I think it's very likely. I think he stumbled on proof of a conspiracy to defraud the company, and he spoke up like the honest man he was. What did he say in his letter to Wheeldon? "I found it necessary to condemn what they have done as deficient both in honesty and good

262

business. By so doing I have raised a Nest of Hornets about me." He just didn't realise what danger he was putting himself in. Or perhaps he knew that too, but had to do it anyway. Maybe he felt responsible.'

Well, maybe. But it wasn't as if there was any concrete evidence that William Buckley had been murdered. How could there be?

And then the front page of the *Lichfield Echo* caught my eye, the headline about human remains unearthed during excavations at Fosseway Wharf. 'Police say the body has not been identified and may have lain undiscovered for some time.' Did 'for some time' mean centuries rather than months?

'That's it for now,' said Rachel, closing her notebook. 'I need to get my head round all this.'

'You know, Chris, this could be what Samuel was aiming to prove all along – he wanted to clear his ancestor's name, prove that William Buckley was murdered.'

'Perhaps. Let me think about it for a bit.'

She nodded, resignedly. 'No problem.'

I cast around for another subject to distract my thoughts, which were getting bogged down in the barrage of information and the sudden possibilities that had opened up.

'How was *Miss Saigon*, by the way?' I said.

'Brilliant.'

'And the matinee of *Cats*?'

'Great.'

'I've heard performers dressed as cats pop up among the audience and you can end up with one of them on your lap or something.'

'Yes, that's right,' she said vaguely.

'And did you?'

'What?'

'End up with one on your lap?'

'Not really. What else has been going on while I've been away? Did you go and see Godfrey Wheeldon?'

263

I shrugged mentally, noting that she was the one now changing the subject. If she didn't want to talk about the musical she'd gone to see, it didn't matter. I was only making polite enquiries. I'd expected her to be full of the subject.

So instead I told her about Godfrey Wheeldon, neglecting to mention the presence of Laura.

'He sounds a sweet old man.'

'Sweet? I suppose so.'

But Rachel was impatient. She didn't want to talk about *Cats* or Godfrey Wheeldon.

'So come on, what do you feel about it all now? Do you still believe that William Buckley was a crook?' She was leaning close to me over the papers, and I straightened up suddenly, feeling the beginnings of cramp in my legs from kneeling on the floor.

'According to history, he was.'

'But what do *you* feel? This was one of your ancestors. What does your heart tell you?'

'Well . . .'

'Samuel didn't think he was guilty.'

'How do you know?'

'You can tell by the way he writes. Read between the lines.'

'But there's no evidence of anything else,' I insisted. 'Not in the manuscript.'

'I'm not so sure. There are the letters. If you put them side by side with the manuscript, I think they tell a different story.' She thrust a transcribed letter at me. 'Read again what he writes to Reuben Wheeldon. This man was in trouble.'

'Look, I know all about money troubles. If William Buckley siphoned off a bit of cash from the canal company to solve his own short-term problems, I've got every sympathy. I need money too. If it wasn't for Great-Uncle Samuel's ridiculous legacy, I wouldn't be touching this project with a barge pole.'

Rachel snorted again. 'I don't believe it's just the money. You're family, Chris.'

'Family? None of these people really means anything to me. Not William Buckley, and not Josiah. Not even Samuel. I didn't know any of them. And if it comes to that, my own parents and grandparents leave a lot to be desired, judging by the way they kept things from me.'

Rachel looked at me as if I was a backward child. 'It doesn't matter whether you knew them or not, or if you hated them. They're still your family. You carry their genes, you're made up of the same chromosomes. You might reject them intellectually, but it isn't physically possible to deny the connection. And it certainly isn't possible emotionally.'

'What have emotions got to do with it, for God's sake?'

She didn't answer. She had that sceptical look on her face again.

'You're involved with these people, Chris. You're involved, whether you like it or not.'

I opened my mouth to argue, but she was already on her way out of the door, back to number four. Her back was held rigid, as if she'd spoken the last word on the subject.

Damn the woman for being right.

35

So I bit the bullet. I phoned the police station and reported that I might have some information on the body found at Fosseway Wharf. After a moment on hold, I was asked to come straight in to the station and ask for DS Graham. Of course it would be him.

I was put back in the same interview room where I'd made my statement about Samuel's death. At least this time I had the attention of someone more senior. Did this mean that Graham was taking me seriously?

'Mr Buckley. You're getting quite a regular customer, aren't you?'

'Not out of choice, I promise you.'

'Have you got over the attempted burglary? Did our chap come round to take fingerprints?'

'Oh yes, you've gone through all the motions.'

'And the lady, your neighbour? I hope she's recovered from her ordeal.'

'She's quite well.'

'She seems a useful sort of neighbour to have. It's nice when you get on well with your neighbours.'

'I came about the body that was found at Fosseway,' I said.

'Ah yes. An interesting case.'

'I wondered if you'd established the cause of death?'

'Well, we don't normally give out such information. But we've recently released details to the press, so I suppose I can tell you. First of all, we're fairly certain the remains are those of an adult male.'

'He was murdered, wasn't he?' I blurted.

'Well, hold on,' said Graham, looking at me curiously. 'Let's take one thing at a time.'

I forced myself to appear relaxed. 'Yes, I'm sorry.'

He looked happier. 'Well, we may know a bit more when the forensic anthropologist has finished his work. But one thing is clear. The back of the victim's skull had been smashed with several heavy blows. Then his body was concealed in a heap of lime, which must have preserved it for a while. It looks as though the lime was never moved. There were the remains of some wooden barrels nearby too.'

'A forensic anthropologist? I know there are all sorts of specialities these days, but I'm not sure what that one involves.'

'Oh, we call him in when it's a question of old bones. You see, there was nothing left but a skeleton. We're talking about an ancient crime here. Two hundred years, by initial estimates.'

I felt nervous, and had to swallow rapidly before I said: 'I think I know who it is.'

'I thought that might have been what you were getting to. You have some information for us?'

'Well, it's more of a deduction.'

'Deduction?'

'I've been putting two and two together. And I think the remains you found may be those of one of my ancestors.'

'Does he have a name?'

'William Buckley.'

Graham wrote it down. 'A distant ancestor, I take it?'

'He disappeared in mysterious circumstances in 1800.'

'I see. I presume you have some particular reason to think he might have been at Fosseway Wharf?'

I told him the known facts about William Buckley's

disappearance and Rachel's theory to explain it. What had once seemed far-fetched when she first aired it had slotted into place when the remains were unearthed, as if the proof had been produced on cue. But now, as I repeated it in that soulless room to DS Graham, it all felt horribly tenuous again.

'I'd say that wasn't so much deduction as guesswork,' he said when I'd finished.

'Well – it seems a possibility. I'd thought I'd better tell you.'

'Oh, quite right. But you understand that, due to the age of the remains, we aren't able to identify them in any of the usual ways?'

Despite his cool response, I blundered on with an idea that had occurred to me when he mentioned the anthropologist.

'Yes, obviously. But there is one way you could establish for certain whether the victim is my direct relative, isn't there?'

Graham tapped his pen on the desk and stared at me. 'How is that, Mr Buckley?'

'A DNA test.'

'Well, but I'm not sure . . .'

'According to what I've read, all you need is just enough marrow left in the bones of the skeleton to get a DNA profile. If I give a sample of my DNA, then you can see if there's a familial match. That would prove it fairly conclusively. Of course, if there isn't a match . . .'

'Well, in theory it might work.'

'Absolutely. In fact, it was done in the case of the Tsar Nicholas II and his family, the Romanovs. You know – the Russian royal family?'

'Of course.'

'I read about it in one of the Sunday papers. They were killed following the Bolshevik uprising in 1918. Their bodies were left buried in a mass grave for years and years, because the Communists didn't want to know about them. But with *perestroika* and all that, people got interested again, and the bodies were dug up. Some said they weren't the Romanovs

268

at all. But in the end they were identified by a DNA match to a blood sample from the Duke of Edinburgh, no less. He's a distant relative of the Romanovs via Queen Victoria. I'm a bit weak on the history of the royal family, I'm afraid.'

'I believe Prince Philip is related to the Tsarina Alexandra, Nicholas's wife,' said Graham, surprising me.

'There you are then,' I said. 'It works all right. If it's good enough for the Duke of Edinburgh . . .'

He smiled. 'Nice try.'

'Can we do it?'

'I'm sorry. I don't think there's any justification for it at the moment. But we'll bear your suggestion in mind.'

I sagged back in my chair. 'You're not interested in finding out who it is.'

'It's purely of academic interest. There's hardly going to be any prosecution. On that basis, we couldn't justify the cost.'

'I see. It all comes down to money, in the end?'

I got up, ready to go.

'By the way,' said DS Graham, looking as if he suddenly felt sorry for me, 'would you be interested in knowing what possessions were found with the remains?'

'I doubt it.'

He shrugged. 'Well, there wasn't much, admittedly. A few coins, pretty worn away. Part of a shoe, a buckle. I'm sorry they're not more interesting.'

'No.'

I was already putting on my coat to leave.

'But there was this. It's the best preserved item of all.'

He was holding a small leather pouch, wrinkled and rotting into holes.

'It doesn't look very well preserved,' I said.

'I meant what's in it. It's survived pretty well.'

'What has?'

'The water has got to the handle a bit,' he said. 'But it's basically okay, even after all this time.'

269

'But what is?' I was aware that I was starting to sound like a parrot, but I hadn't a clue what he was talking about.

And then I had a blinding surge of conviction. I knew what was in the pouch.

'It's a key, isn't it?' I said.

But DS Graham frowned. 'A key? Why would you think that? No, it's a hand stamp. The SOCOs tell me it's made of rosewood and brass. Look, Mr Buckley. It's a stamp for making wax seals.'

36

In the post next morning was a manila envelope with my address showing in a little window, except that it was simply headed to 'The Occupier'.

The letter came from an Executive Officer in the Traffic Management and Tolls Division at the Department of the Environment, Transport and the Regions, who was writing in response to a printed card I'd signed and sent in protesting against the link road. He informed me that the statutory decision could not be altered, but that the Secretary of State had weighed all the various material considerations in taking his decision.

The tone of his letter was very reasonable. The thing that annoyed me most was that they hadn't bothered with my name. I was sure the card had included my name as well as my address. Addressing me as 'The Occupier' made me feel like a statistic rather than an individual. It diminished me, and denied my identity.

I wondered again about Samuel's name change. Why had he done that? He'd deliberately denied his identity as a Buckley. It didn't make sense for a man who'd been so concerned about family. It was just one of the contradictions in my great-uncle's life. I had bits and pieces of information in my hands, but could see no way to fit them together, like an incomplete jigsaw. And the more I found out about Samuel's life, the further away it seemed to lead me from the truth about his death.

Rachel came in almost straight after breakfast and found me looking glum.

'Chin up, number six,' she said cheerfully. 'What's the matter?'

I showed her the ancient stamp DS Graham had given me. It had a nicely turned wooden handle – rosewood, Graham had said. And at one end was an impression of the Ogley and Huddlesford Canal Company's seal set into brass, the image of a pit-head with a stylised beam-engine.

Rachel cooed over it as if it had been a diamond-encrusted tiara.

'So much history right here,' she said, turning it over in her hands and stroking its blackened sides.

'And none of it good.'

'Where did you get it?'

'From the police. I went to see them about the body that was found at Fosseway Wharf.'

'So you do think William Buckley might have been murdered. And the body could be his?'

I shrugged. 'It was a theory, that's all. We'll never know, since they won't do a DNA comparison.'

I was conscious of Rachel studying my face, but I avoided meeting her eye.

'Well, there's something I want to ask you about anyway,' she said. 'That's why I called round.'

As if she needed any excuses to 'call round', I thought. But of course I didn't say it.

'Oh, what's that?' I asked.

'*This continuing feud.*'

'What?'

'In one of his letters, Samuel has written a phrase I don't understand: *This continuing feud.* What feud was he talking about?'

'There was some kind of dispute within the Buckley family. The split between the two brothers, Samuel and my grandfather.'

Rachel wrinkled her nose. 'I don't think he means that. He seems to be talking about a feud between two families.'

'But who could that be?'

'I don't know. Rivals to the Buckleys? Somebody William upset over the canal scheme? A family angry with Thomas over some girl he got pregnant? And wasn't Josiah supposed to have got into a fight with someone? It could be anybody.'

'Hold on, there's something there – an idea at the back of my mind.'

'Best place for it, probably, given the sort of trouble your ideas land you in. It's getting a bit dangerous, Chris.'

'Find the first bit of Samuel's manuscript. It's in the file there.'

'Yes, boss.'

'There's a name on the tip of my tongue.'

She pulled out the file. 'What exactly am I looking for?'

'Go back to the beginning of the manuscript. Look for the names of the canal company proprietors.'

'Okay.'

She turned over the pages until she reached the beginning. She didn't need to read the opening paragraphs, because I could remember the exact words. 'Major international events in the closing years of the eighteenth century were the key to the future of Britain's inland waterways system.'

'There was Anthony Nall and his brother Joshua, who was Deputy Lieutenant,' said Rachel. 'There was the doctor, James Allwood. Edward Wilkinson, an apothecary. Adam Henshall . . . Now that Nall – he sounds a nasty piece of work.'

'No.'

'Or there's Robert Sykes the publican. John Frith the solicitor, and his partner Daniel Metcalf, who was company secretary. The Parker family – Seth and Isaac, the bankers. Did you know that Seth's son Francis was transported to Australia for theft? That must have caused a bit of upset. And then there was the visionary, the Reverend Thomas Ella, of course.'

'Parker.'

'What?'

'The Parker family. I knew there was something ringing a bell. What were their names? Seth and Isaac?'

'Why them?'

'Leo Parker, that's why. There's the connection.'

'There are nearly two hundred years between them.'

'So? There's the same amount of time between William Buckley and me. And why else should Leo Parker turn up now? Of course there's a connection. That man did his best to get the manuscript and the letters off me when he came here. And with that break-in, I think he's succeeded.'

'But why? I don't understand. It's all ancient history, isn't it?'

'There's at least one person who doesn't think it is.'

First of all, I tried Leo Parker's number from the card he'd left me, but I got his voice on an answering machine and had to leave a stumbling message.

I knew Laura was back in London, but she'd left me the phone number at a house she shared in Shepherd's Bush. I'd imagined a couple of girls, and I was taken aback when a man's voice answered and offered to fetch Laura for me.

'Who was that?' I asked, rather abruptly.

'Just one of the people I share with. His name's Ian.'

'Oh.'

She laughed at the tone of my voice. 'Are you jealous, Chris? Don't worry, Ian's gay.'

'Yeah, okay.' I couldn't say any more, for fear of presuming too much on our new relationship.

'But you weren't phoning to check on my sex life, I suppose,' she said.

'I'd thought you'd want to know about the developments here.'

'Ah. Do tell.'

274

She listened intently as I told her about the remains found at the wharf and about Frank, and summarised the information Rachel had come up with, which led me to think that the body might be William Buckley's. I almost told her about the hypothetical feud, but hesitated, and kept it to myself.

'She's been busy, this Rachel, hasn't she?' said Laura.

'I think she's got interested in the project. She hasn't much else to do, you see. Not since her divorce.'

'And this woman is living right next door to you? It sounds as though you might need protection.'

I realised I'd told her nothing of the break-in. But I reflected that it might sound as though I was too concerned about Rachel's welfare, and I kept quiet.

'Is there an inquest then?' she asked. 'Even though the body is so old?'

'Er, I don't know. DS Graham didn't say.'

'I suppose there might have to be, by law.'

'They can only give evidence of cause of death anyway. There'll be no formal identification.'

'Unless you have this DNA test.'

'Even that wouldn't prove conclusively it was William Buckley,' I said. 'Only that it was someone related to me. It could be – I don't know – Thomas Buckley, say.'

'Who?'

'My great-great-uncle. Rachel says he died in the Great War.'

'Was there a famous First World War battle fought at Lichfield then? Will they unearth thousands of dead Germans at Fosseway?'

'I'm only suggesting him as an example.'

'I know.'

She sounded vague, as if she was doing something else while I was speaking. 'Laura, are you listening?'

'I'm just checking my diary,' she said. 'I could run up to Lichfield this weekend, if you think I can be of any help.'

'Yes, I think you could,' I said, trying unsuccessfully to

hide my delight at the prospect of seeing her again. 'Will you book into the George again?'

'I expect so.'

'Laura – have you managed to call at the Family Records Centre?'

'Oh yes,' she said. 'I've got a few things to share with you when I see you.'

'I'll look forward to it.'

The *Lichfield Echo* that Thursday also contained my article and a spread of photos on the visit by Lindley Simpson to Fosseway. I cringed slightly at what they must have said at the *Echo* office about my report making no mention of the sensational developments at the end of the visit, when the excavator had unearthed human remains. What sort of a reporter missed that?

My professional reputation must be pretty low with the *Echo* now, just at a time when I might need to call in old favours. But at least they'd used the feature, which meant a bit of valuable income. It was a good spread, too, which the restoration trust would be pleased with.

As if to emphasise this, a call came from Andrew Hadfield, who'd seen the *Echo*.

'Your piece was brilliant, Chris,' he said. 'Exactly the sort of publicity we need. The committee are delighted with it. They're all ordering prints of the pictures showing them with Lindley Simpson.'

'It didn't get the same prominence as the other story, I'm afraid.'

'Oh, the old skeleton. Never mind. There's no such thing as bad publicity.'

'Have the police mentioned anything to you about who they think it is?'

'No,' said Andrew. 'Presumably it's just some Irish navvy. They died in droves on the old canal projects.'

'Yes, that's probably it.'

'Anyway,' he said briskly, 'thanks again for the article. I thought I came out of it particularly well. Remind me some time that I owe you a favour.'

Dan Hyde had left two more messages on the answerphone asking me to contact him urgently, and finally I had to face up to it. He wanted to tell me that he'd made an appointment to see the bank manager in a few days' time to discuss our loan for the start-up – specifically, our inability to pay it back.

'If he's in a bad mood, it could be curtains, you know, Chris.'

'Yes, thanks a lot.'

'Had the house valued yet?'

'It won't come to that,' I said, trying to sound more confident than I felt. 'Anyway, I wanted to ask you something. About this anonymous backer.'

'Yeah?'

'Did this person ever exist?'

'That's hurtful. Of course he existed. It's just that he made it a specific condition of the agreement that he should never be identified. Don't ask me why. In fact, I don't even know it was a "he". I only ever dealt with a lawyer anyway – and you know what lawyers are like. They're almost as bad as bank managers.'

'Right.'

It was all very unsatisfactory. I no longer felt I could trust my business partner, or anyone else for that matter. The world was shifting around me, and it felt very uncomfortable.

Later that day, Leo Parker returned my call.

'I believe you've been trying to contact me,' he said. 'Is there something I can help you with?'

'I need to talk to you. Not on the phone.'

'Well, my diary is rather full. I could give you half an hour later in the week.'

'Tomorrow.'

'I'm afraid that's out of the question. I'm very busy.'

'It's about your father.'

'I see,' he said, with an uncharacteristic pause.

I hurried to press home my advantage. 'Do you know Stowe Pool in Lichfield?'

'I think so.'

'Meet me there, opposite St Chad's Church. Ten o'clock tomorrow morning.'

'It will be difficult.'

'Be there if you want to know what I've found out about your family.'

I put the phone down. It made me feel good to speak to Parker like that. I knew he would come. He'd already made it clear how anxious he was about the book touching on Samuel's link with his mother.

I could sense the fear growing around me. And at that point I still thought it possible I could make use of it to my own advantage. It hadn't dawned on me yet that the fear would be my own.

There was a cold wind blowing across Stowe Pool when I walked up the steps from the corner of St Chad's Road. I was grimly pleased to see that Leo Parker was there before me. He'd arrived early – that must mean he was keen, and therefore co-operative.

Wrapped up in his waxed coat and a thick sweater, he looked brawny and powerful. The buttons strained across his barrel chest and his dark brow was threatening. I reassured myself by noticing the bald furrows running back from his forehead.

'Before you say anything, I think I know the purpose of the book,' said Parker.

'Do you?' I said, annoyed that he'd already seized the initiative from me.

'Yes, Samuel was going to claim that my ancestors not only arranged the deaths of William Buckley and Josiah Buckley, but also that of Samuel's own son.'

I was stunned for a moment.

'His son? But Samuel had no son. At least,' I corrected myself, recalling the depth of my ignorance, 'no one has ever mentioned a son to me.'

'No? Well, the old man was clearly mad anyway. You have to understand that, Chris. He was unhinged. He'd developed a delusion that his wife, Alison, was deliberately killed in that crash on the A38. Nonsense, of course.'

'But I don't see—'

'Listen, and you'll see. According to Samuel, his unborn son also died in that crash. He'd always desperately wanted a son, to carry on the family name. He said he'd revert to being a Buckley once he had a son. He could have done that, too, with his own brother dead. But there was to be no son for Samuel. It was that knowledge that turned his mind in the end. And all the rest followed on from that. It was all delusion, part of a fantasy world he'd slipped into. He was chasing shadows through history, looking for someone to blame.'

'My feeling was that he blamed himself for that accident.'

'Deep down, of course he did. But it's a lot easier to look for someone else to blame than to face up to your own guilt, isn't it?'

I turned away to look at the cold water of Stowe Pool, afraid that my face might give away how close to home his words had come, how deeply the truth pierced. My own guilt was like a knife twisted in my stomach, and Leo Parker had just given it another turn.

'There's no mention of that in his manuscript,' I said. 'He talks about the deaths of William and Josiah, yes. But not about Alison, not a word. And even in William and Josiah's cases, he doesn't name the Parkers. He only hints at some feud between the families.'

'So? It simply means that there must be another part of the manuscript somewhere. Otherwise, where else was the story heading? William and Josiah Buckley are historical curiosities, no more than that. They're not the purpose of the book. Samuel had a point he was working up to, a big climax. Come on, you're an intelligent man. You must have figured it out for yourself. The missing section is glaringly obvious.'

'Not to me. I think you're wrong.'

'So what has he called the book?'

'*The Three Keys.*'

'Ah, yes. Three mysteries and three keys, but one big secret. That's the way the old man's mind worked.' Parker sighed and shook his head at me rather sadly. 'I know it's all about money as far as you're concerned, Chris. There's no need to pretend to me it's anything else.'

'There are such things as family loyalty, pride, conscience,' I said, and hoped the breeze would take away the sound of my pomposity.

'Yes, I know about those. But what do they mean to *you*? You owe no loyalty to your family, not even to Samuel Longden. As for pride and conscience, they're luxuries you can't afford.'

'What do you mean?'

'I understand that you're badly in need of money. A little matter of a failed business venture and several creditors demanding payment. Being declared bankrupt would hardly do much for the Buckley family name now, would it?'

'Get to the point.'

'Look, I'll pay you to drop the project. Give me the third part of the manuscript and in return I'll pay you an amount equivalent to the bequest you expect to get from Samuel's will. Isn't that much more suitable to all concerned? You'll save yourself a lot of trouble, and you'll get the money sooner too. Perfect, eh?'

'Go to hell.'

Parker raised an eyebrow and looked displeased. 'Holding out for more?'

His talk of a missing section of the manuscript had left me in no doubt that Parker had been behind the break-in at Maybank, and the thought of Rachel's injuries made me want to lash out wildly.

I stood up, trembling slightly with the anger growing inside me. 'I think it's time I went.'

He came after me. 'You've got my phone number,' he said, 'for when you change your mind.'

'You still haven't got the message, have you?'

'Oh, I think I have.'

I left Stowe Pool deeply dissatisfied. My suspicions about Leo Parker had been confirmed. But the worst thing was that he'd voiced the niggling feeling that I'd felt so strongly myself after reaching the end of Samuel's manuscript. There had to be more.

'But if there's a missing section, why is it missing? He must have intended you to have it,' said Rachel that night when I told her. 'Samuel was relying on you to see the book was completed and published, wasn't he?'

'So he said.'

'So where is it, Chris?'

'I don't know.'

'Samuel must have given you a clue of some kind.'

'Not that I'm aware of.'

'Well, think. Remember how eccentric he was. A letter, a cryptic note? A key to a desk or a drawer where the manuscript might be hidden?'

I shook my head. 'Believe me. I've been through everything he left me. There's nothing of that kind. Except—'

'Yes?'

'Well, there was a note that his solicitor passed on to me.'

'What did it say?'

'It didn't mean anything.'

'Chris – what did it say?'

'The exact words were: *Here is the second key. The third is in the lock.*'

She cocked her head on one side to think. 'The three keys. That obviously refers to the book. But what lock?'

'I don't know. I told you it didn't mean anything.'

'But it must do. What lock? One of the locks in the canal owners' box? But that one would be the first key, wouldn't it? Not the third.'

'It occurred to me . . . well, that he was having a joke. That he wasn't referring to the sort of lock that a key usually goes in. He was a waterways man, after all. I thought perhaps he meant a canal lock.' I shrugged. 'Perhaps that he'd thrown the key into a lock somewhere. I thought when that leather pouch was recovered from the body . . . well, I was convinced it would be a third key.'

'But it wasn't.'

'No, of course not. So who can say what Samuel meant? Leo Parker said he was living in a fantasy world. He may have decided to throw the key away and was just toying with me in the end. It's obvious he loved being manipulative. He's played me on a line right from the start.'

'I don't think it's likely. He definitely wanted you to finish the book.'

'Oh, maybe. I don't know any more.'

Finally, Rachel lost patience with my mood and left me to stare at the flickering fish and listen to the tick of the carriage clock.

How on earth had I ended up in this situation? How had I become a man haunted by images from the past? I'd always believed that what happened in the past was over and done

282

with. But during these last weeks I'd spent far too much time looking in the rearview mirror.

I'd begun with what I thought was just a bit of interesting historical research. But, once set in motion, the history of the Buckleys had come rushing up on me from the past like a train whose brakes had failed. There was no stopping it now. Not until the train finally hit the buffers.

And somewhere, in the middle distance, I thought I could already hear the warning sound of its scream.

37

When the phone rang that evening, I was surprised to hear the hesitant voice of Mrs Wentworth.

'Mr Buckley?'

'Hello, Mrs Wentworth. What can I do for you?'

'I'm sorry to bother you, but I thought I ought to let somebody know. I can't get hold of Caroline, you see.'

'Is something wrong?'

'I've rung the police twice now, and a car came past earlier on, but I'm still worried.'

'Worried about what?'

'I'm probably being silly. But I keep thinking there's someone hanging around Ash Lodge. Well, when a house is empty like that, it attracts attention, doesn't it?'

'Have you seen somebody?'

'I thought I did the first time, but it was already going dark. Then there was a noise. I had a look at the house, but I can't see that anybody's got in. It's more of a feeling now, and I daren't ring the police again. They would think I was neurotic. But I'm worried. I'm frightened to go out again.'

'It's Caroline's affair really. The house is nothing to do with me.'

'Oh, I know, but I thought . . . you seemed to be concerned before. You said you were a relative. And since I can't get hold of Caroline . . . There is nobody else but you.'

Her words were such a close echo to what Great-Uncle

Samuel had said to me, that I could almost hear his voice repeating it. There had been only me, and I'd let him down.

'All right. I'll come over and take a look.'

On the way to Whittington, I passed the barracks of the Staffordshire Regiment. There was a double row of barbed wire round the perimeter of the camp, and the Escort's headlights picked out the signs along the shooting ranges, which said 'Danger – keep clear when red flags are flying'.

There were two likely looking pubs in Whittington, and it was the time of the evening when they were starting to get lively. They both looked tempting as the light from their windows began to spill out into the darkness. I might treat myself to a pint after I'd done my duty. But they'd have to wait until later.

The driveway at Ash Lodge looked a little more untidy, the shrubs a bit more overgrown. The house had a general air of neglect, despite the fact that it had been empty for less than three weeks. It seemed to know that it had been abandoned, not just left for a week or two while its owner went on holiday. I could see that Mrs Wentworth was right about it attracting the attention of burglars and vandals, or even drug addicts and squatters – if they got as far as Whittington. Or maybe it was merely a question of a wild animal trying to find somewhere to escape the cold.

I saw the lady herself watching for me from her window, and I gave her a reassuring wave as I got out of the car. I'd taken the precaution of bringing a torch with working batteries, and I was glad I had, because I'd forgotten quite how total the darkness would be. Though I was only a few yards from the street lights, the yew tree and the tall shrubs shielded the garden and driveway from most of the light. With the house itself in darkness, I could barely see where I was putting my feet as I walked up to the front door.

I went through the motions, shining my torch through all

the windows I could reach and checking the doors and a scattering of outbuildings at the back. I checked particularly carefully on the little side windows. They were very much the size of mine back home, which had only just been repaired. But there was no sign of any break-in at Ash Lodge, of course. All I saw was a glimpse of the interior of Samuel's house – an opportunity that had been denied me so far.

Belatedly, I remembered Mr Elsworth's offer to allow me access to the house to look for more papers relevant to *The Three Keys*. From what I could see in the torchlight, it looked as though I was too late to get any sense of my great-uncle's life. The downstairs rooms were stripped almost bare, apart from a few items of dark, heavy furniture. There were pale rectangles on the walls where pictures had been taken down, and patches of brighter colour on the carpets where rugs had been rolled up and removed. There were no clocks, no mirrors, no coats hanging in the hall, no personal items on the mantelpiece or in the empty display cabinets. Samuel's presence had been erased.

I could easily picture Caroline Longden going through the house like a hurricane, no doubt with a small army of helpers at her command, clearing out the memories of her father and preparing the house for sale so she could add its value to her suddenly burgeoning fortune. It seemed a desecration.

Or was I misjudging her? True, our first meeting hadn't been a friendly one, but the circumstances had been difficult, to say the least. Then I thought of her fiancé, Simon Monks. That was certainly a black mark against her. I couldn't trust anybody who'd chosen him as her future husband.

The cold was beginning to strike through my clothes now, and my fingers and toes were going numb. I waved my torch around the garden for a few more minutes, then walked round to The Laurels and knocked on the door.

'All clear, Mrs Wentworth. There's no sign of anybody around.'

'Oh, I'm so glad you came, Mr Buckley. I suppose you think I was imagining things. I'm sure the police do.'

'Not at all. It's best to be sure.'

I thought it was a good idea not to tell her about my own break-in and the assault on my neighbour. The poor woman would never sleep at night.

'You've just been round the house and garden, have you?' she said.

'And the outbuildings.'

'I did think I saw something moving about in the back garden, near the path.'

'It might have been a cat, mightn't it?'

'I suppose so,' she said cautiously. 'But the path leads down to the canal.'

'Yes?'

'I was thinking about the boat.'

'*Kestrel*?'

'It's not unknown for people to break into boats on the canal. It's very quiet down there. There's a couple who live on their boat a bit further along, but that's all.'

I pictured the deserted canalside, too far from any streetlights to be safe at this time of night. I was no hero. That kind of job should be left to the police.

'Well, I don't suppose there's anything worth stealing,' I said.

Mrs Wentworth gripped my sleeve. Her hand was trembling with anxiety. 'You never know. It would be such a reassurance to an old lady. Would you, please—?'

I sighed, realising I'd have to spend a few more minutes on this nonsense before I could go to the pub. 'All right, I'll go and check.'

'Thank you. I do appreciate it. And I'm sure Caroline will, when I tell her how concerned you were.'

'Don't hold your breath.' But I said it entirely to myself as I walked down the path between the two gardens towards the Coventry Canal.

Mrs Wentworth was absolutely right – it was deathly quiet on the canalside. All I could hear was the soft movement of water against the bank, and somewhere nearby a tawny owl calling that eerie cry that sounds like an animal screaming in terror.

The surface of the canal collected a little of what light was available from the overcast sky, and I could just make out the outline of *Kestrel* moored against the bank. In fact, I could smell it better than I could see it, because as I got closer the scents of bitumen and varnished wood mingled with the dankness of the water in the cold air.

Careful to avoid unseen mooring lines, I walked along the length of the boat, shining my torch onto the steel shutters that covered the windows. Everything seemed secure. The stern and fore-end lines were firmly fixed, and the small door that opened onto the fore deck was tightly locked. I began to wonder what the inside of the boat was like. For years, this had been Samuel Longden's favourite plaything. He'd travelled many miles in it, according to the boaters I'd met at his funeral. And even after he'd grown too old, he'd spent a lot of time down here. Mrs Wentworth herself had told me that.

The hull was bituminised, with a thick coat of gloss paint to protect it from the weather, though in places it was starting to wear thin. All the exterior fittings looked solid and new, and I wondered what had made anybody doubt that it was in useable condition.

Now that I looked closely at the metal plate bolted to the side of the stern cabin, I realised that it was not a restored narrowboat, but a modern one made in traditional style at a well-known boatyard near Tamworth, where there was said to be a twelve-month waiting list of potential boat owners. From what I'd seen in the waterways magazines, a sixty-foot boat with something like a Beta BD3 Tug engine from that particular boatyard would cost in the region of £80,000. And

Kestrel was the full narrowboat length of seventy feet. That represented quite an investment by Great-Uncle Samuel. But then, he could afford to indulge himself.

Returning to the stern, I examined the double doors on the back cabin. They were fitted with a Yale lock, and a sizeable padlock on a hasp across the middle. There were small windows in the upper part of the doors, but these too were shuttered, so that the interior was invisible. I tried to shine my torch through a narrow crack between the shutter and the window frame, but I could see nothing except a few patches of wooden panelling and the occasional gleam of brass. The light reflected off the shutter, and I could see my own breath in a cloud before me.

Everything seemed to be secure. With that in mind, I almost turned back towards the house and the safety of streetlights. But something stopped me. Examining the exterior of the boat so closely had made me feel differently about it. It sat there now taunting me, as one more mystery to be solved.

Suddenly, I was consumed with a desire to see inside the boat. I felt sure it could tell me a lot about Samuel's life and character. Then it occurred to me that it might tell me even more than that. What more logical place for him to conceal some documents than on his boat, where no one ever went but himself? What had Mrs Wentworth said that day? *'He still spent a lot of time down there. Tinkering about, I suppose. As men do.'*

Surely if Samuel had been here with me now, he would have been delighted to have shown me round his boat. So it wouldn't be disrespectful for me to take a look now that he was dead. I pulled at the handle of the door and rattled the padlock, but neither of them shifted.

Frustrated, I switched off my torch and shoved my frozen hands into my coat pockets, ready to return to the house. My fingers encountered something metallic in one pocket, and I'd already walked a few paces back along the towpath

289

before I realised what they were. Keys. Not my own car keys – I always kept them on a leather fob in my trouser pocket. So what—? Of course. These were the keys Godfrey Wheeldon had given me, which had lain in my pocket since the previous Sunday. It had been obvious that neither of them fit the canal owners' box, and so I'd forgotten about them until now.

I shone my torch on them. One key was a gold-coloured Yale, the other a silver key with a square end. I hurried back to the boat and clambered back onto the stern hatches, steadying myself on the gunwale as the boat rocked slightly. Sure enough, the silver key slipped in effortlessly and the padlock sprang open with a click. Then the Yale key went into the door lock.

'Eureka!' I almost gave a little skip. Samuel was here helping me after all.

38

As I stepped inside the boat, my first glimpse of the interior of the back cabin almost left me breathless. It was two steps down into the cabin from the hatches, with a deep, drawer-like coal box forming the bottom step. The floor of the cabin seemed a long way below me. But when the beam of the torch hit the walls, I had to sit down on the step to take it in properly.

The place was fitted out as a reproduction of a traditional cabin on a working narrowboat, and it was in exquisite condition. My torch flashed off gleaming brass and the glossy surfaces of walls and cupboards that looked as though they'd been scumbled – the decoration used by the boat people, involving scratch combs to create a woodgrain effect in the fresh varnish. To my left was a vast black stove with brass handles and rails, and lace-edged plates hanging over white crochet work near the chimney.

The cupboard doors were decorated with red and green Roses and Castles designs, the fairytale landscape scenes made famous by canal boat enthusiasts. When I turned round, I could see that the doors I'd come through had similar designs, so they'd be visible from outside when they were opened and folded back.

The golden colour of the scumbled walls and ceiling gave the cabin an unearthly glow in the torchlight. It looked more like a three-dimensional work of art than a living space. Then

I realised this was probably an accurate description. This stove hadn't been used for a long time, not by Great-Uncle Samuel or anyone else. Its surfaces were spotless. When I touched my fingers to the wooden panelling, there was barely a trace of dust. The padding of the bench seat was smooth and undented, as though no one had ever sat on it. It was many years since there had been fuel in the coal box below me, or food supplies in the cupboards.

It was no more than five feet across the cabin to a doorway that led into the rest of the boat. Yet this area would have comprised the entire living space for a family of boat people, even fifty years ago. They would have cooked, eaten, washed and slept in this space, adults and children together. They would have made love and died here, and the women would have given birth in the 'bed 'ole' across the forward end of the cabin, where the doorway was. They were people like Josiah Buckley, Samuel's grandfather, the number one who'd died trapped behind a lock gate. These few square feet would have been home for himself and his family. No wonder Alfred had been put 'on the bank' when the family got too big.

I stood up again on the top step and looked over the cabin roof towards the fore-end of the boat, almost seventy feet away. This was where the steerer operated from, and close at hand were the engine controls. On a small shelf near the steerer's position was a heavy steel windlass, the vital L-shaped tool used for opening and closing lock sluices. It fitted onto the end of a spindle and worked the ratchet and pinion mechanism on the paddles.

I remembered the story told at the funeral in St Giles, about the Captain leaving his windlass slotted onto the paddle spindle – a cardinal sin in boating circles. The ratchet had been worn, and it had slipped, sending the spindle spinning so fast that the windlass flew off, narrowly missing Samuel's head and vanishing into the water of the lock. A boater is helpless without his windlass, and, according to the story,

292

the Captain had made sure he never let go of his again while he was with *Kestrel*. Now, the sight of the windlass resting on the shelf was somehow symbolic of the fact that he'd let go of life.

Alongside it was a British Waterways key, the type they called a Watermate, which is used to operate powered locks and bridges, to open locked gates, and to get access to sanitary facilities at moorings and boatyards.

I stepped down again into the cabin and walked across to the doorway in the opposite bulkhead, flashing my torch ahead of me, until I found myself in the engine room. There were more golden scumbled walls here, but it was the engine itself that took pride of place. It sat in splendour in the middle of the floor, a bright green monster that threw complicated shadows on the walls, with three brass rocker covers on its upper surface that must need constant polishing.

On the wall behind the engine was a day tank, where the fuel was hand-pumped from the main tank. It was decorated with the same Roses and Castles design and the name of the engine manufacturer stood out in ornate script – Lister. I looked again, and realised this was no Beta, but a genuine Lister JP3, a vintage engine much loved by boaters. I immediately began to revise the value of *Kestrel* upwards from my original £80,000 estimate to something closer to £100,000.

At first glance, there seemed to be no evidence of the modern requirements of an engine room and the other systems that a boat of this kind would undoubtedly have. But I opened a hatch in the floor and a corner cupboard to locate batteries, diodes, a boiler and an electrical distribution board, all tucked discreetly out of sight.

I felt the boat dip and sway on the water, bumping gently against the bankside. I looked at the blank windows, expecting to hear another boat passing, but there was nothing. Even if I'd been able to see past the steel shutters, it was totally dark outside.

Forward of the engine room I came to more familiar surroundings. From here on, the accommodation was comparable to a luxury caravan. There was a small bathroom with decorative tiling around the bath and vanity unit, and in a cubicle was a toilet with its flush operated by a foot pedal. The dining area had two bench seats and a central table that looked as though it might convert into a double bed, and a surprisingly large bedroom contained a wardrobe and dressing table and an end column to the bed which gave it the appearance of a four-poster. I passed these rooms fairly quickly and followed the narrow passageway into a galley which had yards of worktop area, as well as an oven, hob and refrigerator.

Finally, I entered a spacious saloon, set out with pine rockers and book shelves and a coffee table with the inevitable Roses and Castles. I began to open the cupboards and peer into the drawers. Like a caravan, every bit of space was used to its utmost and there was storage in the oddest of places. By now, I felt no compunction at searching through the items left behind by Samuel. But they were remarkably uninformative – just the normal clutter of a life lived in an enclosed space.

Then I sniffed. For the first time I noticed there was a strong smell of diesel fuel. I wondered where the main fuel tank was on this type of boat, and whether there were still spare cans on board. Marine diesel is tax-free and therefore cheap, and it has a tell-tale pink dye added to distinguish it from the heavily taxed stuff that has to be used in road vehicles. But fuel is only sold at boatyards, and diesel engines can't be allowed to run out of fuel. So boaters using diesel engines like the one on *Kestrel* will invariably carry at least one spare can to make absolutely sure they can reach the next boatyard to find a fuel line.

I found where the gas supply was stored, in a locker at the fore-end, in front of the saloon. There were a couple of gas bottles standing there, and at least one of them was pretty full. But it wasn't gas I was smelling. I thought I'd finish checking the fore-end of the boat before working my way back to the stern and looking for the fuel tank.

Then I noticed a section of the wooden deck that had been formed into a small hatch, no more than a few inches square. Using a knife from the cutlery drawer in the galley, I eased it open. I found myself peering down into the hull of the boat, with a peculiar damp, green smell rising up to greet me. I shone my torch into the darkness, so I could make out the shape of the hull curving below me. It wasn't as far down as it had seemed at first. If I reached out an arm, I could probably touch the planks.

I realised this was the famous weed hatch. Just below the planks was the shaft of the propeller, and any weeds or other debris tangled round it could easily be removed by hand via this hatch. If the engine was water-cooled, you also had to check the filter near the water intake regularly to make sure it was free of weeds that might block it and make the engine overheat. There were so many things to remember – it was no wonder life on the water could be hazardous if you got old or forgetful.

As the blackness at the bottom of the hatch settled into varying shades of grey in the torchlight, an extraneous object sprang into focus to one side, and my heart gave a jump. It was a package. I stretched out my hand as far as I could and just managed to get my fingers to it. Gradually, I eased the package towards me with the tips of my fingers until I could grasp it. It barely fit through the gap in the floor of the saloon, but eventually I had it, and I was able to sit back on my heels and examine what I held. From the feel and the weight of it, it had to be exactly what I'd been looking for. The missing section of Great-Uncle Samuel's manuscript.

The boat dipped again. But I was too pleased with myself to worry about a bit of wash or current moving the boat, or the faint creaking overhead in the superstructure that may just have been *Kestrel* shifting gently at its moorings.

Eagerly, I pushed the section of deck back into place and studied my prize. The light from my torch was starting to fail now, and all I could see was a thick white envelope sealed with parcel tape and staples. There was no point in trying to open it and look at the contents in such poor light, so I shoved it inside my coat and began to head back towards the stern. I made my way through the galley, past the bedroom and bathroom and through the engine room, where the Lister glowed green and almost alive in the gloom.

When I entered the scumbled back cabin, the smell of diesel was even stronger. I peered over the counter to locate the brass capping stud to the fuel tank on the stern-end. It seemed to be firmly in position. But as I stepped up from the cabin, with my foot on the coal box, my eye fell on the little shelf below the hatches. I froze half way up the step and frowned in bewilderment. Samuel's steel windlass had gone.

Before I could begin to puzzle this out, I heard a movement above me – no more than a faint whistling like something passing through the air at speed. I turned my head just in time to see the end of the windlass flash across my sight.

A split second later, a stunning blow landed on my skull and I fell backwards onto the floor of the cabin, unconscious.

As I came round, my first feeling was an excruciating agony at the back of my skull, which seemed to spread tendrils of pain through my head and neck, and numb my shoulders and arms. Then came the nausea, and I had to swallow painfully as I fought to keep the contents of my stomach down.

I was lying face down on the floor, and the planks were cold against my cheek. The smell in my nostrils should have been of wood, but it wasn't. The reek of diesel was almost overpowering. But there was something else too that I thought I ought to be able to identify. Though my ears were ringing, there was also a noise somewhere that my brain couldn't put a name to.

I don't know how long I lay there waiting for the pain to subside. But my senses seemed to come alive before my brain did. The smells and sounds suddenly registered and became recognisable. Frightened, I moved my head too suddenly, and the pain erupted again. But now I was reacting automatically, driven by the adrenaline that was surging through my body and the unreasoning fear that gripped my limbs.

Fire. The acrid smell filling the cabin was smoke, and beyond it was the crackling of flames. Behind me, the boat was burning. I turned my head as I lifted it from the floor and saw fire leaping and sparking over a pile of paper and rags in the corner near the hatches. The flames were just beginning to creep up the steps, where a trickle of diesel was about to gain the impetus to run downwards to meet it. Without my torch, the blazing objects were all I could see in the smoke-filled darkness.

Somehow I was on my feet. My head was spinning, but I knew I had to get out, and fast. Instinctively, I headed away from the fire, through the door of the cabin, back towards the galley. No sooner had I got the door shut behind me, than I heard the diesel fuel ignite and felt the boat rock as an explosion filled the cabin. Heat seared the door, and the wood twisted and blackened.

I kept going, past the bedroom, cannoning off the doors and bulkheads, and found myself in the saloon. I knew that just in front of here were the gas bottles, and it wasn't the place to be in a fire. When the flames and heat reached this far, *Kestrel* would be blown to bits, even if the fuel tank didn't go up first.

At the fore-end was a small door out onto the bow. It was padlocked on the outside, but the only other way out was through one of the tiny windows. I threw myself desperately against the door, feeling the frame give slightly under the impact. I tried again and again. The wood began to splinter. I could hear the boat burning fiercely behind me, and I glanced back to see flames licking under the saloon door.

With one final, desperate lunge, I crashed through the hatch and stumbled helplessly out onto the bow. With a roar, the fuel tank exploded, and fire leaped out to scorch my back. I threw myself forward into the darkness and plunged instantly into freezing water. The shock drove the breath from my lungs, but I managed to keep my head for a minute or two as I pumped my legs and thrashed my arms to put as much distance between myself and the blazing boat as I could.

Finally, I was forced to come up for air. The night was lit up like daylight by the flames roaring towards the sky. I could see the stern cabin had been blown away completely, and the missing roof exposed a glowing inferno.

I splashed about until I was on the far side of the canal and within reach of the pilings on the bank. My wet clothes were weighing me down, and I was conscious of the bulk of the package slipping down inside my coat. With one hand, I reached in and pulled out the sodden envelope and tossed it onto the bankside.

Even then, I found that I lacked the strength to pull myself up. All I could do was cling to the pilings and watch *Kestrel* burn.

39

Detective Sergeant Graham and I were both wrapped up in coats and scarves as we stood on the towpath next day and watched scenes of crime officers in paper suits go over the blackened wreck of the boat. Our breath steamed the frosty air as I waited for Graham to speak. But for a while he seemed content to let me stew. His expression was more worried than ever, and his face was pale with cold under his stubble.

'Did nobody see anything?' I asked at last.

He gave me an impatient glower. 'The couple who pulled you out of the water saw nobody. And the lady in the next house over there only remembers you, Mr Buckley. The same neighbour who told us you'd visited Ash Lodge previously.'

'Mrs Wentworth.'

'That's the lady's name.'

'Yes, you know perfectly well I visited Ash Lodge. I didn't deny it. I came to see Samuel Longden, but he wasn't here.'

'Remind me, was that before or after the time you were supposed to meet him in Lichfield market square?'

'Before, obviously. Afterwards—'

'Afterwards, he was dead. Of course. You seem to have had bad luck trying to meet up together. But looking for him on his boat nearly three weeks after his death seems a bit desperate, sir.'

I gritted my teeth to prevent myself from getting angry at

the insinuations. I wasn't in the best of moods. As far as I was concerned, I'd been brained with a windlass and then almost burned to death before nearly drowning in the canal. Was it too much to expect a bit of sympathy?

It was the owners of *Rose Marie*, moored further along the bank, who'd come to my rescue with a life belt and a boat hook. Having dragged me to the towpath side and onto solid ground, they'd tried to persuade me to go to hospital for treatment. But apart from a few minor burns and scratches, the worst injury was the gash in my scalp where the windlass had hit me, and the raging headache it had left me with.

In another few minutes, I might have yielded to common sense and gone for a check-up. But the policeman who'd turned up with the fire brigade had been interested only in getting my name and address and my garbled version of events. He'd questioned me suspiciously as I sat and shivered in front of the stove on *Rose Marie*, wrapped in a blanket.

In the end, the policeman's attitude had made me feel so angry that I could think of nothing else except sneaking off to collect the package which I'd dropped in the long grass on the far bank, and which I desperately hoped might contain something that would give me a clue why all this was happening. Only when I'd done that, I thought, would I feel able to get off home to a couple of paracetamols and a warm bed.

But it had been hours before I was able to get away. I'd been forced to stay and watch while the firemen performed the futile and ironic task of pouring water into a boat, a paramedic patched up my wounds, and my new boater friends had hunted round to find me some dry clothes. Even after the firefighters and the police had left, I'd waited in my car until I was sure that the *Rose Marie* people were settled down for the night. Then I'd walked along the towpath to the nearest footbridge, a quarter of a mile along the canal, before I could work my way along the edge of the fields and locate my package – a soaking mess in the grass.

By then, I'd been nearly blind with weariness and pain. I'd driven back to Lichfield in a stupor, like someone drugged. A few hours later, I'd woken up lying on my bed in my clothes, soaked in sweat and stiff with bruising, whimpering with terror – only to be called back to the scene and forced to explain myself all over again to DS Graham on a freezing canal bank.

'If you've talked to Mrs Wentworth, she'll have told you that the reason I came out here last night was because she rang me,' I said.

'Yes, she did,' admitted Graham.

'And she rang me because she couldn't get any satisfactory response from the police.'

'I've checked with the control room. She did make two calls, but the information she gave was very vague. A patrol came by during the evening, but everything seemed to be quiet.' He shrugged. 'We get a lot of calls like that. Especially from householders in this sort of area. Strange noises at night, you know. Very common.'

'So she rang me instead, and I came. But there seems to have been someone else here too. Doesn't there, sergeant?'

'If your version of events is correct, Mr Buckley.'

I knew I was fighting a losing battle. Everything that happened seemed to conspire to convince the police that I was a one-man crime wave. For the moment, Graham would have to be allowed to believe that I'd set fire to *Kestrel* myself. I had no evidence to prove otherwise. Moreover, I hadn't even got a theory about why any of it had happened.

But I knew that I had an accurate memory of the smell of diesel, as well as the subtle movement of the boat like someone stepping on and off the stern. Had the fire been meant for me personally? If so, why? Had this unidentified person realised I'd find something on board *Kestrel*? But who had known I'd be there at the boat? And who'd known that Godfrey Wheeldon had given me the keys? There was no one person that fitted the bill for both questions, which made the whole thing impossible.

'And you say you got the keys to the boat from a gentleman in Cheshire?' said DS Graham with a disbelieving rise in his voice.

'His name's Godfrey Wheeldon. I've given you the address. He said he was sure Great-Uncle Samuel wanted him to pass the keys on to me.'

'Even so, that doesn't make the boat your property, Mr Buckley. At the very least, we're looking at illegal entry.'

Caroline Longden appeared at the end of the path at the back of Ash Lodge. She spoke to neither of us, but merely gazed coolly at the wreck of *Kestrel*. She was wearing a red fleece, and her face was flushed a clashing pink.

'I'll need to talk to you later, Miss Longden,' called DS Graham.

'I'll be in the house,' she said, with a cold stare in my direction. Then she disappeared again.

Graham turned back to me. 'Naturally we asked Miss Longden to make sure everything was all right in the house.'

'Naturally?'

Gradually, under his penetrating gaze, the message began to sink in. The police did not believe my story about why I'd been on the boat. They thought I might have ransacked the house, too, looking for valuables. Had Caroline told them something that would give them this idea?

'She's rather upset, of course,' said Graham. 'Who wouldn't be? But we've got somebody up at the house with her to check on the contents.'

'Funnily enough, I'm quite upset as well. It was me that someone tried to kill, you know. If I'm not mistaken, that's generally considered attempted murder in English law.'

'We'll be conducting a full investigation, sir.'

And from the way he said 'sir', I could see that I would get no further.

*   *   *

302

When Graham had finished with me, I walked up the path to Ash Lodge and knocked at the front door, like a polite visitor. Caroline was reluctant to let me in. The chill that struck outwards from the dark hallway wasn't entirely due to the fact that the house had stood empty for weeks. She regarded me with a hostile expression as I tried to explain falteringly what had happened.

'Really?' She raised her eyebrows. 'Are you feeling quite well?'

'Well, just a few cuts and bruises—'

'I was thinking more of your mental health.'

'You think I'm making it up?'

'It's all rather far-fetched, isn't it? People following you and trying to kill you? I suppose you'll say that none of it is your fault.'

'Well—'

'You must admit that rather a lot of things have gone wrong since you came into my father's life. What is it going to be next?'

'Caroline, you can't blame me for—' I was about to say 'for what happened to the boat', but I saw from her eyes that it was more than that. I felt a sense of shock, and the words came out as if someone else had spoken them. 'But of course. You blame me for your father's death.'

'Well, it's in the blood, isn't it?' she said, a trifle defensively. 'The famous split in the Buckley family.'

'I never knew anything about the damn, stupid split until Samuel told me.'

'How can I believe that?'

She was right, of course. It *was* unbelievable. Unbelievable that I should have known nothing about the division in my family, even about the very existence of half of it. I could barely believe it myself. And if my credibility with Caroline was already undermined from the word 'go', why should she believe me about anything else?

Before I could say any more, a figure appeared behind Caroline, a dark shadow in the hallway. He glowered ferociously when he saw me at the door.

'Mr Buckley,' said Simon Monks, managing to load my own name with a dripping weight of menace. 'It must be a little while since we met at Fradley.'

'Two weeks,' I said, grimacing at the prospect of even more unpleasantness.

'Really? Long enough to forget what we were talking about, was it?'

'I've come to explain to Caroline—'

'Yes, I heard what you were explaining. And I heard her say she didn't want to know.'

How could Caroline stand him? Couldn't she see the potential for violence that oozed from his every pore?

'It doesn't matter,' she said. 'Chris was just going anyway.'

'Excellent. Then you won't mind if I walk you back to your car, Mr Buckley.'

Caroline watched us for a few moments. But before we'd gone ten yards I heard the front door close behind us. The slam sounded like the door of a prison cell closing behind the condemned man as he walked to the gallows. Though Caroline could barely bring herself to be civil to me, I desperately missed her presence as soon as I was alone with her fiancé.

Monks fell into step with me, walking close by my elbow – much too close for comfort. I could smell his sweat, mingled with a cheap deodorant. He was six inches taller than me, and I found myself gazing down at my feet to avoid having to look up at him. I noticed the heavy toe caps and thick soles of his black boots. They must have been size ten, at least.

As somebody who'd just escaped a violent death, I ought to have been able to stand up to crude intimidation, but I couldn't account for the irrational fear he instilled in me. I wondered where the police officer was who DS Graham had sent to the house. If there was ever a time I wanted to see a policeman, it was now.

Monks's voice was low and threatening when he spoke. 'You're on a slippery slope, Chris,' he said. 'When are you going to see sense?'

I tried to quicken my pace to get ahead of him as we neared the bottom of the drive.

'Is that your car?' he said. 'It's seen better days, I'd say. A bit like you, old pal.'

I was ashamed to see that my hand shook as I slid my key into the lock. My body was tense and painful, as if it was expecting at any moment to get a punch in the kidneys or a hand slammed in the door. That was the way Monks made me feel with every word he spoke. It was a dread and apprehension made familiar in my childhood by a certain note in my father's voice.

I wondered if Mrs Wentworth was watching from her front window, and whether she'd report it if she saw Monks attack me in the street. She must know him as Caroline's fiancé, while I was reduced to the level of a suspicious person again, a definite undesirable. For all I knew, she might be the kind who longed for tough vigilantes in size ten boots dispensing summary justice to keep the riff-raff out of the area.

Monks placed his hand on my shoulder before I could get fully into the car, and I found myself unable to move, crouched at an awkward, undignified angle that sent spasms of pain shooting through my aching legs and back.

'Be careful,' he said.

Finally, he let me get into the car. It didn't give me any reassurance to be able to see him in my mirror, watching me as I drove away.

Back at Stowe Pool Lane, the front room was starting to look like an explosion in a library. Sheets of paper lay limp and crumpled on almost every surface, with the gas fire left on to provide enough heat to evaporate the water that had soaked into them. There were damp patches on the table and the seats of the chairs, and drips had landed on the carpet in dozens of places. The windows had steamed up, and condensation was running onto the ledges.

Inevitably, I hadn't been in the house more than a few minutes when there was a knock on the back door. Rachel had called to see how I was.

'Have you still got a headache? How's the lump on your head? That burn could do with some cream on it.'

'I'm all right, Rachel. Don't fuss.'

'All right? You look a wreck.'

I felt it, too. But I didn't want reminding of my injuries, because I was trying to keep my mind off the events that had caused them. It was proving very difficult, and I needed something to distract me. I was hoping the last bit of Samuel's manuscript would do it.

'What are the police doing? Have they got any clues who it was?'

'As far as I can gather, they seem to think I cracked my own skull, tried to set fire to myself and then nearly drowned, just to annoy them.'

'Useless! I presume they've made the link with the break-in. It must have been the same man who broke into your house and attacked me. Well, mustn't it?'

I groaned pitifully as her voice got louder and more piercing. 'I really don't know, Rachel.'

Then she saw the snowdrift of damp paper. 'Good lord, what's all this?'

'From the writing, I think it's more of Samuel's manuscript.'

'Wow. The missing section?'

'Could be. Though whether it's going to be legible, I don't know.'

'Whoever attacked you could have taken their chance to get the manuscript,' said Rachel. 'I wonder why they didn't.'

'Perhaps they didn't know it was there. Or they took the easy way and decided to destroy it, along with anything else on board *Kestrel*.'

'And you.'

I nodded. 'The fire would have burnt the manuscript to a cinder, if I hadn't grabbed it.' I looked again at the soggy, faded mass of pulp. 'As it is, they pretty much succeeded anyway. I don't think they wanted the manuscript for themselves. They just didn't want anyone else to have it.'

Rachel lifted a page from the edge of the table, and a pool of water ran from under it onto the floor. She screwed up her eyes to make out the writing, which was beginning to smudge and blur.

'Be careful with it.'

'This looks like page one,' she said. 'What's it about?'

'I haven't attempted to read it yet.'

'If you don't read it soon, it's going to disappear altogether.'

I looked over her shoulder. The black scrawl was fading in front of my eyes. 'God, you're right.'

'It's water-soluble ink. He never seemed to use a ballpoint pen, did he?'

A feeling close to hysteria took hold of me. The ordeal on board *Kestrel* and my enforced dip in the canal had only seemed tolerable as long as there was something worthwhile at the end of it. But if the manuscript became illegible, it would all have been for nothing. The pounding in my head was like the worst hangover I had ever suffered – except that when I had a hangover I knew that I'd already enjoyed my pleasure beforehand. This was different. My reward for what I'd suffered was about to be snatched away from me by the effects of a bit of canal water.

'We'll have to make a copy, quick.'

'It's too late,' said Rachel. 'There are barely any fragments still legible.'

'Tell me it's not true,' I pleaded.

307

'There is one name here I can make out,' she said. 'Not a Buckley though.'

'Yes?'

'Sounds a bit familiar. Lindley Simpson. Who's he?'

It was about this time that I began sleeping badly. Fear and guilt are insidious, and they do strange things to your mind. Sometimes, in my dreams, I imagined myself responsible for the violent deaths of my ancestors – not only Samuel, but also his grandfather Josiah and even the distant William.

I saw myself rather like the central character in that old Ealing comedy, *Kind Hearts and Coronets*, who bumps off his relatives one by one so that he can inherit the family title. In the film, all the relatives are played by Alec Guinness. And in my disordered mind, all my ancestors became a blur, too – they all had the face of Great-Uncle Samuel. Then I would awake from the dream and realise that it wasn't me who'd been destroying my Buckley ancestors, but someone else. And I was a Buckley too. I would be next on their list.

At other times, there was a different dream. For weeks I'd been plagued by images of Great-Uncle Samuel dying in the road at Castle Dyke. But now there were other scenes mingled with it in a terrifying panorama of death.

First I seemed to see a horse, and to hear a man with a wheeze in his throat. I heard a whistling sound, like something passing through the air . . . Then it switched to *Kestrel*, and the impact of the windlass hitting my skull, the stench of diesel fuel in my nostrils and the sound of flames around me as I faced the prospect of my own death. But suddenly I was out of *Kestrel* and on the hatches of a strange boat, moored by a lock gate, watching the water boil in the darkness, seeing a spreading stain and a shape rising from the depths . . . And once more I was back to the day before, floundering helplessly in the cut, ready to go down to the muddy bottom for the second time as *Kestrel* burned above me.

308

They say that it's possible to regress to an earlier life, and even to remember your own death. This dream was like dying three times over. Samuel, Josiah, William.

Was it just an over-active imagination? Or was it some kind of genetic memory? Great-Uncle Samuel had planted the idea in my mind, and my subconscious had taken over. Now I was living the deaths of my ancestors over and over.

The effect was peculiar. An attack on an ancestor felt like an attack on me, and it gave me a new outlook on the idea of vengeance. Few people can be presented with the opportunity of avenging their own death.

40

Pipehill, Lichfield, Staffordshire. Friday 17th Jan. 1800.

To Reuben Wheeldon Esq., Warner Street, Ellesmere, Cheshire.

My dear friend,

I confess I am utterly confounded. Every thing gives me additional disturbance. Yet I am loath to think myself of so much importance as to suppose every one in a plot against me. After all, I hope the best; but if this should turn out to be a plot, nothing, I fear, but a Miracle can save me. Can the heart of man be capable of such black deceit?

I have passed two days at Burton and in the Neighbourhood, during which I have had occasion to call on my brother. I fear he passes his time swallowing doses of oblivion, as I found him more full of blue ruin than good manners. And he said, in an indirect way, that I had no Business there.

As for my Friends in Lichfield, I am heartily sick of them, for they have deceived me sadly. Do we not see hypocrisy, selfishness, folly and impudence succeed while Merit is trodden underfoot? The web of human life unravels into threads of Meanness, Spite and Cowardice, want of feeling and of indifference towards others. I have been mistaken in my public and private hopes, always disappointed where I placed most reliance. I am a bitter bad judge of the characters of men.

The grievous affliction I am now suffering under is of the bitterest kind, because it is proceeding from a cause which no time can remove. Now my Enemies spread calumny about me. I have become the butt for paltry spite. If they take away a man's Character, there is no degree of turpitude or injustice that they may not introduce into the measures and treatment which we consider as most fit for them.

My friend, this is a trying time. It is now the heart sickens, as I think what they are about and how short a time will determine my Fate. Mr P. has presumed too much on himself, but I haven't done with him yet.

Your friend,
Wm Buckley

41

Although I had been out of work for only a matter of days, I'd already fallen into the habit of getting up late. The dreams I was having didn't help. I spent the night tossing restlessly in my bed, tormented by formless anxieties, and occasionally waking up with a jolt of panic. The result was that I got up in the morning feeling sweaty and drained. Thanks to whoever had wielded that windlass so effectively, I now also had a constant thumping headache, and a churning nausea to go with it.

The sick feeling in my stomach made me feel as though I'd swallowed too much canal water. But in fact, it was caused by the memory of fear. It was a continuous, writhing terror in my guts that came every time I recalled how near to death I'd been, how somebody had coldly and deliberately attempted to cremate me on board *Kestrel*.

Some people seem to be able to brush off fear. But not me. I was an ordinary man who'd lived a quiet, even sheltered life. I'd experienced nothing more threatening than the face of a pub landlord calling last orders, or a white envelope containing my P45. Violence was alien to me. Or it had been since my childhood. I'd always hoped it would never touch my life again.

It was an irony that I'd spent the last few weeks thinking about death. The deaths of William and Josiah Buckley, and particularly the untimely death of Great-Uncle Samuel, which had been painful enough. Events had even made me reflect on the passing of my own parents, sad and unpleasant deaths in their own particular ways. But it takes a moment when death stares you personally in the face to make you recognise what it really is.

It was something for which I had been ludicrously unprepared. The shock of it had jolted me from a deeply ingrained complacency. And it had taught me what true fear was.

When I answered the door that morning, clutching my temple against the excruciating racket of the bell, it was in full expectation of finding Rachel on the doorstep, full of overwhelming sympathy and bright new ideas. But instead I saw a face whose expression held a fear that I recognised as if it were my own.

'Frank!'

He was fidgeting and nervous, casting glances down the street, and his clothes looked as though they'd been thrown on in any order. He was pale, and his hair stood up on end as if he'd been running his fingers through it.

'Chris, can I come in?'

He was asking plaintively, as if he fully expected me to say no and send him away. But how could I do that when I recognised a fellow sufferer? Here was another man who'd discovered that life was not as benign as he'd always been led to believe. He was a man whose fragile defences had failed to cope with the real world, and I was beginning to know how he felt.

'Have you been home?' I said as he entered the hallway. 'Does Sally know where you are?'

'No, I haven't been back,' he said, and shivered as if he was remembering a night spent sleeping rough on the street.

'You've got to talk to her.'

'I will. But I've got to do this first.'

'Do what?'

'Tell you what you wanted to know, that first day you came to Chasetown. I thought if I didn't help you, I'd be able to keep out of it. But I got frightened. It was after you came that second time, and you saw me by the reservoir, I realised that I was in a more vulnerable position than I thought.'

I frowned at him, trying to work out what he meant. 'Did you think I might try to put pressure on you once I knew your little secret? Well, don't worry about that. I'm not into blackmail.'

'No, no, it's not that. Please don't be angry with me, Chris. This is very hard for me. I've had a very bad couple of days. For a while, I thought . . . well, I thought there was only one way out.'

His shoulders slumped, and I could see in him the classic case of a weak man, unable to resist the temptations that tormented him, who'd suddenly seen the prospect of his respectable facade being blown apart. He was facing a future spent trying to explain and justify the unjustifiable.

I took him into the sitting room and turned on the gas fire in the tiled fireplace to fight the chill. Frank stood facing the fish tank as if frightened of contact with the yellow three-piece suite.

'When you left home, what did you intend to do?' I asked.

He stared at the fish without seeing them. 'I didn't know what I intended to do. I was very confused. But frightened too. Frightened of what you might do, and what other people might do. But I didn't have the courage to find a way out. I'm too much of a coward for that. So in the end I went back, with my tail between my legs. And I saw that the only thing to do was tell you everything. Then you might not make the mistake of putting yourself in danger too.'

'I think I've already done that, Frank.'

'Oh, hell,' he said. He followed the movement of a neon tetra with absorption. I recalled Leo Parker standing in almost

314

the same spot admiring the fish in his calculating way, like a visiting salesman.

I told Frank about the fire on the boat and my narrow escape. He listened carefully, his expression growing ever more fearful until I thought he was going to burst into tears.

'Maybe we both need a stiff drink,' I said. 'Then you can tell me what you've come to say.'

'I should have come before. I hope I'm not too late.'

I fetched a bottle and two glasses from the kitchen and poured Frank a large Glenmorangie. At first he spluttered and coughed over it like a man who'd never tasted real whisky before. But the colour came back to his face almost immediately, and his eyes began to lose a bit of their haunted whiteness. I persuaded him to settle in one of the armchairs and turned up the heat on the gas fire. A smell of burning dust filled the air, but neither of us paid it any notice.

While my father's old carriage clock ticked away on the wall and the tetras and mollies flicked restlessly backwards and forwards in their tank, Frank told me that he'd been ten years old when his parents divorced, born when his mother Alison was just eighteen. Though his father had stayed in Burntwood, Alison had taken their son and moved to Lichfield, putting four or five miles between them. Not very far on the map maybe, but enough of a symbol of separation for a young boy.

Then Frank's mother had gone back to work. She'd found a job in the offices of the Sandfields Brewery, which was expanding under the guidance of its new chairman, Samuel Longden. Alison was thirty by then, and an attractive woman, according to Frank, who may have been biased. Within two years, Alison had become the boss's secretary, and Samuel came to rely on her as he finalised plans to sell off the brewery to one of the national companies in Burton-on-Trent.

In 1969, Samuel retired a wealthy man. Alison might well have been out of a job, if he hadn't solved the problem by asking her to marry him. Though she was twenty-three years his junior, Alison had agreed.

'What did Samuel look like then?' I asked Frank.

He stirred uneasily and gulped the last of his whisky. I refilled his glass while he collected his thoughts, thrown out of gear by my interruption.

'He was tall, very upright, with wavy grey hair swept back. Distinguished, I suppose you'd say. He never seemed to laugh much, though. Sally once said he had a mysterious air about him, like somebody who'd suffered in the past. She thought it must be something to do with his time in the navy during the war. And there was something else the women always seemed to go for. He had these blue eyes . . .'

'Was that what your mother saw in him, do you think? A romantic figure?'

Frank bared his teeth in a bitter grin.

'Oh yes. But did I mention that he was stinking rich as well?'

'Go on.'

Frank had been furious at Alison's marriage to Samuel Longden. As a teenager he'd spent a tortured period living in Ash Lodge with his mother and the doting Samuel, shutting himself in his room and playing Rolling Stones records at full volume.

My great-uncle apparently had the good sense to leave the lad to his own devices. Though money was no object, Frank had stubbornly refused to accept expensive presents. Instead, he'd thrown himself into his A levels, and had escaped permanently by earning a place at a polytechnic in Birmingham to study Electrical Engineering. He'd spent his college vacations at his father's terraced house in Burntwood rather than at the gloomy Victorian retreat that Samuel had taken his mother to. There was even more reason for him to stay away from Whittington when his mother became pregnant with Samuel's child – Frank's half-sister, Caroline Longden.

He and Sally married in the late 1970s, but never had children, which was a great disappointment to Sally. There was an underlying hint that she'd been envious of Alison, who now had a new child, nineteen years younger than Frank.

'You don't have to tell me all this,' I said. 'It's Samuel I want to know about.'

But he was well into his second tumbler of whisky, and the alcohol was loosening his tongue. Once he'd started talking, it came in a flood, while his eyes roved the room, staring at the clock, peering at the fish in their tank as if he could read a meaning to his life in their gaping mouths and flickering tails.

When the Chaplins visited Whittington, Sally had been taken by the young Caroline, who was bright and musically talented. More than once, disparaging comparisons had been made between Caroline and Frank. The suggestion that Frank had cause to regret inheriting his character and looks from his father rather than from his mother planted a seething animosity in his heart.

David Chaplin had died in 1986 after a stroke. Frank was devastated, and made no secret of the fact that no relationship went anywhere near the closeness he'd felt to his father.

When his mother was killed in that car crash on the A38 just two years later, his first reaction was that justice had been done at last. Frank had hardly been able to mourn his mother in the way he should have, because there was no room for fresh mourning alongside the grief for his father. In his soul, he became once again that rebellious, long-haired seventeen-year-old. He didn't want to speak to Sally, and certainly not to his stepfather. All he wanted was to be left alone to replay those old Rolling Stones songs – if only in his mind.

'Sympathy for the Devil,' he said.

'I'm sorry?' Was he referring to Samuel? Did Frank really

317

see his stepfather as an evil monster who'd wrecked his life? I was beginning to wonder where Frank had been on the night that Samuel was killed, when he spoke again.

'That was my favourite. Most people go for "Honky Tonk Women" or "Jumpin' Jack Flash" from that period. But I liked the *Beggar's Banquet* album the best. Do you know it?'

'Oh, the Stones? I was more of a Beatles fan myself. Everybody was always one or the other, weren't they?'

'Sure.' He looked at me condescendingly, and for a moment I could see that sneering, bad-tempered teenager. '"Street Fighting Man", that was on *Beggar's Banquet*. But I liked "Sympathy for the Devil" best. Can you remember how it starts?'

'Yes, I think I remember that.'

Frank laughed and looked for more Glenmorangie. 'The number of times I played that at full blast after Mum told me she was going to marry Samuel Longden. Over and over. It must have driven her up the wall. "Please allow me to introduce myself, I'm a man of wealth and taste." She knew who it was meant to be about, all right.'

'Did you lose touch with Samuel altogether after your mother died?'

'For a while,' said Frank. 'But he turned up again.'

Frank had been made to feel uncomfortable at his own mother's funeral. For a start, it was far more lavish than he was used to, and the eulogies were too pious and sentimentalised for his non-conformist inclinations. He knew very few of the people there to mourn his mother. They'd been friends of hers and Samuel's and 'not his type', he said. The salt in his wounds was the contrast between the no-expense-spared extravagance of his mother's sending-off and the perfunctory hymn and a few words as his father's plywood coffin had been shoved into the flames at a crematorium near Sutton Coldfield.

For ten years after that he'd seen almost nothing of Samuel

and Caroline Longden. As Frank put it sourly, 'they didn't move in the same circles'. Once or twice, Caroline had phoned to ask how Frank and Sally were and suggested the Chaplins might like to visit Ash Lodge. But the right time had never presented itself, and perhaps she hadn't meant it anyway, said Frank. There had never been any possibility of the Longdens visiting Chasetown.

And then, out of the blue, old Samuel had appeared at the bowling club one Sunday morning. Frank got the shock of his life when he saw the old man standing on the far side of the green as he was lining up one of his woods. It put him right off his aim, and his partner had made sarcastic comments. Samuel had just stood there, in his black overcoat, leaning on his stick, until the game was over. And then he'd walked over to Frank and had greeted him like a long-lost son. Yes, that was exactly it, said Frank – like a long-lost son.

'When was this, Frank?'

'Last year, towards the back end. September, probably.'

'Just five or six months ago.'

'About that.'

'Okay.'

Frank returned his gaze to the fish tank, switching effortlessly out of the present and back into the past.

Samuel had wanted to take Frank somewhere for lunch. But Frank had refused to go 'anywhere posh' and they ended up eating meat pies in the clubhouse. He often stayed all day at the bowling club, and so Sally wouldn't be expecting him for lunch. It was almost as if Samuel had known this, just as he'd known where to find Frank despite their lack of communication for years.

And then the old man asked for his stepson's help. Frank had been so astonished that he nearly choked on his pie. But as Samuel told his tale, Frank had become increasingly sure that his stepfather had turned senile and lost his marbles completely. It was a complicated, rambling story that went back into ancient history and was all about people Frank had never heard of being murdered by other people he'd never heard of. There was a feud, Samuel said, lasting two hundred years – and it was Samuel's job to set the record straight and take revenge. That was the first time that Frank had ever heard the name Buckley mentioned.

'You told me at Chasetown that it was your mother or father who mentioned Samuel once being a Buckley,' I said.

'So I was lying. You might think it was for your own good, Chris, when I've finished.'

Despite my prompting, Frank was hazy on the details of the feud that Samuel described. Yes, he remembered there had been a William Buckley a long time ago who was an engineer of some kind, connected with the canal. He'd been a good man, but had upset the wrong people and they had him disgraced and murdered. That was Samuel's very phrase – 'disgraced and murdered'. And there was another one who was something to do with the canal, with a strange name. Yes, it could well have been Josiah. Murdered too, Samuel had said.

But it had all passed over Frank's head. At least until Samuel mentioned Alison, Frank's mother, and 'the murder of another Buckley'. The old man said the feud had pursued him for centuries, and that it claimed the life of his son. Of course, Frank had no idea that Samuel had a son, and made the mistake of laughing when the old man explained that it was his unborn son. Because Alison had been fifty years old when she and Samuel's secretary, Karen Mills, had died on the A38.

Samuel became angry at the laughter and told Frank that there was just one thing he needed him to do. There were documents, Samuel said, which proved what he'd been saying, which implicated those responsible for the murders. He wanted Frank to look after them until they were needed. Samuel believed it was too risky keeping them at Ash Lodge. He thought the documents would be safe in the hands of someone like Frank, who was 'family'. Safe – but on one condition.

'He told me then about how he'd been a Buckley until he had changed his name,' said Frank. 'And he told me who the other family were in this feud.'

'Yes.'

'Don't you want to know?'

'It was the Parkers, wasn't it?'

'Oh.' Frank looked disappointed, as if his whole story had been in vain. 'Yes, he warned me that I'd have to be wary of anyone called Parker, that they might come after me if they thought I had the documents. He told me to watch out for anyone asking around about my connection with Samuel Longden, that I should tell him straightaway, so that he could decide what to do. Anything else would be very dangerous, he said.'

'At least he was honest with you about that, Frank.'

'Oh yes. But when somebody did come asking around the bowling club one day, Samuel was already dead. So I didn't know what to do. Suddenly it seemed as though it must all be true. I thought "They've killed Samuel, just like he said they would, and now they're going to kill me because they think I've got those documents." I was still a bit upset after you saw me on the heath, and I sort of panicked.'

'You should have come to see me sooner.'

'Well, I thought of you, of course. After what you said at the funeral, about the book, I knew you were carrying on where Samuel left off. So, of course, I did try to find you. I didn't want to come to your house at first, in case they were watching. But I saw your car, and I followed you to that old canal place.'

'The wharf at Fosseway.'

'That's right. I was going to try to attract your attention and tell you what I've told you now.'

'So what went wrong? Why did you run off?'

Frank dragged his eyes away from the fish tank and shuddered. He hunched closer to the gas fire, seeking warmth. But it wasn't the cold that had made him shiver.

'Just at the last minute, I recognised him,' he said.

'Who?'

'The bloke who was asking about me at the bowling club. It was him. I saw him at the club, and I saw him again at Fosseway. He's one of them, isn't he?'

'Leo Parker,' I murmured.

'Samuel warned me to watch out for the Parkers.'

'Did he mention the MP, Lindley Simpson?'

Frank shook his head. 'Only the Parkers. He said they're dangerous.'

'I'm sorry you've got so involved, Frank. It isn't really your fight.'

'You're right, it isn't. But they don't know that, do they? I want you to get them off my back. That's why I came. That's why I've told you all this stuff. You can see it's nothing to do with me.'

'If you give me the documents, that would be a lot safer for you.'

'What?'

'Let me have the documents Samuel gave you for safe keeping. Then I can look after them instead. I might know what to do with them.'

'You're joking. I haven't got any documents.'

'But you said—'

'Do you think I'm stupid? He wanted me to take the documents, yes. But as soon as he told me how dangerous it was, I said "no" right away. Why should I put myself at risk? He was no relative of mine, not really. I didn't owe old Samuel Longden a thing.'

I stared at Frank, amazed. 'Still no sympathy for the devil then,' I said quietly.

'You what?'

But his attention had drifted back to the tank. Something in there was fascinating him, as if it reflected his own doubtful future.

'By the way,' he said at last, 'did you know one of your fish is dead?'

42

I can't say the visit to the bank manager was an easy one. For a start, the atmosphere between Dan Hyde and myself was decidedly cool. He was under no illusions that I blamed him for the financial disaster we were facing. But, as far as the bank were concerned, we were equal partners, jointly responsible for repaying the debt. We just had one chance to convince them we'd be able to pay, before they took us to court.

In a tiny, overheated office, the bank manager made it quite clear from the outset that he had no faith in any prospect of reviving the fortunes of our dot-com business. He shook his head sadly at the foolishness of suggesting that it might be a going concern. It was difficult to believe this was the same man who'd accepted our proposal with keen interest and handed us the loan to launch our start-up. Now, he said we had no proper business plan. And he was right.

It was an ill-fated project, of course. For my part, I thought my biggest mistake had been trusting Dan to have the finances under control. You can't stint on investment in the early days of a new venture. We'd poured money in, full of optimism. But in the excitement of our own enthusiasm, we'd badly overestimated. If we'd managed to keep afloat for a few months longer, things might have been different. There's nothing like the appearance of stability and success to attract money. But we were destined never to make it that far.

While the bank manager lectured us on the art of cash-flow analysis, I found I could hardly concentrate on what he was saying for worrying about my own future, which was very much on the line. Re-establishing myself as a journalist was an uphill task I found daunting.

I'd wanted to look to the future, but somehow the past had crept up on me and I couldn't escape it. My one positive inheritance from the venture was a good computer set-up at home, which was at least paid for. Now I'd have to go back to the beginning and re-learn my trade, if I wasn't to starve as a result of my folly.

When it finally became obvious from the direction of the discussion that the axe was going to fall, I knew I'd have to throw in my one final ace – the book, and Samuel Longden's legacy.

'Well, well,' said Dan afterwards, as we emerged into the drizzle, sweating from the suffocating heat and anxiety of the meeting. 'That was a bit of a surprise, Chris.'

'I shouldn't have had to do it.'

'Still – fifty grand. Very handy.'

'I haven't earned it yet. I've got to publish the book first.'

We stood on the pavement on the corner of the market square. Dan was carrying a document case with our accounts, unpaid invoices and failed business plan all neatly collected for inspection. In front of us, the market was in full swing, and Dr Johnson's statue looked embarrassed among a stack of orange crates and bags full of cauliflower trimmings.

'Well, maybe we can come to an arrangement there,' said Dan.

'What do you mean?'

'A little business proposition.'

'You're joking.'

'Why?'

'After the dot-com?'

'That was just a bit of bad luck, Chris. We got the timing wrong, that's all. You'll see, somebody else will get in there in a year or two and take the market. It's a pity. Perhaps we ought to have another go some time.'

I snorted. 'Count me out, Dan.'

I began to walk fast towards Bore Street, where I'd found a space to park the Escort near Sarah Siddons House and the shops in City Arcade. Dan ran to stay at my elbow, talking all the while, trying to convince me of some new dream. He was the same old Dan.

'All right, forget that. But I was thinking of diversifying anyway, Chris. Putting online retail on the back burner for a while.'

'Found another market to corner, have you?'

'That's right. Heritage.'

'What?'

'Heritage. Local history, nostalgia, traditions. All Your Yesterdays, Your Town in Old Postcards, The Way We Were. You know.'

'I see. And that's big business, is it?'

'It certainly is. There's lots of money floating round in the grey sector these days, and the demographic trends are definitely indicating a growth in market opportunities.'

'I don't know what the hell you're talking about, Dan.'

'Look, take my word for it, nostalgia is the thing in publishing these days. Business is booming, I can tell you. I thought you'd be interested, Chris. Your project sounds just the sort of thing.'

I stopped in front of the tourist information centre and turned to face him.

'Do I take it you're offering to help publish my book?'

'Well, let's say I'd be available to discuss terms. Do you want to meet up some time?'

'No.'

'Family history. Unsolved mysteries. Memories of the canal trade. It's good stuff – lots of local interest.'

326

'I don't think so, Dan.'

'We could team up. I'll handle the printing and marketing. Maybe we could make it a real seller. What do you say, Chris? History is the future.'

'Forget it.'

I could almost have laughed then, as we stood in front of the elegant Georgian facade of Donegal House and the half-timbered Tudor building next door that had been converted into a restaurant. A few yards away was the Guildhall, where you could still ring the bell and ask to see the dungeons. History was all around us, and here was the man who'd nearly ruined me telling me that it was the future. He ought to have teamed up with Great-Uncle Samuel – they'd have made a good pair with their big plans for my life.

By the time I reached the car, Dan was starting to fall behind. I had my keys in my hand before I had a sudden thought.

'Dan – that anonymous backer.'

'Chris, I've told you—'

'No, wait. This is important. Just tell me who the lawyer was that you dealt with.'

'Oh, it was some stuffy old bloke from a local firm. They've got offices in Lichfield. Just round the corner from here, in fact.'

'Surely you know the name.'

'Yes, hang on. I've got it here. There's a letter somewhere.' He unzipped his document case and shuffled through the papers in it. 'Yes, here it is. Elsworth and Clarke, that's it. I dealt with a Mr Elsworth.'

I'd reluctantly agreed to let Frank stay for a day or two in the spare bedroom at Maybank while he made his peace with Sally and 'got his head together'. I was glad that he seemed happy to keep to his room and not get in my way, because when I got home I couldn't wait to use the phone to try out

327

the idea that had just occurred to me. Luckily, I got straight through to the man I wanted.

'Mr Elsworth? Christopher Buckley.'

'Ah, Mr Buckley. Are you phoning concerning Samuel Longden's bequest?'

'No, something else. An anonymous donation made through you to our business start-up, *winningbid.uk.com*.'

Mr Elsworth was eloquently silent for a moment. I could almost see his raised eyebrow down the phone line. 'May I ask what your interest is in this matter?'

'I'm one of the partners in the venture. Or I was, until you pulled the plug on us.'

'Really? I dealt with a Mr Hyde on that matter.'

'My so-called partner.'

'Mmm.'

I'd never heard anybody put so many meanings into one sound. It wasn't even a word, yet it was infused with surprise, interest, courtesy, an unasked question, and a good measure of professional caution and reticence.

'I hope you're not going to ask me on whose behalf I was acting, Mr Buckley.'

'Yes, of course. That's exactly what I'm going to ask you.'

'But I'm sure you realise that I can't tell you. My client insisted on strict anonymity. That was made clear to Mr Hyde, I'm sure.'

'But, Mr Elsworth, it seems to me that I have the right to ask why the funding was withdrawn.'

'I'm sorry, but I'm not at liberty to discuss it with you. It was purely a business arrangement, and there was a clear condition allowing my client to withdraw at any time.'

I was obviously getting nowhere, so I decided to try a full-frontal assault. 'Was it Samuel Longden?'

'Really, Mr Buckley – client confidentiality is paramount in my considerations. I can't possibly answer your questions.'

'Well, thanks very much, Mr Elsworth,' I said sarcastically.

'I'm sorry I can't be of any further assistance.' He changed the subject smoothly. 'How's the book coming along, by the way?'

'Somehow there seem to be far more obstacles in my way than I ever imagined possible.'

'Oh dear. I do hope you manage to overcome them. I'm looking forward to receiving a copy when the time comes for you to claim your bequest.'

A few minutes later, Rachel bounced into the house singing 'Memories', with her notebook clutched to her bosom. She was smiling and had put on some make-up. I'd never seen her look so happy and glowing as she did just now.

'Good afternoon, number six.'

'Number four. Is that more research you've got there?'

'Ah yes. More revelations about the Parkers. The pieces are falling into place, Chris.'

'Do you reckon so?'

'Get the coffee made and pin your ears back.' She flourished the notebook. 'It took some time going through the parish records to find this. But I traced William Buckley's marriage back to 1796. He and Sarah were married at St Michael's. Have you ever seen the handwriting those old vicars used in the eighteenth century? I think they invented some of the letters themselves. And as for the spelling—'

'Why are we interested in his wedding? There was nothing odd about it, was there?'

'Not the wedding, but the bride.'

'Sarah? She was the daughter of one of the canal proprietors. That was in Samuel's manuscript.'

'Hasn't it dawned on you yet that there was a lot Samuel Longden left out of the manuscript? I think he did that deliberately. He expected you to find these things out for yourself. It was part of the way he manipulated you.'

'Okay,' I sighed. 'Tell me.'

'Well, what he doesn't say is which canal proprietor Sarah was the daughter of. Now, does he?'

I thought back. 'No, he doesn't. He never refers to her family by name. "Sarah's father" and "Sarah's brother" he calls them.'

'Right.' Rachel paused for dramatic effect. 'But the fact is, they were Parkers.'

I sat up suddenly. 'The Parkers. Do you mean Seth Parker, the banker? He was Sarah's father?'

'Right. And Francis Parker, who was transported—'

'He was her brother?'

'You've got it. They were all Parkers.'

'And so was Sarah herself.'

'Obviously.'

'And when William disappeared . . . "When he was murdered", I suppose you'll say . . . Sarah went back to live with her father. So little Edward was brought up in the Parker household. Yet William Buckley had blown the whistle on corruption and embezzlement in the canal company. It was William's evidence that got Francis Parker convicted and transported.'

'Yes.' She looked at me meaningfully. 'So what do you think that means?'

'That he was a man to whom honesty and integrity were more important than anything. More important than his wife's family, certainly. He took the honourable course of action and exposed Francis Parker's crime.' I thought it through a bit further. 'But to the Parkers, it must have seemed like a betrayal.'

'You can just picture old Seth, with his favourite son languishing in a prison hulk at Portsmouth. Imagine him plotting how he could take revenge on the traitor, William Buckley, without alienating his daughter. It was very convenient for the Parkers that William disappeared amid all those rumours about the work on the Colliery Arm. It meant he

330

was out of the way, and Seth got his daughter and grandson to himself. I don't doubt the rumours about William were put about by the Parkers.'

'And William was murdered by them?' I said. 'By the Parkers.'

She nodded. 'It looks very like it. Or by someone employed by them at least. You believe that now, don't you?'

Instead of answering, I quoted a line from one of William's letters: '"*Nothing, I fear, but a Miracle can save me.*"' Then I looked at Rachel. 'And there was no miracle, was there?'

'The accepted story was that William had absconded with the missing funds,' said Rachel. 'And nothing could be proved, because he was never found, alive or dead.'

'Until now,' I said, thinking of the human remains resting somewhere in a mortuary, still officially unidentified.

Rachel met my gaze. 'The next thing I looked at was the dispute many years later between Edward Buckley's son Josiah and the other canal carriers over a coal contract. We have William Buckley's letters. But we don't know as much about Josiah, do we?'

'Well, he was a boatman. Josiah and his family lived on the canal. I don't suppose he wrote letters very much. Perhaps he wasn't even literate.'

She nodded. 'Alfred was the child who went on to do well. He was the one who got an education, living on land with the Bensons. The family has gone through some ups and downs.'

'That's an understatement.'

'So you remember Josiah was found drowned in the canal?'

'Of course. His head had been battered against the wall of the lock when the sluices were opened. They said he fell in, and couldn't swim.'

'That's right.'

I detected some implication in her tone. 'Are you going to tell me Josiah was murdered by a rival?'

'Well, I checked on the companies he was competing with. Would it surprise you that one of the companies he beat to that contract was owned by the Parker family?'

'Bloody hell.'

'There's more,' she said.

'Really?' I could see her expression was more serious now. I sensed that her researches had come closer to the present than 1796.

'Another wedding. This one in 1949. Matthew and Mary.'

'What about them?'

'According to the parish register from Stonnall, there was a wedding there between Matthew Parker and Mary Parker, both of Stonnall Court. You see? The interesting thing is that they were not only Parkers after the wedding, they were both Parker before it.'

'So Mary was calling herself Parker already by then? Before she married Matthew? That's very odd. Why did she take his name so early?'

'She didn't,' said Rachel. 'She'd reverted to her maiden name.'

'Sorry?'

'Don't you get it yet, Chris? Matthew Parker was Mary's second cousin. She didn't need to change her name to his. She already had it. Mary was a Parker too.'

43

'It really didn't occur to you?' said Rachel. 'That Mary was a member of the Parker family?'

I slumped down in my chair. 'Of course not.'

And it hadn't at all. My image of my grandmother had been something quite different, a woman who'd made a difficult decision at some time in her life, but had done it out of love. I'd pictured Mary as someone who'd been vilified for an action we would hardly think unusual these days. Yet she'd been a Parker, of all things. It changed the whole picture.

'It all fits though, doesn't it?' I said. 'It all ties in. Apart from that mention of Lindley Simpson in the manuscript from *Kestrel*.'

'That may have meant nothing,' said Rachel, 'since we couldn't read the rest of it. And we know Simpson is connected with Leo Parker anyway. They're old business associates, and Simpson uses Parker as an advisor.'

I stood up and sat down again, suddenly restless and nervous. 'What I don't understand is – did Samuel want me to inquire into the lives of William and Josiah? Or did he want me to investigate his own death? Because there's no doubt in my mind that he foresaw it was going to happen. He told Frank as much.'

'But aren't they all connected?' said Rachel. 'The three deaths. William, Josiah, Samuel. What if there's a link? By answering one mystery, you could be answering them all. Josiah was William's grandson. Samuel was Josiah's grandson.'

'Okay, so there's a pattern.'

'And you . . .'

'Me? You can't include me. I'm not Samuel's grandson.'

'Oh? Think again, Chris. It seems to me you're the grandson he never had.'

Her words stumped me. Samuel had produced no son, despite his crazy delusion about Alison being pregnant when she died. Caroline might be expected to produce children one day – presumably by the loathsome Monks. But they wouldn't be Buckleys, and they'd be far too late for Samuel anyway. But it was irrelevant. The question was, what had Mary been up to? That was what Samuel had asked. It was the question that had tormented him most. Why did she do what she did?

'It should have occurred to me, shouldn't it? That Mary was a Parker, I mean. Everything that's happened to the Buckleys has happened through them. What she did – was it all part of the damn feud?'

Rachel had no answer. I paced across the room, my mind turning, looking for things to distract me. I paused at the carriage clock, opened its glass front and moved the hands carefully to a position that matched the time on my watch. Then I closed it again and brushed some dust off the top with my hand. Rachel watched me as I moved on to the fish tank. I bent to stare in at the fish, counting them as they went by – one fewer now since the neon tetra had died. A small tub of food stood by the tank, and I tapped some of it onto the surface of the water, watching the fish rise to intercept it. I counted them again as they gathered.

As I returned to my chair and sank into it, Rachel was laughing at me.

'Chris, you're just like your father. Arthur always did that with the clock and the fish.'

I thumped the arm of the chair so hard with my fist that the coffee table jumped an inch off the carpet and coffee spilled over the edge of a cup.

'I am NOT like my father!'

Rachel recoiled, staring at me in bewilderment and embarrassment. She'd never seen me lose my temper before, and I knew it wasn't a pretty sight. I breathed deeply, trying to control the rage that had swamped my mind from nowhere, and attempting to relax the trembling in my arms.

'I didn't mean to upset you,' she said quietly.

'Just don't say any more, please.'

After a moment I was able to reach out to pick up my coffee, not daring to meet her eyes. The bottom of the cup was wet where it had spilled, and I rubbed ineffectually at a splash on my trousers until the uncomfortable silence had gone on too long. In another minute, it would be too late to repair the damage my outburst had done.

'I'm sorry, Rachel. I shouldn't have shouted at you.'

'I didn't realise you were so sensitive about it.'

She tried to laugh it off, though she didn't look convincing. 'It's everybody's nightmare, isn't it? That they'll end up just like their father or their mother. At my age, I look in the mirror every morning for signs of it, don't you?'

'Not really,' I said.

But I did. I'd seen my father only this morning, staring back at me from the bathroom cabinet with the frightened, angry eyes of a person who was being driven inexorably to violence. They were the eyes of a man who'd terrorised me throughout my childhood, the father I'd been forced to face up to when I came home from Stafford.

When I returned to Lichfield, it was to a place only half recalled. By the early 1970s the population of the city had doubled with the creation of the first overspill housing estates for the conurbations of the West Midlands. By the 1990s, it had trebled. Yet the existence of these estates had somehow escaped my awareness in the claustrophobic atmosphere of my youth in Stowe Pool Lane. My landscape had been dominated by the cathedral, the Minster and Stowe pools and the seventy-eight acres of Beacon Park, with the shops of the city centre a few yards away.

So the things I'd previously taken for granted as part of normal life had begun to seem strange and unreal. Only then did I fully realise the determination of the city to hang on to its past. History lived and breathed in the streets. There were the endless performances of ancient customs, from the Greenhill Bower procession and the Sheriff's Ride to the Court of Arraye and the View of Frankpledge, whose very names seemed to be relics of the past preserved like insects in aspic.

Medieval buildings alternated with Georgian facades in a determined rearguard action against the encroachment of McDonald's and Superdrug. The market square where Edward Wightman became the last man in England to be burned at the stake was a few strides from WH Smith's and Allsports. In the Cathedral Close, the sounds of a choir seeped from oak doorways and the remains of fortifications still stood where they'd been left at the end of the Civil War. If the past was another country, you'd need a passport to enter Lichfield.

In my parents' house on Stowe Pool Lane, yet another part of the past had been preserved. Here, the air was redolent of the 1950s and early 60s. It almost came as a surprise to see a colour television in the corner of the sitting room, to glimpse the occasional CD among the vinyl Frank Sinatra records stacked by the stereo. The trouble was, this was my past. It was where I'd been brought up, where I'd spent the years when my beliefs and attitudes had been formed, for better or worse. The years when I learned what nightmares were, and I'd come to fear my father.

In my heart, I was afraid of relationships because I was afraid of becoming like him. Rachel might see the unconscious similarities in the things I did. But consciously, I'd tried to be as unlike him as I could. My father used to take me

336

to see Wolves play. Now I supported Aston Villa. I'd moved away from my home city, only to be drawn back again. Instead of a safe, boring job, I'd opted for a high-risk venture that had failed. I'd never married, and now I was learning what loneliness was. I preferred not to think of the past, of school, of my old schoolfriends. I even avoided the pop music from my teenage years because of its unpleasant associations. I'd tried to live in the present and look only to the future.

Now Great-Uncle Samuel had taught me a hard lesson. You can ignore other people's pasts, if you want to. But you can't turn your back on your own.

I came back to the present to find that Rachel had moved closer and was perched on the arm of my chair with an expression of concern. She touched my hand, and for once I didn't feel inclined to pull away. A shiver of dread had run through my body when my thoughts touched on those child-hood memories. There are times when contact with another human being is vital, whoever it may be.

'What were you thinking about then?' asked Rachel. 'Something awful.'

'My father,' I said.

She nodded. 'Did you really hate him?'

'Hate him? I was afraid of my father, yes. But I didn't hate him. I didn't resent him as much as I did my mother. It was my mother I expected to protect me, and she didn't do that.'

'Poor Chris. I wonder if your Great-Uncle Samuel realised what he was doing when he decided to make you look into your family and your past.'

'Oh, I think he realised that all right.'

Yes, Samuel Longden had deliberately set about re-awakening what he called my 'genetic memory'. He'd wanted me to face up to things that I thought I'd never known about, or had managed to forget. But you can't wipe things out of your mind altogether. You can only push them deeper into the dark corners of the subconscious. Forgetfulness is only a pretence of the mind, an implicit acknowledgement of unwelcome memories.

'But look at it positively,' said Rachel, still clinging to my hand. 'You've discovered another family now. One you never knew you had. You should talk to them. Talk to Caroline.'

'I don't need a family, thanks. I was always fine on my own.'

'We'd all like to think we're independent, but no one lives in isolation. You can't repudiate kinship. It's a fact of life. You're one of them, whether you like it or not.'

'We're not exactly going to gather round the piano for an old-fashioned family sing-along, are we? What's done is done, and it's nonsense to think we can go back and make it come out any different.'

'I've been wondering, though, Chris . . .'

'Yes?'

'What if the body they retrieved from the canal wasn't William Buckley?'

'We'll never know for certain, if the police won't get a DNA test.'

'No. But that might be for the best.'

'What do you mean?'

'Well, what if it wasn't a Buckley at all,' she said, 'but one of William and Josiah's enemies, a Parker? Francis maybe.'

'No, Francis was transported to Australia. How would he end up in a canal in Staffordshire?'

'Do we know he was transported permanently? Sometimes they were sent for a specific period, then allowed to return home.'

I hadn't known that. It unsettled me to think that Francis Parker, the real criminal, might have been allowed back to Staffordshire after serving his sentence.

'Well, perhaps not Francis,' said Rachel. 'But some other Parker. There were plenty of them, by all accounts.'

'But why are you suggesting this? What are you trying to say?'

338

'I'm just suggesting that both families might have been as bad as each other. You've been focused on the idea of William and Josiah being murdered, and that's understandable. But you've never considered a Parker might have been murdered by a Buckley.'

'As bad as each other?'

It was a hard thought. But I had to acknowledge that Rachel could be right again. I didn't know what else might have happened in the feud over those two centuries, what acts of violence could have kept it alive. An eye for an eye, a tooth for tooth. Some of the Buckleys might have believed in that. Perhaps I was one of them.

'It's academic anyway,' I said. 'There's no way they could identify the body without having some idea who it was, and then obtaining a DNA sample from a living relative for comparison. And even then, the best they could hope would be a familial match.'

Although I tried to dismiss the idea, Rachel had planted a doubt in my mind. I resolved not to mention the idea of a DNA test to the police again. If they'd written it off as too old a crime, it probably *was* for the best.

'Also,' she said tentatively, 'I've been wondering whether you're missing the point about what Samuel Longden expected you to do. Are you sure he wanted you to finish the book and publish it?'

'Of course. That's what he said.'

'When?'

I thought back carefully. 'Well, he didn't say it to me in person. He hadn't got round to explaining properly what he wanted when he died. But he left me the manuscript and all his notes, didn't he?'

'From which you assumed that he wanted you to finish it off. But he didn't actually say so.'

'Ah, but there was the letter he left with Mr Elsworth. That was clear.'

She raised an eyebrow. 'Was it? Have you still got it?'

'Somewhere here.'

'Find it and read it again.'

'But, for heaven's sake, what else could he have meant?'

'There might be another way that you could "finish it", other than publishing the book,' she said.

'You've lost me.'

'Well, ask yourself, finish what? You assumed he meant the book. But couldn't he just have easily meant he wanted you to finish the feud? There would be one way to do that – to decide you weren't going to take revenge for the wrongs you think you've been done, to wipe the slate clean. That would finish the feud. You could consign it to history, where it belongs. Wouldn't that be better than prolonging it?'

I thought of all that I'd gone through over the past few weeks. From Samuel's death to my own near-incineration on board *Kestrel*. It would be an immense relief to have it in my power to put an end to it all now. But could I? Was I able to turn my back on the history of my family, on Samuel himself, who seemed to be crying out for revenge? But the voices crying to me were personal, and I didn't know how to put these thoughts into words that Rachel would understand.

'There's Samuel's fifty thousand pounds,' I blurted out, though it was really the last thing I was thinking.

'For God's sake, Chris,' she said angrily. Then she subsided. 'I'm sorry. I keep forgetting that the money's important to you. I suppose you could talk to Samuel's solicitor and see if there's any possibility of interpreting the conditions of his will in such a way that the book doesn't have to be published.'

'I could try, I suppose.'

'It's worth it, isn't it? Well, I think it is. I'd be very glad, Chris, if you could bring yourself to do it. It would be the right thing.'

'I've never quite been able to figure out what the right thing is,' I said.

She lowered her voice, almost to an intimate whisper. 'Sometimes we have to follow our instincts.'

My hand was getting warm where Rachel held it. She was wearing a different scent today, something expensive that was teasing my senses into life.

'Of course we can't change the past, but we can change what happens next,' she said seriously.

'It's too late.'

'You sound so bitter.'

'No, not bitter – realistic.'

She turned my face towards her, and her fingers burned on my cheek as she gazed fixedly into my eyes. 'Please, Chris, please – go and talk to Caroline.'

It was ridiculous. The more I pieced together the fate of William Buckley, the deeper became the mystery around my great-uncle's death. It was as if the two events were inextricably linked across two hundred years, tied together with an irremovable knot. They were opposite ends of a line looped over a pulley – if you pulled hard on one end to draw it towards you, the other end moved just as rapidly away. Somehow there had to be a means of grasping both ends at once and seeing what it was that I held in my hands. But was it feasible that a feud could survive for so long, to burst back to life nearly two hundred years later?

I'd thought the Buckley family tree to be diseased. But over the years, it had been slowly strangled by a parasitic growth that had grown alongside, attaching itself to the tree's roots, winding itself through its boughs, snapping off its branches, and smothering its shoots. This parasite had drained it of life with a suffocating embrace, like two lovers locked in a suicide pact. Here and there a bough had withstood the insidious, creeping menace. But not for long.

That night, my head was filled with images of William Buckley, and the people who surrounded him, people who

341

were no more than names to me. Seth Parker and the dishonest Francis, who'd ended up in an Australian penal colony. Sarah Buckley and the infant Edward, less than two years old when his father had vanished. What had Edward felt about William when he'd grown up?

Then there were all the others – the Nall brothers, Daniel Metcalf, Adam Henshall and the Reverend Thomas Ella. And Reuben Wheeldon, William's friend in Cheshire, who had come as a surprise to old Godfrey, ancestor or not. A memory of Godfrey Wheeldon came to mind and made me smile.

But there was one sentence of William Buckley's that seemed to echo in my mind still. It was a sentence whose resonances touched something deep inside me. It was no mere platitude – it seemed to have a painfully personal meaning for him. *Outwardly he is all politeness, yet at every turn he seeks to thwart me.* Who had it referred to? It was the question that filled my mind as I drifted off to sleep.

I didn't know that a hundred miles to the north, in Cheshire, the staff of the Old Vicarage nursing home were talking about Godfrey Wheeldon's latest visitor.

44

I felt ridiculous having to obtain Caroline Longden's phone number from Mrs Wentworth, but it was too late to put off doing anything purely because of pride or embarrassment. It was long past the time for prolonging family divisions and propping up the walls that had been built between us. It was time to be putting things right.

I was surprised to recognise the phone number as a local one. For some reason, I'd assumed that Caroline lived away from the area, and that this was the reason she was so seldom seen at Ash Lodge. But now it occurred to me there must be some other reason for her to stay away. No doubt she wanted to get on with her own life, even though that involved Simon Monks.

I managed to get hold of her on the third attempt. As expected, she was cool, and reluctant even to discuss a meeting. But eventually I persuaded her I might have some genuine information about her father's death and the fire that destroyed *Kestrel*, and she agreed to meet me. She gave me her address, which turned out to be in Alrewas, an attractive village only a few miles north of the city and very close to Fradley Junction, where our first conversation had taken place.

'Oh, and Caroline – you will be alone, will you?'

For all I knew, she might be living with Monks. Or she might feel she was safer with him alongside her when we met.

She'd obviously already considered the point. 'If you really have information, I'll have to discuss it with Simon. You realise that, don't you?'

'Yes, fine. It's just that—'

'Yes, I know.' She sounded faintly amused. I didn't like the idea of Caroline laughing about me with Monks, but I restrained a sarcastic jibe. 'All right, I'll be alone,' she said.

Caroline lived in the end cottage of an attractive row of late-eighteenth-century properties, with a tiny front garden that was starting to produce spring flowers, crocuses competing with the snowdrops. Inside, the rooms were furnished very simply, almost sparsely, with an eye for the exact position of a bentwood chair or a rag rug.

While Caroline served coffee in a little sitting room with white-washed walls and a cast iron fireplace, I noticed a music stand and a cello case in one corner, and remembered that this was the girl who'd been so musically talented.

Caroline was smartly but casually dressed in a cashmere sweater and jeans, with her hair tied back in a yellow ribbon. Her manner seemed to say she wasn't going to make too much effort for me, and that coffee was all I would get. There weren't even any chocolate biscuits.

She sat in silence while I told her about the Parkers, though her eyebrows rose when I described a two-hundred-year-old feud as being at the heart of our problems. She sat sipping her coffee with one foot tucked underneath her, until I told her about Frank and repeated his story. Then she put her cup down and her coffee grew cold.

'You've met this Leo Parker then?' she asked at last, the first question she'd put since I arrived.

I told her about his visit to Stowe Pool Lane.

'He was concerned about his family's reputation,' said Caroline cautiously. 'His father and stepmother. And his stepmother was—?'

'Mary. My grandmother. George's first wife.'

'I see. The old story. It was all before my time.'

'But you must know what happened between George and Mary?'

'No. Mum told me some things, but not about George and Mary. She was more interested in an affair that Dad had when he was younger.'

'Really?'

'It was some sort of romantic liaison that their families didn't approve of. I don't know the details, but apparently they ran off together. To Ireland, I think. They lived together for a few years, but they never married. I think Dad must have been very much in love with this woman – it was a tragedy in his life that he never got over. So Mum told me. It seemed to add to his attraction, as far as she was concerned. But Dad never talked about it. Not to me, anyway.'

'So both brothers had heartbreak and betrayal in their lives. Mary left my grandfather and married Matthew Parker, her second cousin. She was already a Parker herself.'

'And all this is evidence of your great feud, is it?'

'I know it sounds incredible. But there are far too many Parkers involved with too many things that happened to the Buckleys. It's no coincidence.'

'If you say so, Chris.'

'But tell me about Mary. What happened to her? When did she die?'

'Chris, I don't know. Dad never mentioned her.'

'My God, this family,' I said irritably. 'There seems to have been an awful lot of things that were never mentioned.'

'Perhaps there were a lot of things you never asked.'

'Should I have to?'

I stood up and paced across the room, picking up a pile of musical scores, shuffling them, dropping them on the stand again. After discovering that I'd been kept in the dark for so long by my own parents, I thought that Great-Uncle Samuel

345

had come along to throw a great shaft of light into the dusty corners of my family's recent history. It was never what I wanted, but I hadn't been given any choice, and I'd come to accept it. But now I was finding many things that even Samuel hadn't told anyone.

'I suppose you'll have to ask Leo Parker,' said Caroline doubtfully. 'I don't suppose she could still be alive?'

'Surely not.'

'Well, she'd be about the same age as Dad. And he could have lived a few years longer.'

I looked at her, and mentally kicked myself for my insensitivity. It had never occurred to me to think how she'd feel about me digging up the family history. I'd trampled over Caroline's life enough. I didn't want to make her resent me any more than she already did.

'I could just leave it alone,' I said.

'Oh, you've got to know the facts now, haven't you, Chris? You're not going to be able to leave it at half a story.'

'Is that what you feel too?'

'I suppose it's inevitable.'

She moved almost absently towards the corner of the room and sat down with her cello. She fingered the bow and stroked the curves of the instrument's wooden sides. I wondered if I was interrupting her practice night, or whether contact with the cello helped her think.

'Caroline, I don't know how to explain this – but it's been eating away at me that I never got the chance to apologise to your father. I know I let him down. This is the only way I can try to make it up to him.'

'Yes, Dad would have been very disappointed in you, but not surprised,' she said. 'He came to you as a last resort, because he was terrified that you would reject him, that the past would have as huge a significance in your mind as it had in his. He would never have imagined that you could let him down so casually, because you couldn't be bothered.'

I hung my head. 'There's nothing I can say to that.'

'Dad was quite different, you know. All the time I knew him, he would never let anybody down. He carried enough guilt from what happened fifty years ago. It tortured him all his life and preyed on his mind every day. He could never have born it if he felt he'd let anyone down again. That's what it is to have a conscience, Chris.'

'Tell me about it,' I said, with a spasm of irritation. I was willing to eat humble pie up to a point, but Caroline was piling it on too thick. 'But it isn't quite true to say Samuel would never let me down. He was the anonymous backer who invested in our dot-com start-up, wasn't he?'

'Who told you that?'

'Nobody.'

'It can only have been Mr Elsworth,' she said grimly. 'It's totally unprofessional of him.'

'I worked it out for myself, Caroline. It wasn't all that difficult. Samuel put money in to help our business establish itself in the early stages. I suppose he must have seen my name in some of the promotion.'

'He'd always kept an eye on you. He wanted to support you in some way, and that was his opportunity. Dad felt responsible for you.'

'For me?'

'For everyone,' she said. 'For everything. As far as you were concerned, he wanted to pull you out of the shadow of your father.'

'I didn't need Samuel to do that.'

'Didn't you, Chris? But you haven't always been like this, so they tell me.'

'Like what?'

'So serious, so morose. You used to have friends, you were fun to be with. Isn't that right? I find it hard to believe that now. Dad said you'd become a loner, though you don't seem to like your own company. You certainly drink too

347

much – I've seen that for myself. You've lost control of your life. And it all happened when your parents died. That's what Dad told me.'

I scowled at her. I didn't like being told such things. They were much too close to the truth. But just because you recognised that you'd sunk into a dark time in your life, it didn't mean you could see the way to pull yourself out of it.

Suddenly, I saw more clearly the efforts people had been making on my behalf. Dan Hyde trying to enthuse me with an exciting new project, Andrew Hadfield encouraging me to join in with the canal volunteers, the HR manager who'd thought I might need help to cope with my redundancy. And, of course, Rachel persuading me to go to Gilbert and Sullivan performances, singing their songs all the way back in the car until I couldn't get a jaunty tune out of my head. They'd all seen more in me than I had myself. People around me had never given up hope of getting the old Chris Buckley back. And Samuel had tried to do the same, in his own way.

I'd lowered my eyes in that moment of reflection, but then I looked up again.

'But the book,' I said. 'Why did he want to pass the project on? He tried Frank first, then me. Did Samuel know he was in danger? Did he expect someone to try to kill him?'

Caroline shook her head. 'No, it wasn't that. He didn't expect to last much longer, true. But he wasn't afraid of a violent death. Dad was already dying. He was in the late stages of terminal prostate cancer, which had already spread into his bones and lymph nodes. Didn't you notice how ill he looked?'

'Of course.'

'Yes, even you couldn't have failed to see that. So the fact is, Samuel didn't have long left to live. He knew that very well. And you were his last hope, Chris.'

45

By that time, I didn't need Caroline Longden to lay any more guilt on me. I'd gone past that stage. There's only so much blame anyone can take.

But had Great-Uncle Samuel really been so concerned about me? I frowned as I thought about what Caroline was telling me.

'But then,' I said, 'your father pulled his backing from our start-up, just when we needed the money most. I'm facing bankruptcy now, did you know that? All because Samuel withdrew his funding. I can only think he did that because I told him I didn't have time to help him with the book. He forced me into accepting the terms of his will. No doubt if he'd lived a bit longer he would have made me a similar proposition himself. He wanted to make absolutely sure that I needed the money so badly I couldn't turn it down.'

Caroline looked suddenly uneasy. She drew her bow across the strings of her cello, releasing a couple of sharp, discordant notes.

'It wasn't Dad who withdrew the funding,' she said.

'What?'

'He would never have done that. I wouldn't want you to think that he would, whatever else you think. Once he'd decided to support something, he stuck to it. And you were family, after all. He would never have let you down like that.'

'What then?'

'It was me. As soon as we began to look at my father's estate, I persuaded Mr Elsworth that, as joint executors, we could pull out of the deal.'

'So you did it to punish me?'

'If you like.'

'But it didn't work, Caroline – it only made me more determined to complete the book.'

'The book, the book! You're as obsessed as Dad was. That's all I ever heard from him in the past few years, "the book".'

'It was close to his heart.'

'Oh yes. He never stinted on things that were close to his heart. The trouble was that anything that came by and interested him could become close to his heart very quickly. Charities and appeals, boat clubs and restoration schemes. Do you realise how much those waterways restorations cost?'

'I've a pretty good idea.'

'Dad poured his money into them, all over the country. I only found out about most of them when I started to go through his papers and his bank accounts for probate. The Ogley and Huddlesford Canal seems to have been a particular pet project.'

'There was a good reason for that. He wanted it to open again because he felt he helped to close it.'

'How could he have done that?'

'When he took the transport business from his maltings and brewery away from the waterways to the roads, he dealt a death blow to the Ogley and Huddlesford. That was the last big contract on the canal, and it put many small carriers out of business. Traffic declined so rapidly after that, the canal had already fallen into disuse by the end of the 1950s.'

'I didn't know that,' she said. 'How did you find out?'

'By asking the questions that I never asked about my family before.'

'He never talked to me about it,' said Caroline sadly.

I saw that I wasn't the only one who'd suffered from a

breakdown of communication within the family. 'It was one of the things he was trying to put right, in his own way, before he died. You might call it conscience, I suppose. But he had the money, so he decided to put it to use.'

Caroline sighed and caressed her cello. 'But he didn't have the money. Not really.'

'Of course he did. He was rolling in it, wasn't he?'

'That's what I'm trying to tell you, Chris. A lot of the money has gone. When Mr Elsworth and I went through the accounts, we discovered there wasn't anything like as much as we thought. Not by a long way. Poor Dad. He used to be so clever with money. He made big killings on the stock exchange in the 1970s and '80s. But in the last ten years it's all gone.'

'All? Not all, surely?'

'He stopped keeping track of his investments. He might have thought he still had a lot of money tied up in shares, but they were the wrong shares for the 1990s. Almost all of them were manufacturing companies, heavy industry. They were what he knew best, but in this country they were already dying in the 80s, weren't they? We haven't worked out the full value yet, but it's pitifully small. And he gave so much away. You'd be amazed at some of the things he spent his money on. In the end, he was totally indiscriminate in what he did with it. You weren't the only lost cause he left a legacy to, either. There was all the money he spent on the woman . . .' She shook her head. 'I didn't really mean to tell you all this, Chris.'

I stared at her, my mind whirling with a confusion of thoughts. 'Does that mean that the fifty thousand pounds—?'

Caroline flushed angrily. She raised her hands, and for a startled moment I thought she was going to attack me with her bow. 'I was right! That's all you're thinking about – yourself. Well, don't worry – there'll be enough in the estate for your little windfall. The specific legacies come first,

Mr Elsworth says. Your fifty thousand pounds will be there for you all right, though I'll probably have to sell Ash Lodge to provide it. After that, there'll be precious little left. Dad was so concerned about setting up your scheme and pouring money into his other projects that he left me nothing. So I hope that makes you happy.'

By the time I'd reached the gate and walked to my car, the sound of music was coming from the window of Caroline's cottage. It was something I didn't recognise – a melancholy tune with deep, powerful surges of aggression that made me think uncomfortably of Simon Monks. I looked around the street, expecting to see him waiting for me in the shadows, ready to finish the job that someone had started on board *Kestrel*.

My long overdue meeting with Caroline Longden had left me feeling anything but happy. One more illusion had been undermined. I'd carried a picture in my mind of Great-Uncle Samuel as a self-made man of means, a canny businessman who'd been one of the most successful of the Buckleys, even though he'd chosen to change his name. Frank had added an image of an earlier Samuel, a mysterious and romantic figure with an unhappy past, attractive to women and very much in love with his new wife.

But now Caroline had painted a different picture – one of an old man with failing abilities who'd become obsessed with trivialities and allowed his fortune to drain away. A man who, in the end, hadn't been concerned enough about his daughter to safeguard her future.

I regretted that our meeting had ended acrimoniously. It had deprived me of the chance to ask Caroline about the other mystery of her father's later years – his apparent belief that his wife had been pregnant when she died. For that, there seemed to be no explanation.

I knew that Rachel would be watching for me to arrive

home. And for once I was looking forward to having some-body to talk to who'd understand. Talking to Rachel had helped enormously to get things clear in my mind.

So I put the coffee on as soon as I got home to Maybank and left the side door ajar. Then I noticed that the light was flashing on the answerphone. As Rachel stepped through the door with a tentative smile, I was listening to the news from the Old Vicarage nursing home that Godfrey Wheeldon had died the night before, of a stroke.

'It was very sudden,' said the disembodied voice on the phone, a person who had identified herself as the chief care officer. 'But we were concerned that Mr Wheeldon seemed very agitated after he had a visitor yesterday.' The caller hesitated, and became more cautious, as if measuring exactly what she said. 'If you happen to know who his visitor was, we'd be very grateful if you could let us know. For some reason, we don't seem to have kept a record of his name and address, which is our usual procedure.' It sounded from her tone as though someone would be in trouble for that. 'And we'd like to let him know about Mr Wheeldon.' There was a crackly pause, and I thought the message had finished. 'We wondered if his visitor had brought him bad news. He really was very agitated.'

Rachel went pale when she heard. 'Poor old man. He sounded very nice from what you told me about him.'

'He certainly didn't deserve this.'

'Do you think somebody did bring him bad news?'

'Bad news? No, I think somebody went there to frighten him. Maybe they threatened him. But it seems as though they succeeded in frightening him to death. But who was it?'

'Somebody clever enough to avoid leaving his name and address. Did you have to sign in a visitors' book when you went?'

'Of course. That's how they found me to tell me about Godfrey.'

'Let's think logically,' said Rachel. 'There must have been somebody else who knew about Godfrey.'

'Who? Who?' I demanded.

'Well, Caroline Longden knew her father had visited him. Didn't you say she'd phoned the Old Vicarage to tell him Samuel had died?'

I stopped pacing abruptly. 'You're right.'

'But it wasn't Caroline. It was a man. Could she have sent somebody?'

'Damn right she could.' I glared at the wall, my mind working furiously. 'Or he could have gone on his own initiative. That would be more in character. He's the sort of bastard that would terrorise an old man and not think twice about it.'

'I take it you've got somebody specific in mind?'

'You bet. A bloke called Simon Monks. I'm going to love it if I can nail him.'

'Who's he?'

'Caroline's fiancé. The slimiest object you've ever seen. I wonder . . . I wonder if she's told him about the money.'

'Which money?'

'The money that she's not going to inherit. When they got engaged, he must have thought she was a real catch, an heiress with a wealthy, elderly father. The truth would come as a bit of a shock to him. He must have thought that as soon as Samuel died—'

I stopped dead again.

'Chris?' said Rachel. 'Are you all right?'

But I didn't hear her. I was seeing a scene in my mind, a familiar scene that I'd lived through many times since that day I sat in the Earl of Lichfield and watched Samuel walk away to his death. I was seeing a car hurtling down the ramp from the multi-storey car park into the junction of Castle Dyke, ploughing down a frail old man and leaving him lying broken in the road.

But now there was a difference. Now I saw a face behind the windscreen of the car. I was picturing the face of Simon Monks. A man who just couldn't wait for Samuel Longden to die.

46

Unearthing the past had become an obsession, just as Great-Uncle Samuel had known it would. Had he trusted in my Buckley blood to ensure the past would get its hooks into me so effectively? If so, he'd judged me well.

For a man like me, who had believed he looked only to the future, it was a bitter, unsettling reversal of the natural order. It felt as if the ghosts of my ancestors were conspiring to destroy me. I wondered if there was something in Samuel's 'genetic memory' that amounted to a death wish, an urge for self-destruction. Could William and Josiah Buckley have brought about their own ends? Did Great-Uncle Samuel walk into the path of that car by pursuing his single-minded obsession with an ancient feud? Did his desire for revenge bring about his own extinction?

And now it was my turn. Even from the grave, Samuel had led me, step by step, towards the point where I had no alternatives left. There was nothing left to do now, except to face directly the source of the danger that had already threatened me. If Monks was involved in the deaths of Samuel Longden and Godfrey Wheeldon, I felt sure there was another hand that had guided events.

As I left the house next morning, I found a visitor on my doorstep.

'Mrs Wentworth. What a surprise. Come in.'

'Oh no, I can't stop. I've just brought you this.' She thrust a package towards me, a buff padded envelope. 'Mr Wheeldon insisted you should have it.'

'Godfrey? You spoke to him?'

'He rang me on Sunday. Very pleased with himself, he was. He said he'd been doing a bit of detective work of his own to track me down. He decided that he didn't want the envelope to go to Caroline, but that you should have it. So I agreed to bring it round for you, in case it was something valuable. Things can get lost in the post. He sounded quite a nice old man.'

I took the envelope from her. 'He's dead, I'm afraid.'

'Oh no.'

For a moment, I thought she was going to faint on the doorstep. 'But I only spoke to him the day before yesterday,' she said. 'How can that be?'

'When was it he rang?'

'In the morning some time. About ten or half past, there-abouts. He sounded fine. In very good spirits, I'd say.'

'He died on Sunday night. A stroke, they think. He'd suffered one before, but this was a bad one.'

'Well, perhaps it was to be expected then. The poor old man.'

'Did he mention anything else when he rang?'

'Not really. He just said he'd been thinking about the envelope since you visited him. He didn't want anyone else to have it. I suppose he meant Caroline, but that was the way he put it – he didn't want anyone else to have it. He was quite emphatic on the point. And then he laughed and said something about not being able to escape any more. I don't know what he meant by that. Perhaps he had a presentiment, do you think? But he sounded remarkably cheerful about it, if he did.'

'I think he was the sort of man who kept his spirits up, no matter what.'

'That's good. Well, I'll leave you to it, now I've done what I promised.'

357

'Thank you, Mrs Wentworth. It's much appreciated.'

'Not at all.' She hesitated before she turned to walk back to the road. 'Poor old Mr Wheeldon. It can happen suddenly with old people, can't it?'

'Yes,' I said. 'Very suddenly indeed.'

I looked at the envelope in my hand with a horrible suspicion. Given all that had happened, I couldn't help wondering if Godfrey Wheeldon's death was more than the natural consequence of old age that Mrs Wentworth imagined.

Had someone tried to shut Godfrey up before he could pass on information to me? If so, they'd been too late, it seemed. The old man had beaten them in the end.

I'd rung Leo Parker's number first to make sure he'd be home before I made my way out of Lichfield. The tiny village of Hints lay south of the A5, opposite the radio mast and gravel pits of Hints Hill. I had to stop in the village and ask for directions to Leasow Court. Then I found myself driving through a ford and heading southwards on a single-track road that wound its way towards the A38 and the site of Canwell Priory.

Leasow Court was behind a set of tall wrought-iron gates which stood open on a raked gravel drive and curved lawns, providing a clear view of a house you couldn't help but admire. It had the perfect proportions of a classical Georgian facade, with a fanlighted front door and small-paned sash windows, and its walls were a subtle shade of cream. Part of an old stable block had been converted to garages, and a BMW stood on the gravel near a terraced paved with York stone.

The immediate sense of affluence was so striking that I was surprised when Leo Parker answered the door himself. He was dressed in a business suit and gave the impression of being ready to go out as soon as he'd dealt with a bit of incidental detail.

'I don't have much time,' he said straightaway. 'Come through to the office.'

I took my time following him down the hallway, determined not to be put at a disadvantage. Through an open door I caught a glimpse of a huge drawing room with a Turkish carpet, an Adam fireplace and some beautiful old furniture. There were dozens of watercolours and prints on the walls, and on a table near the doorway stood a tall Chinese vase.

Parker waited impatiently to lead me into a handsome study ruined by a row of grey metal filing cabinets and a vast mahogany desk, which he sat down behind. He took off his watch and laid it in front of him as an unsubtle hint that he was a busy man and I was an intrusion on his day.

'You said you had some information about my stepmother. Is this something that Samuel Longden discovered?'

'In fact, I came to ask you a question.'

'Oh? And that is?'

'What will it take for you to leave us alone?'

'Could you explain that?'

'Too many innocent people have suffered,' I said. 'People who have nothing to do with all this. Nothing to do with you and me, and what's between us. Frank Chaplin, for example. He isn't a Buckley. And poor bloody Godfrey Wheeldon was nothing to do with it. Neither of them was ever any part of your stupid feud.'

Parker clenched and flexed his fingers as his eyes widened. 'I really don't know what you're talking about.'

But I continued my prepared speech. 'And my Great-Uncle Samuel. That was your big mistake. Whatever he knew about you and Lindley Simpson, he wasn't putting the information away for future use. The fact is, he just wasn't interested. It was irrelevant to him. It had no bearing on his book, you see. I suppose you thought the book was an excuse for doing some digging, exposing all those old skeletons. And you thought I'd taken over from him – another troublemaker from the Buckley family. But you don't seem to be able to grasp that my great-uncle was genuinely only interested in the book. He never kept anything that didn't relate to the story of William and Josiah Buckley.'

'But there were letters he had—'

'There's no trace of them. It seems he didn't keep them, so your secrets would have been safe. If only he hadn't died.'

That seemed to get through to him. And it was true, too. If Samuel hadn't been killed, I wouldn't have gone through everything I'd experienced since, and I wouldn't be here now.

'I don't believe it,' said Leo. 'He was a Buckley, like you. The Buckleys have always hated our family. Always. And I don't believe Samuel was any different. Not if he had Buckley blood.'

'So what did you do? I don't believe you'd have run him over yourself. I can see you're not the type to get blood on your own hands. Who did you hire? Simon Monks?' I watched his face carefully for a reaction, but there was none. 'That would be a wonderful irony, wouldn't it? A typical Parker masterstroke – you'd have it in your power to destroy Caroline too. Are you hoping that I'll do the job for you? Well, I'll do whatever I must to achieve what Great-Uncle Samuel wanted – to bring the Parkers down.'

I stood up to leave, feeling my limbs trembling with the anger that had built up in me. I'd almost given him enough to be thinking about for now. But not quite.

'Perhaps my family had good reason to hate yours,' I said. 'Did you ever think about that? One thing I've discovered is what Mary did to Samuel and George. I don't care about all the rest, William and Josiah and all that. That's ancient history. But what Mary did was enough. And now all you're concerned about is protecting her reputation. I believe you'll go to any lengths to do it. My Great-Uncle Samuel knew that, too. And I intend to prove exactly how the Parkers were involved in his death.'

Parker heard me out impassively as I blurted out this claim. I'd intended to make it my exit line, to leave him stunned by the strength of my anger, puncture his complacency and leave him in no doubt that I was a man to be afraid of.

But before I could reach the door of the study, he spoke calmly.

'Christopher, there's something you need to know. When you've heard it, you might think differently.'

There was authority in his words, but an odd compassion too, which completely disarmed me. Immediately I weakened and subsided into the chair, feeling suddenly apprehensive. Too many people had told me there were things I needed to know, and it invariably preceded some awful secret that had been kept from me. Something that I needed to know, but didn't want to.

'I suspect, from what you've been saying,' he said, 'that you still don't know the reason for the estrangement in your family, the rift between Samuel and his brother George. Perhaps it's time you were enlightened.'

I waited submissively. How could I possibly admit that he was right? My pride wouldn't let me accept for one moment that a man like Leo Parker could be in possession of knowledge about my own family that had been denied to me. In fact, I had to suppress a ridiculous surge of gratitude that he was willing to share this information with me. With just one sentence, he had me eating out of his hand.

He looked at his watch. 'I really am out of time. I must walk down to the stables to look at a horse. But if you want to hear the truth and you promise simply to listen, you can come with me.'

I trailed after him down the passage and into a utility room with a quarry-tiled floor, where he put on wellingtons and a waxed jacket over his suit, instantly transforming himself into a gentleman farmer. He picked up a stick and we went out through a back door onto a gravel path that led towards the stable block.

Parker didn't specify where he'd got the information he based his story on. He didn't need to. It was obvious that his family had never made it a secret in the way mine had. As he spoke, his words raised tears of frustration at the fact that I'd been reduced to relying on a stranger for details of my own history. Because it was *my* history. It was where I'd come from.

47

The story began with Mary Parker. She'd been trained as a teacher, said Leo. Though she taught for a while at the girls' grammar school, Lichfield Friary, she'd never really intended to make a career in education, being more interested in finding a well-off husband and living in comfort for the rest of her life.

Leo showed me a photograph of her that he'd brought from the study. She was posing with a class of teenage girls who were dressed in dark tunics and white blouses with wide collars. Mary was tall and elegant, with a narrow waist and thick waves of dark, burnished hair that fell round her ears. And there was that direct gaze I recalled so well, eyes that seemed to burn through the lens of the camera.

Mary had married my grandfather, George Buckley, in 1938. George had been a brilliant young corporate accountant and had just been made a partner in a Birmingham firm when Mary was introduced to him in Beacon Park after the annual Bower Queen parade. George had been smitten from the start, and proposed within a few months.

Mary must have been banking on a husband with a guaranteed high-flying career. Accountancy was a safe profession, and corporate accounting was where all the money was. This illusion survived for about twelve months, during which time Mary give birth to Arthur, my father. He was born in July 1939.

'Less than two months before the start of the Second World War,' said Leo.

We walked across a terrace and past some kind of annexe attached to the back of the house until we reached a concrete yard.

At the stables, Leo Parker paused in his story. A teenage girl in jodhpurs and a hacking jacket was leading an elegant hunter into a railed-off paddock on a long rein. She glanced only once at Parker, who nodded, then ignored her.

'I know that Great-Uncle Samuel joined up,' I said. 'I suppose my grandfather did as well.'

'Yes, but they went their separate ways. George was three years older, you know, and for a long time Samuel hero-worshipped him. But the two boys were very different. George had gone for a safe career, but Samuel was more adventurous. When they joined up, it was almost like a competition. They'd both been in the cadet corps at school, and they went straight into commissions. I'm explaining to you what my stepmother told me, of course.'

'I understand.'

He told me that my grandfather had been recruited into the Pay Corps, which seemed a natural route for one of his talents and training, and would have meant a safe billet away from the Front. But Samuel had scorned such easy options and had surprised everybody by joining the Royal Navy. After a period of training in Devon, he'd become a junior officer on a minesweeper operating in the killing grounds of the North Atlantic supply routes. A few months later, my grandfather had obtained a new posting for himself. He'd transferred to the South Staffordshire Regiment, which was then serving in North Africa, resisting the Italian invasion of Egypt. By the summer of 1940, both the Buckley brothers were in the thick of the action.

For a while, life was as exciting at home as on the Front. German raids on Birmingham continued through to the spring of 1941, and reports came back of the mixed British fortunes in North Africa and the danger of German U-boats in the Atlantic. But by 1943, encumbered with a four-year-old son and frustrated by worsening shortages, Mary was getting bored.

It was difficult to imagine, at such a distance, that women could be envious of the excitement their menfolk were experiencing as they fought in the war. But for Mary, when Samuel was invalided home with shrapnel injuries to his leg, it was the best thing that had happened for four long years. Samuel was a lieutenant commander by then – he was never an actual captain, though he'd gained his own command. In his naval uniform, with his battle wound, he was a stirring and romantic figure on whom Mary's attentions centred.

Whether there had been any attraction between them previously, Leo didn't know. But the fact was that by 1945 Mary and Samuel had begun a passionate affair which was the scandal of the neighbourhood. To escape the gossip, they sailed to Ireland, where they stayed for twelve months.

So when George returned home at the end of the war, it was to find his house empty. The son he hadn't seen for over three years wasn't there to meet him. George's wife had left him for his own younger brother.

'"She left him in the cruellest way possible",' I said. '"But there was a worse betrayal than that . . . Much, much worse."'

'I beg your pardon?'

'It was something Samuel said to me when we first met. I didn't understand what he meant at the time.'

He was watching the horse keenly as it trotted round the rail with the stable girl. To my eye, the animal seemed to move with a power and grace no human was capable of. Its sides began to gleam as it ran, and each time it passed close to me I could smell its sweat. I wondered if Leo Parker was considering buying it.

'My stepmother might have betrayed George,' he said. 'But so did his brother. It's not for me to say which was the worst.'

365

'Samuel wasn't in any doubt which was the worst. I think he was consumed by his own guilt.'

'That could have been because of what happened later,' said Leo.

He told me that George had come back from the war a major, having distinguished himself with the South Staffs in the Sicily landings, and later in Burma fighting the Japanese. But he'd also come back with a debilitating nervous condition caused by experiences in the Far East that he'd always refused to talk about. The double blow dealt to him by the treachery of his wife and brother had left him a broken man, and he put up no resistance to divorce proceedings.

My grandfather's old firm had taken him back on in his pre-war job, out of loyalty to a returning hero. But George was no longer the capable young accountant who'd gone off to the war. His promise had died in the Burmese jungles. He was incapable of concentrating on any task, but refused to admit his deficiencies. For a while he'd succeeded in covering up his errors, until eventually he was found illegally transferring funds from a client's account and falsifying the records. The firm had been regretfully obliged to dispense with his services, though it refrained from a criminal prosecution because of his exemplary war record.

Meanwhile, Mary and Samuel returned from Ireland, along with Mary's son, my father. Their affair was over almost as soon as it had begun, but not out of choice as far as Samuel was concerned. Mary had decided to move on, renewing a liaison with her second cousin, Matthew Parker, who ran an engineering company with three big factories in Birmingham and the Black Country. Within six months, they were married. And Samuel no longer felt worthy to be a Buckley – he'd gone to his solicitors, Elsworth and Clarke, and obtained a notarised certificate taking the surname Longden.

Because there was one last thing, a final straw that had led my Great-Uncle Samuel to change his name. In February

1948, his brother George had blown his brains out with his old service revolver.

Leo Parker left me for several moments to digest the information while he spoke to the stable girl. I didn't doubt for a moment the accuracy of what he'd told me. It filled in a huge blank so precisely that it had to be true. It was what my parents had concealed from me for so long. This was why I'd never known of the existence of my disgraced Great-Uncle Samuel.

The horse was led back towards the stable, snorting and steaming.

'He looks fit enough now,' said Leo complacently.

'My father . . .?' I said, not sure what question I wanted to ask of the many that crowded into my mind.

'Oh yes, your father. My stepmother kept Arthur with her throughout, both when she was living with Samuel in Ireland, and later when she married my father. Who can say how much he understood of what was going on? He would have been ten years old when Matthew and Mary married, so he must have known some of it. I understand that sort of upheaval and uncertainty can affect a child quite deeply in later life.'

'Yes.'

'I'm sorry that I didn't have more contact with him later on,' said Leo. Then he shrugged. 'But you know how it is. You drift apart. Inevitably, in our case. He was six years older than me, and he never wanted a little brother.'

In Leo Parker's paddock, it was raining again. Leo was beginning to look at his watch and stir restlessly.

'Chris, I know all this must be a shock. But unless there is anything else you want to ask—'

There were, of course, a million questions. The one that popped to the forefront of my mind was one that had been niggling me ever since Leo Parker had first raised the subject.

'A week ago you told me you thought Samuel blamed your family for the death of his son in that car crash.'

'That was one of his fantasies, yes.'

'But do you realise how old Alison was by then?'

'Oh, over fifty, I suppose.' He smiled without humour. 'I did say it was a fantasy. Perhaps you knew Samuel for too short a time to realise how he'd lost touch with reality. He was obsessed with having a son. It consumed him to the end, I think.'

The stable girl came past, struggling with a wheelbarrow heaped with soiled straw. Leo snapped the strap of his watch and slid it back and forth on his wrist, a sign that the conversation was over. He turned and walked towards the house, and I was forced to follow. In his waxed jacket, his back looked solid and self-assured. But as we re-entered his study, I felt obliged to make one last, feeble attempt to puncture his complacency.

'I suppose you're proud of what Mary Parker did to the Buckley brothers,' I said, when we got back into his study.

'I don't have to justify what she did. I think I'm safe in saying that family has always meant more to me than it seems to have meant to you. And that is my justification.'

A framed photograph stood on his desk, and he turned it towards me. It showed Leo Parker himself with a handsome, fair-haired woman and two fair children, laughing at the camera in front of a mellow brick wall planted with espalier pears. Leo's arms were held protectively around the shoulders of a boy of about eleven, while a girl a few years older stood arm in arm with her mother. The perfect happy family.

My eye was caught by a second photograph. It showed a woman whose face I'd seen before, a face I couldn't help but remember. She'd been with Leo Parker and Lindley Simpson at the link road protest meeting in Boley Park.

Leo noticed the direction of my gaze. 'My sister Eleanor,' he said.

368

'It must be nice to have a close family.'

I could hardly believe I'd uttered those words. The thought would never have occurred to me a few days ago. But this glimpse of Leo Parker's life had stirred some unaccountable worm of envy.

He gazed at me for what seemed like an eternity, glanced once more at his watch, then stood up.

I thought he was getting rid of me, but instead he said: 'Come and meet one more relative.'

'What?'

'Follow me.'

So I followed Leo Parker as he led me towards the annexe at the back of his property. As we entered, I noticed the handrails on the walls, the ramps instead of steps. Which relative of his was I about to meet?

Parker knocked on a door. 'It's Leo,' he called.

He didn't wait for an answer, but walked into a sitting room that struck a jarringly old-fashioned note out of keeping with the rest of the house. My eyes took a moment to adjust to the gloom. The curtains were drawn, as if the occupant couldn't cope with too much daylight.

'Here she is,' said Leo.

Then he raised his voice. 'Christopher Buckley has come to see you.'

I saw an old lady sitting upright in an armchair. She turned her head slowly towards me. A second later, I was transfixed by her unnervingly piercing stare. But there was no recognition in her eyes, only a blankness that suggested a total lack of comprehension.

Leo Parker ushered me forward with a hand on my shoulder.

'This is Mary,' he said. 'This is your grandmother.'

48

The old woman looked from me to Leo Parker when he spoke. But I could still see no spark of recognition in her eyes. She had no idea who either of us was.

I tried to speak, but my mouth was dry. Why hadn't it occurred to me that Mary might still be alive? It had been Rachel who pointed out that she'd be about the same age as Samuel. And here she was, alive and, well . . . not exactly kicking.

I could sense Leo's eyes on me, watching for my reaction. I cursed him silently for putting me in this situation without any warning. But then I realised it was entirely my own fault. I recalled his first visit to my house. It was his step-mother he'd been most concerned about, not his father. He didn't want to cause any further distress, he said. And he'd dismissed my remark that it was all in the past and couldn't mean anything to us now. *That's where you're wrong, I'm afraid.* I could hear Leo speaking to me in that tone, as if I was stupid. And it was true – I had been very stupid.

Mary hadn't spoken at all, and I realised she wasn't going to. Despite the superficial directness of her stare, I could see there was no expression behind it, no emotion or thought. No understanding. I'd found the woman at the centre of the Buckleys' story, yet she wasn't really here at all. Those piercing eyes were gazing beyond us to something that had happened long, long ago.

'She has good days and bad days,' said Leo.

'And this is a bad day, I gather.'

He shook his head. 'Not the worst. At least she's calm.'

'Does she understand what we're saying?'

'Who can tell? She doesn't let on if she does. The only way she ever communicates is through screaming and lashing out. It's frustration, of course. So there's probably some level of understanding, but she's unable to express it.'

I was feeling very uncomfortable standing in this room that was so obviously hers. I knew I'd intruded into her world without permission. She met my eyes as I studied her face, looking for a family resemblance. Did she have my father's mouth, the fleshy pout that I'd known so well? But no. Despite everything, I could see that she'd been a handsome woman. She still bore herself with a poise and dignity belied by her vacant gaze.

'Hello, grandmother,' I said slowly, as if the words were every bit as unfamiliar to me as the person herself.

I waited in vain for a response. I was craving the smallest acknowledgement from this old woman more than anything else I'd ever wanted in my life. But it didn't come.

What was going on inside her head? Did Mary sometimes remember the three men in her life – her first husband George Buckley, who she'd betrayed while he was away fighting in the war, or his brother Samuel who tempted her into a fling, that impulsive flight to Ireland with the young Arthur in tow? Or was her real love her second husband, Matthew Parker? Had her dalliance with the Buckley brothers been a mistake, the impulsive actions of a passionate young woman?

Or was there something more to Mary Parker? Perhaps a deliberate cruelty that was unfathomable to me, but which might be the source of the old woman's anguish on her really bad days. Mistakes could come back to haunt your conscience in the most painful ways, especially when it was far too late

371

to put things right. Samuel had told me her actions were unforgivable.

Perhaps my grandmother had never forgiven herself. Yet I couldn't ask her.

I wondered why Samuel hadn't mentioned she was still alive. Didn't he know himself? Or had it been one of his deceptions, a vital piece of information that he'd decided to keep to himself, a tidbit he hoped I would discover for myself. I felt as though I was following a path he'd ordained for me. Visiting Leo Parker today hadn't been my choice, or fate, or coincidence, but something Samuel Longden had anticipated. For a man obsessed with the past, he'd seen the future very clearly.

Leo touched my arm. 'We'd better leave her now, Chris. She gets tired very easily.'

'Who looks after her?'

'She has a nurse who comes in every day, and full-time carers. She's very well looked after.'

I let him lead me out of the room and back into the open. It was only when I breathed in the fresh air that I realised the room had been thick with some kind of scent, an old-fashioned aroma redolent of lilac and jasmine. Stepping through that door had been like physically passing from the present into the past. The sense of relief at being back in my own time was overwhelming.

'You can come and see Mary again, if you want to,' said Leo. 'But let me know. As I said, there are bad days.'

A few minutes later I was driving home up the A5 and through Lichfield in a daze, trying to digest the story that Parker had told me. The rain had become heavier, veiling the roads and traffic in a stream of water that ran across the Escort's windscreen. And there was another, more painful, blurring in front of my eyes that the windscreen wipers could never touch.

Perhaps I was right about the diseased Buckley family tree, after all. It certainly looked unlucky. An ancestor disgraced and possibly murdered, another drowned in suspicious circumstances. A son ruined, two brothers forced permanently apart by betrayal and jealousy. One driven to suicide, the other to a renunciation of his Buckley blood. My father, emotionally scarred by his childhood upheavals. And myself, an ineffectual end product of one of those embittered branches.

My Great-Uncle Samuel, it seemed, had been unhinged by his fixation with the past. The man they called the Captain had been all at sea by the end of his life. His brain had silted up and his keel was holed. From the grave he was doing his best to send me the same way, to undermine the mental certainties of the very last of the Buckleys.

I could understand the guilt that Samuel had been devoured by when my grandfather had killed himself. The bigger the breach with someone, the harder it is to cope when they die. And Samuel had been partly responsible for driving his brother to his death, it couldn't be denied. George's experiences in the war may have begun the rot, but the great betrayal by the two people he'd trusted most in the world must have kicked the skids out from under a damaged psyche, pushed his reason beyond the limits where normal life became impossible.

Who knew what he had been thinking when he took the money from his clients' accounts to cover his accounting errors? Had he seriously believed he'd never be caught? Or had he just not cared? Did he, in fact, hope that he'd be found out, bringing an end to a situation that he was powerless to control? With clinical depression, the mind loses all sense of proportion, and small problems can seem immense beyond all coping. George had reached a stage where nothing gave him enough reason to carry on living in the face of betrayal, despair and ruin.

373

And then there was Mary, the woman right at the heart of everything.

I phoned Laura to reassure myself that she was coming to Lichfield the next day, and to report on my meeting with Leo Parker.

'And she's actually still alive?' she said, her voice rising to an incredulous pitch, the way mine must have sounded when I stood in that room at Leo Parker's house. 'It must have been a shock after all these years.'

'You can say that again.'

'And so the story is that Mary left your grandfather for his brother while he was away fighting in the war?'

'So it seems,' I said. 'While he was lying injured in a field hospital in Burma, she got bored and decided to find somebody else. That was a fine hero's welcome for him when he came home, wasn't it? To find his faithless wife had left him, taking his six-year-old son with her – a son he hadn't seen for three years, who he must have dreamed about night after night while he was fighting his way towards Singapore. It wasn't the war that killed my grandfather, it was Mary Parker. The Germans and Japanese damaged him, but Mary destroyed him. That was why he killed himself.'

If I was expecting sympathy from Laura, I didn't get it. Perhaps it was the distancing effect of the phone that made her sound detached. I felt sure it would have been better if I could have been there with her, to get comfort from her presence.

'But what about Samuel?' she asked.

'Samuel became rich, but he was an old man riddled with guilt, who wanted to atone for it before he died. Now he's atoning to the tune of fifty thousand pounds. He thinks he can carry out his penance through me,' I said. 'This is blood money.'

'Yes, I suppose that's true.'

'And now he's made me feel the guilt.'

'Why, Chris?'

I stared out of the window at the houses in Stowe Pool Lane.

'Because my pride makes me want to turn it down. But I can't afford to. The fact is – I need his blood money.'

And later I had to explain the same thing over again to Rachel.

'What's the matter?' she asked as soon as she set eyes on me. 'What happened?'

She stared at me as I pulled off my coat and shoes, and collapsed into a chair.

'I've just met Mary,' I said.

'Mary . . .?'

'Yes, that Mary,' I said. 'You were right, she's still alive. Well, physically at least.'

'Do you mean she has dementia?' she said, when I described her.

I realised I hadn't asked Leo Parker what Mary was suffering from.

'Yes, I think so. She doesn't seem to be able to communicate or recognise anyone. She's living in Hints with her stepson, Leo Parker.'

'That's why he was worried about protecting her reputation, then. Not just an interest in the past, but a concern for the living.'

'I suppose so.'

'You don't sound convinced, Chris.'

'I don't know. There's still something not quite right.'

When Rachel heard the story Leo Parker had told me, she was appalled at the thought of the misery that had been caused, and all the grief that had been stored up for future generations.

'It's amazing the things that people will do to themselves,' she said thoughtfully.

It was an aspect that hadn't occurred to me. 'Yes, you're right. Samuel brought everything on himself.'

Rachel looked at me for a moment. 'That wasn't quite what I meant.'

But I was following my own train of thought. 'Samuel's problem was that he caused trouble for everyone around him as well.'

'Yes, Samuel,' she said. 'It's an odd thing, this business about him thinking he had a son who was killed in that car crash. An unborn son.'

'Oh that. I can't believe that Samuel ever said it.'

'You think Leo Parker was lying? But you believed everything else he told you, Chris.'

'Yes. He's a clever man, of course. I think he slipped a big lie in among a series of appalling truths, in the hope that I'd accept it without question.'

'But why?'

'Don't you see? He wanted me to be convinced that Samuel had become mentally unbalanced since the crash. Let's face it, there is plenty of evidence pointing that way if you choose to see it in that light. Leo wanted to be sure that I did see it. No doubt he'd like everybody to see it that way.'

'Ah,' said Rachel. 'So that the will could be challenged.'

'Exactly. On the grounds that Samuel was no longer of sound mind when he made it.'

'Caroline Longden seems to have been trying hard to give you that impression too. And she's the one who stands to gain, isn't she? Not Leo.'

'Yes,' I said. 'It's what I'd call a very interesting alliance.'

Back at my desk, I remembered the package Mrs Wentworth had brought. What could Godfrey Wheeldon have been sending to Samuel? Could it be more letters? But if so, why hadn't he mentioned them?

I ripped open the package and unwrapped the newspaper

inside. At first, I almost laughed at what I found. But then I felt more like crying. It was a set of cigarette cards depicting famous cricketers from the 1920s, the ones that Godfrey had told us Samuel was interested in. The cards were a gift from one old man to another. And both of them were dead before the gift had been received.

I looked at the cards for a while before I put them away. Then I decided to go through my photos again. The shots of the visit to the Fosseway site by Lindley Simpson and Leo Parker were now added to the earlier ones. Leo could be seen talking to the MP, to the chairman of the restoration trust, to Andrew Hadfield and some of the other members. He was recognisable mostly by the set of his shoulders, as he seemed to have managed to keep his back to the camera throughout. But Frank must have seen him clearly from the banking above the wharf to recognise him as the man who'd been asking questions at the bowls club.

I had got a blow-up done of one of the earlier pictures of Fosseway. It was the one that showed Samuel looking towards me across the restored lock, but in the enlargement only Samuel's face and the shoulders of his black coat were visible. I stared at my great-uncle's photograph in bafflement, the questions colliding with each other as they rushed into my mind. Captured by the lens, Samuel's weary face was gaunt with sorrow and guilt, and etched with a bitterness that had lasted, undimmed, for over fifty years. As I looked at him, I tried to picture him as a handsome young man, who'd been so tempted by desire for his own brother's wife that he'd committed a desperate act.

I stuck the picture on the corkboard over my desk, along with the square black and white print of George and Samuel as boys.

There was also another good photograph of Samuel at Fosseway, but more in the distance. He was pictured across the lock, on the far side of a black gulf. There was a pleading expression in his eyes, as if he were still appealing to me from the grave.

Then I noticed an even earlier shot from that same day. The yellow dumper truck was in the foreground, backing up to the spoil tip near the tailgates. I'd taken the picture because of the contrast between the yellow of the dumper and the black of the damp earth, as well as the sense of movement and the serious expressions on the faces of the workers. But in the background of the photograph was Samuel.

I hadn't noticed him when I was taking the picture, because I'd been focusing on the activity around the lock. But there he was, and he'd evidently just arrived at the site, because he was standing with his back to the open door of a car, leaning slightly forward as if caught in the very act of getting out. The car was a light green saloon, but I couldn't tell the make. Surely Samuel hadn't arrived in a car – he didn't even have one. But then I realised it was the passenger door he was getting out of. Someone had brought him to Fosseway that morning.

I went into the sitting room and rummaged through the drawers of the sideboard. Somewhere among the old postcards and spare fuses and bits of string I knew there was a magnifying glass. I couldn't remember it ever having been used for anything, but it was one of those bits of clutter that my parents had refused to throw away. After a few minutes of tossing things aside, I finally found it and took it to the front room.

The magnifying glass was enough to increase the clarity of the bit of the car that I could see past Samuel. I could make out the grille, and a distinctive badge. Then I knew the car was a Mercedes. A lime-green Mercedes. I'd ridden in that car myself, after Samuel's funeral. It was Laura Jenner's car.

I dropped the photo, engulfed by a cold, sick feeling of apprehension. So Laura had been the one who brought

Samuel to the Fosseway site that morning, when he'd first sought me out. Samuel had never mentioned it. More to the point, Laura had never mentioned it either. She'd deceived me all along about knowing Samuel. What else had she lied to me about?

My heart felt like a stone as I contemplated the awful truth. Laura had known about the entire thing. She'd led me on to feed her with information, to keep her up to date with everything I found out. And she'd been clever enough to let me think it was all my own idea.

Another thought struck me. Caroline hadn't been the only one who knew where to find Godfrey Wheeldon. I'd actually taken Laura with me when I went to see him. Had my desire to spend a day with Laura been a mistake that proved fatal for that lonely old man?

So who was Laura Jenner? That was the big question. But I already knew the answer with devastating clarity. She could only be a Parker.

49

The realisation that Laura Jenner was involved drove me straight back to my car. I made it to Hints in record time, cutting up a cement lorry in the spray on the A5. I'd brought the photograph of Laura with Godfrey Wheeldon at Chester Zoo – the one that showed her with a frank, happy smile and the sun casting a faint shadow where the scar crossed her forehead.

As I approached Leasow Court through the rain-filled potholes, I saw Leo Parker's BMW leaving the gates and heading off southward towards the A38. I knew if he made it to the dual carriageway I'd soon lose him in his more powerful car, so I put my foot down and brought the Escort close up behind his rear bumper, flashing my lights and sounding my horn.

I didn't care about the physical risk I was taking in the treacherous conditions. An unnatural recklessness had come over me. I knew that it was too late for staying on the sidelines and the only way to achieve anything was by confrontation. Even what Leo had told me earlier in the day hadn't changed that – if anything, it had made me less cautious. There seemed to be so little left to lose.

Leo must have seen the Escort, but he seemed intent on ignoring me until he had to slow for a sharp bend near the woods at Canwell Hall. My bumper actually touched his tailplate with a sudden jolt and a screech of metal. He swung over onto a pull-in of flattened earth and his brake lights came on as he skidded to a halt. I just had time to draw in alongside, ending up at a slight angle to avoid his rear wing.

Leo had started to climb out of his door, but my adrenaline was rushing and I was much quicker than he was, leaping out almost before the Escort had stopped, so that the engine stalled. We ended up face to face at the side of his BMW, with the rain driving on our heads.

'Are you crazy? What the hell is this?' he shouted.

I reckoned, in my bravado, that I had the measure of him. He was a man who didn't fear for his own personal safety, but was terrified that I might damage his precious car. So I leaned deliberately on the roof of the BMW with the flat of my hand.

'I think there's something you forgot to tell me, Leo.'

'Is that all? Is there one more question you want to ask? Have you ever heard of the bloody telephone?'

The dual carriageway was only yards away from us, the width of one field, and we had no alternative but to shout at each other above the roar of the traffic and the blustering slap of the rain.

'This one happens to be bloody important. It looks like an unbelievable oversight that you forgot to mention it.'

'I told you everything I know about your family. I'm sorry if it didn't make you happy, but that's just tough.'

'And what about *your* family? Did you tell me everything about them?'

'There's no damn reason why I should.'

'Just tell me this – how is Laura Jenner connected to you?'

'Who the hell is Laura Jenner? I've never heard the name.'

'Well, that's what she's been calling herself while she led me on and got information from me. While she planned her betrayal. But I dare say that's not her real name. I presume she's yet another Parker.'

'I don't know who you're talking about.'

I pulled out the photograph I'd taken at Chester Zoo and slammed it on the wet roof of the car. 'I'm talking about this woman.'

Parker stared at the photo. He looked genuinely puzzled. 'I've never seen this person before in my life.'

'You're lying to me again.'

He took a few deep breaths. He had better self-control than me, and I could see him working out how to resolve the situation to his advantage while I was still burning to kick his door panels in.

'I assure you I'm not lying. I've been very frank with you, despite your aggressive attitude. But the woman in this photograph is a complete stranger to me.'

I faltered, convinced despite myself that he was telling the truth. 'It isn't possible.'

'A lot of things are possible. You ought to know that by now, Chris. I'm intrigued, though,' he said, 'to know how this woman comes to be so important to you.'

I looked at the photograph, remembering how I'd met Laura at Fradley as if by accident, how she'd seemed to understand all about Samuel Longden so easily. It had been one of the things that drew me to her.

'I really wish I knew that.'

'Well, don't expect me to be able to tell you.'

'She's deceived me all along,' I said, talking almost to myself. 'I'm convinced she has something to do with Samuel's death. And Godfrey Wheeldon's. Her *and* Simon Monks.'

'Monks?' Leo gave a barking laugh as he climbed back into his car, wiping rain from his face. 'Do you mean Caroline Longden's fiancé?'

'Yes – do you know him?'

'I know of him,' he said. 'My God, you've really got yourself in a mess, Chris, haven't you? Such a mess that I don't think I can help you any more. So do me a favour – stay away from me from now on, okay? I've heard enough about

382

your family to last me the rest of my life.' He closed the door and started the engine. The driver's window slid noiselessly down as I stepped back from his wheels. 'But I'll leave you with this warning: if you've been lying to me and you try to blacken our family's name in your ridiculous book, it will be me on your tail. And I don't back down.'

After I got home again, I paced around the house for a while, with no clear idea what I should do next. The adrenaline was still flowing, and every time I thought of Laura I felt a fresh surge of anger that flooded my brain and prevented me from thinking logically. Time and again I picked up the photographs and stared at them, willing them to change. I tried to convince myself that there could be any number of green Mercedes in Lichfield. But how likely was it that any of them would be driven by somebody connected with Great-Uncle Samuel?

Besides, once I'd changed my perspective, everything seemed to fit in the picture too well. It had been Laura who sought me out at Fradley after the funeral, not the other way round. I'd been too intoxicated by the wine and her presence to notice, and she'd taken advantage of that. She'd made it seem as though it was my idea to ask for her help with the research for the book, but surely she'd been the one to plant the suggestion in my mind? Of course she had. Her show of reluctance wouldn't have lasted long if I hadn't taken the bait first time, like a besotted fool.

And once she had me hooked, I was truly hooked. I'd been a sitting duck for a seduction. She must have seen me as a pathetic, lonely man with no power of resistance. Which, to my shame, was exactly what I'd been. When I thought of all the things I'd told her on the journey to Cheshire, and everything that had happened between us that night at her hotel, the rage made me smash my fist into the table with frightening violence.

Frank had retreated to his bedroom, keeping out of the way of my bad temper once I'd snapped at him a couple of times in the kitchen as I towelled my drenched face and hair. Boswell had long since disappeared from the house when he sensed my mood. Even the fish in the tank seemed to gape at me in astonishment and derision.

It was as if they all knew what a fool I'd been. I'd passed on to Laura Jenner all the information I'd gathered with Rachel's help, and I'd betrayed Rachel's trust at the same time. As a result, Laura knew about everything – about Godfrey Wheeldon, and Frank, about everything.

I recalled that Laura had known only too well that I'd be away from Maybank on the night it was broken into. She knew because she made sure I was with her at the George. The realisation that she must have planned that night with an accomplice was a torment of outrage and humiliation. She'd planned it with Simon Monks – because I was sure it could only be him. I had no idea what the link was between them. I only knew in my guts that he was the one who'd wielded the windlass against my skull and torched *Kestrel*.

It seemed horribly plausible that Monks had been deceiving Caroline in the same way that Laura had deceived me. But who were they? And what was their purpose? If they weren't Parkers, why were they trying to destroy the last remnants of the Buckley family?

50

Pipehill, Lichfield, Staffordshire. Saturday 25th Jan. 1800.
To Reuben Wheeldon Esq., Warner Street, Ellesmere, Cheshire.

My dear friend,

It is a just and feeling remark of Doctor Johnson's that we never do anything consciously for the last time without sadness of heart. The secret sense of a Farewell Act I carry along with me into every word or deed of this Day.

My friend, I'll fight no more; I've had enough. I hope I have done no more harm than any other man, but the world will do quite as well without me. I do not want to rip up old grievances and live my life twice over. As the tree falls, so let it lie. We shut up the book and close the Account once and for all.

I look not for others to profit by my example, nor do I seek to give moral guidance to others. Yet my behaviour must give no reason to be ashamed, for the World is all too prone to censure and ridicule. I confess I have no hope for the outcome, since Prejudice against me runs so high. I am torn by the utmost anxiety at what I must do, and my mind is in turmoil of a thousand imaginings.

I will not detain you for a minute more. To speak plainly, I have business with Mr P. that cannot be delayed. I have engaged to meet with him this very night, that we might resolve our differences for once and for all. I know that

I go into Danger. If the worst befalls me, Sarah will return to her Father's house, where I trust little Edward will be well cared for. To you, my dear friend, I entrust the documents of which we have spoken. You will understand that they are not safe in my Possession. If I do not return, you must do with them as you see fit.

They say that Mr P. has engaged a pair of bravos, for what purpose they do not know. Let him then send his bravos.

Your obedient servant and friend

Wm Buckley

51

The last thing I wanted in my current state of mind was Rachel asking awkward questions and interrogating me about Laura. She'd demonstrated several times that she could see straight through me. The only thing to do was get out of the house before she arrived home, and there was only one place where I could do my thinking.

It was only a few minutes' walk to the Stowe Arms, and soon I was cradling a pint of Marston's in my favourite corner, feeling the warmth and reassurance of the alcohol creeping through me. A few of the familiar regulars were in, and it seemed likely that somebody would soon buy a round, a game of darts would be started and the evening would take its predictable course.

Before long, though, my thoughts began to drift back to that afternoon I sat in the corner of another pub, the Earl of Lichfield, and did absolutely nothing until it was too late, as my Great-Uncle Samuel walked away to his death. The thought was uncomfortable, and it turned the taste of the beer sour in my mouth. I'd seen where being a coward and failing to act had led me. The time for doing nothing was past. I had to redeem myself in Samuel's eyes, to reclaim my family name.

It was strange that a name could have such power. How could a single word be so important that individuals would sacrifice their lives to it, as Samuel had sacrificed his? And as I had been in danger of sacrificing mine. It was a mysterious power that had lain dormant in me until these past few weeks. But I was no longer in any doubt about its crushing potency.

I ignored the cajoling of my drinking companions to join their circle and headed to a payphone in the passage behind the bar. Laura's number was on a slip of paper in my wallet. But all I got was the male friend, who told me that Laura wasn't at home. When pushed, he said she might already be in Lichfield again. So I dialled the George Hotel, and was put straight through to her.

'Laura, it's Chris.'

'Hi.'

I had to steel myself at the sound of her voice. This was no moment to weaken. I was going to stay cool and decisive. 'I need to talk to you. Tonight.'

'Can't it wait until tomorrow?'

'No, it can't. A lot has happened, Laura. I've found out things that have changed my mind on the whole business.'

She hesitated. 'I see. You sound as though you're confused, and maybe a bit angry too.'

'Oh yes, a bit,' I said sarcastically.

'All right, I can tell. And you probably blame me for some of it.'

'No, not some of it – all of it. You've deceived me all along.'

'No, Chris. It's true that I haven't been honest with you. But if you think I'm the one you need to blame for everything, you're very wrong.'

'You expect me to believe that?'

Laura sighed. 'I can explain.'

'That's exactly what I'm going to insist on you doing. For a start, you can explain why you and the people you're involved with killed Samuel Longden, and why you tried to kill me.'

'It's not like you think,' she protested. 'None of it is.'

'Oh yes? Someone tried to break my skull and turn me into roast meat. I take it that was a member of your family? A Parker? If not, I'm sure you could take a very good guess at who it was. That would have been a really neat ending, wouldn't it? The last of the Buckleys finished off.'

I heard her sigh. 'I'm not a Parker.'

'I don't know why I should believe you.'

'What's been done to you was dreadful, Chris, and I'm as guilty as anybody for deceiving you. But I want to put a stop to it now. Things are very close to an end.'

'Fine. Finish it, then. Call your family off and get out of my life.'

'It isn't as simple as that.'

'Why not?'

'Because of the book, of course.'

'So there's no way out. A stalemate. You'll just have to wait for the book to come out then, won't you?'

'You don't understand. It's very dangerous.'

'Oh, I know,' I said, feeling the bump on my head. 'It was particularly dangerous for Great-Uncle Samuel, wasn't it? Do you know who killed him?'

'Yes,' she said. But she said it so quietly I hardly heard her.

'Then it's time you told me. I want to meet you. Tonight. And be sure you come alone.'

'All right, I will. But for one reason.'

'What?'

'Because you're the one who's most in danger.'

We arranged to meet at Fosseway Wharf at nine o'clock that night. The choice had been mine. It felt like my home ground now, and it would be more than secluded enough for the purpose. Besides, it was somehow symbolic, since it was the place where it had all started.

But I didn't want to go to Fosseway alone. I needed a

witness to what Laura had to say. And, yes, I was a little afraid. I thought of William Buckley and what he had written to Reuben Wheeldon: 'At every turn he seeks to thwart me.' And then that courageous, foolhardy line: 'Let him then send his bravos.'

So I considered my options. Frank was on hand, but he would only be a liability, even if I could persuade him to leave the house. Rachel was out of the question – I didn't even intend to tell her where I was going. Who did that leave? My genuine friends were very few, when I actually tried to count them. There were far too many I'd drifted away from. Excepting the regulars at the Stowe Arms, there was only Dan Hyde, and he was the last person I'd ask for a favour.

And then I thought of Andrew Hadfield. Yes. He owed me one.

Andrew was surprised at the request, but agreed without too much coercion or the calling in of old debts when I explained what it was about. He was a kindred spirit, really – he shared my sense of curiosity, my urge to balance unfair odds. He couldn't resist the chance to learn the outcome of a mystery that had begun when he'd first introduced me to Samuel Longden.

'I remember Laura,' he said. 'Bit of a looker, isn't she? She's the one who latched on to you at Fradley.'

'You might put it like that. She said she knew you.'

'Mmm? I come across a lot of people. I dare say I've seen her about. Do you think she'll tell you anything?'

'She says she will. She knows who killed my Great-Uncle Samuel. I have to hear what she's got to say, but I need someone else there as well. Someone independent.'

'No problem, Chris.'

In fact, by the end of the call Andrew seemed positively keen to be involved, rather than have me wandering around the restoration site on my own in the dark.

'You'd end up right up to your neck in mud in the basin if you weren't careful,' he said. 'That wharf is pretty slippery after the rain, and the edges are crumbling away. You'll be all right with me, though. I know my way around.'

'So I've heard from the WRG girls,' I said, starting to feel more confident already about the meeting.

'Hey, all right. I've said I'll come. As a favour to a friend, okay?'

We arranged to meet in the entrance to the car park at The Friary and go to Fosseway in my car. We had to be there before Laura arrived to find somewhere for Andrew to conceal himself, so she remained convinced I was on my own.

After the call, I had time for another drink at the Stowe Arms before I had to go back to the house to collect the car. The alcohol pushed me just to the stage where I felt charged with confidence and righteous strength, without making me giddy with recklessness.

What it didn't do, though, was take away that nagging fear that had been at the back of my mind ever since the incident on *Kestrel*, since my first encounter with Simon Monks, in fact. I'd strayed into a world of violence that was unfamiliar to me, and the knowledge was a constant nauseous pain that I couldn't forget, any more than I could rub away the swelling on my head where the windlass had connected.

In the front room at Stowe Pool Lane, I found Frank looking at the photographs of the visit by Lindley Simpson and Leo Parker to Fosseway.

'Yes, that's him there,' he announced bitterly. 'That's the bloke I saw at the bowls club.'

'I know who it is,' I said. I was too busy planning the evening to pay proper attention to Frank. 'But what I don't know is how Laura Jenner is connected to him. He denies knowing her, and there's no real evidence to link them. But how do I know who I can believe?'

He frowned. 'But the funeral—'

391

'Yeah?'

'I thought you said—'

He shook his head, staring at the photos. 'I suppose I've got it all mixed up.'

'Don't bug me about it now, Frank. I'm going to sort it out with her tonight. I'm meeting her in half an hour. Maybe I'll have the answers when I get back. Okay?'

'Where are you going to meet?'

'The same place those photos were taken. The old wharf at Fosseway.'

'Chris,' he said. 'You will be careful, won't you?'

I couldn't help but be touched by his genuine concern, despite my low opinion of him. 'Don't worry. Just for your information, I'm not going alone. I'm taking some support she doesn't know about.'

'A friend? It's good that you've got a friend you can trust.'

'It's Andrew Hadfield from the canal group,' I said, putting on my coat and collecting my car keys. 'He's a decent bloke. He'll be watching my back, and acting as an independent witness.'

Frank put down the photos and seemed about to say something else important. Then he wiped his hand across his eyes like a man overwhelmed with weariness. I remembered the stress he'd been through and reminded myself to make allowances. I understood that too much fear and uncertainty could scramble your power to think logically, and wreck your ability to say what you meant.

In the end, Frank kept whatever he was thinking to himself, but followed me as I went to the door.

'I don't know what's wrong with me, Chris,' he said. 'I don't understand any of it now. Not any of it.'

52

The Fosseway Wharf site was totally unlit, and the darkness was palpable. I pulled the Escort into the damp undergrowth and turned off the headlights. The blackness closed around us immediately, and the only sound was the occasional car going by on the road behind us. The rain had stopped, but everything was wet and dripping.

Andrew and I slipped through a narrow gap in the steel fencing and picked our way carefully past the restored lock towards the wharf. Once we were off the towpath, the ground became sticky and treacherous underfoot, and we had to move carefully as we crept past the sheer drop off the edge of the wharf into the excavated canal basin.

Sensibly, Andrew had brought a powerful torch, which he directed towards our feet. He already seemed to have planned the exact spot for the meeting – just behind the abutment of the old bridge, where a fragment of an old warehouse still stood, its tumbled brickwork and overgrown scrub providing a complex of dark corners where he could remain completely invisible while Laura and I talked.

Ahead of us was a cleared section of wharf, and a fenced-off compound where the excavator and giant dumper trucks stood waiting for their next tasks. Beyond them, the earth was heaped up and piled with debris where work had yet to start on clearing the accumulated decades of infilling. There was a long stretch exposed here where the edge of the wharf was crumbling away, its retaining bricks rotten and worn loose. No one knew yet what the condition of the brickwork was under the debris. The area would have to be cleared by hand before it was safe to let the excavator on.

In the darkness, I became very conscious that nature was still in control of most of the site. The reclaimed section was only a tiny portion of the expanse of flourishing birches and sycamores, and the dense undergrowth of brambles and bracken hadn't been touched for nearly fifty years.

'Yes, this will do fine,' I said. 'I hope you don't have to wait long.'

'Don't worry about me,' said Andrew with a grin, as he switched off his torch and slipped back into the shadows. Within a couple of seconds, I couldn't see him at all.

I walked back to the gateway and got into my car. For several minutes I sat alone, watching the clock tick round, until I was startled by a sudden knock on the window. Laura's pale face peered in at me.

I wound the window down to speak to her, but she hushed me and gestured at me to get out of the car. Common sense almost got the better of me then. Why should I trust her after all that had happened? But one glimpse of her face close to mine, and I'd weakened. I knew I would follow her, even if it was into more danger.

'Are you alone?' I asked.

'Of course.'

'This way then.'

'Where are we going?' she whispered.

'We need to get away from the road.'

As we passed the lock and left the towpath to enter the wharf, she slipped on the mud, and I automatically put out an arm to support her. She leaned against me, but I pulled instinctively away.

'You need to trust me, Chris. Please.'

'Tell me why I should,' I said.

394

'We're on the same side. You've got to trust someone some time.'

We were close to the spot where the skeleton had been found by the excavator. I could see the remains of the heap of lime, gleaming white in the darkness, reflecting the small amount of light from the night sky. My eyes were adjusting to the gloom, and I could see the vehicles crouching in their compound like giant insects.

Between us and the compound was a wide, dark expanse of earth and rubble, with the distorted shapes of foundations and fragments of wall here and there. To the left of us was the steep drop into the basin. But it was impossible in the dark to make out where the edge of the wharf ended and the void began. I led Laura forward a bit more until the remains of the bridge appeared, and then the edge of the warehouse ruins.

'Right. This is fine. Now tell me. And make sure it's the truth.'

'This is crazy. What are we doing in this place?'

'It'll do for me,' I said, the alcohol still carrying me through so far. 'First of all, I want to know who killed Samuel.'

'I need to explain properly—' she began.

'Just tell me!'

She pulled her hand away and hugged her arms miserably round her body. 'I was there,' she said. 'When he was killed, I was there. I saw it.'

'So you were the witness. The car park attendant told me there was someone.'

'I saw what happened, but I didn't know who was in the car. Not then.'

'But you do now.'

'Yes. And there's proof.'

We were interrupted by a clumsy crashing in the under-growth back near the gateway, on the other side of the lock. It was the sound of a heavy body floundering in the brambles and trampling dead wood underfoot.

395

'I thought you said you'd come alone?' I said angrily.

'I did. I don't know who that is.'

'You've tricked me again.'

'No!' She listened, trying to peer into the darkness. 'But, Chris – did you bring someone with you?'

'Hello! Where are you?' called a voice out of the darkness. A shiver ran up my back. It was the voice of Simon Monks.

'It's him.'

'I don't know what he's doing here,' said Laura unsteadily.

'Liar!'

'No!'

I scrambled away from the direction of the voice, abandoning Laura in the darkness before she could cling on to me and prevent my escape. I could hear Monks thrashing about, but he seemed to be going in the wrong direction. From the amount of noise and the breathless mutter of subdued voices, it sounded like he wasn't alone either. There were at least two or three of them, and I was badly outnumbered.

I ran along the edge of the wharf towards the vehicle compound, painfully conscious that I was heading deeper into the derelict wharf and further away from the road and my only escape route. I peered anxiously into the shadows of the ruined buildings, but saw nothing that reassured me.

'Andrew!' I hissed. 'Where are you?'

My urgent whisper was almost swallowed by the darkness, but he must have heard me.

'Here.'

There was a strange tone to his voice. I looked around for him and saw his outline close to one of the giant six-tonne dumper trucks. The gate of the compound stood open, and it went through my mind that he was intending for us to escape in the dumper. For a moment, I had a mental picture of ploughing through Monks and his friends, crushing them under the huge wheels.

But my fantasy was very short-lived, as Andrew stepped towards me and I saw his face. I could see he had no intention of helping me to escape.

'This is where it ends, Chris,' he said. 'You've done enough.'

And then he did something that turned my mind upside down in bewilderment. He raised his hand, covered his mouth, and coughed. It was a deep, racking cough, a sound I'd heard twice before. One of those times was at the scene of Samuel Longden's death.

'Andrew?' I said again.

But he didn't answer. He moved in close to my body, laying his hand flat on my chest and leaning his face towards mine as if to whisper some secret. I smelt his breath and saw his teeth gleam white for a moment before he gave a sudden jerk. Then the ground went from underneath me and the horizon disappeared as the world tilted.

Before I had time to realise what was happening, I'd tumbled off the crumbling edge of the wharf and hit the mud in the bottom of the basin, landing so hard on my back that the air was driven out of my lungs. With a great squelch, my shoulders and back disappeared three inches into stinking ooze.

The fall could have injured me badly, if it hadn't been for the steady rain that had turned the ground into a quagmire. The mud sucked at my limbs and spilled over onto my face and chest as I lay there, dazed and winded.

I struggled to get my eyes open. When I lifted a hand to wipe my face, I found I was only transferring more mud. Through smeared lids, I gazed up at the edge of the wharf, where a tall silhouette stood against the sky. Though I couldn't see his face, I could tell from his posture that he was listening, cocking an ear at the sound of Simon Monks across the basin.

As I floundered to get a purchase on the mud, spitting out gobbets of the foul-smelling stuff from my teeth, the figure disappeared. I redoubled my efforts to push myself upright.

Illogically, I was still thinking that my priority was to get back on my feet and get away from Monks, although the crashing in the undergrowth was far away and the real danger was very close.

And then there was a throaty rumble as an engine burst into life, and I looked up again. I could only watch as the monstrous black shape of the excavator appeared, outlined against the stars. It was inching out of the compound and towards the edge of the basin, its jaws swivelling to dig viciously into a heap of spoil and debris until its bucket overflowed. It bucked and lifted its load, spinning on its tracks. I caught a brief glimpse of Andrew bent over the controls in the cab, like an animal crouched over its prey.

Still I scrabbled in the mud, sinking further into the mess every time I tried to move my feet. Panic was only making my predicament worse, and I was becoming exhausted.

Finally, I stopped struggling and stared at the excavator as it trundled noisily along the edge of the wharf. Several tons of mud filled its metal jaws and slopped over the sides in great, slippery gouts. I'd seen Andrew use this machine on the site before, and I knew he was a skilful driver who could drop a load exactly where he wanted it. Right now, he was manoeuvring the excavator directly over my head.

I craned my neck to stare up in helpless fascination as the arms of the machine reared above me. If the weight of that mud didn't break my neck, I would suffocate in seconds, with my lungs full of wet, stinking sludge. For the second time in a few days, I was staring into the face of death.

53

Every time a boat passes through a lock, thirty thousand gallons of water go with it, descending from the summit level, lock by lock, until they reach the end of the canal and flow into a river. The water in the summit pound is kept up to its level by a reservoir. Without that reservoir, the waterway would run dry with the continued passage of boats.

In my mind, that reservoir is a bit like the genetic memory that Great-Uncle Samuel thought he'd discovered. The water is released one surge at a time, flowing imperceptibly through the miles, just as a blood line passes from generation to generation of a family. But there's no way to call on the whole reservoir at once. And there's no way to grasp the entire thoughts and memories of your ancestors, to understand what drove them, what they desired or feared. The system hasn't been designed that way.

I always said I'd never look back. But, in a way, my life had ceased to be a series of random, unconnected trivialities. I was starting to see myself as part of an unbroken strand, an individual segment of a coherent whole that stretched over the centuries and had its own unique significance. I'd begun to believe there was a meaning for everything, after all.

William and Josiah Buckley had both died close to that spot at Fosseway Wharf. Their lives had been cruelly taken from them, their place in the flow cut violently short. I'd seen in my nightmares the way they both met their deaths.

I'd felt their fear, as real as if it were my own. The fate of my ancestors was inextricably linked to mine.

But I'd vowed to avenge their deaths, not to allow myself to die in the same way. I hadn't come all this way to suffocate in three feet of mud. I was the last Buckley, the end of the line, and I carried the weight of expectation of all those generations who'd gone before me. When history's boot is in your face, the only thing to do is fight back.

I can't pretend all these thoughts went through my mind as I wallowed in the canal basin watching Andrew Hadfield manoeuvre the excavator bucket into a killing position. There was really no thinking involved. It was more like a great surge of defiance, a furious rejection of the prospect of death that sent new strength rushing through my body and pulled my limbs free from the clinging mud at last.

My foot found a fallen lump of brickwork. I kicked out against it, and suddenly I was free and moving. It felt as though unseen hands had reached out to pluck me from the morass and set me on my feet.

I didn't waste any more time. With my muscles straining and my breath coming in painful gasps, I thrashed across the sea of mud, feeling fresh rain starting to fall on my sweat-soaked face and wash away the caked muck. I thought I heard a curse from the direction of the excavator cab, then a grinding of gears as the machine began to turn.

I plunged along below the wharf side, feeling the ground get firmer and firmer underfoot. I realised there was more and more fallen rubble in the bottom of the basin the further I went towards the end of the wharf. The brickwork was powdery and disintegrating, broken down and ruined by the passage of time. Looking over my shoulder, I saw my advantage of surprise was rapidly being lost as the excavator kept pace with me on the wharf above.

My burst of energy was already failing me when I saw a brick pier jutting out into the basin from the darkness. The top looked indistinguishable from the rest of the wharf, but from below I could see the brickwork was decayed so much it was on the point of collapse. The packed earth supporting the masonry was bursting through bulging walls. The pier looked as though it could fall at any moment, perhaps as soon as I touched it.

I staggered my way to the end of the pier, and finally the energy drained from me completely. I watched in desperate hope as Andrew stopped and twisted the wheel to send the excavator trundling towards me. The tracks of the machine got only halfway along the pier before the ground began to give way.

For a moment, Andrew didn't seem to notice the danger. His attention was distracted by a running figure that came from the direction of the old warehouse and leaped onto the back of the excavator, shouting and gesticulating. I realised it was Simon Monks, arriving on the scene at last. Having pursued me into Andrew's trap, he was now attempting to avert the disaster that he and I could see, but Andrew Hadfield couldn't.

But Monks was too late. In the next moment, the walls of the pier disintegrated and the excavator tipped precariously. Earth showered into the basin, and I threw my hands over my head to protect myself against the cascade of broken bricks that followed. The giant machine sank with a jolt as the ground subsided beneath it. I could hear the engine whining and the tracks spinning uselessly until the excavator began to topple, the weight of the debris in its bucket throwing it sideways off the derelict pier.

I saw a single figure hurl itself clear before the machine lurched one last time and fell ten feet into the basin. The excavator rolled over onto the roof of its cab and landed in an explosion of metal and splintered brick.

For a few seconds the engine continued to churn and the tracks attempted to grip the shattered side of the pier, driving the excavator further into the mud as lethal fragments rained down on the basin.

Then the engine choked and stopped. And a strange silence fell on Fosseway Wharf.

I seemed to be making a habit of coming round to find myself in even worse situations than I escaped from. When I awoke, it was to find Simon Monks standing over me. He was staring at me with a calculating look, like a butcher trying to decide which knife to use to dispatch his victim.

I began to panic again, thrashing my arms and tossing my head from side to side to see where I was and what was holding me down. Bafflingly, I realised after a moment that I was surrounded by plain white walls and constrained only by bedclothes. I felt a hand on my shoulder, and heard a voice I knew.

'It's all right, sir. You're quite safe.'

The face was too close for me to focus on it at first, then I recognised Detective Sergeant Graham. I grabbed at his arm and pointed wildly at Monks.

'It's him!' I shouted. 'Him! Keep him away from me!'

'Now, calm down, sir,' said DS Graham. 'You're getting a bit hysterical. You've had an unpleasant experience.'

'Unpleasant? He and his friends tried to kill me!'

'I don't think you quite know what you're saying, sir.'

Graham looked worried, embarrassed and puzzled. Monks continued to stare at me contemptuously, a sneer lingering around the corners of his mouth. I couldn't understand what he was doing in my hospital room after what had happened at Fosseway Wharf.

'Why isn't he under arrest? He's the man who killed Godfrey Wheeldon. He tried to kill me, too. I can give you all the evidence you need.'

Finally, Monks had heard enough. He spoke to the bemused Graham.

'See that Mr Buckley understands the situation, sergeant.'

'Yes, sir.'

I gaped at Monks as he leaned closer to me.

'Just one thing,' he said.

'What?'

'I gather Caroline told you she was the one who pulled the funding for your internet business.'

'Yes, the dot-com start-up.'

'Well, it wasn't her. It was Samuel himself.'

I would have shaken my head if it didn't hurt so much. What he was saying didn't make sense.

'Why would she lie to me?'

'Because,' said Monks, 'Caroline didn't want you to think badly of him. What you think of her, she doesn't mind. But she felt protective about her father, and of his reputation. It meant a lot to her what memory people took away of him, so she told you that untruth.' His rugged face softened for the first time. 'That's what she's like, you see.'

Not for the first time since I'd met Monks, I didn't believe a thing he was saying. The word 'liar' was creeping towards my lips, but I couldn't articulate it. Instead, I croaked something incoherent. He smiled as if I'd complimented him.

To my relief, I watched him go out of the door. Then I looked at Graham for an explanation. He laughed out loud when he saw my face.

'You seem to have been upsetting Inspector Monks,' he said. 'Now, that's not a good idea.'

Graham's explanation left me with more questions than it did answers. He referred to 'information' the police had been given by a witness to the hit and run that killed Samuel Longden. The investigation that followed included surveillance of a possible suspect, by the name of Andrew Hadfield. The police had been preparing to move in and make an arrest, but when he slipped out of his house one night, they lost him. They'd been watching for his distinctive Jaguar XJS,

403

but had only discovered it much later in the car park at The Friary. They hadn't been expecting him to be travelling in my old Escort.

But then there had been a phone call from a person Graham referred to as 'the lady who is your neighbour', who'd asked for him by name and informed him that I'd gone to Fosseway with Hadfield, and that she believed I was in danger.

'She was quite right,' said DS Graham. 'Obviously.'

'It sounds as though everybody was right, except me.'

Graham grinned, a small, conspiratorial grin. 'Did you really suspect that Detective Inspector Monks was the man who killed Samuel Longden?'

'Yes. And Godfrey Wheeldon too. And that it was him who tried to kill me in the boat fire.'

'All those were Hadfield. He'd been keeping a pretty close eye on what you were up to, and decided you were becoming too much of a threat. On the other hand, Mr Monks was the man who saved your life at Fosseway tonight.'

I frowned, cudgelling my brain to remember the details of the night. Some of them I didn't want to remember. But it seemed to me that it was Andrew Hadfield's life that Monks had been trying to save, not mine – and that I had, in fact, saved my own life.

'But how did Rachel know to phone you?'

'You've got Frank Chaplin to thank for that,' said another voice.

I lifted my head and saw Rachel standing in the doorway, clutching a ridiculous bunch of daffodils and a box of Cadbury's Milk Tray. What on earth had made her imagine I liked flowers and chocolates? I thought of making a caustic remark, then swallowed it for fear that she might go away. At that moment, I didn't want her to leave.

'I'll let you two be alone for a bit,' said Graham. 'We'll have to talk to you again later, Mr Buckley, when you're feeling up to it.'

He slipped away discreetly, as if we were two lovers, and Rachel came to sit on the side of my bed. She took my hand, and a curious tingle went through my fingers. 'Hello, number six.'

'Morning, number four.'

'My God, you were a mess when they pulled you out of that wharf, Chris. Nobody could have recognised you under all the mud.'

'Perhaps that would be an improvement,' I said.

'I don't think so.'

I looked at Rachel for a moment, trying to remember all the things I wanted to say to her. But only one thought came into my mind.

'Hang on,' I said, 'you mentioned Frank Chaplin. Where does Frank come into all this?'

'Frank told me where you'd gone. He was very worried, because he thought you were making a bad mistake.'

'Don't tell me that Frank had it all figured out before I did, too.'

Rachel nodded. 'He said he tried to tell you it was Andrew Hadfield he'd recognised at Fosseway, not Leo Parker. It was Hadfield who went looking for him at the bowls club. But Frank realised from the way you spoke about Hadfield that you'd got it all wrong. He didn't know what else to do, so he came next door and told me where you'd gone. I phoned Detective Sergeant Graham, and he seemed to know exactly what I was talking about. The police reacted pretty quickly.'

'It almost wasn't quick enough,' I said petulantly.

'You didn't come out of it too badly. Hadfield has two crushed legs.'

'But why did he do all this?'

'He's not saying anything, apparently. But Inspector Monks and Sergeant Graham will work it all out, I dare say. One thing they did tell me is that Hadfield is Leo Parker's nephew, the son of his sister Eleanor.'

'I've seen her,' I said.

'Well, it seems she's going to marry Lindley Simpson, the MP.'

'Jesus, this is making my head hurt.'

'The Parkers did very well for themselves, didn't they? But you were threatening to bring it all down. You and your blessed Great-Uncle Samuel. So Hadfield set about finishing the Buckleys off completely.'

'I never trusted him anyway, not really.'

Rachel laughed. 'I know you didn't. But you men – you don't listen to what your hearts are telling you.'

And then I had to ask her the thing I needed to know most. 'What about Laura?'

She smiled, and her fingertips moved in my palm. 'I'll let her talk to you for herself. She's here, waiting to see you. She has something to explain.'

I groaned. 'Not more explanations. I can't stand it.'

And then she came in, the woman calling herself Laura Jenner. She carried no flowers and no chocolates, not even a bunch of grapes. And she spared no time beating about the bush.

'My name isn't Laura Jenner, of course,' she said.

'I know. You're a Parker.'

She laughed bitterly. 'Not at all. I'm Karen Mills.'

In my woozy state, the name didn't click at first. I knew I'd heard it before, but couldn't place it.

'I was Samuel Longden's secretary,' she said. 'His personal assistant.'

Karen Mills? Who had mentioned that name first? Frank Chaplin? Or had it been Leo Parker? Then I remembered how it fitted.

'You were in the car with Alison when she was killed.'

She nodded. 'I was driving, in fact. Alison was going shopping in Birmingham, spending Samuel's money, but she didn't like taking the train. She used me as a chauffeur sometimes.

I didn't enjoy that very much, but Samuel was always pleased when we were together, and he was paying me well. So I was driving her car that morning, a sporty Toyota that Samuel bought her. Ridiculous, really – she was fifty years old by then, you know. But Samuel still thought of her as his young bride.'

'Go on.'

'Well, Alison was a bit frightened of the car, and wanted me to drive her. We were on the A38, the dual carriageway stretch between the A5 roundabout and Moneymore. I suppose I might have been going too fast, but it was the lorry veering across the central reservation that caused the crash. The car turned over when we hit it. Alison was killed instantly. But it took them about two hours to cut me out of the wreckage.'

'At least you survived.'

'Oh, I survived. With two broken arms and broken ribs and lacerations on my body from the shattered glass. And this.' She flicked back her black hair to show the scar on her forehead. 'But there were also internal injuries.'

'So why did you stay in Lichfield?'

She shrugged. 'I was still working for Samuel. He took me back on after I recovered. But he began to use me more as a researcher than a secretary. I had less and less to do with his business affairs, and I got more and more involved with his other interests. You can guess what I was researching for him, I suppose.'

'The Buckley family.'

'The Buckleys and the Parkers, yes. As well as the family history, Samuel particularly wanted to keep an eye on Leo Parker. But he also kept track of what you were doing, Chris. I was the one who found out about the dot-com venture, by talking to Dan Hyde when we identified him as your friend.'

'Some friend.' I was gradually focusing on what she was telling me. Was she the one person who could give me the answer to a question that had been perplexing me? 'Samuel

407

must have been tormented by the accident that killed Alison. He got a strange idea in his mind, from what I hear.'

'What idea was that?' she said.

'He told Leo Parker that Alison was pregnant when she died. That she was carrying his son. But, as you said, she was fifty years old.'

Karen Mills shook her head and looked away. 'No, you've got it wrong.'

'But that's what he told Frank, too.'

'Frank Chaplin misunderstood. Of course Alison wasn't pregnant.' She paused. 'But I was.'

'You?'

Her manner was cooler and more distant now. I couldn't see how I'd ever found her attractive. She told me the facts without passion, as if they referred to somebody else entirely.

'Yes, I was six months gone at the time of the crash. There were no air bags on Alison's car, and thanks to the impact of the steering wheel I wasn't pregnant any more by the time they got me to hospital.'

'The internal injuries.'

'Exactly. A ruptured uterus, among other things. My unborn baby died in that car.'

There seemed to be little to say that would sound sympathetic. Not that she gave the impression of wanting sympathy.

'But I still don't understand,' I said. 'I might have got that part wrong. But Samuel specifically claimed it was his son who died in that crash on the A38.'

She nodded, her lips held in a tight line, and she began to gather herself ready to leave. I watched her movements, willing her to answer the final question that I didn't want to ask. Samuel had been an old man already at the time of the crash, while Karen Mills had been no more than twenty-one.

'As I told you,' she said. 'He was paying me very well.'

54

Nine months later, *The Three Keys* was published. A local publisher had agreed to take it on, counting on the publicity from Andrew Hadfield's trial. The police had been successful in producing evidence only of manslaughter in Great-Uncle Samuel's case, and of assault on me at Fosseway. There was nothing to connect Hadfield to the fire on board *Kestrel*. And Godfrey Wheeldon, of course, had died of a stroke.

But the details of the case had been enough to provoke interest for a while after Hadfield was sentenced to ten years in prison. There had been a certain amount of speculation in the papers, fuelled by ambiguous references by the prosecution to an ancient feud between the Buckleys and the Parkers. The speculation had been heightened by Hadfield's steadfast refusal to offer a motive for his actions.

The result had been a happy publisher as the book sales took off, if only on a local basis. There was a curious, pleasing symmetry to the structure of the book. It started with William Buckley and his role as resident engineer at the birth of the Ogley and Huddlesford Canal, then dealt with Josiah and Hannah when the canal trade was at its height. Great-Uncle Samuel himself had become the subject of the third part of the book – he was the man who brought the story full circle.

One morning, buoyed by a glowing review in the *Lichfield Echo*, I decided to do a job I'd been putting off for years. I found a roll of black bin bags in the kitchen cupboard, and walked slowly upstairs. I hesitated for only a moment on the landing, bracing myself mentally, then pushed open the door of my parents' bedroom. The trace of my mother's perfume and the sight of my father's suits in the wardrobe were no longer associated with any memories I wanted to keep. It was time to put the past aside.

I worked quickly, and didn't stop to examine anything. It all went into the bin bags. Clothes, shoes, make-up, hairbrushes, even that pair of favourite cufflinks. I'd take everything to the tip.

It was only when I'd finished and the last bag was twisted tightly shut that I stopped, straightened up, and took a deep breath. I found I was sweating, and the room was full of an acrid dust that bit at the back of my throat. I remembered reading once that ninety per cent of house dust consists of fabric fibres or flakes of human skin, and the thought revolted me.

I threw the window wide open, the first time it had been opened for a long time. A cool breeze blew in from the street and stirred the curtains. And suddenly I laughed as I felt the wind on my face. I was sure I could see all those old memories being swept away over the roofs of Lichfield in a swirl of musty air.

There was one other outcome from the successful publication of *The Three Keys*. As required by the terms of Samuel Longden's will, I'd sent one of the first copies off the press to Mr Elsworth. Publication was within the deadline, so I'd met all the requirements for the legacy.

The solicitor's response was prompt, and came in the form of a covering note and a second envelope from Great-Uncle Samuel. Inside the envelope was a letter – and a key.

Dear Christopher,

The fact that you've received this letter means you've completed the task I presented you with. You should now know almost everything there is to know about your family. You should know what I did, and about Mary, and about your grandfather. I make no excuses. It's far too late for that.

I hope you also know about the Parkers. In this respect, I believe I did my best, but it wasn't good enough. I thought I might find there was some justification for the hatred the Parkers had for us. But I found none, Christopher. Perhaps I wasn't objective enough. Perhaps you'll find some cause where I could not. The solution is in your hands. It is in your power to stop it.

Of course, it all goes back to William Buckley. William was as close to me as my grandfather is to you. I can tell you my memories of my grandfather. And my grandfather could have told me his memories of William Buckley. If only William hadn't died too soon.

When I began to explore the history of our family, the fact that one of my ancestors was the resident engineer for the Ogley and Huddlesford Canal seemed to complete a remarkable circle. But then I found more, and yet more.

William died because he exposed the dishonesty of Francis Parker. Josiah died after a dispute over contracts with a rival carrying company, run by a branch of the Parker family. Alfred, your great-grandfather, was a hard man. How could he be anything else after fighting through the Somme and Ypres? He had no sympathy with the malcontents and agitators who sabotaged trains and buses during the General Strike. One man who lost his job after the strike thanks to Alfred was Ralph Parker, Mary's uncle. So a Parker found himself having to go on the Parish and be means tested for charity handouts. Did this justify what Mary did?

George thought he'd ended the feud when he married

Mary, but he was wrong. And I was the one who made him wrong. I prolonged the feud myself by breaking them up.

I know that your father Arthur was made bitter and cruel. For this, I apologise, as for everything else. And so it passed on to you, Christopher. And to how many more generations that follow? It has to be stopped. Once my own son was dead, it was already too late for me. But the Buckley name can't be allowed to die.

There is only you left, Christopher. Don't leave me to take the blame for destroying the Buckleys altogether. I'm giving you the power to stop it.

Your Great-Uncle Samuel

While I sat and stared at the letter, Rachel had carefully cleaned and oiled the third key. She also dripped some oil into the empty keyhole of the canal owners' box and insisted on waiting for it to work.

'So this is the third key,' she said.

'No,' I replied. 'It's the first.'

'What?'

'Remember Samuel's will? He said he'd left me the second key and "the third was in the lock". It didn't make any sense at the time.'

'But it does now?'

'Of course. *This* is the first key. It's William Buckley's key.'

I was fidgeting with impatience, despite the fact that I'd waited so long already. I told myself there wouldn't be anything in the box anyway. But I didn't quite believe it.

Finally, Rachel allowed me to turn the key. It moved stiffly, but it moved, until it clicked into position with its two companions. Slowly I lifted the lid, marvelling at the smoothness of the action, the craftsmanship that had produced this object. I hardly dared to look in the box when it was open.

It was almost as empty as I'd feared – but not quite. In

the bottom lay a sheet of what my mother would have called greaseproof paper, faded like parchment. And just showing through was something I recognised. A red blob of wax, with the image of a pit-head and a stylised beam-engine. The Ogley and Huddlesford Canal Company's seal.

'What can it be?' asked Rachel.

We unfolded the paper and pulled out the documents that nestled inside. The contents made me sit back on my heels before I'd even begun to take in the details. They were recent, and devastating. There were letters, a contract full of mind-boggling figures and copies of certificates listing the directors of companies. I'd never heard of the companies, but some of the directors' names were familiar, as were the signatures on the letters.

'Well, that's it. It looks as though we've got the complete evidence on the Parkers.'

'And Lindley Simpson,' said Rachel. 'It doesn't come as a surprise any more that MPs should be tied up in shady financial dealings.'

'When the new link road goes through, they both stand to make a great deal of money.'

'But Simpson is in the Ministry of Agriculture, isn't he? Could he have any influence on the road scheme?'

'I don't know. But that's probably beside the point. In the present climate, the mere fact that he's in the government would be enough to create a scandal. He'd be hounded into resigning if this became public knowledge. It was what Andrew Hadfield was concealing. Leo Parker can hardly deny being involved. So Andrew had three people to protect – his uncle, his mother, and his future stepfather. No doubt he was deep into it himself somehow – there's enough money in the pot to make them all millionaires.'

'It was about money after all,' said Rachel. 'Not family.'

'They must have found out that Samuel had this information, and they thought he was going to publish it.

413

Parker and Simpson needed to stop the book to make sure their scheme went through.'

I realised Great-Uncle Samuel must have gone to great lengths to get hold of the material he'd hidden in the box. Probably he'd poured much of his resources into employing private investigators. Maybe he'd paid bribes to obtain some of the confidential documents. But they'd been important to him. They were what this was all about – obtaining the power to destroy the Parkers. He'd dedicated the last years of his life to it. And finally he'd laid his plans to pass the information on to me.

Rachel looked at me, and at the papers I held. 'So what are you going to do, Chris? Send them to the newspapers? That would complete your revenge.'

'Yes, it would.'

I thought about it for a long while, clutching in my hands the means to hit back at the Parkers. I pictured Leo Parker's face, his impotent rage when it all came out, the disgrace of Lindley Simpson, the sensational stories in all the papers. And I felt a physical glow of satisfaction, the thrill of knowing that I'd brought retribution on behalf of my family. I smiled at the thought. It would be the culmination of everything Samuel had worked for, a justification for everything I'd gone through. Revenge. It was a sweet concept.

But then I met Rachel's eyes, and the vision vanished abruptly. What was the point? What would I achieve by perpetuating the feud? I would ruin the final years of a sick old woman, and store up more animosity and bitterness for future generations to deal with. Presuming, of course, that there were going to be future generations of the Buckleys. Events had focused my mind on this issue like never before. When you lose your parents, you're suddenly in the front line.

Meeting my grandmother had changed my perspective too. The Buckleys and Parkers no longer seemed like two rival families locked in conflict over the generations. As Leo himself had said, we weren't just related, but inextricably entangled. I'd even been back to his house in Hints to visit Mary again, and had taken her some flowers for her room, hoping for a flicker of recognition, desperate to draw back the curtains and let in the sunlight.

And I knew that a continuation of the feud wasn't what Samuel had wanted. He'd given me the power to stop it. That was exactly what his letter said. Two hundred years were enough. Instead of a weapon to be used, he'd bequeathed to me a deterrent that would ensure peace. All I had to do was reconcile myself to keeping quiet about the dealings of Leo Parker and Lindley Simpson, and the true motives of Andrew Hadfield. It was a sacrifice. But it was nothing compared to the sacrifice that Samuel had made himself.

And he hadn't just given me this power, had he? He'd given me the choice to use it, or not. Was this what it had all been about? Great-Uncle Samuel had forced me to grow up, to take responsibility and make my own decisions. Caroline said he'd been keeping an eye on me. And perhaps he was still watching over me now.

'No, they won't go to the newspapers,' I said. 'I think a safe deposit box in a bank somewhere would be the answer. And a carefully drawn will. No doubt Mr Elsworth could help me with that.'

'So that's it, then?' asked Rachel.

'Yes, that's it,' I said. 'It's all over.'

415

55

A few days later I was in London to see the editor of a new magazine covering 'green' issues, trying to persuade him that my services would be valuable to him. It seemed as though I'd convinced him with my presentation, and I came away with a small clutch of commissions that would mean a few hundred pounds in my pocket. With the book selling well back home, things were starting to look up for my future career as a freelance writer and journalist.

I'd set off from Trent Valley Station that morning on the 7:59, the direct service via Tamworth Low Level and Nuneaton, taking an hour and forty-five minutes to Euston. I'd been intending to catch the 17:25 to get back to Lichfield, but there was another train later, and I had nothing to rush back for.

I don't know what made me think about it just then. Maybe it was the idea of having something to celebrate at last that put anniversaries and birthdays in my mind. But it had been niggling at me for some time that I didn't know Great-Uncle Samuel's exact date of birth. Among all the mass of information we'd collected, it was one detail that seemed to be missing.

Of course, I'd entrusted the research into the registers to the woman I knew as Laura Jenner. But if she ever took the trouble to find out, the information had gone with her when she disappeared after visiting me at the hospital. Caroline Longden had been refusing to speak to me for some time.

And only the years, not the dates, had been on Samuel's headstone at Whittington.

But now I found I had time on my hands before catching the evening train back to Birmingham. So I took the tube across London to Islington, emerging at Angel, and asked the way to Myddelton Street, which turned out to be near Sadler's Wells Theatre. The General Register Office was in a large building called the Family Records Centre. Since it was a Thursday, the centre was open until seven o'clock. More than enough time for what I wanted.

I found there were four huge red-bound volumes for births registered in 1916, which divided the year into four quarters. There was nothing for it but to start with the January to March volume and work my way through.

I tried to recall the events of that year. April had seen the Easter Rising in Dublin, Lloyd George became Prime Minister, and sixty thousand men had been killed on the first day of the Battle of the Somme. But that was about all I could bring to mind. They seemed to have so little personal significance compared to the birth of Samuel Buckley, the man who'd wreaked such havoc in my life.

I settled myself down and began to go through the names in the first volume. Would Samuel have been a winter baby or a summer one? There was no way of knowing, but at least I was looking for a fairly unusual name in Buckley. It wasn't as if I was searching for one of the ubiquitous Parkers.

I passed from March to the June volume, and then to September. All too soon I'd reached December and the end of the four volumes for 1916. I frowned, sure that I couldn't have missed the name Buckley. But I decided that my concentration must have wandered at the wrong moment, so I turned back and went through them again more slowly, making sure I read every name. There was no Samuel Buckley entered.

An assistant saw that I was getting frustrated and came

417

over to help me. She suggested trying the years either side of 1916, as a mistake could easily be made. She asked me whether Samuel had been specific about his year of birth. And even if he had, she said, old people could sometimes get a little confused about their own age.

It sounded reasonable to me. A little reassured, I took the new volumes she gave me and went carefully through 1915. That was the year Alfred Buckley had joined the Army Ordnance Corps, the year the *Lusitania* was sunk by a German U-boat and tanks were invented. Then I went through 1917. The Russian Revolution.

Increasingly anxious, I tried 1914 and 1918. Nothing. After a couple of hours, I'd reached as far back as 1913, when George was born, and as far forward as 1919, when I found the birth of Mary Parker. Those five years in between were a yawning gap, with no Buckleys registered.

By now, the assistant had taken pity on me. Or maybe she was worried that I'd still be there at closing time, turning the pages madly with a desperate stare, like a man haunted by some obsession. She diplomatically suggested trying a year or two earlier still, before Alfred and Eliza had married. She refrained from pointing out that my Great-Uncle Samuel might have been a bastard.

But that was impossible. Samuel had been the younger son, and I'd already identified George's birth, registered in 1913, two years after the wedding. I tried again. My notebook and pencil lay unused on the table, and my eyes were tired and beginning to water from the effort of staring at the lists of names for so long.

'We'll be closing quite soon,' said the assistant, probably wondering whether she'd made a mistake in encouraging me to stay.

'It's all right,' I said. 'I'm nearly finished.'

I started again from the beginning, going through the lists a third time, refusing to believe what my eyes were telling me, still convinced I'd made some stupid mistake, a simple oversight. Laura had done this research, and she never mentioned such an omission. But then I remembered who Laura was. She'd lied to me all along, so what was one more untruth?

But no matter how many times I went through the index, there was no birth registered for Samuel Buckley. There was no birth registered for anyone by the name of Buckley, not after George in 1913. There had been no Samuel Buckley born in South Staffordshire in nearly a decade. There was nothing. The man I'd thought to be my great-uncle simply didn't exist.

'Well, there could be an explanation,' said Rachel that night. She'd found me unshaved, with a bottle of beer in my hand and several empties on the floor by the armchair. There was a great heap of papers scattered around, where I'd thrown them in a rage. It seemed as though I'd wasted months of my life.

'Yes, of course there's an explanation,' I said. 'I've been conned again. What a bloody simpleton I am. They've had me for a complete fool, the whole lot of them. And all because I didn't bother to check properly. Christ.'

'Look, there could be a mistake in the records. It does happen sometimes. Or he might have been registered some-where else, and just forgotten about it.'

'Forgotten?'

'His family could have been out of the area when they registered him.'

'Is that possible?'

'Yes, I'm sure.'

But I could see that she didn't look convinced. 'He told me he was born in Tamworth Street,' I said.

'Did he say that specifically?'

I paused, trying to think back to the old man's words, while Rachel glared at me impatiently. But my brain was fuzzy. And anyway I didn't want to think about it, not for a while.

'Well, did he?' she repeated.

'I can't remember,' I said, slumping into my armchair.

'Well, there you are. You can't remember what you were told in the last few months. And yet you expect an old man to remember the details of something that happened eighty-three years ago.'

'It's different.'

She shuffled through her notebook with her head down, so that I couldn't see her eyes. Her tenseness made me suspicious. Over the months, we'd become so close that I'd learned to read her thoughts as easily as she read mine.

'Rachel,' I said, 'there's something you're not telling me.'

She nodded reluctantly. 'I never thought you were right to trust that woman you called Laura Jenner. All that research she said she'd do . . . well, I went and did it myself.'

'Did you?'

'Yes. It was while I was visiting my sister. I never went to the matinee of *Cats* – I was at the Family Records Centre that day instead. I went over all the same ground that Laura Jenner said she'd covered. At first I thought she was a poor researcher, that she was missing too many things. But of course she was lying to you all along, Chris. Everything she did was intended to mislead. I'm sorry.'

'It's not your fault,' I said feebly.

She was looking down at her notebook, and I still couldn't see her eyes. I experienced the sort of awful feeling in my stomach that I'd only ever read about – a sinking, a plummeting, a dreadful wrench in the belly that foretold bad news. Her manner warned me that there was another revelation to come, just when I thought the whole business was over. And right now I was in no fit state for any more nasty surprises.

'Get it over with, Rachel, please.'

'All right. Yes, I checked the indexes myself a long time ago and found there was no Samuel Buckley entered. I went through the actual registers, and there was still no Samuel.

I looked hard, Chris. I really looked very hard, in every conceivable place. But the fact is, there's no record for the birth of anyone called Samuel Buckley. There's no doubt your great-grandparents only ever registered the birth of one child, and that was your grandfather, George.'

She looked up at me then, watching my face for a reaction. But I was beyond reacting now. I'd already been to the bottom of this pit, and concluded that the whole awful business had been for nothing.

'It would have been easy at that stage to give up and decide Samuel Buckley didn't exist,' she said, 'that the man claiming to be your great-uncle was a fake. But why should he do something like that? And who was he? It didn't make sense. I thought there had to be another answer.'

'And so you made sense of it, did you? You found an answer where I couldn't?'

She flushed and turned back to her notebook. 'I found the answer here in Lichfield, in the County Records Office. In the records of the Thomas Ella Trust, in fact.'

'Hold on. Thomas Ella?'

'Yes, the Reverend Thomas Ella.'

'The canal proprietor?'

'The same man.'

'Samuel wrote more about him than any of the other proprietors,' I said. 'He described him as a visionary, who was almost single-handedly responsible for getting the Ogley and Huddlesford Canal scheme under way. He was a prominent personality, the headmaster of a local school.'

'He also said that Ella was "a real gentleman and scholar", generous, public spirited, a conscientious teacher and a good father,' Rachel added.

'Yes, all that and plenty more.' I could see the appropriate page of the manuscript in front of my eyes as I spoke. 'The Reverend Thomas Ella took snuff, gambled at cards and enjoyed brandy and wine. He bought silver buckles for his shoes and had silk handkerchiefs. He raised pigs. He was secretary of a circulating library and took an active interest in local politics. Oh, and his first wife had died, but he married again and had five children. It's all imprinted on my memory after the book. Samuel made him sound like a hero.'

'And with good reason, I think.'

I watched Rachel carefully. 'Go on.'

'There was another thing Samuel wrote about Thomas Ella. Do you remember the death of his son, who lived for only three weeks?'

'Ella baptised him at a private service, but he died ten days later. Yes, of course I remember. But what has that got to do with anything?'

'Something came from Thomas Ella's desolation at the loss of his son. Ella wasn't just a clergyman, a headmaster, and all the rest. He also founded charities. One of them was a charity for orphans. It was called the Thomas Ella Trust. It survived into the 1930s, then fell into disuse. Until then it had been very active.'

'Doing what?'

'Well, bear in mind that the Adoption of Children Act didn't come in until 1926. That was the act that made adoptions legal in England and Wales. Before that, they had to be arranged privately via the Poor Law Union, or through certain charities. Charities like the Thomas Ella Trust.'

I let my head fall back onto the chair. I felt exhausted, drained of all energy. It seemed to have run out of me in floods since I nearly got myself killed for the second time at Fosseway Wharf.

'So Samuel was adopted,' I said. 'After all that, Samuel was adopted.'

Rachel nodded eagerly, glad to get it over with. 'You see, Chris, that was why family was so important to him. He was so grateful to have been taken in as one of their own that he put his heart and soul into being part of the family.'

'Yes, all right. I can see that.'

'But when he ran off with Mary, he betrayed it all. Of course, the Buckleys never forgave him. But Samuel accepted that as a right and natural outcome of his actions. He understood that George and his family didn't want to know him any more. The worst thing by far was that Samuel never, ever forgave himself. Right until the end.'

She was right, of course. 'He was carrying a huge burden of guilt,' I said. '"There was a far worse betrayal". Those were his words. He'd been trying to put it right ever since. It's funny, really, that in the end he had to rely on another generation to finish the job for him.'

For a moment I saw myself as Samuel must have seen me – the next in a long line of ordinary human beings who happened to carry the same genes as William and Josiah Buckley. I was just an average man with many weaknesses, to whom he had to pass on the baton. And yet he'd trusted me not to drop it. He'd been sure I would carry out my part. Because I was one of the family. I was a Buckley.

Rachel closed her notebook and came to sit next to me on the sofa, her face full of concern.

'That's it, Chris. There's no more.'

'It's enough. More than enough.'

'I'm sorry. But it's best to know the truth, isn't? There have been enough secrets and lies.'

'You're right, Rachel. Thank you.'

Even after all these months, I hadn't escaped the images that haunted my thoughts. At night I still saw the old horse emerging from the fog under the bridge, hauling the boat that had brought William Buckley to Fosseway Wharf for that fatal meeting. I still saw the figure in the darkness, waiting to crush his skull with a boat hook and conceal his body in a heap of abandoned lime. And I saw that terrible oily swirling in the water behind the lock gate as Josiah Buckley's wife Hannah watched her husband's battered face float to the surface.

And, of course, I would never be able to rid myself of the image of that old man left to die in the road at Castle Dyke, his body broken by the cold, unyielding steel of a car that had come out of the night. Death was in the unreachable corners of my mind, and it would never be removed.

But as Rachel and I sat in silence together, I found my thoughts were no longer whirling in that pit of despair. Daylight had entered at last, and a little flicker of hope was spreading through my life. In the end, it had been Rachel who brought me that release – she'd been the only one who stood by me all along, in spite of everything that I'd done. And now I found that I felt no uneasiness about our companionship, no defensive urge to drive her away.

'So Samuel wasn't a Buckley at all,' she said. 'Now, that's what I call a con.'

I realised that Rachel was sitting very close to me, her hand on my arm. She was completely at ease and comfortable with me on the old sofa in the untidy Victorian semi, with the carriage clock and the worn rug and the cabinet full of Wedgwood figurines. For the first time, it occurred to me that I didn't have to be the last of the Buckleys, after all. But there had to be a clear understanding between us on one thing.

'Not a Buckley?' I opened my copy of *The Three Keys* and looked at the picture of Samuel on the inside of the dust jacket. Surely she could see the determined set of Samuel's jaw, as well as the pain in his eyes? She must be able to understand that he was a man who'd sacrificed himself so that future members of his family could live in peace? So that *we* could live in peace.

'No, you're wrong there, Rachel,' I said. 'As far as I'm concerned, Great-Uncle Samuel was the finest Buckley of them all.'

ACKNOWLEDGEMENTS

I'd like to thank my agent Teresa Chris and editor Ed Wood at Little, Brown for supporting this book, and all the readers who were willing to try something different. Thank you! My appreciation also goes to Lichfield International Arts Festival and renowned Lichfield bookseller Ralph James for the original inspiration and encouragement.

Drowned Lives is set in the late 1990s, which feels very much like a historical period due to the speed of changes in the last twenty years or so. As a writer, I'm particularly conscious of the changes in language. For example, the term 'cellphone' appears in this book. The word was in common use in the UK in 1998, and it wasn't until the following year that we began to abandon the American term in favour of 'mobile phone'. So, although I'm sure I'll get emails from readers who pick up on the terminology, 'cellphone' is very 1990s. Likewise, the 18th century letters from William Buckley are as close to authentic as I can get them while still being intelligible for 21st century readers.

The Ogley and Huddlesford Canal and its proprietors in *Drowned Lives* are fictional, but a real-life restoration project is currently under way in the South Staffordshire area. Members of the Lichfield and Hatherton Canals Restoration Trust are working to re-open a seven-mile link between the Birmingham Canal Navigations and the Coventry Canal:

www.lhcrt.org.uk. This is a huge task for a group of volunteers. Their current Tunnel Vision fund-raising appeal, led by *Poirot* actor David Suchet, can be supported at Total Giving: www.totalgiving.co.uk/appeal/TunnelVision.